BEN ANDERSON

The McGunnegal Chronicles

Book 1 – Into a Strange Land

4th Edition

Copyright (c) 2013, 2014, 2015, 2017 by Ben Anderson

Edited by BZ Hercules, Shane Caswell, and others.

D0684966

For Janet, Sam, Luke, Rachel and Katie.

All my love.

– Dad

BEN ANDERSON

ACKNOWLEDGEMENTS

Thanks to everyone who helped me with editing, ideas, and encouragement, especially Frederica, Mary Beth, Sharon, Doris, Katie, Rachel, Jannie, and others.

Thanks to BZ Hercules, Shane Caswell, and others for their great editing help.

Special thanks to my dear wife, Janet, who has been so patient with me on the journey of writing The McGunnegal Chronicles.

Thanks also to all of my heroes of ages past, whose teachings whisper through these pages.

Chapter 1 – Grandpa's Secret

Frederick glanced over at his cousin, Colleen McGunnegal, and did a double take. For a moment, the wind had whipped Colleen's hair into a golden-red frenzy, and with her form silhouetted against the sun, she seemed to be transfigured into some mysterious elemental with hair of fire. Then the gust died as they walked into the shadow of her great grandfather's hut, and she was just herself again – a thirteen-year-old girl, half-starved from the famine.

The old porch steps sagged and creaked as Colleen climbed them. She motioned for Frederick to follow, but he hesitated, eying the broken shutters, crumbling mortar, and the strange carving on the door – three interlaced spirals. A crow sat on the roof, ruffling its feathers, a black shape against the orange western sky. It squawked, a sickly croaking sound, as Colleen pushed the door open and rusted hinges groaned in protest.

"Come on, Frederick," she said, waving to him. "He won't bite, you know. He doesn't have enough teeth left. I've got to warn you, meaning no disrespect, but he's, well, a bit... old."

"You mean he's a bit corr in the head?" asked Frederick as he climbed the steps.

Colleen frowned at him, turned, and went in. He took a breath and followed. Inside, the hut was dark except for the glow of a fire on a stone hearth and the fading light of day filtering in through several draped windows. Scant furniture lay about the room – a wooden chair beside a small table, a lidded wooden box, a cot covered with thin blankets, and a rocking chair, in which sat a hunched old man smoking a corncob pipe. Frederick wrinkled his nose at the smell of bad tobacco.

"Grandpa!" said Colleen, her voice full of joy.

She went to him and gave him a hug and a kiss on the cheek, at which he waved her away and wiped his face on his sleeve. When he spoke, his voice reminded Frederick of walking through dried leaves – brittle and crumbling, crunching underfoot.

"You'll give me the *kootinanee*, girl, with all those kisses!"

"Oh, Grandpa, you know you love it," she said. "Look who I've brought to see you – it's our cousin Frederick. He's come all the way from Wales to visit Ireland with his family. His pa and Dad said they had business to discuss and for us to find something to do, so I told him we would come see you."

Grandpa McLochlan turned slowly in his chair. Frederick had never seen a face so wrinkled, a nose so large, or ears quite so stretched and drooping. The old man grabbed his shillelagh from beside the chair, a black stick with a knobby head and, with a grunt, stood and shuffled slowly over to Frederick.

Although Grandpa's back and neck were so bent that his chin nearly touched his chest, he still managed to hobble around Frederick, looking him over and sniffing, as if inspecting a piece of fruit. Frederick froze, following the old man with his eyes.

"Well, what's the matter, boy? Are you dumb or something? Cat got your tongue?" Grandpa prodded a gray cat that had appeared at Frederick's feet, and it meowed and ran under the rocking chair. The old man cackled with delight and looked Frederick over once again.

"Say, young feller, don't I know you from somewhere? Where ye be from?" he said.

"Uh, I'm Colleen's cousin, Frederick – Frederick Brendan Buttersmouth, as she's said, and I'm just now come from Wales. My father has business with Colleen's dad – your, uh, great son-in-law."

"Well, then!" shouted the old man. "What's your picture doin' on me wall?"

He lifted his cane and shook it at a faded oil painting hanging above the fireplace.

"Now, Grandpa, you know that's Mom and Aonghus, not Frederick," said Colleen. She had seen it many times, and now that her mother was gone, she often came here just to look at it.

"Ha!" he said, a note of victory in his voice, though over what, Colleen was not sure. "That's not yer mum nor yer brother! It's been hanging there since I was a lad, and when my grand was a lad, and before him as well. It's *him*, I tell ye, and you'll know it soon enough!" He shuffled back to his chair, plopped himself down, and stared into the fire.

"See," whispered Colleen to Frederick. "I told you, he's old - a hundred and three, actually."

She led him over to the fireplace, and they sat at her grandfather's feet.

"Tell us one of your tales, Grandpa, one about the olden days," she said.

He narrowed his eyes at Frederick, glanced up at the picture, and said, "Well, since *he's* here maybe I'll tell ye at last. No, I can *show* ye the *secret* where all the stories began. Follow me."

He rose once again and went to one corner of the room. "Franklin, move this here rug for me. Just shove it aside."

"It's Frederick, sir," said Frederick, but he grabbed one end of the round braided rug and pulled it away. There in the floor was a square trap door with an iron ring for a handle.

"I've not been down there for some time," the grandfather said. "Too old. 'Cept for once back when..." He mused for a moment then muttered, "Taters are probably all spoiled by now, though they might be better than those in the fields, what with the blight and all." Then, in a hissing whisper, he said, "But *it* was down there. Yer mum found it that night. That's why she's been away." His eyes grew wide, as if some memory suddenly became lucid to him.

"Mom found what?" said Colleen. Her mother had vanished without a trace eight months ago. She had come here to visit her grandfather, but he said she had gone down into the potato cellar and never came back. Something else had come in her place – something dark that the old man said he only *smelled* and caught a glimpse of before it dashed out the door. Not a day had passed by that Colleen had not thought about her mother, wondering what had happened.

"Go and see!" the old man said.

Colleen reached down and heaved on the ring. It moved a few inches, then fell back with a thud.

"Give her a hand, Farman," said Grandpa, and whacked Frederick on his backside with his shillelagh.

"It's Frederick, sir," he replied, his voice rising in agitation. But he bent down to help.

Together, they lifted the door and leaned it against the wall. A wooden ladder descended into darkness, and the musty smell of rotting potatoes wafted up to meet them. Frederick turned away and coughed.

"Grab a lantern, Frederick," said Colleen. "And hand it down to me, then come down yourself."

"I'm not going down there," he said. "Who knows what's down in that musty old cellar? It's probably full of poison spiders and rats and such."

"Oh, just hand me a lantern, then, if you're too scared. There's nothing down there but old sacks of potatoes," she said, although she felt a queer chill at the thought of going down into the dark cellar – the last place her mother had been seen.

Frederick retrieved a lantern from the wall and lit it while Colleen climbed down the wooden rungs. Halfway down, she paused and said, "Now hand it to me."

He did so, and watched as she descended the remaining few steps to the dirt floor. She paused, holding up the lantern and looking around. Then she looked up at him and said, "Oh come on, there are just a load of old sacks and such. Grandpa, what was it that you wanted me to see down here?"

"Under the blankets, girl, over to your left," he called down to her.

Colleen looked. A piled heap of crates covered in old, thin blankets lay against the wall. Frederick watched as she moved out of sight, and suddenly felt ashamed that he had not gone with her.

"Ye best git down there, Ferdinan," said Grandpa. "Ye wouldn't want her going *there* all alone, would ye?"

"It's Fred... Oh, never mind." He gulped, looked one last time down into the shaft, then got on his knees and slowly backed into the hole. The old man wore an eager toothless grin, and his deeply

7

sunken eyes followed Frederick as he descended.

Off to the left, he could see the glow of the lantern sitting on a crate and Colleen's flickering shadow dancing about as she dragged boxes away from the wall.

He made his way over to her, and then turned to look back at the trap door. He jumped and yelled out – the old man was standing right behind him.

"How did you..." he began, but Grandpa moved past him to where Colleen had now cleared the debris away from the wall.

There, engraved on a single massive stone at least seven feet high and four feet wide, were three interlaced spirals.

"Why it's the same design as on the front door. When did you carve this?" asked Colleen.

He lifted the lantern in one hand and leaned heavily on his cane. He frowned, and his face looked eerie in the dim light. "Old, it is," he said. "Older than me. Older than the farm. Older than the Celts themselves. Much older."

"What is it?" whispered Frederick. He was getting a strange feeling in this place, as though something was watching him. He looked about, but could see nothing in the dim light other than vague shapes.

"A marker," replied Grandpa. "A marker to an *entrance*."

Colleen's eyes grew wide. She suddenly remembered another place where she had seen the triple spiral before. There was one on the passage tomb up at Newgrange. She had seen it several years ago when they had gone to visit her mother's cousin.

"It's a grave, isn't it, Grandpa?" she whispered.

He slowly turned his bent neck and looked sidelong at her. "Maybe. Maybe they're *all* dead."

"Who?" said Frederick.

"The *Others*," he hissed. "Maybe *it* was the last one – the one that came that night."

He paused, looked at Colleen, then at Frederick, as if considering something.

"*It* lives in the bog now. But some nights, it comes. I can *smell* it. It wants to go back – back to its place. Back to where the old tales all began."

Placing the lantern back on the crate, he fumbled for a moment in his sweater pocket. Removing a small box, he held it next to the light.

"This is the McLochlan family secret, child. *You* have to keep it now."

He glanced at Frederick and said, "Fandrick must help you. *It* must not get it!"

"Why, it looks like a tiny treasure chest," said Colleen.

"Yes. An ancient treasure."

The old man removed a thin chain from around his neck. On it was a tiny golden key that bore the triple swirl pattern. With this, he unlocked the box and opened it. Inside was a perfectly round crystal ball. Colleen looked up at her grandfather, and he nodded.

"Take it," he said.

She carefully lifted the ball from its red velvet seat and held it in her palm near the lantern. Inside the clear two-inch sphere was a tiny forest scene with perfectly formed trees that all appeared to be dead. A scattering of minute leaves littered the ground. In the midst of the hunched trunks, jutting upward from the forest floor, was what appeared to be a broken section of a stone wall. On one side, a large mirror was hung, and on the other side, a triple spiral design was delicately carved.

They all drew their faces close to the crystal, staring into its intricate depths, illuminated by the lantern's flame. Frederick's palms were beginning to sweat, and he wiped them on his pants.

"What is that?" he asked. "It looks like a haunted wood or something."

"Haunted?" whispered Grandpa. "Yes! Mothers whisper tales to their children about it. They say that dragons and poisonous beasts lurk there – all the treasures of evil! There are other things as well – beings and cities of light and marvel that men dream of seeing – all the treasuries of unstained kingdoms that the Haunts have never fouled. There are doors and paths that one must take – but one must first find an entrance. And it's said that if mortal folk dare to tread those lands, they find their true selves there."

"Sounds too deep for me," said Frederick, trying to push away a growing sense of dread.

"Deep calls to deep!" whispered the old man.

"That's just a bunch of fairy tales and superstitions," said Frederick. "My father is an archaeologist, and he says..."

He was interrupted by the sound of creaking floorboards above them. Dust sprinkled down on their heads.

The old man sniffed the air and wrinkled his nose. He snatched the crystal ball from Colleen's hand, and held it up for a moment in front of the spiral on the wall. He stared hard into its depths, then put it back in its box, locked it, and handed it to Colleen along with the key.

"Hide!" he whispered. "And no matter what you hear, don't come out, and don't tell anyone about the secret!"

"But why, Grandpa? It's probably just one of my brothers, Bran or Aonghus, come to fetch me," she said, putting the box in her pocket.

"Hush! It's none of the McGunnegals! Hide now, quick!" he said. "*It* is here."

"What?" asked Frederick nervously.

"A *superstition!*" said the old man. "Now hide!"

He turned once again toward the spirals on the wall and said, "Go on now, and close your eyes and count to a hundred before you come out."

Colleen and Frederick ran behind several large sacks that reeked of mildew. Frederick wanted to gag. He was getting a bit irritated with the old man's crazy antics and had a mind to say something about it all. However, something deep inside, whether fear or curiosity or some other instinct, also told him to stay put and see what would happen.

"No peeking!" said the old man, and he cackled as if he had made a marvelous joke.

They crouched down, listening intently. It sounded as though Grandpa was climbing the ladder. There was a bang that sounded like the trap door had been shut, and then a moment later, there was a grinding sound, like stone on stone. A rush of wind blew through the cellar, stirring up a cloud of dust. The old man laughed giddily, and then whispered, "Farewell! I'll send help." Something flashed, the grinding noise ceased, and all was still.

They sat frozen, hardly daring to breathe, when suddenly from the room above them came a good deal of scuffling and bumping. The muffled screech and hiss of the cat could be heard, and then there was a loud thud, followed by a shower of dust.

"That's it," said Colleen, jumping from their hiding place. The old man was nowhere to be seen. "Grandpa could be hurt!" she said, and she ran to the ladder.

"But, he said to hide!" said Frederick.

She ignored him and began to climb.

"Brilliant!" he muttered, and ran after her.

Colleen pushed on the trap door, but it barely moved. "I think something is on top of it!" she whispered.

They listened and could hear someone shuffling about, and then the sound of the iron ring being fiddled with.

They scrambled down, grabbed the lantern, and ran back to their hiding place, dousing the light just as the door in the ceiling cracked open.

Frederick shuddered as a bare, gray, misshapen foot stepped down on the first rung of the ladder. A second mottled, gray-green foot with bulbous toes followed, and a small figure, no larger than themselves, draped in a tattered and hooded black cloak, slowly descended into the darkness.

A smell that reeked like rotting meat filled the room, and the two children watched with wide eyes as the stinking creature stood swaying back and forth in the dim shaft of orange light that shone from the room above.

Every hair on their necks stood on end, and their hearts began to pound. A cold sweat broke out on Frederick's brow, and he felt as though he was going to be sick.

He looked at Colleen, and in the dim light, he could see her face was a mix of emotions, but whether fear or outrage and indignation, he could not tell.

To his utter surprise and terror, she stood up and shouted, "What have you done to Grandpa?"

She lifted the lantern and somehow it flamed to life. Frederick shielded his eyes from the sudden light, which for a moment appeared to spread all about Colleen, making her seem to be shining. The darkness that had been descending on his mind snapped and vanished.

The creature hissed and crouched down, spreading its arms across its hooded face. Gray-green clawed hands with dirty brown nails knotted into fists. It peered through its arms at them, then dashed up the ladder in a flurry of ragged black robes and was gone.

Colleen sprang from their hiding place and raced after it, leaping over the potato sacks, knocking one of them to the ground. Neither of them noticed that as she leaped up, the little box and key slipped from her pocket and fell to the floor, and the falling sack tumbled right on top of them, hiding them from view.

Frederick blinked, and then ran after her, but when he climbed up into the house, he found her standing in the living room, the lantern burning dimly in her hand. The furniture in the room was toppled over, and the gray cat sat on the shelf above the hearth, its fur all standing on end. It growled and hissed, then leaped down and ran out the open front door.

"Grandpa?" Colleen called. No one answered. She ran to the door and looked out. For a moment, she thought she saw a dark shadow run away southward, then it was gone. But an eerie wailing came floating across the field from its direction. "Grandpa!" she called again.

They searched the house, but the old man was nowhere to be found.

"I'm getting out of here," said Frederick, and he ran out the door.

Colleen paused for a moment, looking desperately around the room. Then she too ran from the hut and caught up to Frederick.

Together, they reached the farmhouse and burst through the door. Everyone inside turned and stared.

"It's happening again!" said Colleen breathlessly, her face terrified. "Just like before, when Mom disappeared!"

Chapter 2 – The Decision

"They're just downright unnatural," said Frederick to his rather portly, ten-year-old brother, Henry. "In fact, that old O'Brian fellow who lives down the way from them said this sort of thing has happened before – I overheard Dad talking to him in the pub last night."

Henry shrugged and took a large bite of chicken.

"There's more," said Frederick. "Get this – O'Brian also said that the McGunnegals have a bunch of giant grave mounds on their side of the farm, but the McLochlans – Colleen's mother's side of the family – they have no graveyard at all, and none of them are buried at the church either."

"So?" said Henry through a gulp of juice.

"So, isn't that weird? I mean, where do they bury their dead? That old geezer said the disappearances explain it – they're all cursed or something. And those McGunnegals – every one of them has something strange going on. It's just unnatural, it is, being so impish and all. O'Brian said that's what happens when a McGunnegal marries a McLochlan – their children all have this *strangeness* about them."

"Impish?" said Henry, now working on a melon.

"I mean, it's been four days since their grandfather disappeared and they've been out and about the countryside searching for him without a speck of sleep and barely eating anything. How do they do it?"

Henry stopped eating for a moment. His cheeks were covered with grease and jelly, and melon juice dripped down his chin. "You mean they haven't eaten or slept in four days?" he asked.

"That's what folk are saying. And what about that black creature?" said Frederick. "I've been thinking that it was probably some Irish kid who ate too many bad potatoes. They say people all over the country are sick and dying from eating them. I'm glad I'm not Irish. At least I'll never look like *that*."

He was about to say more, when their mother, Mabel, poked her head in the door.

"Time to be going, boys," she said.

"But I'm not done eating yet!" complained Henry.

Mabel looked at the biscuits, pulled her considerable bulk through the door, and helped herself to one.

"Yes, yes, well, you can have a snack later. We have a meeting with the McGunnegals. It shouldn't be long," she said.

With a heavy sigh, Henry pushed himself away from the table, grabbed a biscuit, and put it in his pocket.

Frederick followed his mother and brother out to a carriage where their father, Rufus, and their cousin, Helga, waited. Rufus was a short man with quick, intelligent eyes that took in everything at a glance, and Helga was a large German woman with a square jaw and a sour, distrusting expression. Both carried themselves with confidence and purpose, but did not smile.

They climbed aboard and, a moment later, were rolling down the bumpy dirt road toward the farm.

In the farmhouse, Mr. Adol McGunnegal had gathered his children in the living room and was studying their worried faces.

"The Buttersmouths and Helga should arrive shortly, children," he said in his deep, booming voice. "I was going to tell you this before, but then Grandpa disappeared and it just didn't seem like the right time. I've agonized over it for days, but now my mind is made up. Helga contacted my cousin Rufus in England some weeks ago, telling him of our plight, and he has offered to do us a favor."

"What kind of favor, Father?" asked Henny as she crawled up on his lap. She leaned her golden head against his massive chest and looked up at him with her strange violet-blue eyes.

He sighed deeply and said, "You all know that the farm is not doing well. The potato crop failed last year in the blight, and things are not looking good this year either. Our neighbors are going hungry, and some are sick. We've managed to sell some things to buy food, but it's not enough."

"Dad, what are you saying?" asked Colleen.

"We're out of money, children," he said, his voice cracking and his eyes growing wet. "And I have to do something to feed you. Rufus Buttersmouth has offered to take you all to Wales, and there pay for a full year of boarding school."

A chorus of protests filled the room as the children all spoke at once. Adol held up a hand and began to say more, but there was a knock at the door and it swung open. In strolled Helga, followed by the Buttersmouths.

"Hello, Helga, Rufus, Mabel, Henry, Frederick," said Adol. "I'm glad you're here. I'm just telling the children what we have been discussing."

When they were all seated, he took a deep breath. There was an uncomfortable silence for a moment, and then Colleen's sister, Bib, spoke. "We'll make it somehow, Dad," she said. "We can all do odd jobs for the neighbors and such, and I hear the Brits will be sending corn over soon."

"The Brits!" said Helga, disdain in her husky voice and thick accent. "No offense to our kind cousins, but let us be frank about the situation. The British government cares nothing for the Irish. They say that this *Irish problem* will take care of itself one way or another. You are out of money, out of food, and out of things to sell. Your neighbors are starving to death, and you don't know how long this famine is going to last. Your countrymen are dying or fleeing to America or other shores, and now it is time for you all to do something as well."

She paused for a moment, looking them over, and then continued. "I recently came into an inheritance, and have enough money to pay the taxes for one year, and Rufus has been so kind as to offer to take you to Wales and give you a decent education. There really is nothing to discuss."

"Please, Helga," said Adol. "Let me explain our plan to them."

He was about to go on when Henry piped up. His voice whined and sounded as though he were holding his nose. "Father, this hut stinks and I'm very sleepy. We're not staying *here* tonight, are we? And I'm hungry!"

"Quiet!" snapped Rufus. "We'll be staying at the village Inn this evening, and we'll be done here soon enough!"

He looked at Adol and said, "I'm quite sorry about that. The boys have had a long day, and they're a bit cranky."

"Aye, that's all right. I quite understand," he said. "I have considered your offer, but I've hardly had time to discuss it with my children. I've only just now begun to tell them."

Rufus looked at the six children and then his eyes glanced about the room again, lingering for a moment on a picture frame hanging above the fireplace. "They will be well cared for, well fed, well housed, and well educated, Adol," he said. "My time is very precious, and I shan't stay and try to convince you that this is the best and only opportunity that you have to provide them with more than poverty and starvation. You recall my terms, I assume?"

Adol nodded. "Give me this evening to explain to them, Rufus. We'll meet with you in the morning."

"Early then," said Rufus. "The ship leaves at one o'clock. Come, Mabel, Frederick, Henry. Helga, how about spending the evening at the Inn with us? We could discuss... a few things."

"Certainly, cousin," she said. "Adol, we'll see you in the morning. Do consider our offer, hmm?"

With final goodnights, the lot of them left, and the children could hear the horse-drawn carriage drive away.

"Father," said Bib. "What did Cousin Rufus mean by his *terms*? What is he asking for? And what was that about a ship leaving at one o'clock?"

Adol looked at the floor, then at each of them. "He wants the farm as collateral for paying him back."

"The farm!" said Aonghus. "But, Dad, this farm has been owned by the McGunnegal family for generations! We can't give it up just because of one failed potato crop. We'll make it somehow."

"I've agonized over this for days and days," Adol said. "Think about it – if the potato blight ends and the crop goes well this year, we'll make enough to pay the taxes. We won't need Helga's money, and I think in six or seven years, I can pay Rufus back, and you all will have gotten a good year of schooling. If the blight goes on, though, we'll have nothing, and we'll lose the farm anyway. At least this way, it goes to someone in the family. Besides, what happened this week has helped me make up my mind. I can't risk any of you with that *thing* having come back. I'm sure it had something to do with your mother's disappearance, and now with Grandpa's – I won't risk losing any of you while it haunts our farm. This will give me a chance to find it and … take care of it."

There were more protests and arguments, with many reasons why they should not leave Ireland, and all sorts of ideas of how they might make money, grow other food, or do this or that. In the end, however, Adol shook his head and said, "I love you all, my precious children, and I would sacrifice anything, except you, to save this farm. You are more important to me than all the world, and I'll do what I must to save you first. The ship leaves tomorrow at one o'clock in the afternoon."

"Dad, why didn't you tell us sooner?" said Aonghus, a hint of anger in his voice. "We've got no time to properly pack, or say goodbye, or anything!"

"The ship wasn't expected to arrive until next week, but the captain's plans changed and he arrived yesterday. I'm sorry, children, but this is our last, best hope," he said sadly. "I need you all to help me with this. It tears me up inside to send you away! See here, now, let's all get to bed early and get up before the sun. We'll spend what time we can together."

They sat for a long moment, then Aonghus rose and walked away without a word. Adol could see the frustration on his oldest son's face. Then, one by one, the others got up and followed him upstairs.

In the girls' room, Colleen turned to her sisters and said, "Something is rotten about all this. It just seems wrong that all these cousins should suddenly show up and take such an interest in our farm, especially when it's in such bad shape. What are they up to?"

"I don't know," said Abbe. "But let's get to sleep. Father won't let us down. He'll do what's best for us."

"True," said Bib. "But I don't trust Helga or the Buttersmouths. Colleen is right – they're up to something."

"Well, I'm going to find out," said Colleen, and she slipped on her shoes. "I'm going to run to the village Inn and listen at their door. Maybe they'll be talking about the whole affair."

The three sisters watched as Colleen quietly opened the window, swung her legs out, and grabbed a branch of the tree that grew next to their house.

"Be *careful*," whispered Henny.

Colleen made her way toward the trunk and then climbed down to the ground. With a wave, she dashed into the night, down the dusty street toward the village, her long hair flying behind her.

She ran as quickly as she could down the dark road for a good ten minutes, and then, to her surprise, she rounded a bend and almost immediately came upon the carriage. It had stopped, and there were voices coming from it. She quietly slipped forward and hid behind a tree, straining to hear what they were saying.

Rufus was speaking. "... yes, but did you get the *map?*" he was asking.

Helga laughed. "Of course, I got the map. What do you think I've been doing all this time at that miserable hut?"

"Fine, fine," said Rufus. "And what does it show?"

"I have it here with me," she said. "Look!"

Colleen could hear the rustling of paper, and a bit of jostling going on.

"Let me see!" said the voice of one of the boys, which was followed by a howl. She could imagine Rufus pulling him back by his ear.

"Just sit still and you'll get your chance!" said Mabel, and the boys went quiet.

"Now look here!" Helga was speaking again, and the light of a lantern shifted inside the carriage. "This is only a copy of the map. The real one is hanging over the fireplace in the living room. I did not dare take that one – there was no chance to do it. Those children don't like me very much, and they were always watching me. However, I did manage to make a copy of it, a bit at a time. Look, here it is."

There was silence for a moment, and Colleen could imagine them all looking at the map – a copy of Father's map of the farm that hung above their fireplace.

"There is clearly a trail leading from the hut to this hill, just on the north end of the farm. Look here – here is the key to it all! There is a clue written on the map that I cannot read. That is where you come in, Rufus, you are the expert in ancient languages."

There was silence for a few moments and then Rufus spoke. "It seems to be written in a combination of ancient Norse and old Gaelic. One moment…"

Long minutes passed, and Colleen crept closer, just under the back end of the carriage. Standing on her tiptoes, she peered over the edge of the back window and could just see through the nearly drawn curtain. Rufus was scribbling on a parchment, looking at the map, and then scribbling more, until, after a long while, he spoke again.

"There, I've roughly translated it, and not too badly, I think. It's entitled *The Lathe of Atsolter.* Here it is."

"Under the hill lay eight doors.
Some lead to sun, and some to moors.
In one, you find the Little Folk,
With treasures hidden under oak.

There I found the lady sleeping fast,
And broke the spell that had been cast.
But, no princess prize was she,
Indeed, a witch turned out to be.

Oh, what treachery was this,
That I should wake her with a kiss?
Door two finds Trolls, their cruel hearts long
To rob and steal and do folk wrong.

20

Once architects and builders tall,
Now under bridges they do crawl.
A third finds gold and gems and ale,
And treasuries and spear and mail.

Magic ax and armor bright,
And carven halls of dwarven might.
Four is where the Giant roams,
Beware him lest he crush your bones

Into his bread and nasty meal
To feed his lusty gullet's zeal.
The fifth you must not pass, be sure!
For demons wait beyond that door.

Your soul they seek! From them I fled!
Do not open! This I have said!
The sixth leads home, remember it when,
You wish to return to the world of Men.

And there find rest and peace at last,
When you return from the looking glass.
The seventh finds Elf and tree and song,
Spells and laughter all day long.

Bright never-dying folk and friend,
And maids so fair your heart will rend.
Open eight and find sure gloom,
An ancient plague, the Goblin's doom.

And there the Worm that brought the blight,
Calling all into its pits of night.
Behind these doors such perils lie,
And lo, no keys to these have I!

Yet to these worlds I yet have passed,
Through a simple looking glass.
The portal to a perilous maze
Into which I have dared to gaze.

No simple trek around a wall,

But beyond it, I have placed it all -
A king's ransom, oh, and so much more!
Things of might and magic stored.

Things too great for mortal men,
Things so great that I, a brigand, send
Them far away from mortal lands
Into, I hope, far wiser hands.

Yet three things I dare not leave
Lest too our world become bereaved.
The first, this map to mark the place
That leads beyond our time and space.

The next an orb so small, yet rare!
With it you travel, but oh, take care!
And last, a looking glass to see
Wherever the traveler may be.

And at special places you may pass
And step through the looking glass.
What secret powers these things possess,
None have fathomed, none have guessed.

Yet with simple folk who have no cares,
I leave these things from wizards' lairs."

As Rufus finished, a cold wind blew from the woods, bringing with it a fog that snaked and swirled about the road. A chill ran down Colleen's spine and she shivered. She turned and looked behind her, sensing eyes upon her, but no one was there. The horses stamped their feet and neighed, and those inside the carriage must have felt it too, for they were all silent for a long moment, until Rufus spoke again.

"So there it is," he whispered. "The last of the riddles. But this one speaks of eight doors under a hill."

"Yes," said Helga. "Like the other maps, there is a hill. This must be the last one. The artifacts must be here. Once we have the farm, we can begin digging."

"How many years have we searched?" asked Rufus. "It seems a lifetime."

"Think of it!" said Helga. "The wealth and relics of a lost world! We must keep this secret!"

"Who is Atsolter?" whined Henry suddenly. "That riddle said there was buried treasure somewhere. Is that why you want to steal your cousin Adol's farm, Father?"

"Hush!" hissed Rufus.

"Now, Rufus," said Helga. "Let the boys in on our secret. They will be rich with us soon enough."

"Oh, fine," said Rufus, and his voice lowered so that Colleen had to strain to hear.

"Well, boys, before you were born – some twenty years ago – I was on an archaeological dig in Germany. That is where I met our friend here, Baroness Helga Von Faust. We were, with her permission, digging at a site around her family castle when we broke into an old vault. Actually, it was a tomb and, in a stone box in the tomb, we found a skeleton."

"A skeleton, as in a dead man?" said Henry.

"Of course, you ninny," said Frederick. "That's what a skeleton is!"

Rufus continued. "In the hand of the skeleton was an old parchment. It was so brittle that it nearly broke to pieces when we finally dislodged it from the bony hand. But it was the first piece of the map, and it spoke of the other three pieces and of fabulous treasure, and told a tale of a certain Viking commander named Atsolter, who somehow acquired an incredible amount of wealth and hid it somewhere that the whole map would reveal."

"Real treasure?" said Frederick, sounding in awe.

"More than that!" said Rufus, rather pleased with himself. "The riddles always mentioned things of *magic* and *might*. You know that I am not a superstitious man, but I have investigated many ancient legends and cultures, and they all speak of such things – relics that were revered by the people, and around which strange things happened. I, myself, have seen strange things…"

He paused for a moment, unconsciously touching a smooth blue ring on his right hand, and then seemed to come to himself, and continued.

"The scroll that we found said that one of Atsolter's men had gone to Norway, there to hide another piece of the map. Immediately, Helga and I entered into a partnership, and we have been searching for these twenty years for the other three parts. It took us nearly twelve years of excavations along the Norwegian coast and various ancient sites. Dig after dig, dead end after dead end, until finally, we found it. Again, it was at the ancient ruins of a castle on a hill, just as in Germany, and there, in a vaulted grave, we found a second skeleton gripping the second piece of the map."

"What did it say?" asked Frederick.

"Well," said Rufus, who was obviously enjoying telling the tale. "It pointed to a province in Spain for the third piece."

"But no treasure?" asked Henry, sounding disappointed.

"Some," he replied. "But not what we expected, so we kept searching. It took us nearly six years to find the third, and we focused our digs at ancient castle sites on hills. Once again, we found the grave, hoarded wealth, and a piece of the map. That last piece pointed to Ireland, to this province and, for the past four years, Helga has been here searching, while I pursued the site in libraries and old archives, looking for hints. We performed a number of digs, but found nothing, and it was only by chance that one night in a pub that I was inquiring of the locals about ancient sites and maps, and one of the men mentioned the old map over Adol's fireplace."

"That's the fourth piece, isn't it!" said Frederick.

"Yes!" said Rufus, barely able to contain himself. "How remarkable that it was my own cousin who owned it! After all these years of searching, it was right within my own family! Helga and I came up with the plan that she would pretend to be a long-lost cousin. I would confirm this, and she would befriend Ellie and Adol, pretending to have come here from Germany to escape poverty. Her real job would be to get the last piece of the map."

Then, he laughed. "Now we have it! It is the most important piece of all, because it pinpoints the location of Atsolter's share of the treasure that he had divided among his men."

Colleen's mouth dropped open and she almost let a cry escape from her lips.

"Father, why are you telling us all this?" said Henry. "You never tell us anything about your business ventures, and this one seems like a real doozy."

He paused, considering, then said, "I have a job for you two. I need you to make friends with those McGunnegals and find out as much about their farm as you can. They've lived here all their lives, and they no doubt know every inch of it. They might know about this key of which the riddle speaks. If there truly is some sort of door, we just might need such a key. Often, old things are passed down by families through the years and people have no idea what they were originally used for. I want you to start asking questions and keep your eyes open. Who can say what ancient relics lie buried under their land?!"

Helga laughed. "Your father is interested in relics. I just want the money!"

Colleen had heard enough. Her heart was beating so hard that she almost felt it would burst as she slipped away from the carriage and then sped back down the lane toward her house. She ran across the yard, then climbed up the tree, and back through the open window.

The girls were still awake and had been watching for her.

"Get Aonghus and Bran," whispered Colleen breathlessly. You'll never believe what I've found out!"

Chapter 3 – A Song on the Hill

"They want the farm because there's something valuable buried here, Dad," said Colleen as she and the family ate a breakfast of stale bread early the next morning. "We just can't let them get it. I think we should stay and catch a later ship. Maybe we could find whatever it is and be able to pay the taxes without Rufus' help."

Adol took a deep breath, considering, and then said, "No. I've made up my mind, and this doesn't change it. I'll keep my eyes open, you can be sure. That map over the fireplace is old – older than this house, probably. It's been passed down for generations and generations. I can see why Rufus would want it, being an archaeologist. But, all that about strange creatures and such... honestly, that's a bit much. At any rate, it's become much too dangerous for you to stay."

He paused, his brow furrowed, then went on. "Well, come on, then. We'll walk around the farm and up to the Hill and watch the sun rise, then we'll come back and get packed."

They left the house and walked together in silence as Adol led them across the quiet fields of their farm. Colleen thought how this place was all she had ever known. This land and their old house – these were hers and her family's, and somehow they had to find a way to keep them. But her father was right – they had little food left and precious little to sell. They were better off than most, though – at least they still had a home. So many were being evicted by greedy landlords, or were sick and dying. Rumors were spreading that disease was rampant in the south, especially in Skibbereen. What was becoming of her precious Ireland in this Spring of 1846?

After walking for some time, they neared the wall that bordered their property. It rose up before them in the darkness, six or eight feet high in parts, a jumbled mass of broken white and gray stone.

Colleen brushed her hand along a chunk of cold rock, and her fingers traced the edges of an ancient rune engraved into its surface. Even in the dim light of the stars, she could see many carvings like this one on the piled and strewn stones that had been carelessly tossed in this great heap that was the wall. No one could read them or guess what they meant, and no stories told of their origin.

Henny wrinkled her nose as they walked on. "I smell the bog," she said. "I wonder why it's here, right next to our good farm."

"That's how some things are," said Adol. "Even some people. Seems the bad grows up right next to the good at times."

He looked up, and Colleen followed his gaze. The Milky Way blazed above them, illuminating the long cairn that stretched from east to west.

"You know, now that I think of it," he said, "that old bog never has passed this wall, not in all my years. These stones seem to keep the foulness out."

"What do you mean, Dad?" asked Henny.

He picked her up, placed her on his broad shoulder, and pointed up. Thin tendrils of mist lingered at the top of the pile, reaching toward the farm.

"Do you see that?" he said. "The bog wants to come in, but this bulwark won't let it."

"What if it did?" asked Colleen. "Suppose the wall gave way? What would happen to our land?"

Adol glanced at the stones and then at Colleen. Her golden-red hair shimmered, and her eyes reflected a thousand shining stars as she looked up at him.

"Come on, I'll show you. You first, Henny. Let's climb up and have a look. I'll follow right behind."

Up they scrambled and sat at the top. Colleen waved her hand at the misty air. Thin wisps of slowly moving fog drifted below them among a dense collection of creepers and vines and twisted trees, colliding blindly with the wall, rising, curling about their legs and hands, and vanishing as they sought to pass to the other side.

"You see, lass, it's like this," said Adol. "Sometimes bad things will try to get into what is good. There's something about this barrier, though, that keeps the bad things in the bog from getting over it and messing up our farm. You just keep on being like this wall, Henny. Don't let bad things creep into your heart."

Colleen sat listening to the night crickets and strange croaking and bubbling sounds that the mists seemed to give birth to. *Bad things...* she thought. Was that black creature living in there? Grandpa thought it was. But what was it? He had called it a *superstition.*

"I went in there once," said Bran, interrupting her thoughts.

His face was blank, unreadable as he recalled the memory. Then he breathed deeply, frowned at the putrid smell rising around them, and continued.

"Some ways in, I found a hillock of sorts, with old ruins of a building or something on it. A terrible stench came from it – maybe the source of all the stink in the whole place. But more than that, it made all the hair on my arms and neck stand on end. It was as though something with terrible malice were watching me. I left that place and ran all the way back to the farm, and those invisible eyes were on me the whole way. I was never so glad to see this wall and climb back over and, when I did, that feeling was gone. It was the first time I ever truly felt... afraid."

"Yes," said Adol after a moment. "There's more than bad air and will-o-the-wisps in there, but what, I can't say. Whatever it is, it chills the heart."

How the mists swirl and move, Colleen thought. *As if something were flitting about beneath them.* Then she started, for she was sure that something *had* moved down there, and that she had caught a glimpse of two pale eyes peering through the gloom at them. She was about to say something, but Aonghus spoke first.

"Let's walk by the graves before we go to the Hill," he said.

The others began to climb back down to the farm, but she lingered, gazing into the haze. But the mists had returned to their lazy drifting, and the eyes were gone. At last, she too climbed down and followed them.

They walked along the long line of stones eastward for some way before coming to two great mounds that were nearly as high as the wall.

"I love this place," said Aonghus. "I feel a closeness to our kin here."

"Aye," said Adol. "Here are the graves of our ancestors – Geer, Laar's son, and his sister Aililli - the tallest people in Ireland, if tales be true. It's said that after Geer died childless, Aililli married the steward of their house, Aeden McGunnegal, and so here we are, their descendants, untold generations later, standing by their graves."

"I've sometimes wondered where Laar's grave is," said Aonghus. "If he was as tall as the legends say – nine feet – he would have been the tallest man in the world, much less in Ireland."

"There are other stories about big people – even in the Bible," said Bib. "Some called them the Nephilim."

"True," said Adol. "We really don't know how long ago Laar and his children walked the Earth, nor why they came to the Emerald Isle. It's said that Laar brought things of great magic to Ireland with him, and that his children buried most of them in his grave, save a few that they kept for themselves. Who knows what the truth of all that is? One thing's for sure, their descendants were always big people."

Colleen looked at her brothers and father. They were rather like giants, especially Adol, who towered above other men at six-foot-eight. Bran and Aonghus, at seventeen and nineteen years old, were well on their way to matching him.

She walked over to the great mound of Aililli and ran her hand through the tall grass that covered it. *What is buried under this mound*, she wondered. *Just old bones from ages long past?* Or were the stories true, that they had possessed magic from the Old World, and took it to the grave with them? *Is that what the riddle on the map had spoken of? Could there be relics and treasures of the past lying beneath her feet?*

She looked out across the other graves, some marked with Celtic crosses, some with standing stones, and others with older blocks whose inscriptions had worn away long ago. The McGunnegals of untold generations lay here, now all silent beneath the eternal sky. A vision flashed in her mind of tall men and women working the fields, year after year, century after century, passing on stories and songs to their children's children, preserving the traditions of their fathers. It made her heart ache to think that she and her brothers and sisters might be the last generation of their family to live and die here. She bowed her head for a long moment, then turned to the others.

"Come on," she said. "Day is dawning, and I want to greet the sun from on top the Hill. Today may be our last morning in Ireland for a long time."

Leaving the graveyard behind, they headed back north, past Grandpa's hut, and toward the Hill that loomed in the distance.

As they came to its base, Aonghus said, "I wonder if this hill could be the grave mound of Laar. It is strange that so large a hill would sit on these flat lands."

"I've wondered that myself," said Adol as they climbed its steep green side.

At the top, Colleen climbed up onto a low branch of a great oak tree and stood facing east. The dawn was beginning to break and the stars were fading.

"This is where I first met your mother," said Adol. "We were youngsters then - just ten years old. I remember seeing her standing on this hilltop under this oak, and she was singing some love song about an Irish maiden. Fifteen years later, I married her, and we still came on occasion. She loved to sing songs on this hill. What a magical voice she had."

Colleen's thoughts drifted to her mother – her beautiful face, her golden-red hair, her slim form. She sighed and climbed down from the tree as the first sliver of red fire slipped above the horizon and flooded the world with light.

A deep red filled the sky, lining silver clouds with pink and orange. She walked to the edge of the hill, her slight frame silhouetted against the brilliant colors, and her long, golden hair fluttering in the breeze.

"My, Colleen, you do remind me of your mom," said Adol. "Would you sing us a song before we go back home? It would make me so happy."

She hesitated, but then decided to do it. She thought for a moment and then began to sing a song that her mother had taught her. Her voice was strong and sweet and, with perfect notes, she sang.

"Long ago from distant lands
A magic people came to see
The Emerald Isle so fair and old,
A land unstained by mortal feet.

There they lived in joy and rest
And wove their spells among the trees.
Until the mortal men did show
Bold faces on their shores of peace.

With happy hearts, they welcomed all
Until sad treachery was seen.
From their fair city they did go
And leave the Emerald Isle to me.

But in the blood of mortal men
Their fair semblance at times 'tis seen.
For one did choose a bride so fair
And wed her in that very Spring.

So if you see fair golden hair
Blowing softly in the breeze
That maid may have within her soul
The magic lost so long ago."

As her song ended, the morning rays sliced higher over the horizon and filled her golden hair with fire. They all stared, transfixed at the sudden transformation that had taken hold of her. For her voice had been that of their mother, only younger, and standing there, surrounded by the sun's radiance, she just seemed to *fit*. She was in her element somehow, as natural here as the tree and the grass and the stars and the morning light. Somehow, in this place, singing that song, she was changed from a simple girl to a young woman knowledgeable beyond her years, a master of song and nature, with a power and wisdom that lay hidden just beneath her slim frame. For several long moments, no one stirred.

Then, suddenly, a strange sound rose from the south – a shrieking, like a crazed animal that screams a menacing cry when threatened. The eerie sound rose to a desperate pitch as the sun crested the horizon and blazed in all its glory on the farm. The howl seemed to rise and blow across the hill, dispelling the magic of the moment and sending chills down their spines.

"What was that, Daddy?" asked Henny, clutching him tightly. "I saw a little black thing down by the wall a minute ago." She pointed south where, far away, the bog stretched out, a dark field beneath the brightening sky.

"You have sharp eyes, little one," said her father. "I've been hearing it now and then in the night since..."

Colleen thought he was going to say *since your mother disappeared*, but instead he said, "Oh, it might be that old fox down there. He gets cranky sometimes."

But they all knew that it was no fox. They knew exactly what it was – it was that *thing*.

"Let's go home, Dad," said Colleen.

They rose together in silence, Adol carrying Henny in his massive arms, and walked down the hill and through the fields, listening to the sounds of the morning. But they did not hear the strange cry again.

Finally, they came to the farmhouse and their horse trotted up to greet them as they came through the gate.

"Poor Badger," said Colleen. "Let me take you to your stall and get you some hay."

"I'll come with you," said Aonghus, and they led the old horse toward the barn.

"Don't be long," called their father. "Time is moving along and we need to pack."

"Yes, Father," they called, and walked on.

After a moment, Aonghus spoke. "You know, Colleen, you seemed different up on that hill this morning."

"How so?" she said.

"I mean, you were, well, I can't explain it. Just different, that's all. Not in a bad way, in a really good way - like you *grew* or something. You seemed a lot like Mom when you were singing out there. Something good is happening to you, Colleen." Then he gave her an unexpected hug, which he rarely did to anyone who he wasn't trying to crush in a wrestling match.

She led Badger into the barn and put him in his stable. There wasn't much hay left to give him, so she gave him a few mouthfuls, left the stable door open so he could wander back outside, and walked back to the house.

Before they went in, Colleen said, "Aonghus, I'm really glad we all spent the morning together. You know, I did feel different up there on that hill. I hope you're right. I hope something good is happening. We need something good for a change."

Chapter 4 – Departure

Adol bowed his head and sighed deeply. Then he looked up into the sky, and his heart cried out, *Why must it be like this?* But he knew there was no other way. So he steeled himself, went into the house, and called his children.

"Be quick now," he said. "We can't let you miss the ship."

A few moments later, all six of them had gathered in the living room, their few extra clothes tied in old blankets.

"Well, I guess this is it, then. We're actually leaving," said Bib.

Adol took her in his huge arms and hugged her. "Bib, my lass, even at fourteen years, with the mind that you have, you'll find yourself the smartest in the school. I'll be expecting great things from you when you return next year."

He smiled weakly and kissed her on the forehead, and then one by one, embraced each of his children.

"Come on, now, we don't want to be late. I've already hitched Badger to the cart – go and put your things in it. Aonghus, sit up front with me," he said.

For a time, they rode in silence, each absorbed by their own thoughts as they passed broken down huts, old men walking feebly down the road, young men meandering aimlessly, kicking stones and looking downcast, some hacking and coughing, beset with sickness. Sodden fields, ruined by too much rain, lay barren or unplanted, destined to become grazing land for foreign-owned cattle. Withered leaves of potato plants filled others, a portent of bad things to come at harvest. It seemed that the whole land around them groaned under the weight of the Great Hunger that had beset Ireland.

Ahead of them, Adol could see a young mother holding her little girl's hand. Both were barefoot, and the girl was thin. They walked with their heads bowed.

Adol recognized them and stopped the cart as they rode up beside them.

"Orla MacLeish, where are you and little Sarah going this

morning?" he called.

Orla slowly looked up. Her face was dirty and streaked with tears. She opened her mouth to speak, but nothing came out. Then she stumbled and nearly fell. Adol leaped from the cart and steadied her.

"Orla, what's wrong? Where's Shane?" he asked.

"Daddy went to heaven," said the little girl. "Mommy says we've nowhere to go, so we're going to try to get on a ship."

"Come, both of you get up in the cart and ride with us. We're going to the docks as well. Bran, jump down, lad, and give them a place to sit," said Adol.

Bran jumped from the cart, and Adol lifted Sarah and put her next to Henny. He marveled at how thin and frail the little girl had felt.

"There you are, lass. Don't you worry, now. You're going to be just fine," said Adol.

"Thank you, Adol," said Orla as she weakly climbed into the cart, helped by Bran. She leaned back heavily and shut her eyes. Sarah laid her head in her mother's lap and, within moments, both were asleep.

Adol climbed back into the front seat and flicked the reins.

"Poor things," whispered Abbe to no one in particular as the cart started off again. "We've no room to complain about our lot. Loads of folk are far worse off."

Adol, overhearing her, smiled at his daughter. Then he leaned over and whispered to Aonghus.

"Son, you've seen the folk on the road. Look hard at these dear ones we've just picked up. Do you understand why I'm sending you all away for a time?"

Aonghus looked back at Orla and Sarah. Even in sleep, lines of care and grief were etched in their thin, hungry faces. He nodded, but said nothing.

An hour later, they arrived at the village and watched as a few dilapidated old carts rolled by, and various shopkeepers stood in their doorways, watching the seven McGunnegals as they made their way to the docks.

"'Ear you're sendin' 'em all away, Adol," said a thin, gruff-looking old man leaning on a lamppost. His face was drawn and emaciated, his eyes sunken.

"Shame. Real shame," said the man. "Too many of us leaving." He shook his head, looked down at his worn and broken shoes, then turned and shuffled away.

Adol did not reply, but continued on toward the docks. A single tear spilled down his weathered cheek, which he quickly wiped away.

"Here we are, Miss Orla," said Abbe, shaking her slightly to wake her.

Oral opened her eyes with effort, looked around, and said, "Wake up, Sarah. It's time."

She thanked them and weakly climbed from the cart.

"Is there anything we can do for you and Sarah?" said Adol.

"No, no," she said. "We'll be boarding the next ship to Canada."

"Well, good luck to you," he said. "I pray you'll find you way safely there and back again one day."

"Thanks, and you as well," she said.

She took Sarah's hand, and they walked slowly down the docks. The little girl looked back once, her face uncertain and fearful. She waved her tiny hand, then turned again and walked on.

Adol wondered if he would ever see them again.

"Ah, there you are at last!" said a harsh voice, interrupting his thoughts.

The large form of Helga appeared in the street in front of them.

"Hurry now, the ship is nearly ready to go. Come, come!" And she waved for them to follow.

"Go on, boy," said Adol, and the horse pulled them forward.

Helga turned down the next street and led them three more blocks through a row of old buildings, only two of which were not boarded up, and out onto the wooden docks where a large sailing ship was tethered. A rather rickety-looking gangplank stretched from the deck of the ship to the docks.

"Ho there, Adol, children, come aboard, come aboard!" called a man from the ship, and they could see Rufus Buttersmouth waving to them.

Adol tied Badger to a post, and the children all gathered their belongings, then they carefully walked single-file up the plank and to the ship's deck.

"Well, here we are at last," said Rufus, smiling broadly at the children. "A grand adventure is about to begin for you. I just know that you will love Wales. And see, you are to board a true sailing ship – one of the last of its kind, I dare say. They'll all be replaced by steam ships one day, you know."

But their sad faces and silence said that they certainly did not plan to have any grand adventures in Wales, and he stared at them awkwardly for a moment before saying, "Well, that is... Yes! And let me show you to your cabins now." He turned and walked toward a door that opened to stairs leading down into the lower parts of the ship.

All three of the McGunnegal men had to bend down to avoid hitting their heads on the low ceiling, and Adol's and Aonghus' shoulders were actually too wide to fit down the hall, forcing them to move sideways while ducking their heads. Henny giggled to see her father and big brothers squeezing through the hallway with such trouble. Her laugh lightened their hearts and they smiled.

The accommodations Rufus had arranged for them were certainly not the best and were rather crowded, with all four girls packed into one cabin, and Aonghus, Bran, Frederick, and Henry in another. Mabel seemed to have acquired a cabin of her own.

"Well, now, isn't this cozy!" said Rufus a bit too loudly. "You should all be quite comfortable here for a few days."

"I suppose it's not too bad," said Colleen, trying to make the best of it, and she dropped her sack in one corner of the room.

Four hammocks were arranged for them, two on either side of the room, which itself was not much larger than a good-sized broom closet.

"At least we'll be out of the open air," said Bib.

"Yeah," said Aonghus, poking his head in their door. "At least you'll fit in your hammocks. Ours are way too small for us. Guess we'll be sleeping on the floor."

He waved to them and they squeezed out into the hall and to the room opposite the girls. Peering into their equally small room, they burst into laughter as they saw Bran attempting to lounge in his hammock, his long legs draped over either side, his knees hitting one wall and his head leaning against the other.

"Well, at least I have a place to sit!" He grinned.

"You're all taking this quite well, children," said their father, who was now smiling.

"Well, I guess it's like you always say, Dad," said Abbe. "There's no sense in crying once the milk is spilled."

"Right!" he said, and continue to grin, though his smile didn't entirely reach his eyes, and they all knew that they were only making the best of a bad situation.

"And I do have some good news for you," he said after a moment. "Rufus has informed me that those old stones around the farm with writing on them might be worth something to collectors back in England and here in Ireland. He might be able to sell them for a few pennies each, and has already packed a few of them with Cousin Mabel's things. The museum in London might be interested and, if they are, they'll gather more and split the profits with us."

"That's ... really great, Dad," said Colleen, although her mind was racing. She simply could *not* let those stones get to anyone. What if they were old – really old? If they were, she was sure that an entire army of treasure hunters, scientists, and greedy land owners would descend upon the farm and find some *legal* reason to take it from them.

"Yes, and in fact," Rufus put in, "your father and I must be going.

We have a meeting with the curator of the museum in Dublin quite soon. We're dropping off the horse at the farm and then meeting him half way. I sent a message to him some days ago, and he has agreed to come and examine some of the pieces himself."

Colleen and the others gave each other a knowing glance, and then Aonghus said, "Well, might we have a few moments with our father alone – to say goodbye?"

"Of course, of course," said Rufus. "Mabel and the boys are up on deck. Meet us up there, Adol, as soon as you can." He squeezed past them all and disappeared up the steps.

"Well, this is goodbye for a time," said their father. "I shall miss you all terribly. But do write to me when you can. And you can be sure I will write to you as often as I can buy the postage."

They all hugged him, doing their best to put on smiles, until Henny burst into tears and clung to his neck as he picked her up in his massive arms. But at last, he passed her to Abbe, and they all went back up on the deck.

With many waves and goodbyes, the children watched as their father walked down the gangplank after Rufus and Helga, got into the cart, and drove down the street, following a carriage that Rufus and Helga had gotten into.

Just before he rounded a corner and rode out of sight, he waved one last time. They heard his booming voice call out a last farewell, and then he was gone.

Chapter 5 – Captain Truehart

Colleen stared down the empty lane. Her father was gone, and even though she was surrounded by her five brothers and sisters, she could not suppress feelings of hurt and abandonment. She understood their need – the starvation they would soon face, the sickness that was spreading across Ireland, the lack of money – but her heart still ached. Soon they would sail away, leaving their home for an entire year. Beyond that, she feared for her father's well-being, and knew that when they left, he would have to deal with Rufus Buttersmouth's schemes all alone.

She wiped her eyes and turned away, thinking that she would go below deck, when a voice said, "Well, then, would you like to see the rest of the ship?"

She and the others all turned to see who had spoken, and Henny took a step back, reaching for Aonghus' hand. The appearance of the man before them was so striking, even disturbing, that for a moment, she forgot her grief and concern and, in spite of herself, simply stared.

His face was weather-beaten and pitted, and tanned dark from countless hours on the open sea. Terrible scars ran down the right side of his face, as if he had been burned, and the eye on that side was covered with a brown patch. Colleen could not help but follow the line of scars down his neck, to his right hand that was missing its pinky, and down to a wooden post where his leg should have been. He smiled at them, but only the left side of his face seemed to work – the other was frozen in a grim scowl.

"Truehart's the name," he said through the left side of his mouth. "Captain Truehart. It's a pleasure to have you all aboard."

His voice was rough, and the accent that of an English commoner, but somehow jovial in spite of his appearance.

Suddenly, a flurry of images danced in Colleen's mind – rough seas, blistering suns, long starry nights, dreadful storms, shipwrecks, battles with pirates, and high adventure – all this she read in a moment's time in the eyes of this man.

Henny also seemed to see something unusual in him, beyond his appearance, and she cocked her head to one side, looked him thoroughly up and down, and then walked up to him and took his mangled right hand.

"You had a bad accident, didn't you?" she said.

Truehart wrinkled his brows beneath his captain's hat, leaned down to her, and said, "Aye, lass. That I did. Years ago. But don't you be troubled by it."

"Oh, no," she said. "I see that the scars don't touch your heart."

"Do ya now?" he said, standing straight and raising his one eyebrow, "Let's hope that it's true. I wouldn't want me inner self wrestling with old wounds. Dealing with them in the flesh is trouble enough. But come now, let me show you around the ship."

He winked at Henny.

"I've owned the *Lady* for near twenty years now. Got her from me own dad, rest his soul. She's a mighty fine ship, and near dances across the water when the wind is full in her sails." He removed his hat and ran his thick fingers through his mop of brown hair that was streaked with gray, and beckoned for them to follow him.

He led them up a broad-stepped ladder to the upper deck, where a large steering wheel turned the rudder, his peg leg thumping on the wide rungs as he went.

"Now, you're a strapping young man," he said to Aonghus, who stood at least six inches taller than he did. "Do ya think you could steer the *Lady Wave* on the open seas? It takes a strong arm to hold her."

Colleen exchanged a knowing glance with her sister Abbe. Aonghus *strong* enough?

"I've never been on a ship," he replied. "But I'd love to try."

"All right then, when we set sail here shortly, you come up here with me and I'll teach ya to steer the *Lady*. Looks to me that you'd make a fine sailor."

He paused, looked at the rest of the children, and then walked in front of each of them, eying them up and down with his one good eye, as if inspecting them.

41

"Aye, a fine lot you are, fit for the sea!" he said.

Upon coming to Henny, he bent down to her with some difficulty, looked in her face, and said, "And how old might ya be, young lass?"

"I'm seven," said Henny.

"Seven!" he bellowed. "Why, you look at least ten, what with all that golden red hair and ... and ... well, the most unusual eyes I've ever seen."

He then glanced from one child to the next and, rubbing his grizzly brown and gray speckled beard, he said, "Well, you all have those eyes. Blimey if I've never seen eyes like you lot have! Blue and ... lavender, or I'm a bald parrot! Now where did you get those from?"

"From our mother," said Colleen. "She's been missing for nearly a year."

"Oh," he said, pulling himself back and frowning, and still scratching at his beard. "Yes, that's what Mr. Buttersmouth said. So sorry."

But then he smiled a half toothy smile at them and said, "But on the *Lady Wave*, you'll be my guests. And you can help me out for the next day while we sail southeast to Wales. I'll have some jobs for ya all, if you've a mind for it, even you, young... young... now what was your name?"

"Henny," said Henny.

"Henny, it is!" he bellowed again. "And for you, I think ya might need to help your big brother steer this ship tomorrow."

Henny grinned up at the captain, looking excited.

"Well, off with ya now. We'll be shoving off within the hour. Why don't ya have a look around? Just don't climb the masts or ropes and stay out of the cargo hold and the crew quarters. Other than that, you're free to go wherever ya like. But I would ask that you boys keep an eye on your younger sisters," he said.

This they promised to do, and as Truehart limped away, yelling orders at his crew to make ready for departure, Colleen wandered away from the others and over to the side of the ship. Some twenty feet below, waves lapped at the side of the ship, and in the sky, the sun had begun its westerly descent over Ireland.

Her thoughts returned to her father and their farm, and she looked out at the town for some time, until suddenly, a bell began to clang, and the gruff voice of the captain called for all hands on deck, and all ashore who were going ashore.

Not wanting to watch Ireland slip away, she found Aonghus and told him she was going below to her room. As she descended the steps, a thought struck her and she put her hand in her pocket. It was empty. She checked her other pockets and realized that it was missing – the little box containing the crystal ball that Grandpa had given her – it was gone.

Frantically, she thought where she must have put it. Was it in her room? No, she couldn't remember having it at the house. It must still be...

She dashed back up the stairs and nearly collided with a startled Frederick.

"Hey, what... I was coming down to..." he began, but she ran past him and back up on the deck.

Looking around, she saw Mabel, Henry, and all of her brothers and sisters on the upper deck milling about.

Henny spotted her and came running, climbed down the ladder to the lower deck, and said, "Colleen, Captain Truehart is quite nice. He's given us each a silver penny to spend when we get to Wales!" And she held out her hand, showing Colleen the silver penny that the grizzled captain had given her.

"Listen to me, Henny. I've got to get off this ship. I forgot something really important, and I've got to go and get it. Look, can you cause a bit of a distraction for me. I need to get off without being noticed. Can you play a bit of hide and seek, just like you do at home, so that no one can find you?" she said.

Henny nodded and said, "But you've got to come with us!"

"I'll come on the next ship with cousin Rufus and Helga. They're not coming on this ship, remember? It will be okay. Father will understand too. Now, can you keep this a secret until you're well out to sea?"

"Well, all right. But you have to promise to come on the next ship," she said.

"I promise," said Colleen. "On the next ship I'm able to board."

Henny climbed back up and looked about, thinking about what she might do. Then, walking past the huddled group, she climbed up on the rail of the upper deck and called, "Look at me!"

Captain Truehart stopped in mid-sentence and said, "Now see here, youngster, get yourself..."

But he stopped again as Henny had quite suddenly vanished. The entire group rushed over, expecting to see Henny tumbling into the water below, but upon reaching the rail, found her simply gone.

Colleen took the opportunity and ran down the deck, and, just as a sailor was about to pull the gangplank in, ran across it, down the docks, and up the street toward home.

What she did not notice was that Frederick, seeing her go, paused for only an instant, then darted after her.

Once again, the sailor, who had begun pulling in the gangplank, was interrupted by a second child running ashore and back through town. He shook his head, pulled in the plank, and went about un-tethering the docking ropes.

Henny, in the meantime, had re-appeared behind the group that was gazing at the waters below and said, "What ya looking at?"

Captain Truehart bellowed, "Whoa, there ya be! Don't do that to an old sailor! Now you stay with your big brother here for the rest of the trip and stay off those railings!" He smiled at her and winked at Aonghus.

"Now where was I..." he began, but a bell rang again, and he said, "Ho there, that's me first mate's bell. All's ready to go now. Unfurl those sails, lads, and shove off!" he bellowed.

Away they sailed for Wales, while Colleen dashed back toward the farm, with a panting Frederick running as fast as he could to catch her.

Chapter 6 – Swirls

Frederick, though several inches taller than Colleen, was having trouble catching her. He jogged down the road, holding a stitch in his side. *"How can that girl run so fast?"* he mumbled to himself through his panting breath. He was a fast runner, but he was barely keeping her in sight. *And where was she going?*

I've got to keep after her, he thought. *Maybe she's just scared and running home, but she might be going back for some old relic or something else valuable. Father would want me to follow her. But she's too far ahead!*

Then the thought struck him that if he cut across the fields to the old McLochlan hut, he might beat her back to the farmhouse. He had studied maps of the area with his father the week before and had memorized them. He turned abruptly off the road and ran through a number of barren potato fields until he saw Grandpa McLochlan's old house in the distance. He jogged up to it and bent over, breathing heavily, and then noticed that there was an outside entrance to the basement through two rather large wooden doors that lay at an angle to the ground.

He went over to them and hesitantly pulled on one of the handles. It lifted easily, and the moldy smell of old potatoes reminded him of that night that he and Colleen had seen the dark creature. A ramp went down into the cellar, and as Frederick pulled open the second door, he could see that it was larger than he first thought, and must have been used to let down carts for unloading.

Suddenly, a figure riding on a horse appeared, coming up the trail from the McGunnegal farm. It was Colleen, riding on their old horse. How could she have gotten to the farm so fast? He glanced about and then slipped down into the cellar to hide.

Looking around, he ran to the place where he and Colleen had hidden, then realized that she would see him. He was about to dash to another hiding place when he saw something shiny just sticking out from under a sack. He heaved it out of the way, and there, lying on the floor, was a small box and key – the very same that Grandpa McLochlan had given Colleen. *She must have dropped it,* he thought.

He grabbed them and ran over to the wall where the strange swirl patter was inscribed, stooped down behind the crates that Colleen had piled up that night, and waited, expecting Colleen to come in at any moment.

But she did not come in immediately, and he began to wonder about the little crystal ball inside the box. What was it, really? Could it be that this was the *orb* of which the riddle on the map had spoken? He put the tiny key in the lock and turned it, then lifted the lid. Taking the crystal between his fingers, he held it up to the light shining in through the open doorway. The perfect forest scene lay silent and still inside.

Suddenly, something in the tiny scene moved, startling him. Had it been his imagination? He stared into its depths harder, and then gave the ball a shake. To his surprise, tiny golden flakes swirled around in a circle. He stood, holding the crystal close to his face and watching as the little particles began to take on a pattern – a triple swirl.

His eyes grew wide as he realized what he was seeing. He turned to look at the wall behind him and, as he did, the huge block of stone that bore the same shape began to move. It rotated, a circle of the floor beneath it turning in place, revealing for a moment a black passage beyond. Then it had turned completely around, hiding the passage, and there stood a marvelous mirror as large as the stone block. All about its rim were shapes of branches and roots and trunks of trees. He stared at himself in the mirror for a moment and whispered, "It must have been on the other side of the wall. So that's where the old man went. He's probably hiding in some hidden room back there."

Suddenly, he jumped as someone spoke his name. "Frederick!"

He spun around and saw Colleen coming down the ramp, leading her old horse.

"What on earth are you doing here!" she demanded. "And... what's this?"

He backed away without thinking, right into the mirror, and before he knew it, he was falling backward, and landed with a thud, not on the dirt floor of the basement, not into the dark passage he had seen, but into a pile of *leaves*. He looked around, wondering what had just happened, for he found himself sitting in the middle of a dead-looking forest, staring at a broken piece of wall on which was hung a huge mirror. Or was it a mirror? It looked more like a window, for he could see Colleen coming toward him, leading the horse. She paused, looking puzzled, and then reached out her hand to touch something in the middle of the window. But she did not appear to see him.

Frederick looked at the crystal ball. The tiny golden specks had settled now and were still. He gave it a shake again, and again, they swirled into the triple swirl pattern.

Chapter 7 – Into a Strange Land

Colleen knew she had seen Frederick standing there a moment ago. But he had ... vanished! She thought he was going to fall into the big mirror. Where had it come from anyway? Wasn't this the very spot where the triple swirl pattern had been carved on the wall?

She led Badger over to it and reached out to her own reflection, touching its smooth surface. It was solid enough. What had just happened? She leaned against the glass surface and pushed. Still solid.

Suddenly, her image in the mirror began to shift and swirl like water into three whirlpools, which just as quickly vanished. There before her was not her reflection, but Frederick, sprawled in a bed of leaves and surrounded by great trees.

She reached out again, but this time touched – nothing. She stumbled forward, finding herself falling *through* what should have been the mirror, but was empty air. Grabbing Badger's reins for support, she fell forward and the old horse simply followed her and, before she knew it, the world around her changed.

Badger neighed, reared his head, and his eyes rolled wildly.

"Easy, old boy, easy!" she said, patting his nose and neck. "Easy there."

A confused and uncertain Frederick sat in the leaves before her. He looked about, unsure of what to say. Then his eyes focused, not on Colleen, but on something behind her, and a look of sheer terror swept over his face.

Colleen spun about, and there, hanging on an old ruined wall that stood in the middle of the forest, was a large mirror - a twin to the one through which she had apparently just stepped. But she could see clear through it into her grandpa's basement.

A curious smile crossed her face, and she took a step forward and reached out her hand, which easily passed through, as if there were nothing there at all.

"What good luck!" she said, and turned back to Frederick.

"Colleen," said Frederick. "Get away from that thing! There was something... something dark... I saw..."

"Whatever do you mean?" she said, turning and walking over to him. "It's a doorway of sorts, back to the basement, you silly goose."

But the same look of terror returned to his face as he looked beyond her. His mouth moved, but no words came out.

She smiled wryly at him, then turned back to the mirror – a magic mirror, she thought it must be, and was about to say so, but stopped short. Her smile vanished as a black shadow ran across the doorway and then disappeared.

Suddenly, a gray bony hand slipped around the edge of the brass frame, followed by a dark hooded face.

Colleen backed up a step, pulling Badger with her, and Frederick crab-crawled backward in the leaves until he hit a tree. A chill shot through her as the creature hissed and began to pull itself in front of the mirror, revealing a ragged black cloak covering a hunched form about four feet tall. A horrid odor came from it, making them want to retch. Then it began to inch its way forward, swinging its hooded head back and forth. *It* was back.

Colleen could hear Frederick panting, and she struggled to control her own mixture of fear and revulsion. Yet, she also had a sudden desire to rush forward and grab this thing and force it to tell her what it had done with her grandfather.

She was about to muster the courage to actually do something, when from behind her, Frederick cried out.

"Get out of here you, you... thing!" he yelled in a rather high-pitched voice.

Colleen glanced back at him, and there he was, splayed against the tree, gripping something in his hand.

The creature took a step forward, its mangled gray foot stepping into the leaves. Frederick shouted something unintelligible, then threw what he had in his hand at the creature.

Colleen watched in disbelief as her grandfather's crystal ball, its box, and the little key flew through the air, right at the thing's head.

It hissed and jumped back through the mirror, and the little treasure continued its flight after it, disappeared into the darkness of the basement with a *plink* and a *ding*, and was gone.

The scene in the mirror swirled into a gray mist, and a moment later, Colleen was staring at her own reflection.

Chapter 8 – The Land of the Little People

For a long moment, Colleen stared at the mirror, unsure what had just happened. Frederick moaned, and she glanced over at him. He was standing with his back against a huge tree, gripping great flakes of bark with his outstretched hands.

"Wha... what happened?" he said. "That *thing*... it... it almost came through! And how did we get into this forest?"

Colleen looked around. The trees all about them were gigantic, with great gnarled roots protruding from the ground like knobby knees. Many seemed dead, or dried up, as though it were the middle of winter, though it was warm and stuffy. To one side of the broken wall stood an ancient trunk, its twisted branches reaching outward in frantic chaotic directions, and its rotted heart exposed by a ragged hole that dripped with black sap. A thin fog shrouded the wood, causing everything to fade in the distance into a gray haze.

Colleen leaned heavily against Badger's side. Her mind whirled with the possibilities of what was happening.

"So this is it," she said after a moment.

"This is what?" said Frederick, still gripping the tree. "Where are we? We've got to get out of here."

"Don't you see?" she said. "This is what my grandfather was talking about. We've come through the *entrance*."

"That's a load of rubbish," said Frederick, his voice a higher pitch than usual. "We've come through that revolving door thing in the cellar, and stumbled into a woods on the other side of a tunnel or something, and that sick child or whatever it was has shut the door on us. Yes, that must be it."

"No, Frederick, we just stepped through a magic mirror, I'm sure of it. That's the secret that my grandfather has kept all these years. He must have come through as well that night he disappeared. We're in the Land of the *Others*!"

"Rubbish!" he said again, but his eyes were darting to and fro, as though searching the mist for signs of any *Others* that might be lurking there.

"Now calm down, Frederick," she said. "It's no good going off like that. I'm sure we can't be far from home. But did you... did you just throw my grandpa's crystal ball at that thing in the mirror?"

He looked at the ground and shook his head. "I was ... well, it just happened, that's all. I didn't mean to do it. That was the key, wasn't it? It was our way home. Now it's lost, and that *thing* has it." His voice was growing more desperate now.

"What did you do, Frederick? How did you make the doorway open? Frederick – was it the crystal ball? Did that open this... *entrance*?" she asked.

"I don't know!" he moaned. "I'm sorry! I wasn't thinking. And I'm not sure how I opened it, if that's what I did," he said. "I just shook the crystal and all those little glittery things inside started swirling around in that weird shape and then it happened. It must be the key, Colleen – the key that the riddle..."

Suddenly, he realized what he had said and fell silent. He wasn't supposed to tell the McGunnegals what he knew about the map. He was supposed to get information from her.

"I know, Frederick, about your father's plan to steal our farm," she said. "We all know."

"But... but how?" he said.

"I followed your father's carriage the other night and overheard you talking. There's more to our farm than meets the eye – as we've just found out," she said.

"But the riddle spoke of eight doors, Colleen. *Under the hill lay eight doors.* Did we just find one of them? Which one do you think it is? Or maybe we just found the *looking glass* that it spoke of," he said.

Colleen sighed and didn't reply. Was Frederick right? He must be – the crystal ball must be the key to opening the looking glass. But Frederick had thrown it at that creature, and now it was lost.

A wave of panic threatened to take hold of her, but she consciously stilled her thoughts, forcing herself to think clearly. *Eight doors.*

Had they found one? But which?

"Frederick, didn't that riddle say something about not having a key to the eight doors? If that's so, then how..." she began, but stopped suddenly.

A tiny flash of green and red, a small figure just four or five inches high, had just dashed behind a tree root, startling her. For a moment, she froze, unsure what she had just seen, but then slowly tiptoed toward the tree where the little form had disappeared.

"Wait!" said Colleen. "Wait, please don't run. I won't hurt you. We need your help!"

A little woman peeped over the root so that just her scarf, eyes, and nose were visible.

"I promise I won't... I mean, *we* won't hurt you. Please, do come out and talk to me!" said Colleen.

The little woman slowly came out from behind the root, and then dashed back again as Frederick came lumbering up behind Colleen.

"Who *are* you talking to, Colleen?" he said. "The roots of the trees? We've got to get out of here! We've already missed the ship, for sure. But my father is still in Ireland – we can sail on the next ship with him if we can just get back. Come on now, let's get going. There's got to be another way... what...!"

A plump little lady had climbed up onto the tree root and now had her hands placed firmly on her hips.

Frederick yelled and backed away, his hand in front of his face, as if he was seeing a thing of horror.

"Now, you just settle yourself for a moment, young man," said the little woman. "And sit down right there before you step on someone."

Frederick obeyed immediately and, in fact, not only sat down, but fainted dead away, falling into the leaves and there he lay still.

"In all my days!" said the little woman, and turned to face Colleen, who was glancing back and forth between the woman and Frederick.

"And now, young lady, who might you be, and for heaven's sake, how *did* you get here and what happened a moment ago?" The little woman seemed a bit brazen, but then her expression softened, seeing the look on Colleen's face.

Colleen was rather taken aback and, for a moment, she forgot that she had just landed in a strange wood after falling through a mirror. For there before her was what was obviously one of the little people that she had heard about in so many fairy tales and legends.

"My name is Colleen McGunnegal," she said, "and this is my horse, Badger. And that, well, that's my cousin, Frederick Buttersmouth."

Colleen tried not to stare, but simply could not help herself.

"A bit of a troublemaker at times?" asked the woman.

"Well..." she began. "I mean, he's not as bad as his brother, I don't think. But as to how we got here, we must have fallen through the looking glass! It has to be a doorway of sorts."

"You fell *through* the mirror?" the little woman asked. "But of course, that would be the only place you could have come from."

"But where *are* we?" asked Colleen. "And who are you? Are you ... are you one of the ... little people?"

"Well, first let me say that you are the *second,* or should I say *third* person who has arrived in a most curious way in the past year. The first... why now that I think of it, she looked very much like you! Could have been your sister, in fact. But, she didn't fare too well in these woods. Poor thing! She was taken away with my dear husband, Bhrogan."

The little woman grew silent and bowed her head.

"Taken away?" asked Colleen.

"Aye, taken by the goblins. She fought a good fight, though, and kicked one of them right through that mirror over there, and it plum vanished! I take it she had a bit of magic in her too, to do that trick! But there were five of those evil brutes left. They knocked her cold, tied her and my dear Bhrogan up with magic string, and stole them away through the forest."

At that, she sat down on the root and began to weep with great sobs. She soon recovered, however, and blew her nose on a hankie that she produced from a pocket in her dress.

"Forgive me, young lass, but it grieves me so to think of my dear Bhrogan slaving away for the goblins in their wicked pits. Slaving away with so many others! But here," she said, wiping her nose again, "that cousin of yours seems to be coming around."

Indeed, Frederick lifted his head, looked at Colleen, then at the little woman, groaned, and fainted again.

"Well, maybe not," said Colleen. "But please, what is your name?"

"Forgive me. My name is Mrs. Edna Sofia Wigglepox. I am, of course, one of the Tuatha de Dannan – a leprechaun, to be precise. And you are in Dannan Land – the Land of the Little People."

"You are a ... a Tuatha de ... a leprechaun?" said Colleen, amazed.

"Well, of course I am! What else would I be? Certainly not a gnome or pixie or sprite or ... but anyone can see that!" she said.

"And your husband, Mr. Wigglepox, he was a leprechaun too?" asked Colleen.

"Dear girl, of course he was, I mean, *is*. Those horrible goblins came and took him away, as I said, along with that lovely woman who fought so valiantly," she replied with a sigh.

"But I thought that leprechauns were all little, well, *men*. I've never heard of a leprechaun lady. Plus, I thought that they were all magic, and could disappear and grant wishes, and all of that. Why doesn't he just wink out of their dungeon and come back to you?" asked Colleen.

"It's a long story. Our world is under a dark spell that limits our magic. We don't understand where The Spell really comes from. Some say it comes from the Witch who lives in the South. Some say they have seen the source of the Spell in their dreams, and that it comes from someone they call The Gray Man – a shadowy spirit that dwells under the Witch's dungeons and is her dungeon keeper. Others say that something went terribly wrong in the last Great

War against the Witch, and that the wizards are to blame. We only know that we are small and weak, and have been this way for a long, long time. Even most of our trees have fallen under this Spell. Why, there was a time when the trees were green and the sea was blue and we could grant a wish as quick as anything!"

She sighed and continued. "All of our pots of gold have been stolen, and now we're lucky to have enough magic to make our shoes, and even they're not what they used to be. Most of us have forgotten how to really wish."

She paused, looked sad, and then angry. "That's what those nasty goblins steal away our people for – to make them magic shoes and hats and cloaks and that sort of thing."

Then she sighed again and said, "As for us all being *men*, I assume you mean our *he-folk*, for we are most certainly not Men – humans, that is. And dear child, *of course* there are lady leprechauns, although now that I think of it, I can't recall any of our own tales speaking of our lady-folk going to your world as some of the he-folk did long, long ago."

"Amazing," said Colleen. "What was that you called yourself – *Tuatha* something?"

"Tuatha de Dannan," she said. "It means the *people of Danu.* Danu is the Lady of our land. She is very great and powerful, and if it were not for her, our forest would long ago have completely fallen under the dominion of the Witch and the goblins. She lives near, or some say *in,* a lake many days walk from here. I have never seen her myself, but I have heard that she is very beautiful and is one of the Big Folk, like you. But I fear her power has waned, and the power of the Witch grows."

"You mean this lady is human?" asked Colleen.

"I've heard tell that she *looks* human. But the tales say that she is far older than any human could be. Older than the Forest itself, and that is *old!*" she said.

Colleen pondered this for a moment and then a thought struck her. It was a wild, desperately hopeful thought.

"Mrs. Wigglepox, I don't mean to change the subject, but you said that a woman came here just like we did. Do you remember what she was wearing when she came?" she asked.

"Oh yes, it was a brown dress – like a work dress, and she had on a red apron with a beautiful pattern on it. I'll never forget it – it was like nothing I've seen before," she said.

Colleen reached into her pocket and pulled out her mother's scarf.

"The pattern on the apron – did it look like this?" And she held up the scarf.

"Why, yes, child! It most certainly did! In fact, a piece of her apron tore off in the scuffle and I saved it and made this little scarf I'm wearing now!" And she untied her own scarf and held it up. Indeed, it had the same pattern sewn into it.

"Mrs. Wigglepox, that was my mother! She's been missing for months! Someone must have looked into the crystal ball or something that night and activated it, and she must have fallen in through the mirror, just like I did. But the crystal ball was still on the other side – in my... in my world." She said the last few words slowly, thoughtfully.

"So," Colleen continued, "the mirror *is* a door of some sort. You look into the crystal ball, or do something with it – maybe shake it like Frederick did, and it can take you to the place that you see – you just walk through and you are there! I wonder... did Grandpa use it that night he disappeared? Did he activate this portal and come here, or go some other place? He might also still be alive! Have you seen an old man with a walking stick come through?"

Before Mrs. Wigglepox could answer, a voice from behind interrupted her.

"We've got to get out of here and get back home!" it said.

It was Frederick. He was rubbing his head and staring at Mrs. Wigglepox.

"This must be a bad dream," he groaned as he sat up.

"No, Frederick," said Colleen. "It's not a dream. We've come through a sort of magic doorway or something. And the same thing must have happened to my mother and grandfather! And now those

– those *goblins* have her, and maybe Grandpa as well. We've got to save them!"

"No way," said Frederick. "We've got to get back and tell my dad about this."

He got up then, and Colleen whirled to face him.

"No!" she said, her voice full of anger. "You're going to come with me to find my mother and grandfather or you're going to stay here in these woods alone. Just how do you intend to go back? You threw the crystal ball on the other side, remember, and that *thing* that was coming through the mirror likely took it! You can wait around for it to follow us through, or we can move away from this place."

"Yes, *it* was likely a goblin," said Mrs. Wigglepox. "They are wicked creatures that roam the night, casting spells of fear and dread and plague. You mustn't face them alone."

"Let's not talk nonsense," said Frederick. He was trying to sound brave, and his father had always said that logic and clear thinking could solve every problem that one might face. "There's a logical explanation for all of this. And those things you're calling *goblins* are nothing but a bunch of outlaw thugs that have been roaming the countryside – or maybe the children of thugs, by the size of that one we saw. My father warned me of them – a band of homeless misfits who can't find jobs and are all in a huff because they've lost their land. They roam about stealing and robbing from anyone they can. That's what that thing was in the doorway – it was one of them. And I say it was one of them that stole away your mother, Colleen, and maybe your grandfather as well. Father told me about the whole thing before we came."

"Lawless misfits and robbers – yes, they are that, my boy," said Mrs. Wigglepox. "But they are not men. They are goblins. And they have dark powers, or at least some of them do. You would do well to stay clear of them. As for your grandfather, Colleen, I've not seen anyone else. I'm sorry."

Frederick sniffed and said, "Well, you can believe what you want, but even so, how do you expect to do anything about them? And, if they've kidnapped Mrs. McGunnegal or your grandpa, what can we do about it anyway... two kids and a ... a... a l...leprechaun!"

He stumbled over the last words, and began to mumble about not believing in little people. "Must have hit my head... that's it... it's all a hallucination... I'm imagining it all. Yes..." But he sounded most unconvincing, even to himself.

"Well," Colleen said slowly, "you may have a point - about us just being kids, I mean. I hadn't thought of that. But perhaps Mrs. Wigglepox can guide us, and we can rescue Mr. Wigglepox as well. We've got to try to do something!"

"Yes, in this place, you will most definitely need a guide. Those who know how to guide well are rare at every season, but in this time of darkness in our land, a good guide would be hard indeed to find," said the little woman. "I am certainly not fit for such a venture, and as for going to the strongholds of our enemies – that is far too dangerous. Why, it would take a troop of strong men and a wizard to break into the fortress of the goblins, and even then, you would have to face the Goblin King, Gruazard, and his Court Witch. I've never seen them myself, but it's said that the Goblin King is horrible and huge, and does things to his prisoners that just can't be mentioned. And the Court Witch – it would take a powerful wizard to face her. Plus, the goblins roam about these woods and try to snatch away what few of us are left."

"See there," said Frederick. "Now, let's just try to get home and... and, well, you can tell your father and big brothers all about it, and the police too, and bring them all back here to take care of this... king and witch and ... goblins ... if that's what they are. I suppose if there are really little people, there *might* be goblins. But really, Colleen, we're just kids! We have to get some adults to help."

Colleen started to protest, but Frederick was making a bit of sense. Surely Father, Aonghus, and Bran were more than a match for any goblins. Why, they were the biggest men in the whole territory, and were wonderfully strong and even a bit frightful when angry.

"But it seems," said Mrs. Wigglepox, "that you have lost the way back. You will need to find another way."

Colleen thought for a moment and then said, "If this mirror is a doorway, it might lead to other worlds as well. There's an old map over my fireplace back home that has a riddle on it. I think it speaks of other worlds where the maker of the map went to. Maybe there's a different key for each world or something. If we could find another key..."

They were all quiet for a moment, and then Frederick said, "It was the pirate."

"The Pirate!" said Mrs. Wigglepox.

"The map back at your farm mentions a pirate named Atsolter. He must have come here the same way. That means that the crystal ball *is* the key and he must have hidden the treasure *here* somewhere!"

Colleen noticed a strange gleam in his eyes when he spoke of treasure.

"Yes," said Mrs. Wigglepox. "There are tales of someone called the Pirate. But they are old, old tales, though not as old as the tales of the wizards, or even so old as the witches coming to our land. But yes, there are tales of someone called the Pirate."

"I think the crystal ball is the only key that there is," said Frederick. "At least if that riddle is right. And I'll bet *this* was the last place that Pirate went to – that's why we ended up here and not somewhere else. Imagine having the power to go anywhere in the universe right from your living room! Someone with the mirror and the crystal could..." He stopped mid-sentence, pondering where he might go and what he might do.

"But we came through a mirror on the other side, Frederick," said Colleen, interrupting his thoughts. "I think it will only take you through to another magic mirror. Whoever made these mirrors must have gotten here somehow in the first place to put them here. If we could figure out how they got in, maybe we could go back that way too. Mrs. Wigglepox, you mentioned the wizards - how did they ..."

But before she could finish her sentence, Badger gave a whinny and stamped his feet. Off through the mist came the distant sound of cracking branches and rustling leaves.

Mrs. Wigglepox gave a shriek and leaped from the root to the ground. *"Goblins!"* she whispered. "We must hide!"

Chapter 9 – Goblins

Colleen froze, squinting through the fog, trying to see any movement in the direction where the noises were coming to them. But the mists hid whatever it was.

"We can't just hide under the leaves," said Frederick. "We've got to get out of here."

"Badger," said Colleen, pointing at the horse. "Come on."

Mrs. Wigglepox looked up at the horse. "I'm afraid you'll need to carry me," she said. "Quickly now, put me in your pocket."

Colleen hesitated only a moment before carefully picking up the little leprechaun and sliding her into her dress pocket, then she mounted Badger.

"Frederick, come on. Climb on behind me," she said urgently.

"I'm no good at riding!" he said in a whisper. "I'll fall off!"

"Just get on the horse and hold onto me. Hurry now, they're coming!" she said.

Frederick glanced in the direction of the noise coming towards them and then ran to the horse. Putting his foot in the stirrup, he swung his leg over and nearly fell, and was only saved by Colleen steadying him.

"Now hold on around my waist and don't crush Mrs. Wigglepox – she's in my pocket!" she said.

She heeled Badger and off they went at a dead run. The sound and smell of the goblins seem to put speed in the old horse's stride. But the trees were close, and even as they started out, a long, hanging branch snagged Colleen's shawl and snatched it from her shoulders. She glanced back at it, but kept going.

Mrs. Wigglepox peered out from Colleen's pocket and said, "There's a path up ahead that your horse could run on better, and it leads down to the old bridge across the river. The goblins use it sometimes, but I think that's our best bet."

Within a few minutes, they were at the path, and Mrs. Wigglepox directed them to the left. Badger seemed to be enjoying the run, somehow, and Colleen hadn't seen him so lively in years. He galloped along at a good speed until they came to the bridge, and there they stopped.

For an instant, Colleen gazed in amazement at the structure – a massive bridge with intricate workmanship, although obviously quite ancient. Its huge stones were perfectly shaped and fitted together, forming a single span across the deep chasm. The path, however, did not cross it, but continued on along the side of the gorge.

Colleen began to move Badger toward the bridge, but Mrs. Wigglepox said, "No! Not that one! That was the Troll Bridge. I don't trust it. See, there, down the trail – the wooden bridge to the right – that's the one we're taking."

"But ..." began Colleen.

But Mrs. Wigglepox cut her off and said, "I'll explain later, Colleen. Just run Badger across the wooden bridge and up the trail a ways, and then ride back to the bridge."

"But why?" she insisted.

"We're going to try to fool them into thinking that we went up the trail. Be quick!" she said.

Reeds grew along the banks of the river in the chasm, and there seemed to be a small side trail of sorts on the far side of the wooden bridge that appeared to run off the main path and down to the riverside. The strong smell of rotting grasses and cattails reached their noses.

Colleen said, "Run, Badger, run!" And the old horse took off, a glint in his eyes, and clattered across the wooden bridge.

"Slow down!" wailed Frederick as he bumped up and down. "I'm going to fall off!"

"Just you hold on if you don't want those goblins catching you," said Colleen, and he clung tighter around her waist.

Up the trail they flew, then, after about a quarter mile, she turned and they raced back, but this time on the side of the road until they reached the bridge again.

"Now, quickly, we must get down and walk Badger down the side trail and under the bridge!"

Off the horse they jumped, with Frederick sliding down Badger's back side and falling on his own.

"Frederick, grab that bunch of ferns there and try to wipe out our footprints," she said.

Frederick obeyed, grumbling.

Colleen paid him no mind and led the horse down the embankment and under the bridge. Frederick threw the ferns into the brush to one side, looked anxiously across the bridge and down the path, and then followed where Colleen had gone.

They hurried into the shadows, and not a minute later came the sound of tramping feet and rough voices above them on the bridge.

"They came this way," said a gruff voice. "Look here, their trail goes on down the path. It's a bit confused, but they ran off that way, for sure."

"Maybe the Old Troll scared 'em off," grunted another.

"Or ate them," said another, which brought a chorus of harsh laughter.

"Maybe we should send Bones down there to check," said another.

"Yeah, go on, Bones," jeered a rather high-pitched voice. "You know you like to pick over the carcasses."

"On with it, you gloats, we're almost on 'em," shouted the first voice. "Get down the trail or I'll throw you to the Troll myself. Get on!"

Colleen listened as the voices faded in the distance, and then they were gone.

"That won't fool them for long," said Mrs. Wigglepox. "We've got to make our way back to my tree. We should be safe there. Come now, we'll stay in the river so that we don't make tracks. Hurry along."

Colleen mounted Badger again, and Frederick climbed unsteadily behind her.

"We'll have to go under that... Troll Bridge," said Frederick.

"Yes, we shall," said Mrs. Wigglepox. "The goblins will never suspect that we went that way. They fear the bridge."

In a few moments, Badger was nearing the massive structure. Its impressive arch loomed high above, and they stopped before entering its dark shadow.

Colleen looked where Frederick was pointing, and there in the mud were huge footprints, at least two feet long. Frederick opened his mouth to say something more, but Mrs. Wigglepox spoke first.

"Colleen, you must have Badger run for all he is worth under the shadow of this bridge. Do not let him stop!" she said.

Colleen didn't question why, but said, "Hold on, Frederick," and spurred Badger.

Badger took a step, then hesitated, neighing and tossing his head. But then there was a distant sound of harsh voices, and Colleen kicked him again and said, "Go boy!"

The old horse leaped forward, and as they passed under the arch, Colleen saw why the goblins feared the Troll Bridge. Beneath one side of the arch, a massive black shadow moved. She could not see it clearly for the darkness, but its muscled bulk sat hunched, and as they bolted by, it rose from its place and lunged at them.

Colleen's blood ran cold, and Frederick blathered something unintelligible as the great shape flung itself after them, its breath coming in harsh gasps with every step.

Just as they passed into the light on the other side of the arch, it stopped, a huge green-scaled hand reaching outward, but quickly withdrew with a dreadful cry of anguish and rage.

Colleen looked back as they ran on, and she could see the thing standing in the shadows, its great shoulders heaving, its breath labored.

"Was... was that a troll?" said Frederick, his voice weak.

"It was indeed," said Mrs. Wigglepox. "It was a very old troll. I thought surely it was dead by now. I am sorry."

"A troll!" he wailed. "A troll! We were nearly eaten by a troll!"

Colleen urged Badger on up the stream as quickly as she dared. When they had gone for some minutes, the river bed began to grow rockier. "I think we better slow down a little. It wouldn't do for Badger to break an ankle. But why did the troll stop? Why didn't it chase us?" she asked.

"I think they fear the sunlight," Mrs. Wigglepox replied. "But why that is, I don't know. Legend has it that it got trapped here long ago during one of the wars."

Colleen slowed Badger, and for a good hour, they made their way up the water course, until finally, Mrs. Wigglepox said, "This is where we need to leave the river. I think we'll be safe now."

They climbed the bank on the left and Mrs. Wigglepox said, "Now we've got to make it to my house before nightfall. It's not safe anytime, but it's especially dangerous after dark."

"Why do you say that? Will the troll come after us?" said Frederick.

"Maybe, but the goblins love the darkness too. Actually, I'm quite surprised to see them out even in the fading daylight. It's very unlike them. But they won't stay out in the day for long. I think it actually hurts them in some way. But at night – that's when they grow fierce and do terrible things. You mind yourself, young man, and don't go slipping away from us," she warned him. "There are worse things than trolls and goblins that haunt the forest when the sun goes down."

Chapter 10 – The Wigglepox Tree

Colleen rode on through the mists, guided by the little leprechaun perched in her pocket. They had doubled back on their trail several times to elude any goblins that might still be tracking them. Dusk was heavy upon the forest, and the great trees loomed before them like vast giants with outstretched arms.

Mrs. Wigglepox urged Colleen to ride faster.

"My tail bone is surely bruised," said Frederick with a moan.

However, they didn't slow, but rode on through the deepening gloom, until eventually, Mrs. Wigglepox said, "Here we are at last – the Wigglepox Tree."

Colleen drew Badger to a stop and gazed in awe at the most enormous tree she had ever seen. Great branches near the ground, as thick as Badger was tall, reached outward from the vast trunk and ran in crooked paths through the surrounding wood before raising themselves haphazardly toward the sky. Her eyes slowly followed the hulking growth upward, through a great tangle of massive gnarled arms.

Frederick let out a low whistle. "My whole house would fit inside that thing," he said.

Then he gripped her waist tighter, and she felt an involuntary shudder run through him.

"What's wrong?" she said.

"There are faces in that tree," he whispered.

She looked up again, and the many knobs and contorted twists and turns of bark seemed to cast the illusion of eyes and noses and great mouths frowning down at them.

Then, suddenly, another vision came to her. It was more than just a face, but a sense that something in this tree was deeply *aware* of them – a mind that gazed down and considered them with deep, slow thoughts.

"Please, Colleen, put me on the ground," said Mrs. Wigglepox.

Colleen blinked, and the vision vanished, but the feeling of watchfulness in this tree lingered on. She and Frederick dismounted, and she carefully placed the leprechaun on the ground.

Mrs. Wigglepox walked beneath the massive branches right up to the base of the tree. Cupping her hands against the bark, she appeared to whisper something.

With an earsplitting sound of creaking and grinding and thrashing of branches and leaves, the great tree began to change. Two of the huge branches nearest the ground began to writhe, moved apart, and formed a passageway through the tangle. Then a large opening appeared in the trunk between the branches, big enough for Badger to walk through easily.

"Welcome to the Wigglepox Tree," she said. "My family has lived here since before anyone can remember."

"You live in a rotted-out hollow tree?" said Frederick.

"My boy, this is *not* a rotted-out tree," she said sternly. "For your information, the Wigglepox Tree and its little people have lived in harmony, protecting and caring for each other, for ages and ages. The tree has *opened* itself up to us, and you're fortunate that it doesn't give you a good thrashing for such an insult."

Frederick took a step backward. "I didn't mean..."

"Never you mind," interrupted Mrs. Wigglepox. "But you just mind your manners, since we'll be sleeping inside it tonight. Come along."

Mrs. Wigglepox disappeared into the tree, and Colleen led Badger through the aisle of branches toward the opening. Frederick hesitated, looked around at the deepening darkness, and quickly followed.

As Colleen passed into the great tree, a dim light greeted her that seemed to come from the wood of the tree itself. As her eyes adjusted, she saw that, although the tree was hollow, the wood was not rotted at all, but rather clean and smooth, not at all like other hollow trees she had climbed into that were full of sawdust and ants and crickets and spider webs. This tree seemed more like a house – or at least the room of a house – and it was spacious, comfortable, and welcoming.

"Well, let me just check in," said Mrs. Wigglepox.

She hurried over to one wall and disappeared through a small hole.

A moment later, they heard her voice call from above them and they looked up. There she was, looking out a window of sorts about ten feet above their heads.

"Everything is fine, my dear, and word from the forest is that the goblins have lost our trail and have gone on south, back toward their holes, no doubt to report what they've discovered," she said.

She disappeared again and re-emerged at the base of the tree, and behind her came two even tinier people.

"Colleen, Frederick, I would like you to meet my two daughters, Lily and Rose," she said.

"How do you do?" said Colleen. Frederick grunted and nodded his head.

The two tiny girls, no taller than Colleen's fingers, curtsied and said in very small voices, "Fine, thank you. Very nice to meet you."

"And you," she said.

Meanwhile, Frederick had gone over to the far wall and was poking his fingers into more holes in the side, when he suddenly said, "Hey, see here, let me go!" and was pulling frantically at his hand. Apparently, his finger had gotten stuck in one of them.

"Help! It won't let me go! It grabbed me, I tell you!" he cried.

"Well, it serves you right," said Mrs. Wigglepox. "How would you like it if someone went poking their fingers in your belly?"

She watched him jump about, trying to pull his finger free, and finally, with a chuckle, said, "Lily, how about helping the boy? He's really got himself into a fix."

Lily walked across the floor until she was just a few feet from the struggling and now moaning Frederick.

"Now, boy," she said. "You must stand still. I shan't help you if you're going to dance all over the place like that. I do not wish to be stepped on!"

Frederick stopped his dancing and looked down at the little girl.

"Now be still," she said, and walked next to him and leaned close to the tree. She cupped her hands against the wall and said something that Frederick could not make out, but almost immediately, his finger popped out of the hole and he fell backward in a heap.

Lily giggled and walked over to him. She was a very pretty little girl with brown braided hair and tiny freckles across her nose.

"How old are you?" she asked him.

"Well, I'm... I'm fourteen," he said to her.

"I'm nine. And I think you're cute," she said, and she ran back to Mrs. Wigglepox.

Frederick actually blushed for a moment and then got to his feet.

To change the subject, he said, "Have you got anything to eat? It's well past tea time."

Mrs. Wigglepox frowned. "Yes, we do have food for folk our size, but one small meal for you would clean out our cupboards! I am sorry, but I'm afraid we're going to have to find you something in the forest in the morning."

She thought for a moment and then said, "There's a berry patch not far from here, least ways not far for your kind to walk to, and a few hickory and chestnut trees as well. That won't be much, but at least it should fill your bellies."

"Can't we go now?" asked Frederick.

"At night?" said Mrs. Wigglepox. "No, no, we mustn't wander about in the dark, not in this wood. The Haunts come out at night."

"What are the haunts?" asked Colleen, and she glanced at the open doorway.

Mrs. Wigglepox looked down at her daughters and said, "That's what we call a person who has fallen under the Spell. Ah, but let's not speak of it in the darkness. Bright morning is the best time for such tales. I'm sure you must be exhausted. Please, make yourselves as comfortable as you can. It's time to close up for the evening."

With that, she spoke to the tree, and Colleen watched as the entryway began to close with an echoing sound like thunder, grinding stone, and great creaking boards. Then the doorway was gone, and no crack or crevice could be seen in the place where it had been.

She turned to Frederick. His eyes were wide and his face was ashen.

"Well, we might as well settle in," she said. "Come on, help me with Badger's saddle."

He stared at the blank wall a moment longer, then said, "What? Oh, all right," and helped her unsaddle the horse.

"Best get some sleep," he muttered.

"Here, we'll share the saddle as a pillow. You sleep on one side and I'll take the other," said Colleen.

"You two sleep well," said Mrs. Wigglepox. "We'll see you in the morning."

She led Lily and Rose back to the hole in the wall, and they disappeared, but not before Lily lingered a moment longer, staring out at Frederick. Then, she too vanished.

Colleen lay on the soft pine needle floor of the tree, her head resting on one side of the saddle.

"How about this?" she said. "Who would believe it if we told them?"

"Not my family, that's for sure," replied Frederick. "I wouldn't have even a few hours ago."

"It's maddening and terrifying and, well, exciting, all at the same time," said Colleen. "Still, I do hope we can find another way back soon."

They said no more that night, but stared up at the high ceiling above them, each lost in thought about the strange things they had seen. It was a long while before they slowly drifted to sleep.

Neither of them noticed the little faces of Lily and Rose peering down at them from a high window, their tiny lips forming innocent smiles as they beheld their first glimpse of the big people. Mrs. Wigglepox joined them for a moment, then shooshed them to bed. Then, going to her own room and gazing out a knothole into the night, she made a wish.

"Let these be the ones," she said to the listening night. "The ones who will break the Spell and set us free."

Chapter 11 - Oracle

"Wake up!" said a little voice in Frederick's ear.

He opened one eye and jumped. Lily was sitting on the saddle right next to his head. She was dressed in a mottled brown dress that made her look remarkably like a leaf with a head.

"Don't scare me like that!" he said and sat up. "It's not every day you get woken up by a little person."

His stomach growled, reminding him that he had not eaten since lunchtime the day before.

Colleen was already up and looking as fresh and perky as ever, as though falling through magic mirrors, being chased by goblins, and sleeping in haunted trees with a family of leprechauns was something she did every day, and was of no account.

"Up at last, sleepyhead?" she said. "We've been waiting for you. The sun is up already."

He stood and stretched, then realized he was covered with pine needles.

Both Colleen and Lily laughed, and Colleen helped him brush himself off.

"Best be going for breakfast," said Mrs. Wigglepox as she came out of her tiny doorway. "Come on now, we'll show you the way. Colleen, will you carry us?"

"Mother," said Lily. "I want Frederick to carry me. Can't he, please?"

At this, Frederick looked quite surprised and even a bit taken aback.

"I, uh, well, that is, I..." he stammered.

Mrs. Wigglepox looked hard at him and then nodded to herself. She walked over to him, leading Lily by the hand.

"Frederick," she said. "Do you see my daughter here?"

He nodded.

"Do you know how valuable she is to me?" she asked.

He shook his head.

"She means more to me than all the treasures in Fairyland, more than all the pots of gold at the end of all the rainbows in the world. You've not shown yourself to be a very trustworthy young man. But I trust my daughter's judgment of you. Apparently, she thinks you worth trusting, so I put her, literally, in your hands. Mind you, I'll be watching, and if any harm comes to her, you shall have me to deal with, and I shall have this tree take hold of more than your finger to squeeze!" At that, she stepped back a few paces, leaving a beaming Lily staring up at him.

"But, but..." he began.

"Come on, Frederick," interrupted Lily. "It will be grand fun. You'll carry me and I shall tell you stories of the woodland."

He paused a moment, and then said, "Well, all right. Why not? It's not every day you get to carry a leprechaun in your hands." So he knelt down and held them out.

Lily stepped onto his palm and, with a care that Colleen thought him incapable of, he raised her up and held his hands close to his chest, where she sat down cross-legged and leaned back against him.

"Off we go!" she squealed happily.

Colleen carefully picked up Mrs. Wigglepox and then Rose and put them each in a pocket.

"Shall we ride Badger?" asked Colleen.

"Let the old boy sleep," said Mrs. Wigglepox. "He's had quite enough excitement for a while."

"What fun!" cried Rose. "I've never been carried by a giant before!"

"They are not giants," said Mrs. Wigglepox. "If you, a little seven-year-old leprechaun, ever came across a giant, you probably would not even know it, because his shoes alone would seem like a huge mountain to you."

She paused a moment, smiling at her daughter, then called out, "Open, please!"

The noise of the tree opening filled the room for a long moment, sunlight streamed in, and there before them was a pathway through the great branches. The fog of the previous night had vanished, but the sense of heaviness in the forest remained.

Still, the Wigglepox children giggled and called to one another as they walked along and, after a short time, they came to a large meadow where there was a spring and many berry bushes. In the center of the clearing was what appeared to be a broken tower of sorts, its stones crumbling with long years of disrepair.

At first, Frederick started to run toward the berry bushes, but at a scream from Lily, he remembered that he was carrying her and immediately stopped.

"Oh... sorry," he said in a low voice so no one but she would hear him, and he walked over to a berry bush that was laden with fruit.

He picked a particularly juicy one and popped it in his mouth.

"Mmmm," he said, and reached for another one.

"Frederick!" said Lily. "Doesn't a lady get any?"

"Oh, sorry," he said and, looking about, picked a small but juicy one and put it in his hand next to her.

She grabbed hold of one of the juicy knobs and twisted it free from the rest of the fruit, and then took a bite. Purple juice came squirting out and dotted her checkered dress. Frederick laughed.

"Uh, here," he said, and reached in his pocked, pulled out a hankie, and handed it to her. "It's not used or anything," he said. "Maybe you could use it like an apron or something."

She smiled at him and said, "I have a grand idea. Put me down in the grass here and we'll spread this out like a picnic cloth. You can get yourself a handful of berries, and I'll just have this one. It will be more than enough for me."

To Colleen's amazement, Frederick Buttersmouth, the boy of whom she had so many bad impressions, sat down in the grass, spread out his hankie, and piled a handful of berries on it, and sat eating and talking to a three-inch tall little leprechaun girl. He even went to the spring and drank deeply, then brought back a bit in his hand for Lily to drink.

"Would you look at that!" whispered Colleen to Mrs. Wigglepox as she put Rose down on a large toadstool, where she happily sat to watch. "Who would have thought?"

"Amazing what a little trust can do for someone," Mrs. Wigglepox replied. "Sometimes a person just needs someone to believe in them. But the proof's in the pudding, as it's said."

For a moment, Colleen munched on her berries in silence, and then said, "Mrs. Wigglepox, what's this old stone heap here in the meadow? It looks ancient."

"I believe it goes back to the time of the wizards," she said. "It was a tower or house of some sort once, but it has not been used in our living memory, and even the forest has forgotten how it was used. Some say that a beautiful princess with the most extraordinary hair was trapped in it once, but she escaped through some sort of magic and ran off with a prince. Others say that dwarves built it, and some that wizards lived here once, but no one knows for sure. It was long, long ago."

After they had eaten their fill, Colleen said, "Frederick, I'm going to climb to the top of this broken tower and have a look around. Want to join me?"

He looked up hesitantly, then nodded.

Up the pile of ruined stone they went and, as they did, Colleen noticed many strange runes and carvings on the rocks.

"Frederick," she said. "Look at these carvings. They look very much like ones I've seen back home. They're all over the broken rocks that make up the wall that borders our farm."

Frederick looked closely at the odd letters carved on a large stone block that he was leaning against.

"Could be," he said. "Father went walking about your farm while you were all looking for your grandfather. He brought a whole sack of them to the inn and had me look them over. He said I was to help him decipher them when we got back to England. He always makes me do that sort of thing. He says he's preparing me to take his place when he retires."

"He was taking stones from our farm without permission? Well!" she said.

She was exasperated at the thought of Rufus taking things that were potentially of great value without even asking, especially when they were so poor and needed money to save the farm.

"I suppose there's nothing for it now. So, can you read these things?" she asked.

"No, they're not in any language I've ever seen," he said. After a moment, he said, "Say, maybe Mrs. Wigglepox could read them."

"Let's see," Colleen replied. "But first, let's get higher. We're almost over the treetops now."

As they neared the top, Colleen could see a vast brown carpet that stretched in all directions, dotted only occasionally by a lonely green patch. Far to the south, she could barely make out a distant range of high hills that ran from east to west and beyond them a brown horizon.

"What's that?" asked Frederick, squinting as he peered southward and pointing. "That shiny thing way off in the middle of the forest."

Colleen looked where he pointed, and there was a tiny speck of something shining in the sun.

"Must be a lake or pond or something," said Colleen. "It certainly is shining."

"Colleen, this is pretty scary," said Frederick. "This forest must stretch for hundreds of miles all around us. There's no place like this that I know of anywhere in Ireland or England. We've *got* to be in some other land. And it looks like our only way home is going to be the same way we came."

Quite suddenly, there was a sound, and a very strange sound indeed, for a large round stone that was sitting on the peak of the mound began to speak.

"The spelpy forest strunes frightibly round. But farder lies the

76

Landu ground. There brines the spectvelous light! The Leople's hope amid the night!"

Colleen and Frederick both jumped and nearly went tumbling down the rocky hill.

"What was that?" said Frederick.

Colleen looked upward at the gray rock, and realized that it was not a rock at all, but a small hunched man wearing a tattered gray cloak. He had been sitting very still on the highest point of the pile, with his back to them and his head bent down. Now he slowly uncurled himself and turned to meet their astonished expressions.

His face was neither old nor young, and he was rather bald with strands of gray-white hair strewn across his head. He had a short, scraggly beard but no mustache, and the clothes under his gray cloak were faded green britches and a tunic with a brown belt that had a dull brass buckle. He looked as though he might stand about two feet high in his worn, black, brass-buckle shoes if he were not so bent.

He squinted his large brown eyes at them and said in the same scraggly voice, "Helves and Smen, come to the Leoples land again!"

Colleen had no idea what he had just said, so she just stared at the little man, not knowing how to reply. After an awkward moment, Frederick spoke.

"Uh, please excuse us, sir, but we didn't quite catch that."

The little man closed his eyes and said, "Trechangers and frighty times may lie ahead, for Fredersmouth and Colligal shall besperience the dead."

Colleen and Frederick looked at one another, and then she said, "Please sir, what is your name? My name is Colleen McGunnegal, and this is my cousin, Frederick Buttersmouth. We've only just arrived in your land."

But the man picked up a cane that was lying next to him, stood up, and began slowly to descend from the mound, glancing at them as he passed them by.

They watched him as he made his way from rock to rock, grunting at times, but muttering a tune as he went.

"When chidescents of oldient king
Clascend the broashed tower again,
The time to rejelbate has come
For Leoples will get liberdom."

He kept repeating this, with an occasional laugh of glee between the verses.

"He's loony," whispered Frederick. "Maybe that Spell that Mrs. Wigglepox was talking about has gotten to him."

The little man seemed to hear this, for he stopped and turned, looked Frederick in the eyes, and shouted, "Imachievable!" then continued on down the mound singing his tune.

"Best follow him," said Frederick.

Colleen nodded, and they began to follow him down, being careful not to knock any of the loose rocks down on the little fellow as he picked his way toward the meadow.

When they finally reached the bottom, the bent man sat on a rock and called loudly, "Pigglewoxes!"

Mrs. Wigglepox, Lily, and Rose all looked up with a jump of surprise. They all dashed behind a large mushroom and peered out.

Frederick walked past the man and over to where they were hiding and bent low to talk to them.

"There is some sort of mad fellow here," he said. "We can't understand a word he says."

All three of the Wigglepoxes climbed up on the mushroom and looked across the meadow where Colleen was stooped down, trying to talk to the hunched man.

"Did he say who he was?" asked Mrs. Wigglepox.

"Just went on with a bunch of nonsense," said Frederick. "I was wondering if you might know him."

"I've never seen him before," she said. "My, but he is a big fellow."

"Big to you," he said. "Rather a midget to me."

"Well, at any rate, he's not a goblin, I can tell you. But my eyesight isn't what it used to be. Let's go meet him," said Mrs. Wigglepox.

They slid off the mushroom and made their way quickly across the meadow. As they drew near, they could hear Colleen talking to him.

"Please, sir, won't you tell me who you are? What is your name? Do you live nearby?"

But the man didn't say anything in reply, and only watched as Frederick and the Wigglepox family made their way toward him.

When finally they drew near, Mrs. Wigglepox exclaimed, "Well, bless my soul! You are a leprechaun!"

"Coursitutely!" said the man, and he winked at her.

"If he's a leprechaun, how come he's so big?" asked Frederick.

The strange little fellow turned slowly toward him, pointed at the Wigglepoxes, and said, "Questery is, why's them so miniscuall?"

There was an awkward moment of silence before Colleen said, "Well, at any rate, won't you tell us your name?"

But the bent little leprechaun slid from his rock and hobbled over to the Wigglepox family, bent down even lower to them, closed one eye, and gazed at them with the other one, which he opened quite wide.

After looking them over, he nodded to himself and said, "You'll do."

"I say we call him The Oracle," said Frederick with a laugh. "He seems to say a lot of nothing in a rather mysterious way."

The little man rose from his examination of the Wigglepox family, hobbled over to Frederick, and whacked him in the shin with his cane.

"Ouch!" said Frederick. "What was that for?"

But the leprechaun said nothing, proceeded over to a berry bush, began to pick some low hanging fruit, and placed them in a shoulder pouch that he had produced from somewhere.

Colleen could not help but giggle at the sight.

"I think he's rather charming," she said. "But I do wish he would tell us something of himself."

"Well, at any rate, he does have a good idea - we best gather as much fruit as we can, and be getting back to the Tree," said Mrs. Wigglepox. "And Mr. ... Mr. ... well, if you won't tell us your name, then we *shall* call you Oracle. So then, Oracle, would you join us back at our tree?"

He paused in his berry picking, looked at her, winked again, and then continued picking berries and humming a little tune.

Frederick rolled his eyes, but Colleen wondered about this fellow. He was odd, but there was something about him that made her instinctively trust him.

Suddenly, a strange feeling swept over her, as though his frail frame and gray cloak veiled a hidden – *something*. But she could not put into words what she felt. Then he flicked a berry through the air, grinned, and hobbled down the trail.

"He's a loon," whispered Frederick as they followed him.

But Colleen was not so sure.

Chapter 12 – Another Night in the Land of the Little People

The mysterious little man lagged behind as Colleen and Frederick made their way back to the Wigglepox Tree. Soon they were back, where they found Badger still contentedly sleeping.

Oracle went up to the tree and gave one of its massive roots a hug. It gave a slight quiver, and then was still. Mrs. Wigglepox looked at the leprechaun and rubbed her chin for a moment, then shrugged.

"I guess you'll want to be making plans today, and spend at least one more night with us," she said.

Spend the night! thought Colleen. All the events of the prior day and night came rushing back to her, and she realized that they did need to get back home. Her mother was here, and she was being held captive by terrible creatures. She had to get back home and bring back her father and brothers, and then they all could rescue her. Besides, her family would be getting terribly worried by now... or would they? No, actually they would not be worried, not for some days at least. Henny would tell the others that she was home, and Father... he would not even know that she was missing. These and other thoughts whirled about in her head as she walked into the huge tree.

Mrs. Wigglepox interrupted her thoughts and said, "It's a mighty shame that you lost that crystal ball. I'd hate to think of a goblin having the power to move from world to world through that mirror."

Oracle grunted and looked very serious and, in a somber tone, said, "Hoblgobs and Witlcore mustn't get the keydloore, or Fredersmouth and Colligal shall see their middangeard go ill."

"What *is* he saying?" said Frederick.

"I think I actually caught that one," said Colleen. "I think he might have said that the goblins and the Witch mustn't get the key to the door or something bad will happen to our world."

Something bad will happen. Suddenly it hit her. Something bad *was* happening back in their world. The black blight had arrived in

Ireland the very year that her mother had disappeared and the goblin had come through the mirror.

"Frederick, we have *got* to get that crystal ball back somehow, and get that goblin out of our world. I think it plans to turn Ireland into *this!*" she said, pointing out the doorway at the dead forest.

For a few moments, they all sat in a depressing silence, then she whispered, "I think it's already started."

Frederick was not sure what to say. He had seen the sick and starving people in Ireland firsthand, but he had never stopped to think much of what was happening to them. He had overheard old O'Brian say that he had seen mortiferous vapors rising out of the swamp near the McGunnegal farm, and he speculated that those fumes might be to blame for the failed potato crop and the sicknesses that were spreading. Could it be that this goblin was somehow involved as well? And what if it spread to England?

The very thought of it made him feel sick and helpless, and so, to change the subject, he asked, "Mrs. Wigglepox, how is it that just the three of you live in this huge tree? It seems as though it would hold many more folk of your size."

Mrs. Wigglepox bowed her head and said, "Once there were more of us here. And... well... once we were... bigger, or so our legends say. Something like..."

She glanced over at Oracle, and then said, "But never mind that. The goblins have taken all the others. Once this tree was the home of quite a few of my people – a veritable village of leprechauns, and all related to the Wigglepoxes! My grandmother told me of the days when many a rainbow ended at this tree. But now all are gone, and all their pots of gold are stolen away. I suppose that one day, we will be gone too, and the old tree will close itself up forever."

"But I thought leprechauns were magic and all that. Couldn't you just zap those goblins with lightning bolts or something when they came near?" asked Frederick.

"It's the *Spell*, Frederick. It has robbed us of our gifts, and if they want, sometimes the Witch's people can actually *hide* within the Spell, sneak up on you, and catch you off guard," she said.

"But how could they hide inside a spell?" asked Colleen, joining in the conversation.

"It's hard to explain, but it seems that they can sort of blend in with it at times, like a fox hides in the grass until a mouse comes by, then it leaps out and gobbles it down," she said. "I'm afraid the Spell sometimes makes the Witch's folks rather hard to spot. They become like shadows, especially at night when the darkness deepens. They don't like the sunlight, you know. They can't seem to blend in with the Spell so much when the sun is shining on them. I think it might even hurt them somehow.

"But so many of us have been stolen away and cast in their dungeons because we just didn't see them coming in time. We wandered out at the edge of night among the lengthening shadows, and there we found them waiting for us. At first, we didn't know what was happening, but by the time we did, we were weak and had little strength to fight back."

"Blazight!" said Oracle from the place where he had seated himself. "Scalurns and healooths!"

"Loony," said Frederick under his breath. Then a thought struck him and he said, "Earlier, you said that there were stories here about the Pirate that came to your land. What do those stories say about him?"

"There are quite a few of such tales. They tell of a man who called himself a pirate who came long ago through that very mirror that you came through, and caused great havoc among the little people. He stole our pots of gold and they granted him wishes to get them back. With some of his wishes, he gained great treasures and wealth and power. But for his final wish, something within him changed."

"What did he wish for?" asked Colleen.

"It's said that he wished for great wisdom. He disappeared for some time after that, but returned later, bringing with him all the pots of gold he had taken and all the treasures he had wished for, along with a good many other things that he had taken from our land. He left them here, disappeared through the mirror, and was never seen again."

"So there is great treasure here somewhere!" said Frederick.

"Alas," said Mrs. Wigglepox. "The goblins have taken it all long ago. It was not long after the Pirate left that the goblins came in force. Some said that it was he who somehow led them here from their deep places under the Earth. They had come from time to time before, but now they began to come with greater numbers and with dark magic."

After a moment, Colleen asked. "Mrs. Wigglepox, tell us more about the goblins. I mean, why are they here in your land? Just what *are* they?"

"'Tis a sad tale, lassie," she replied, "but I suppose I should tell you at least some of it. Long ago, there were no goblins in the Land of the Little People. We all lived in peace and were quite content. All the leprechauns and fairies and gnomes and pixies and such – why we had such wonderful times! The grandmothers of our grandmothers used to tell us marvelous tales of the Good Old Days, as we call them, before the Great Wizard opened the Gates."

"The Great Wizard?" interrupted Frederick. "Who was that?"

"Ah!" said Mrs. Wigglepox. "That was Anastazi the Great. He comes into many tales, as does his daughter, Mor-Fae. He was a great Elf Elder, perhaps the greatest of them all, besides their king. And he built the Timeless Hall, as he called it, and in it made the Gates of the Worlds. And when he opened the Gates, the way to each other's worlds was open!"

"You mean that you had never seen anyone besides the little people before then?" asked Colleen.

"That's right, child," she replied. "No one except the Dryads and other such folk, and the Lady, that is. We didn't even know that anyone else existed until one day, a great silver gate appeared in the forest and through it stepped a giant! Or so we thought. It was the Great Wizard himself, all clad in shining blue robes. He had a crown on his head and a white staff in his hand. My people hid from him at first, but soon they found that he was friendly and good, and it was not long before we were freely visiting all the worlds, and learning from them, and they from us. Ah, those were the Good Old Days."

"So, is that how the goblins got here?" asked Frederick.

"Indeed it is," she said. "But the stories say that they were not evil at first. Something terrible happened to them. I don't know the whole story, but it has something to do with the Great Wizard's daughter. A sad tale, at least the part I know. But suffice to say, after Mor-Fae came, it was but a few hundred years before the evil goblins came too. Some say she let them loose from some awful place, and some say she cursed them and they became evil, while others say that she let loose something in *their* world that made them evil. I don't know what the truth is, but she is always in the tales when it comes to the goblins. She's all mixed up in it somehow. But now they are long gone - all of the elves and wizards that is, the Gate is closed, and we are left with the goblins and the Court Witch," she said sadly.

"Gone?" said Frederick. "But where did they go, and why did they leave?"

"Who can say where they went?" she replied. "Probably through the Gate, and they seemed to have locked it behind them. Some say the Gate was destroyed in the Last Battle, for it was supposed to have been at the Wizard's Castle that once stood far to the south of here."

"Do you think that castle is still there?" asked Frederick, a look of wonder on his face.

"Perhaps, but wherever the Gate was, or is, it's said that some of our people were on the other side when it disappeared. We never saw them again. I suppose they made their way to the other worlds and made homes there as best as they could."

"And some *must* have gone to our world," said Colleen excitedly. "Why, we have *loads* of stories of little people where we come from. Those tales must have come about long ago when your folk came to the lands of Men."

"Now those would be stories worth hearing," she said. "You must tell them to me some time soon."

"But what of the elves and wizards?" asked Frederick. "Why did they leave?"

"I think it was because of the Court Witch," said Mrs. Wigglepox. "She's in many a tale too. The elves and wizards fought against the goblins and the Court Witch for many, many years. Over a hundred years, I think! But somehow, in the last battle, a terrible thing happened. It's said that the Witch unleashed some dark magic that nearly destroyed the wizards. They fled for their lives, leaving behind a great many treasures, and after that battle, it was thought that the Court Witch was gone for good, for there was peace for a long while. The castle was laid desolate and was lost, though legends say that it now lays empty in the Burning Sands – a great desert that lies south of the forest. Few tales come out of those lands, but those that do say it's a mystical place. People that go there are *changed* by it. The Court Witch is powerful, but I guess she still couldn't *undo* all the magic that once dwelt there."

"That sounds *marvelous*," said Colleen. "A magic castle with a gate to other worlds!"

"Yes," the little woman replied. "It was, supposedly, a wondrous place. Anastazi the Great, and Mercurus the Wise Wizard, and all sorts of fair and terribly powerful folk all laboring there and inventing magic things and keeping the goblins away from the Forest... But, alas, now they are gone."

"Mrs. Wigglepox," said Colleen, "if we could get to that castle, then maybe we could find that gate and get through it. That could be our way home!"

"It could be, child, but that would be a very long journey. You would have to travel through the whole forest even to reach the desert's edge, and then somehow you would have to find your way through the Burning Sands to the castle. No one knows for sure where it is," she said.

"Do the goblins ever venture into the desert?" asked Colleen. "Where do they live?"

"Somewhere far to the south," she said. "No one goes there. It's far too dangerous."

Frederick didn't like the idea of potentially having to travel right into goblin territory.

"So is that when the goblins started coming into your forest and taking away your people – after the war, I mean?" asked Colleen.

"Well, it took a while and, as I said, we thought that the Court Witch was destroyed. The final battle was a dreadful one. It devastated the whole land south of the Great Hills. It wasn't even a desert before that war. It was green and growing – beautiful fields and meadows and hills and woodlands, and the Great Sea was not so wide. But the dark power that the Witch unleashed laid it bare – or perhaps it was the clash of the powers of the Witch and the wizards that destroyed it, and a great piece of the land just *sank*. It's said that a terribly huge wave swept across the land almost to the Great Hills when that happened. Perhaps it was from that dreadful wall of water that the wizards fled.

"After that, there was no sign of the Witch or goblins for a long, long time. And then the Pirate came, and that is when the Witch showed up again.

"But the goblins began to come slowly – and we were not defenseless, no! The little people had magic too! Why, whenever they would come, we would weave spells of forgetfulness on them and make them lose their way in the forest. We would lead them through paths that ended up back at the desert, so that they never found us or our trees," she said.

"But they are here now," said Frederick. "What happened to your magic?"

Mrs. Wigglepox sighed. "It's the Spell. It overshadows everything in the Forest, and our magic is ever so weak because of it. The goblins and cluricauns and gremlins came, slinking within it like ghosts and shades, and began to take away our pots of gold. That's when our magic began to wane.

"It's also said that she has done something to the Waking Tree, and because of that, all the forests in all the Land are fading. And her spell is spreading. It's like a slow-moving fog that creeps farther and farther year by year. One day, we fear that it will cover the whole world, from the Great Sea in the South to the Northern Ices and beyond."

"The *Waking Tree?* What's that?" asked Colleen.

"Ah!" she said. "The father of the fathers of the fathers of the trees.

It was the first tree in our world, you know, and from it all the forests were born."

"Why is it called the *Waking Tree?*" asked Frederick. "Does it keep the other trees awake?"

"Well, not exactly," she said. "It was in that tree that our first ancestors *woke up*, you see. They awoke and found themselves there, inside it, much like we are inside this tree, and it spoke to them and they to it. It was from there that we and the forest spread out to cover all the land, oh so many ages ago. It is said that the Creator planted that tree himself, then made the first little people – two of each of our peoples – and placed them inside it. He placed wisdom and knowledge and power in that tree for us to learn from and use. From there, we and the forest spread across the world.

"But we have not seen the Waking Tree since the war, and we were afraid that it was destroyed. But we think now that it was not destroyed, only lost. We wonder if the Court Witch has found it and cast her black magic upon it. Some say that it was the Pirate who actually found it, sailing the South Sea, and it was from him that the Witch discovered its location. If that's true, maybe we could go and somehow free the Waking Tree from her spell, then our own magic might return. Then we would deal with these goblins!"

She made a fist and slapped her hand with it, looking defiant. But a moment later, a look of hopelessness washed across her face.

Oracle stood and joined their little group. He looked at each of them and said, "Wæcan it, Colligal. Bereofan the Sorcergic, and snatch, scratch the Leople's folclond from the hobgobles."

Frederick rolled his eyes, but Colleen looked hard at him.

"I do wish you could make yourself plain, Oracle," said Colleen. "You are rather hard to understand."

"Mph!" said Oracle, and then in a sing-song voice he chortled out a rhyme.

"Colligal and Fredersmouth!

Side and ring and sail far south!

88

Amid the sea, lies Witcherisle,

Place of doom and grief and mother's smile."

Having said this, he returned to his place and sat hunched, staring at his shoes.

Mrs. Wigglepox looked at him, sighed, and said, "I have heard tales of long ago that when the gate to *your* world was open, we found the magic of your world mostly faded too. Did some witch or evil sorcerer cast a spell there as well?"

"I don't know about that, but we have many tales of magic in our world. Most people think they are just fairy tales. But these days, some people believe in it, though I doubt that anyone has actually *seen* any magic," said Colleen.

"Never seen magic? Surely there is still *some* magic left in the lands of Men! Or perhaps some wicked witch did cast some vast sleepiness over your world too. How terrible a thing, to live in a world with no magic at all!" said Mrs. Wigglepox sadly.

"Most people think that magic is a bad thing," put in Frederick.

"Well, I suppose that may be true, if you're talking about the Witch's kind of magic – power for the sake of power, no matter its source, or for personal gain or glory. Some of that sort of thing comes from dark powers that ought never to be sought after," said Mrs. Wigglepox. "But the magic of the little people isn't *that* kind of magic. Maybe it ought not to even be called *magic* at all, since that seems to make folks think of the Witch's kind of power. It's more like the gifts that the Creator gave our people at the beginning – gifts to be used for the betterment of all of our people, never for our individual selves. I think that all of the races were given some sorts of gifts like that, though each one was likely of a different kind. But some of them went all wrong and turned what powers and gifts they were given into dark desires that ruined them."

"Do you mean that humans once had magic, and now it's gone?" asked Frederick.

"The Noetic Wolf huffed and puffed and blew their house down," said Oracle from his seat, shaking his head sadly.

They all looked at him, but no one knew what to say in response to his ravings. After a moment, Mrs. Wigglepox looked at Colleen and Frederick, and then said, "It is curious, though. We have not had humans visit our world in a very long time, other than the Court Witch – and we are not sure if she is human or not and, of course, the Pirate. But when humans did come, the stories say that they were powerful wizards. I wonder now if they were wizards back in the world of Men, or if they *became* wizards here? I mean, did the magic in our world awaken something in them that had long been slumbering, and they took that back with them? Or did they find their magic in some other source?"

"You mean," said Frederick, "that *we* might become wizards or something if we are here long enough?"

"I don't know," she said. "I don't think that is what your people were meant to be. But as I've said, our magic is fading too. Once the Wood was alive with magical trees and creatures and little people, and there were rainbows and ..."

They talked on and on through the day, and Mrs. Wigglepox told one tale after another of leprechauns, fairies, gnomes, pixies, goblins, and trolls, of wizards and the Witch. Frederick and Colleen in their turn told her as many tales as they could recall of the same people that appeared in the legends back home.

At last, Mrs. Wigglepox glanced out the door and said, "See here, I'm rambling on and it's getting late. Look, dusk is coming, and the mists are settling. We had better have a quick meal and drink from the spring, then get some rest."

They ate a brief meal of nuts and berries, and then went outside to drink from a small spring that ran near the Wigglepox Tree.

Then Mrs. Wigglepox said, "Lily, Rose, come along, off to bed with you. And you, Colleen, Frederick, get some rest. Oracle – rest well. Tomorrow promises to be a day of adventure!"

After many goodnights and with much fussing about wanting to stay up a little longer, the girls followed their mother through a tiny door and disappeared.

When they had been gone a few moments, Frederick said, "That's just amazing. I still can't believe it. I *wouldn't* believe it if I hadn't seen it with my own eyes. *Little people! Goblins! Wizards and elves and witches!*"

"And more than that," said Colleen. "We're in the *Land* of the Little People. It's all like a dream, somehow. But think of it! My mother is *here*. You can't imagine what that means to me. I've got to get back home somehow and bring my father and brothers to rescue her. I mean, what if those *things* - those goblins - are doing something awful to her? And that evil Court Witch... I just can't imagine what they..."

At this, she began to sob. The full realization of all that had happened to them that day and the knowledge that her mother was here and was in danger came rushing into her heart and mind all at once.

Frederick did not know what to do. He was not good at comforting people, and he knew it. In fact, he couldn't remember ever trying.

But it seemed to him that he ought to say or do *something*. Here was his cousin sitting across from him, crying her eyes out because her mom had been missing for months, and the very day she finds out she is alive, she also finds that she's in the dungeons of some horrible creatures that were apparently quite *evil*.

That word – *evil* – seemed new to him too. He had never really thought about what evil *was* before. But he now supposed that it was what *they* were – the goblins. They were brutish people who took advantage of others for their own pleasures or greed and didn't care, really, whether they lived or died, so long as they got control of them for their own purposes.

And then it dawned on him that *he* was that way. So was his whole family. They had always lived just like that – taking whatever they wanted without regard to what other people thought or needed. And now, somehow, he felt very sorry about it all.

He moved over next to Colleen and put his hand on her shoulder.

"Don't worry, Colleen," he said. "We'll rescue your mom somehow."

"I do hope so," she cried. "But I'm *so* worried about her. And I feel so *small*. We're just kids, Frederick. What can we do to help her?"

Oracle was at her side as well, his hunched form looking up into her lavender eyes.

"Courageroic Colligal must be," he said.

Colleen took a deep breath and nodded. She wiped her eyes and sniffed, steadying herself.

"I'll be okay," she said after a moment.

Frederick fidgeted with a pine needle, unsure what else to say. Then, to break the silence, he said, "Oh, look, Badger needs a bit of grass. Oughtn't we get him settled for the night?"

Colleen wiped her eyes once more, nodded, and together they went outside, pulled up tufts of dry grass, and gave it to the old horse.

"I guess we don't have a brush to brush him down with," said Frederick.

"No, I'm afraid not," said Colleen. "But he'll be all right for a few days. Hopefully, we'll be home by then."

They talked for a while more about their strange day, and Oracle sat quietly, listening. Soon they grew tired and lay down once again, sharing the saddle for a pillow. The tree creaked and groaned as Mrs. Wigglepox bid them goodnight one last time and closed the door. The ground was as soft as moss and both of them fell fast asleep almost immediately.

Late in the night, Frederick woke with a start, sat up, and looked around. But seeing nothing, he lay down again.

He did not know that, just outside, strange eyes glowed in the darkness, and a misshapen nose sniffed around the base of their tree, smelling something new, but finding only strange footprints.

Chapter 13 – Journey to Wales

Aonghus stood beside his brother and sisters on the aft deck as Ireland shrank away in the distance. He studied their faces, seeing the ache of their hearts in their eyes. This journey would be especially hard on Henny, he knew – no one so young should lose their mother and be forced to leave their father all in a single year.

He understood his father's reasons for sending them all away – good reasons – but everything within him cried out against the injustice of it all, and he wondered what kind of Ireland he would return to in a year.

"Say now, where's that other sister of yours... what was her name?" said a voice behind him.

He turned to see Captain Truehart coming across the deck toward them.

"Colleen is her name. She must still be below deck," said Aonghus.

At this, he noticed that Henny looked at the boards on the deck and pretended to study them.

"She's missing a good part of the trip, she is. Why don't you go below and fetch her up here? Perhaps she could steer for a while," said Truehart.

"I'll get her," said Abbe.

"I think I'll come along too," said Henny.

Aonghus watched them go to the door that led below deck, where Henny stopped Abbe and whispered something in her ear. Abbe's eyes went wide and her jaw dropped. They rushed below deck and returned a few moments later without Colleen. Abbe beckoned for Aonghus, and he hurried over to them.

"Henny has something to say," said Abbe, a worried expression on her face.

Henny folded her hands in front of her, shrugged her shoulders, and rubbed her shoe on the deck.

"Well... Colleen isn't on the ship. She got off just before we left," she said quietly.

"What?" said Aonghus rather loudly. "What do you mean, she got off?"

"She told me not to tell," said Henny, her eyes a bit fearful. "She said she had forgotten something and that she would catch the next ship to England with Cousin Rufus and Helga. She promised me she would."

Aonghus stared at her, disbelieving. "Are you sure?" he said.

"Yes, I watched her go. And Frederick followed her too," she said.

"Frederick too? I wonder if Mabel knows?" said Aonghus, worried. "We better go tell her. But first, let's tell the others."

He waved to Bran and Bib, and they excused themselves from Captain Truehart and joined the others.

"What's wrong?" said Bran. "Is Colleen sick or something?"

"No, not sick," said Abbe. "She's not on the ship!"

"What!" said Bib.

"That's right. Henny says she got off just before we left, and Frederick followed her. She said she'd catch the next ship with Rufus and Helga because she forgot something," said Abbe.

"That's just like Colleen," said Bib. "Father is going to ground her for a month!"

"No, he won't," said Aonghus. "I think Colleen had a good reason for going back. What was it, Henny? What did she go back for?"

"She didn't say," said Henny. "But it was really important. I know it was."

"Well, Colleen can take care of herself. It's not that far from the docks back to the farm – just a few miles. But Frederick is another matter. He's liable to get himself lost or something. We better go tell Mabel," said Abbe.

"Right," said Aonghus, and they all headed out to find her.

After looking about the decks, and just double-checking to be sure

94

Frederick was nowhere to be seen, they decided to check her cabin. Upon knocking on the door and hearing Mabel's drawling voice call "Enter!" from within, the five children piled into the room.

Mabel's room was much larger than theirs was, and she was not lying on a hammock, but on a large bed that was adorned with a fluffy-looking mattress and several large pillows. Lovely paintings of sea birds and lighthouses adorned the cabin walls, and a bowl of fruit sat on a lace-covered table, several half-eaten pieces of which lay on a dish of blue china. Mabel herself was eating another piece as she lounged comfortably on the bed.

"Ooh, it's you, children," she crooned. "Come in, if you must. What can I help you with?" She took another bite of her fruit.

"Thank you, Cousin Mabel," began Aonghus. "We need to talk to you about Frederick."

"What has he been doing now?" she said, her mouth still somewhat full. "Is he climbing the masts or swinging from the ropes? I hope not. He's like that, you know – the adventurous type like his father. Why, I remember when..."

"He's not on the ship," cut in Abbe.

For a moment, Mabel looked shocked and stopped chewing. She swallowed, looking hard at their faces, and then chortled. "Don't be silly, of course he's on the ship. Why, I left him up on the deck some hours ago."

"We've looked up there, ma'am," said Bib, "and he's not to be found. Colleen is gone as well."

"Whatever are you saying, child!" Mabel said, a bit more loudly. "Quickly now, spit it out."

"Henny said that the two of them left the ship just before we set sail," said Aonghus.

"Henny, come here, child. Tell me what you saw, quickly!" Mabel's voice was quite aquiver now, and she listened intently as Henny told her that Colleen had forgotten something and said she was going back to get it, and that she would come on the next ship with Cousin Rufus.

"Those little rats!" said Mabel, growing angry. "I'm sure Colleen egged Frederick into leaving the ship. Why, when I get my hands on them, I'll give them a tanning!"

She rolled from the bed, squeezed out of her room, stomped up to the upper deck, and fairly shouted at the captain that both Frederick and Colleen had gotten off the ship and that she would have his commission if he didn't refund her entire fare.

"They both got off the ship?" he replied, coming over to her. "Why, we surely would have noticed that. What say we have a look about the ship? I'll have my men look below deck. Maybe they've wandered into the crew quarters or into the cargo hold. I'll have a bit of a scolding for them if that's where they are. I told 'em not to..."

"Yes, you just do that!" interrupted Mabel.

"Right, then," said the captain, and he walked over to the bell hanging from the center mast and rang it.

The men on the deck gathered 'round.

"Now see here, men," he barked. "Miss Mabel here seems to have misplaced her boy, Frederick, and that little golden-haired girl Colleen as well. Have a look about the ship, down below and all, and see if you can find them. Off you go now."

The group of men started to disperse, when one of them spoke up.

"Was the girl about this high," he held up a hand to his chest, "with long reddish-gold hair, and the boy a bit taller with dark hair?"

"That's them," said Aonghus.

"Well, there were two kids like that who dashed down the gangplank just as I was pulling it in. I figured they were supposed to be going ashore, since you had just called for it," the sailor said. "Anyway, they were in a big hurry. Ran like jack rabbits, down the docks and into the village."

Mabel narrowed her eyes and frowned. "What kind of irresponsible crew do you have, Captain, allowing children to run wild. You shall indeed refund my fare and pay a fee for my trouble."

"Now see here, Miss Mabel. Isn't your husband still there? He's supposed to come on the next ship in a few days. Surely your boy and Colleen can come with him then?"

"That's true, Cousin Mabel," spoke up Henny. "Colleen did promise that she would come on the next ship with cousin Rufus and Helga. Frederick can come too."

Mabel blew heavily through her teeth and said, "I suppose that will have to do, but I shall be reporting this incident to the port authorities!"

"Come, let's go down to my cabin and we'll discuss this," said Truehart. "Back to work, lads!" he shouted to his men, and they all turned, shaking their heads and talking among themselves.

He led her away and through the door which led to his cabin. "You children come too," he called, and they followed.

Truehart's cabin was neither as large nor as comfortable as Mabel's was. Its walls were lined with maps and nets and odd driftwood and starfish and other dried sea creatures. An odd assortment of round glass balls dangled from one net in a corner.

He led Mabel to a chair at a small table and sat in an adjacent chair.

"If Frederick misses the next ship, Truehart, I shall hold you personally responsible!" she said, sitting heavily.

"Don't worry, Mabel," said Aonghus. "Colleen knows the way back to the farm, and the town folk know her. If Frederick is with her, they'll be just fine."

"But why would they leave the ship!" she snapped.

Everyone was silent for a moment.

"Well, no matter," said Truehart. "No matter. We can't turn back now, in any case. I'm on a contract that I have to keep. No way around it, ma'am. If I'm late with this shipment, I could lose me ship. And if your boy is safe, as these good folk say, I think there's no reason to sail back. And besides, with the winds the way they are, it might take us twice as long even to make the attempt. Why, it could be eight or ten hours just getting there, maybe more. By then there'd be no tellin' where those kids would be."

Mabel harrumphed and said, "You most certainly shall *not* turn back. I do not wish to be late to the ladies' ball in two days!"

"Don't worry, Cousin Mabel," said Bran, although Mabel looked anything but worried. "Colleen will take care of Frederick and make sure he gets to the farm safely. Then Rufus will bring them both along on the next ship."

With many more words, and not a few promises of decent food and repayment, Mabel finally calmed down and said that she would retire to her cabin. Captain Truehart said he would send her an extra meal that evening, along with some wine and brandy, and deliver it himself, and this seemed to settle her considerably.

After seeing her to her room, Aonghus gathered his brother and sisters in the girls' room to discuss the situation.

"There's nothing for it," he said. "We'll just have to trust Colleen to get them both safely to the farm and to come on the next ship like she promised. The captain won't sail back, and there's no way we could swim back, or even row back in the dingy – we just aren't good on the sea."

"But what if something happens and she and Frederick don't show up with Rufus?" asked Bib.

"We'll just have to cross that bridge if we come to it. If they're not here in a few weeks like they're supposed to be, then I'll sail back on the next ship to Ireland myself and find out what's going on," he said. "But we'll just have to trust in Colleen's good sense and pray she and Frederick will be all right."

They talked on for some time until Aonghus turned the conversation to what they might discover in Wales.

"I hear the headmasters of the schools are very strict," said Bib, "but that they have wonderful libraries."

"And they have great sports, such as rugby," said Aonghus. "I wonder if our school will have a team."

"Do they beat their children at their schools?" asked Henny.

Aonghus picked her up in his massive arms and looked her in the eyes.

"Now don't you worry about that, Henny. If anyone lays as much as a finger on you, they will have me to deal with," he said seriously.

"And me," said Bran.

"And us as well," agreed Abbe and Bib.

"We'll all stick together," said Aonghus, "and have no secrets. Agreed?"

"Agreed," they all said.

After a bit more talk of what lay ahead, Aonghus and Bran headed to their room, leaving the girls to lie in their hammocks.

They found their room much less comfortable, and after unsuccessfully attempting to sleep in his hammock, Aonghus finally curled up on the floor to wait for the dawn. It didn't come too soon.

Chapter 14 – Morning in the Wigglepox Tree

Morning came, and with it, Colleen heard Mrs. Wigglepox singing an opening song. The tree opened with a creak, and sunlight streamed in, waking Frederick as well.

He yawned and sat up, and Colleen giggled at him.

"You have pine needles in your hair again," she teased.

"So do you," he said, grinning.

They both laughed and helped one another pick them out.

"Oh my," said Colleen. "I have no comb with me. I'm sure my hair will look like a rat's nest soon."

"It's fine," said Frederick.

Her hair fell across her shoulders as if she had not slept at all, and he shook his head.

"Wish my mop would behave like that," he said, running his fingers through his tangles.

Colleen only smiled.

"Well, children," said Mrs. Wigglepox. "I can't offer you any hot cakes or muffins, but I suppose there are still some berries and nuts left from yesterday. You had best eat something before we set out."

"Yes, I suppose we should eat something. Badger will need something too," said Colleen.

She and Frederick led the horse outside to where a small patch of grass grew by the spring and set him to graze, and there she found Oracle, standing some ways off on a large, flat stone, facing the rising sun.

"How did you get out here?" asked Frederick.

The old leprechaun ignored him and continued to gaze silently east.

Colleen and Frederick shook their heads, sat down, drank from the spring, and washed their faces.

Then a thought struck Colleen, and she said, "I wonder how that crystal ball ever came to be a family heirloom? It's a *magic* thing, and like we were saying, there's not much of that back home."

"Maybe there's more than we know," said Frederick. "I mean, it's not logical or anything, but maybe a long time ago there was more of it, and some seems to have lingered on from that earlier age – like that mirror and the crystal ball, and those – what did your grandpa call them – *entrances*? Maybe that big stone with the swirls on it really was a marker. It marked the place where the mirror stood."

"And other things seem to have lingered on too," said Colleen. "Just think about where we are! The old legends talk about these things, and here we are walking among them. Little people and goblins!"

"And a nasty lot they are," said Mrs. Wigglepox, coming outside. "They've put a plague on our land, what with their black ooze and all. They spread disease and death wherever they go."

Colleen was thoughtful for a moment and then said, "I've been thinking about it – it was shortly after Mother disappeared that the famine started. Loads of people have been starving since then."

"Oh, dear," said Mrs. Wigglepox. "No doubt it was a plague put on the land by that creature, or it stirred one up that had already started. It must have been a goblin chieftain to have such dark magic. They are horrible creatures, all misshapen and distorted, and terribly cruel, and they carry in their very bodies some disease or evil."

Images of the goblin running about Ireland, cursing the land and its people flashed through Colleen's mind. It was still back there – still performing its mischief. She knew she had to get home somehow and warn everyone – to tell them what had happened, and make them believe her somehow. But she also somehow had to get help for her mother.

"We've got to get to that castle," she said. "We just have to. It's our only hope."

"It will be a hard and dangerous journey, child," said Mrs. Wigglepox. "You will need to find shelter each night for both of you and your horse... and for us."

"You mean you'll go with us?" asked Colleen.

"Well, I could not let you go off on your own. I know these woods as well as any leprechaun around. In fact, we may be the only leprechauns around to help you out, at least for some days' walk."

"Thank you, Mrs. Wigglepox! How can I ever repay you?" said Colleen.

"No thanks are necessary. I've been sitting in this tree hiding long enough. My daughters and I will come along and do what we can. At least we can be your guides, and perhaps you can help us find my husband as well," she said.

"Now, let's talk a bit about the journey," she continued. "If I'm not mistaken, I'll bet your horse could make it to Nidavellir, just south of here, by this evening."

"Where?" said Frederick.

"Nidavellir. Some call it the Dark Fields, or the House of Mysteries. It was built ages ago, during the time of the wizards, but it's been long abandoned. I don't think even the goblins go in there. It's said that it's haunted by the spirits of the wizards who once dwelt there, imprisoned in it by the Court Witch. But I don't know if that's true or not. But it is a huge house – a mansion, really, and legends say that it had dark tunnels far, far beneath it – the Dark Fields that are now haunted. Since the goblins fear it, it just might be the place to head to today."

"Then that is where we must go first," Colleen replied. "If there's any hope of rescuing Mother – and Mr. Wigglepox – then we might as well be on our way."

"Brilliant," said Frederick, not fully convinced that a haunted house was better than a forest full of goblins.

"I'm with you, Frederick," said Lily.

"And me too!" said Rose, clapping her hands.

Colleen and Mrs. Wigglepox looked at them and smiled.

"Well, now, here we are - an old horse, two human children, two little people children, and an old little people woman off to fight goblins and a wicked witch! But maybe we'll have a few tricks up our sleeves as well," said Mrs. Wigglepox. "The magic of the little people may be down, but it's not gone yet. And there are other little people in this forest who have not yet been captured, or so say the birds that are left. Perhaps we will meet some of them along our way."

"What about Oracle?" asked Colleen.

She turned to the little man and said, "Oracle, I can't ask you to come with us. Perhaps you could stay here in Mrs. Wigglepox's tree. You would be safe here."

Oracle was silent for a moment and then turned, climbed from the rock, and hobbled over to them. Then he gazed at them with his deep-seated eyes and waited.

"Does that mean he's coming with us?" asked Rose.

"I'm not sure," said Lily. "But he is an unusual old chap. I think he's quite dear and his company would be grand."

So it was decided. For a long time, they sat and discussed their plans and Mrs. Wigglepox spoke with a bird that happened by and landed on Oracle's head, and with a fox that had silently slipped into their circle, and nuzzled against the old leprechaun. There wasn't much news from the forest. But before long, they had gotten together a plan, of sorts, although they still did not know what chance they might have of succeeding at it.

First, they would go south toward the House of Mysteries, which Mrs. Wigglepox thought they could reach in a single day if they rode Badger hard enough.

From there, they would keep on toward the south, toward the Valley of Fairies, where it was said that the Lady Danu now dwelt, and she might be able to give them some aid, or at least advice. But that would be a three-day journey, and they would need to find help along the way. "We had better," said Mrs. Wigglepox. "We don't want to be caught outside after nightfall."

"And what if this Lady can't help us?" Frederick asked.

"Then we keep going," said Colleen.

And to keep going meant going through the Great Hills, and from there, across the desert of Burning Sands, where the Wizard's Castle was said to be. If they could find this magical Gate of Anastazi and get home, then they would. But if not, they would cross the desert to the sea, where the Island of the Waking Tree and the fortress of the goblins were both said to be.

If there were some way to find the Waking Tree and break the dark spell that enchanted it, then perhaps the Witch's hold over them would be broken. Then they would not be alone, but have all the magic of the little people to aid them. This was Mrs. Wigglepox's one hope, for, she said, there was no way to enter the goblin fortress alone.

"It's a slim chance," said Colleen, "but at least it's a chance."

Frederick said little, but wondered how they were going to get to those hills off in the distance, or how they would ever cross a desert. Even if they did make it to the sea, how in the world would they find a boat and then somehow explore the sea, searching for some lost island? And then, even if they found it, how that was supposed to help them find Colleen's mother, he couldn't imagine. But he kept these thoughts to himself, and gave a practical suggestion.

"We had better map out our whole journey," he said, "so that we can find our way back to the Wigglepox Tree. At least here, we can live on nuts and berries for a while if we have to."

To this, they all agreed. Fortunately, there had been an old parchment in Badger's saddlebag as well as a quill and ink that Mr. McGunnegal kept there to keep track of his bartering. One side of the parchment was blank and, on this, Frederick began to draw his map, beginning with the Wigglepox Tree.

Chapter 15 – A Foreign Land

Abbe opened one eye and looked up, sensing someone watching her. A small gray mouse sat perched on the rope that secured her hammock to the wall. It twitched its nose, sniffing the air as it stared at her.

"Hello there," she said to the mouse. "Come here, let me have a look at you."

The mouse scurried down the rope, hopped onto her leg, and ran onto her outstretched hand. It stood on its hind legs, squeaked, and pawed at the air.

"What a handsome fellow you are," said Abbe.

"Who are you talking to?" groaned Bib.

"This mouse," she replied. "I think we're getting near the shore. He's seems to think the air smells different."

Bib popped open both eyes and looked over at Abbe holding the mouse.

"Ugh, how can you do that?" she said.

"What?" said Abbe.

Suddenly, there was a knock at the door. Henny, who had been watching quietly from her hammock, got up and opened it. Aonghus poked his head in the door.

"Breakfast bell just rang," he said.

The mouse looked over at him, squeaked loudly, and scampered away.

"Thanks, Aong. We'll be there in a minute," said Abbe.

"See you there," he said, and left.

Abbe and Bib climbed from their hammocks, stretched, and combed out their long, red locks.

"Get any sleep, Henny?" said Abbe as they walked down the hall.

"Plenty," she replied, "but those mice woke me up a few times.

They kept running up and down your hammock ropes and sniffing you."

Abbe smiled. "I like mice," she said.

The ship's mess was a large room with wooden tables and benches lined with rough-looking sailors who glanced up at them as they entered. They paused, unsure of the hard looks they were getting, until a weathered old man who sported a wide scar across his forehead rose from his seat and approached them.

"Cap'in told us you'd be joinin' us this mornin'. See that there ugly feller by that big pot?" he said, pointing to one corner of the room. "That's Onion, the ship's cook. He's stirred up some mean gruel if you care for it. Just go over and introduce yourselves."

Abbe noticed the wry smile on the man's face and the sniggers that passed among the sailors. "It's good stuff!" called a gruff voice from one table. "Put hair on your chest, it will."

Laughter erupted around the room, and the tension that had hung in the air vanished. The men went back to their meal, and Abbe led the others over to the man who was stirring the pot.

"Good morning," said Aonghus. "Might we have a bite to eat, please?"

"Don't do it," called a skinny sailor. "We never know what he puts in that pot." The men laughed again.

"Yeah, look what it did to Skinny," called another rather round man, pointing at the first.

"Doesn't seem to have hurt you, Plumps," said another. "You seem to thrive on it pretty well."

"Pay 'em no mind," said the cook, a big man with thick forearms and a broad face. "They've no appreciation for fine food."

He smiled, showing a gap in his brown teeth, then grabbed a bowl from a rack beside him. He wiped it out with his apron, filled it with a white mush from the pot, and handed it to Abbe.

"There are spoons," he said, pointing to a barrel filled with wooden spoons, which looked none too clean.

"Thank you," said Abbe, looking down at the gruel. "I'm sure it's … delicious."

"'Course it is!" shouted another man from the tables, prompting groans and gags and more laughter. As the cook served Bib, Henny, Bran, and Aonghus, the sailors struck up a song about eating the cook's food, singing in loud and raucous voices.

Oh, life on the sea is quite a boon,
The waves and the wind can make you swoon.
Lucky are we to be so free,
And eat from Onion's fine galley.

Onion is fat and his food is fine,
He scrapes off the worms and peels off the rind.
And rarely a rat or beetle is seen,
Swimming in Onion's fine cuisine.

If waves make you sick and spray makes you sneeze,
It's nothing compared to Onion's rare feed.
Colors so rare and smells so unique,
If you can down it, we'll know you're a freak.

Then they started over and sang it even more loudly than before, then lifted their cups in the air and shouted, "To Onion!" then laughed all the more.

"Quite a crew," said Aonghus as they sat eating their breakfast.

"The food's not that bad, though," said Bran, tasting the mush. "Better than some we've had this year."

"True enough," said Aonghus.

They had no sooner finished their meal when a bell clanged and the crew rose from their benches and tossed their bowls and spoons and cups in a great heap on one table.

Abbe looked at the mess, then saw two boys who couldn't have been more than her own age of fifteen come out and begin to pile the dirty dishes onto wooden carts.

One of them with blond hair and blue eyes glanced over at her, removed his cap, and bowed slightly.

"Hello, ma'am," he said, smiling broadly.

His partner elbowed him and they went back to work, but she noticed that he kept glancing her way.

"Come on, Ab," said Bran, pulling her after him as they left the mess.

Abbe followed behind the others, but had a strange urge to go back to the dining hall and help the boys. But as she climbed to the upper deck and looked out over the water to the southeast, she could just make out the outline of land on the horizon.

"I see it!" said Henny excitedly. "Is that England?"

"Wales," said Bib.

"Looks like we'll be there soon," said Bran. "Perhaps this afternoon."

"Aye, aye," said a voice behind them, and they turned to see Captain Truehart coming toward them.

"Won't be long now," he said cheerfully. "And I suppose you youngsters will be going off to school. Even you, Aonghus?"

"Yes, sir," said Aonghus. "My father would like for me to take the opportunity to study agriculture and bring back some new farming techniques to Ireland."

"Ah, a fine, fine thing farming is. Me own uncle is a farmer, one of the best in England," said Truehart. "And what of you, lad – Bran, isn't it? What will you be studying?"

"Well, seeing that I'm a fair hand at hunting – much to my sister's chagrin," he replied, winking at Abbe, "Dad thinks I might look into learning both the blacksmith and weapons-making trade. He says that to make a plow and a bow and use them both will take me far. But I can already do both. Dad thinks that these English folk might have some ideas that we haven't heard of, though," said Bran.

"And what of you, young Abbe, what will you be looking into at school?" the captain asked with a smile.

"The veterinary trade, to be sure, sir," she said. "I love animals." She stuck out her tongue at Bran, but then smiled at him.

"And I will be studying the sciences," piped in Bib.

"And I'm going to learn to read better!" said Henny.

"Good, good for you all," said Truehart heartily. "I think you'll find your time in school just grand." He gave them all a big toothy smile. "And I hear it's the Ismere school that you're off to," he continued. "I know one of the teachers there. Professor Atlas McPherson is his name. A fine old chap... if a bit odd. One of his boys went sailin' with me some years back." The bit about the professor being a bit odd he said rather under his breath so that only Henny, who was nearest him, heard what he had said.

"How's he odd?" asked Henny, her innocent eyes looking up at him.

"Well, now!" he replied. "Nothing in a bad way, you know. It's just that he collects odd things, you might say. Has all sorts of trinkets and oddities in his office."

Truehart then bent down low and whispered, forcing the lot of them to lean in close to hear, "And he's got a door in that office of his where his boy, Charlie, told me he keeps even stranger things – old things that come from ancient civilizations and castles and graves and things like that. I suppose he's some sort of archaeologist, like your cousin Rufus. Come to think of it, that's probably how Mr. Buttersmouth got you all into the school – had a contact there in old McPherson. And, oh! He owns a ship! A bit of an old dumpy ship, mind you, but a ship nonetheless!"

Then he stood straighter with a slight groan and said, "Well, anyway, you say hello to him for me, right? But if he asks about Charlie, tell him that I haven't heard hide or hair of him since he sailed away for Bermuda."

"I've heard strange things about that place," said Bib.

The captain glanced around, and then leaned down again, an odd look in his eye.

"Aye," he said in a hushed voice. "Bermuda is a piece of ocean that gets 'em, it's said. Strange things happen there. Whole ships get swallowed up and are never seen again."

Truehart grinned, glanced about once again, and then continued, "Once, when I was just a lad, and was a deck hand on a ship sailing in the waters somewhere southwest of Bermuda, we spotted something floating in the ocean. We sent out a row boat and found it was a piece of ship, and there was a man floating on it!"

"Was he dead?" asked Henny, her eyes wider than ever.

"No, lass, he was alive, but his clothes were torn to shreds, and he was baked near to death from the salt and sun. We took him aboard and they found he was gripping a stone chest in his arms. Wouldn't let go of it! Kept mumbling about some great door and a throne and a dead man. At times, he would seem to speak in gibberish. We figured he was out of his mind from the sun and the sea.

"But one night, I slipped into the cabin where the man was sleeping and hid behind a barrel to watch him."

"What happened?" whispered Henny.

"Well, quiet as a mouse, I slipped over to the bedside and found that the chest was unlocked. I peeked inside and saw some scrolls and a compass and a dagger. I pulled one of those scrolls out and had a look. It was real strange – written in a funny language with all sorts of symbols, and it was a map of a land I've never sailed to before. Big place, and far as I can remember, it was situated right there between Africa and South America. Must have been some old map made before folk got good at making maps. There's no island there that's that big today.

"Anyway, that's when the man woke up and grew angry. I ran out the door right quick and up on deck again.

"But it was after that the man seemed better and was able to tell his tale. He said that his ship had been sailing to South America, but had lost all wind for three weeks and they sat drifting day after day. In all that time, it never rained and their supplies began to run low. But one night, a frightful storm suddenly blew up and drove the ship like they were in a hurricane. They never saw the rocks that they hit until they were well-nigh upon them, and then it was too late. Their ship was smashed to pieces, and he was swept overboard into the sea."

"And what happened to the crew?" asked Bran.

"He never found out. Never found any of 'em. But he said that he was driven by the waves to the island - was washed right into a rocky cave. He crawled inside to escape the storm and waited through the night, half dead from exhaustion," said Truehart.

"But you said you found him in the ocean," said Bib. "How did he get off the island?"

"Ah, now that's a tale! He wouldn't tell anything about this treasure he had been mumbling about, nor about the door. A huge door in the cave, he had said in his madness. And he wouldn't say much about the chest – said that he had saved it. When they asked him his name, he said it was ..."

But before he could finish, there was a loud clanging of a bell, and the captain straightened himself with a grunt and looked about.

"Ah, sorry, lads, lasses. It's time for inspections. We'll talk more in a bit. A tidy ship gets better trade prices, you know."

With a wink, he limped away toward his first mate, who was waiting for him by the main mast.

"That's quite a tale," said Abbe to Aonghus. "I'm going to ask him what that man's name was just as soon as I can."

"I was thinking the same thing," he replied.

But the chance to speak to Truehart never came. As land drew steadily nearer, the crew busied themselves with cleaning the decks and coiling ropes and folding nets and making the ship look generally neat. Each time Abbe thought she might have a chance to speak to him for a few moments, he spotted something or other that needed doing and was barking orders to his crew.

When at last the port was in sight and it would only be a few minutes before they docked, Abbe took Aonghus by the arm and said, "Come on."

They climbed to the upper deck where the captain was at the wheel, still calling out this or that command.

"Captain," said Abbe, "that shipwrecked sailor you were telling us about – the one you rescued by Bermuda – who was he? Is he still

111

alive today?"

"Of course he is. Didn't I mention it? He's your professor – Professor McPherson," said Truehart.

"McPherson!" said Abbe.

"Aye, the very same," he replied.

"Does he still have the stone chest and all that?" asked Aonghus.

The captain looked sidelong at them for a moment and then said, "Well, that I don't know. His son, Charlie, may have taken it with him. At least, he had a copy of that map I was telling you about when I saw him last. But if you talk to old McPherson about it, mind yourself. He loved his boy very much, ever the more so since his wife passed on some fourteen years back giving birth to their second son, God rest her soul. And when Charlie decided to sail to Bermuda to look for that island, he was at odds with the old man about it. I don't think they parted on very good terms."

"We'll remember that, sir," said Aonghus. "Thanks very much for your kindness."

He extended his hand, which the captain took and shook vigorously.

"My, but you've got a powerful grip, lad!" said Truehart with a grin, rubbing his hand. "You'd make a fine sailor. If you ever want to join my crew, come and look me up!"

"Thank you, sir. Thanks very much!" said Aonghus.

"Well, now, best be getting to business. Look here now, we're bringing her in to dock," said Truehart.

Two dinghies had been let down over the side with ropes fastened to their sterns and tied to either side of the ship. Four strong men in each were slowly rowing, towing the ship toward the docks, where Aonghus could see the dock men waiting to tie her to tall wooden posts.

Captain Truehart busied himself with barking orders and the ship drew nearer and nearer. When they were close enough, several sailors threw thick ropes to the waiting men, who caught them and pulled hard to inch the ship closer.

"I'm going below to get my things together," said Aonghus. "Want to tell the others?"

"Right," she said, and went down to her brother and sisters on the lower deck.

"You'll never believe what we found out," she said to them. "Professor McPherson, who we're going to have at the school, is the sailor that Captain Truehart rescued."

"Brilliant!" said Bib, "What a story he'll have to tell!"

"Well, at least going off to school isn't turning out so bad after all. I just hope Colleen gets here soon enough," said Abbe. "Come on, then, let's get our things together."

She led them below and they gathered up their belongings and then went to Mabel's room to see if she needed any help. They found her sitting in a padded chair directing two sailors who were struggling to haul a sizable trunk toward the door.

"What have you got in this thing, ma'am?" asked one of the sailors, a big brawny man. It feels as though it's packed full of rocks!"

"Those are my personal effects," said Mabel in her drawling voice. "Please be careful with that."

The two men, huffing and puffing, carried the trunk through the door, and the McGunnegal children moved aside to let them through. As they began to struggle up the steps toward the deck, the contents of the chest shifted, and the sailor on the bottom lost his footing and began to fall backward, grimacing with fear and letting out a yell as the heavy box came crashing down on him.

In that moment, Aonghus, seeing what was happening, leaped forward, catching the chest with one hand and the man with another.

"Are you all right?" asked Aonghus as the man stood up and looked at him in amazement.

The other sailor had put his end of the chest down on the steps and gawked at Aonghus as well.

"Here, let me help you with that," he said casually. Taking the chest, he lifted it easily, and the sailor quickly moved out of his way. Up the stairs he went and placed it on the deck while the other children, Mabel, Henry, and the other sailor followed behind.

"Why, lad!" said the man who had slipped. "I've never in all my days seen anyone as strong as you! Name's Jones, Harry Jones, and I'm indebted to you." He held out his hand to Aonghus.

Aonghus took his hand and shook it. "Aonghus McGunnegal," he said.

Harry Jones, who prided himself among the sailors as having as powerful a grip as any man, withdrew his hand and rubbed it. "Good Lord, son! Where *do* you get your grip from?"

"My father, I suppose," he said. "He's a bigger man than I am."

"If I didn't know better, I would swear I've met a hero from the past – like someone who walked out of a legend!" said Jones, laughing. "I've never felt such strength!"

Aonghus looked down, embarrassment rising in his cheeks. "It's just from working the farm all day long."

"Well, listen here, Aonghus. The boys and I are going to the Gull this afternoon for a few rounds after we finish loading the ships. That's the pub right down there on the wharf," said the sailor, pointing to a gray building some distance away that had a chipped and flaking painting of a sea gull on a large sign above the door. "How about you join us? They always have arm wrestling matches, winner takes all that's bet. I'm sure you could beat any man, even Bob Watchford, who's never lost a match."

"I'm traveling with my family here," he replied, "and we're heading to school after we leave the ship. I suppose we will be traveling on now."

"No, no," said a voice behind them. It was Mabel. "After that horrid trip, we will be staying the night at the Five Springs Inn, a fine establishment. You *will* need to earn your room and board for the night. So go and wrestle with the ruffians and earn a few silver pennies. It's that or sleep in the barn."

"The Five Springs!" said Jones. "That'll be a pretty penny for the lot of you to stay at! But if I don't miss my guess, you'll earn that and more if you come down to the Gull. I'll keep an eye out for you."

He winked and bent down to pick up an end of the heavy chest. The other sailor joined him, and together they heaved it up and struggled carefully down the gangplank with their burden and, to their dismay, found that they had to lift it onto the top of a coach.

Aonghus followed them down and, with his help, they easily placed it on top of the coach, which creaked and sagged under the weight.

"What *is* in that chest?" whispered Bran to the others as Mabel and Henry waddled down the plank toward the coach, watching as other bags and chests were loaded on top and in the sagging vehicle.

"Probably stuff they stole from the farm," whispered Abbe. "I'll bet it *is* filled with rocks – rocks that have all those runes and carvings on them. Dad said he took some. My guess is that they're pretty valuable to people like Rufus or he wouldn't have packed away so many of them."

"I don't remember that big chest coming on board with us," said Bib.

"She must have sent it on ahead so that we wouldn't be suspicious," said Abbe.

Mabel heaved herself into the coach, barely squeezing her large belly through the door, and Henry followed behind. Aonghus poked his head in, frowned, and motioned for his brother and sisters to come. He lifted Henny aboard and she climbed in among the bags next to Henry, who scowled.

"Looks like the rest of us will have to ride on the outside," he said, but then saw that there was only room for two.

"Ladies first!" he said to Abbe and Bib, and he helped them climb up next to the driver. "We'll just run alongside."

"It's quite a ways, lads," said the driver. "You can hang onto the back if you like. Only, be careful."

"I'd rather walk," said Bran. "I've been cooped up on that ship too long."

"Aye," said Aonghus. "And I say we race!"

Placing their belongings on top of the carriage, and seeing that everyone was ready, the driver cracked his whip and the four-horse team surged forward, straining at first, but then pulling easier as the carriage moved.

"Where is this Five Springs Inn?" Aonghus asked the driver as he and Bran trotted along beside the horses.

"It's clear across town. You follow this street to Center Circle, then take Roadham Road until it leaves town. The Five Springs is about a mile outside of town," he said.

Abbe watched as Aonghus and Bran looked at each other, nodded, and took off at a run. Seeing the boys speed ahead, she let out a low, fluttering whistle, and all four horses immediately began to gallop at full speed. The road they were on was straight and paved with smooth cobblestones, and Abbe laughed as her long, red hair flew behind her in the wind.

From inside the carriage came a muffled cry from Mabel and a giggle from Henny.

Now the horses were running full tilt and caught up with Aonghus and Bran.

"We're right on your tail!" shouted Bib to the boys, who both looked back in surprise, then looked at each other and, with a great surge of energy, ran even faster.

The surprised coach driver had by now gotten a grip on himself, but could not rein in the horses. He shouted at them and pulled, but they raced on, spurred ahead by some unseen force. For several moments, they ran, until Abbe, seeing that they would not catch her running brothers, whistled again and the horses slowed to a trot.

The driver eyed her suspiciously as he regained control, but she only smiled at him and looked about innocently.

The boys had now disappeared from sight and, for a good while, the coach rode on quietly. When they reached the edge of town, the boys came racing back down the road at a dead sprint, flying past them, with Bran beating Aonghus by a step.

They both trotted back beside the moving coach, breathing heavily but smiling. "Beat you again, big brother!" laughed Bran.

"Only by a step!" he said. "We'll have a rematch in the morning!"

"Whatever you say," he laughed.

"Do they always run like that?" the driver asked Abbe. "They're incredible!"

"It comes from running over the farm all the time," she said. "When you have six children and only one horse, you end up doing a lot of running."

"Still!" said the driver. "They outran the horse team, and I've never seen these horses run so hard!"

Abbe just smiled and shrugged, but that night the driver, over his pint of ale, told of the two boys who outran his team of horses, and many a townsman said that he had seen them racing through the streets like no horse or deer or fox had ever run.

Chapter 16 – Five Springs Inn

Aonghus jogged next to Bran and the carriage carrying their sisters and cousins. He glanced at his brother and shook his head.

"Don't you ever sweat or get tired?" he said, mopping his forehead with his sleeve.

"Can't say I ever have," said Bran, grinning.

"You are a freak," said Aonghus with a laugh.

"Would you look at that?" said Bib from her seat, pointing forward as they pulled from the street onto a smooth, multicolored cobblestone pavement that ringed an ornate marble building.

In the middle of this wide circle were five pools lined with white stone.

"Guess that's why it's called the Five Springs Inn," said Aonghus.

As they pulled up to the front door, a butler, dressed in coat and tails, walked up to the coach, opened the door, and put his nose in the air. Mabel squeezed herself backward out of the coach.

"Welcome to the Five Springs, Ms. Mabel, Henry, and..." he paused, eying the McGunnegals' shabby clothes, sniffed, then said, "and guests. Lunch will be served within the hour, ma'am."

"Good, good. And I need a large bath prepared as well. That ship was wretchedly dusty," she drawled.

"Very well, then. And will your... your guests be joining you for lunch?" he asked.

"Oh. Well, I had not thought of that," she said. "Children, did you bring anything to eat with you?" she asked in a sickly sweet voice.

"No, ma'am," said Abbe.

"Careless of you," she replied, dismissing them with a wave of her hand. "I suppose they could eat with the servants at a reduced fee?"

The butler rolled his eyes and sighed. "Yes, ma'am. I will make arrangements."

"Thank you, my good man," said Mabel, and slipped him a coin.

"Now!" she said more sternly to the children. "Help unload the coach and bring my things to my room for me. There now, that's right."

They all loaded their arms with as much as they could carry, with Aonghus and Bran easily handling the huge chest. It was locked with a large iron key lock, and Bran whispered to Bib, "Do you think you could unlock this thing and get a look inside?"

"No problem," she whispered back, and pulled an old hairpin from her hair. Shifting her load of bags to one arm, she walked beside the trunk on the side with the lock.

"Slow down!" she said as she fumbled to get the hairpin in the lock keyhole. They did, and within a moment, there was a click as the big lock fell open.

By now, Mabel had made her way inside with the butler and, seizing the opportunity, Bib lifted the lid and looked inside.

"Clothes!" she whispered.

"No way," whispered Bran back. "This thing must weigh a couple hundred pounds! Dig around in there, quick!"

Bib handed her bags to Abbe, who was now quite overloaded, and dug beneath the clothes in the chest. She pursed her lips, narrowed her eyes, and pulled out a heavy brown sack.

"It's rocks from our farm, all right," she said, opening it and pulling out a white chunk of stone. "And they all have those runes on them."

"So, we were right," said Abbe. "He took more than a couple of them – he took loads! But quick, shut the lid!"

The butler had appeared at the door, and Bib, not having time to put the sack of rocks back in the chest, quickly locked the chest, and cradled the heavy bag in her arms.

"Lazy child," snorted the butler at Bib. "I can see that you will amount to nothing. You should take a lesson from your sister here, who is carrying at least three times what you are."

Then he looked them over, sniffed again, stuck his nose in the air, and said, "Follow me. And you boys, clean your shoes before you enter."

He led them up a flight of stairs to Mabel's rather luxurious room and said, "Leave the lady's effects here, and then go down to the kitchen. It is in the back of the Inn. The chief cook has jobs for you to do to earn your supper." Then he left.

"Earn our supper?" asked Henny. "What do we have to do?"

Aonghus knelt down next to her and pushed her long golden hair out of her eyes.

"Now don't you worry, little sprite. I'm going to take care of you. It might just be a few dishes or something. It'll be fun, you'll see." And he winked at her and the others.

Following the sumptuous smells of cooking food, they soon found the kitchen, where a very fat cook bustled from pot to pot, mixing, tasting, adding spices, and guiding several other cooks in making lunch for the rich guests who were visiting the inn.

"Ah!" he bellowed as they entered. "Stay out of the way until cleanup time. Over there by that wall will be fine." And he waved them to a far wall away from the stoves.

Soon, plates and dishes, heaped with chickens and roast beef and succulent vegetables were loaded onto carts by servers and rolled out to the dining area.

Henny's eyes were wide, and they all licked their lips as the wonderful smells rolled by. An hour passed, and the carts began to return, laden with dirty dishes and silverware. These were unloaded in the sinks, and re-loaded with plates full of pies and cakes and teas.

"To the dishes now!" bellowed the cook a moment later. "And see to it that you don't chip any of the tea cups! Come on, now, move along!"

"Come on," said Aonghus.

They gathered around the two massive sinks, with Henny standing on a chair, and washed and dried dishes until their hands were wrinkled and their clothes soaked and soapy. As they worked, Bran struck up an old song that their mother and father had taught them, and they all sang together as they worked.

A long ago stranger did visit our land,
Her name, fair Orlaithe the Gold.
No man had ever seen such a maid,
For her beauty was beyond what can be told.

Long did she walk on the Emerald's fair shore,
Greeting many a folk as she went.
She found that war made them glad, but their songs were all sad,
And the maiden she wept when they sang their laments.

Now the Gold One she spied a tall, red haired man.
'Twas Cian, whose strength was renowned.
'Twas love at first sight, and they married that night,
And in that same year, their fair Lucy was born.

But one dark night came a band from the sea,
Forty pirates stole Orlaithe away.
And Cian pursued and did slay all but three,
But mortally wounded he lay. But mortally wounded he lay.

On bloody sands he did watch his fair maid,
As they stole from the shore to the sea.
And the pirates did carry his true love away,
And left him to die as he called out her name.

But Cian did crawl to his home that same night,
And fell by his little lass' bed.
And with his last breath, he did cry out and bless
Little Lucy with all of his remaining strength.

Now Lucy was taken by friends and was raised
And ne'er was so fair a green-eyed maid.
Her golden hair shone in the sun like its rays,
And Lucy McLochlan ran like a deer in the glade.

Lucy could sing and make grown men just weep,
Her voice filled with magic and power.

And all men would stop to hear her fair songs,
And women and children would all sing along.

But Lucy's stepparents told her one day,
How her father was slain and her mother away'ed.
And Lucy did run to the sand and the sea,
And gazed out and wondered where her mother might be.

Then one lonely day, she did sail away
In search of her mother, long lost to the sea.
And the Emerald Isle lost its fairest of maids
To a life of long wandering, hoping, and dreams.

As their song ended, Aonghus noticed that the kitchen had grown silent, and even the fat cook was wiping his eyes on his apron.

"Come, come now," he choked. "Eat something and leave the rest of those dishes for later."

He went over to them, took Henny in his round arms, and carried her over to a table where leftovers had been placed.

Aonghus gave thanks, and they all hungrily ate, thanking the cook again and again.

"I've never heard voices like that before," the cook said after they had eaten for several minutes. "Why, you children could sing for a living and make a mint!"

"You should have heard our mother sing," said Abbe. "Now she could *sing*!"

"And our sister, Colleen, too," said Bib through a mouth full of green beans.

"I'll tell you what, little friends," said the cook. "You sing for the Master here tonight, and you can bet that there will be no sleeping in the barn for you! You just finish up your lunch there right quick and I'll go speak to him."

He smiled a huge grin and waddled out of the kitchen. Slowly, the other kitchen staff went back to their tasks, whispering and talking among themselves.

"Now *that* was a meal," said Aonghus when they were done.

"Amazing," said Abbe.

"I've never eaten like that before," agreed Bran.

Seeing them finished, the cook came over and said, "The Master of the Inn has agreed to hear you sing tonight, and in exchange to give you two rooms for each night that you sing, if you please him and his customers," he said.

"Well, it would be nice to sleep in a decent bed, just for one night, I mean," said Bib.

"Aye," said Bran. "And a bit more of that mince pie wouldn't hurt either!"

"Pie it is!" said the cook. "And tonight you sing! Be sure you are ready and cleaned up and here in the kitchen at six!"

Then he bustled off, humming the tune they had sung.

Chapter 17 – Supper

Aonghus sat on a stone bench outside the Inn, looking at the lush gardens of roses and carpeting flowerbeds. The fragrance was intoxicating, and the late afternoon summer sky was bright and clear. Birds sang in the shade trees, and honeybees buzzed in a blue and white flowering bush beside him. Women in silk dresses and pink umbrellas walked along the path, holding the arms of gentlemen dressed in coats and tails.

"How strange," he said to his sister, Abbe, who was seated next to him.

She looked at him inquiringly.

"It's like a paradise here," he said. "There's food and riches and good clothes – everything you could possibly need and more. Yet just across the Irish Sea, our whole nation is starving. Do these people even know?"

"Maybe," she replied. "Bib says the government knows, but they're so busy planning how to help that no help is coming."

"Not the government, Ab. I mean these folks right here, walking along happily arm in arm and chatting about the sunshine and whether they'll have lamb or steak tonight. I'm not faulting them, mind you, I just wonder if anyone has told them – if they might organize some relief or something if they only knew."

Abbe didn't reply, but only looked at her dingy and worn dress, then at the rich ladies in their ornate gowns.

"You could ask them," she replied.

"I just might do that," he said, and rose.

At that moment, a young freckle-faced boy came running and said, "Master Ted bids you come down to the kitchen and have some supper early. We have roast lamb and potatoes and greens, and pie for dessert!" he said cheerfully.

Spying Bran, Bib, and Henny in the next garden, Aonghus called to them, and they all followed the lad inside and there found five plates all prepared for them.

They all hungrily ate the meal set before them, and Bran especially noted that the pie had been excellent.

When they were done, the cook said, "The guests will be finishing up and wanting some song before bed. Hurry now, quick – off to get your best things on, and be back here in ten minutes! Ten minutes, mind you!"

They hurried off and put on their Sunday best, and when they returned, exactly ten minutes later, the cook eyed them up and down, tsked, and shook his head.

"It's the best we have," said Abbe, looking down at her faded dress.

"I suppose it will have to do," he sighed, and then brightened. "But with your voices, the clothes won't matter a bit. Let's go now. You all will stand together in the middle of the hall and sing us the songs of Ireland!"

As they walked out into the dining room, Aonghus surveyed the guests. At least fifty, he thought, and all of them dressed like noblemen and women. The ladies wore wide dresses made of satin and silk, and carried fans or umbrellas, and the men wore dark suits with red vests and white shirts and carried black canes with golden goose heads.

"I feel like a rotten potato in a pot of golden apples," whispered Bran to Aonghus as they took their place, and Aonghus could see by the look on the other children's faces that they felt the same.

But the Master of the Inn was speaking now, and Aonghus held a finger to his lips.

"My dear ladies and gentlemen," he was saying. "I present to you, all the way from Ireland, the band of singers whose voices will bring tears to your eyes. I give you the famous, no, the legendary, Singing McGunnegals!"

He bowed a deep bow, and passing by the children, he hissed, "You better sing well, young ones!"

"Thank you, kind sirs and ma'ams, for your attention," said Aonghus. "Let me introduce to you the McGunnegals! I am Aonghus, strongest lad in Ireland. This is Bran, the swiftest of foot, and Abbe, our sister, who can tame the wildest Spanish stallion in a moment. And Bib, who can fix anything broken, our youngest, Henny, who can... who can never lose at hide and seek!"

The faces in the crowd were stern, and the women began to fan themselves and whisper. Aonghus caught sight of the Master, who frowned and mouthed the word "Sing!"

"In addition," continued Aonghus, "we all can sing like no one you have heard before!"

Then he whispered to the others, "Follow my lead, just like we do back home at the Old Inn."

He began to sing then, in his deep baritone voice, a song of lovers and war and life and loss, and the others joined him on the chorus, each singing a different part, their voices blending with such perfect harmony that the room grew silent, the ladies stopped fanning themselves, and began to dab their eyes with their handkerchiefs.

When the song was finished, there was a pause of silence and Aonghus whispered something to Henny, and she began to sing in her clear little girl's voice. Like her sister Colleen, Henny too had inherited something of her mother's spellbinding voice, and though only seven, her perfect pitch and sweetness captivated the room. It was a simple song of springtime and rains and flowers and bees, but visions of clear blue skies and green fields filled the minds of her listeners as she sang, and when the others joined her in hushed voices on the chorus, all leaned closer to hear what they sang.

"Oh the green shores of Ireland are calling to me,
To away, far away, to my home 'cross the sea.
Where children are happy and brave and so free.
On the green shores of Ireland that one day I'll see."

Through the evening they performed, with each of them leading a song, and all of them joining in the chorus, and then all of them singing together, or a solo and, as they sang, Aonghus watched the faces of the men and women in the room, noticing their hard expressions soften, and canes laid down on the floor, fans put away, and many a handkerchief wiping a wet eye or blowing a nose.

When they had sung for over an hour, and Henny began to yawn, Aonghus took her in his great arms and sung a few lines of a farewell song, which they all joined in as the five of them slowly walked across the floor toward the kitchen, where they bowed, sang the final line, and left the hall.

For a moment, there was absolute silence, and then a sudden thunderous applause with many a "bravo!"

The Master of the Inn waved to them from the door to come back out into the Hall, where the applause continued. The children shyly bowed again and then retreated to the kitchen. The cook motioned for them to follow him and bustled them to the back door.

"We have not had songs like that in this inn since... well... well we've *never* had songs sung like that here before!" he said, his face glowing. "And did you hear them clapping? *Clapping!* Children, those sour-faced nobles have *never* clapped for *anyone* before tonight, I can tell you that. There's something real special about you youngsters, real special. You keep together, you hear? And Aonghus, you watch over that little Henny there."

Aonghus handed Henny to Bran as the cook took his arm and led him a few steps away.

"You be sure you *do* watch over her," he said. "There's some bad or downright evil folk that dress in those top hats and fancy dresses out there. They'd as soon steal away a little gem like Henny and sell her talents for a pound as look at you. Mind you, watch them all."

"Thank you, sir," Aonghus replied. "No one will touch my brother and sisters as long as I'm around."

The cook looked at Aonghus' massive muscles and said, "No, I don't expect they would. But you watch yourself and them nonetheless. By the way, my name is Corry - Ted Corry the cook. And if you're down this way and need anything, you look me up, see," he said. "But come on, now, I'll show you your rooms."

He led them up the back stairs to a pair of large rooms that had several wide beds with soft pillows and clean sheets.

"It's not fancy, but it's clean and comfortable. You lock the doors tonight and don't answer them if anyone knocks until morning," he said, smiled at them, and waddled away, humming one of the tunes they had sung that night.

Chapter 18 - Breakfast

Aonghus stretched and bumped his head on the headboard.

"They don't make beds for McGunnegals," he said to himself.

His brother, Bran, lay curled up in the bed across the room. He opened one eye, yawned, and proceeded to bump his own head.

Aonghus laughed. "You see?"

Bran rose and stretched his lean form to its full six-foot-six height.

"Might as well get washed and wake the girls. Do you think the cook is up this early?" he said.

"Let's find out," said Aonghus, rising.

He went to the washbasin, splashed water on his face, rinsed his hands, then looked in the mirror and stared. They had sold all the mirrors in their house back in Ireland to buy food, and it had been months since he had seen himself. Even though he was powerfully built, his face was gaunt, even somewhat grim. Hunger had taken its toll. He looked over at Bran, and realized how thin he had grown over the past six months as their food supply had diminished.

"What's wrong?" said Bran, seeing Aonghus staring at him.

"Nothing," he replied, drying his face with a towel. "You should wash."

Bran did so, combed out his hair with his fingers, then said, "Come on, the cook must be up. I smell breakfast."

Stopping at the girls' room, Aonghus knocked, but when no one answered, they went down to the lounge and found them all sitting at a table, talking.

"Slept in, I see," said Bib with a grin as they approached. "Soft mattresses making you lazy?"

Just then, the cook came bustling in with plates and cups and silverware in hand and set the table for them.

"Breakfast will be right out," he said.

"We would like to work for our meal, sir," said Abbe as he put a plate before her.

"No need, no need," he said. "It'll all be paid for."

"But, we have no money," said Bran. "Is Cousin Mabel paying for it?"

The cook looked at him for a moment, and then said, "You talk to your cousin Mabel about that," he said. "It seems you'll be staying here a day or two more, and singing for us again."

"Singing..." began Bib, and then she added, "Mabel decided this, didn't she?"

A cart bearing ham, eggs, cakes, and fruits was rolled out by one of the kitchen hands, and heaping platefuls were placed on the table.

"I only heard a rumor that she and the Master of the Inn talked quite a bit after your performance last night, and I was given instructions to feed you well and tell you to be ready to sing again tonight," said the cook.

Then, in a lower voice, he said, "One of my table servers said he saw the Master hand her a silver coin, but I suppose that's between you and her," said the cook. "Enjoy your breakfast, and call if you need anything."

He bustled back to the kitchen, and when he was gone, Abbe said, "So that's it – She's getting *paid* for us to sing!"

"Well," said Aonghus, "remember that we are under her care for a time and things may not be as they seem."

"Oh, you can be sure that Mabel Buttersmouth is in it for money if money is to be had," said Bran.

"Bran," said Abbe, "you mustn't talk about Mabel like that. We *are* going to get a good education, and we wouldn't have it without her and Rufus."

"Maybe so," he said grudgingly, "but I still don't trust her. She just seems... well... all wrapped up in herself, if you know what I mean. Both her and Rufus, and Henry and Frederick seem to be like that."

"Bran!" scolded Abbe.

"That's just how I see it, Abbe," he replied. "Meaning no harm, mind you."

Abbe was about to say something more, when in through the door came the Master of the Inn. He was dressed in a green smoking jacket and a tall hat and had a black cane in his hand.

"Ah, children!" he crooned, his deep melodic voice filling the room. "I am so pleased to hear that you will be staying another day or two. Apparently, your cousin, dear Mabel, needs rest from her journey from Ireland and has decided to stay on for a bit."

His large dark eyes swept their faces, and a large smile revealed his unusually white teeth.

"You know what white teeth mean," whispered Bib to Abbe.

"What?" she hissed back.

"He probably gargles ur..." she began, but Aonghus' strong hand on her shoulder cut her off.

"That's just fine!" said Aonghus. "But we would like to work to pay for our stay. We can work the barns and the kitchen if you would like."

"No, no," he said. "Your voices this evening will be quite enough. In fact, I have sent word all about to the nearby towns that the, well, the famous Singing McGunnegals will be performing tonight. I'm sure we will triple our crowd. In fact, you can keep any tips that you receive."

"What are tips?" asked Henny.

"Money," said Abbe.

"Oh. You mean you're going to pay us to sing tonight?" she asked, her innocent eyes looking up into his.

The Master's grin broadened, but still the smile never reached his eyes. "You might say that, little one. Why, with your young voice, I'm quite sure the coins will be showering down."

He patted her on the head and then turned to go. "This evening at seven, my Singing McGunnegals. Be ready then. Eat heartily. And do wash properly. And comb your hair." Then he turned and walked away.

Aonghus watched him go.

"Stay together today," he said. "Something feels wrong about this."

Chapter 19 – The House of Mysteries

"It's time," said Mrs. Wigglepox.

Colleen studied the little leprechaun's face, trying to read what she was feeling. A sense of many, many summers living in the Wigglepox Tree washed over her. Memories of bygone years, of generation after generation coming and going, moving on to other trees. Of goblins and darker creatures stealing them away. Fear. All this came to Colleen in a moment as she gazed into Mrs. Wigglepox's eyes, and then it was gone. She wondered how old the tiny lady actually was.

"You don't really want to leave, do you?" said Colleen.

"It's hard, you know," she replied. "This will be the first time this tree will have been without someone living in its heart for many thousands of years. The trees need us, you know. We live in them and care for them, and they for us. A living thing is only half alive when it doesn't have someone else to care for. It's just the way we're made."

"I suppose so," said Colleen.

"Well, let's hope we're not gone for long," said Mrs. Wigglepox, wiping her eyes. "Would you and Frederick mind stepping outside for a few minutes while we say goodbye?"

"Of course," she replied.

Colleen and Frederick led Badger from the great tree and sat down in its shade.

"Can you believe it?" said Frederick after a moment. "I mean, being here – in the Land of the Little People and all. I'm having a hard time getting a grip on it."

"Why's that?" asked Colleen.

"I mean it's not logical," he said. "My father has always said to think things through logically and not believe in superstitions. 'Rational thought will solve all man's problems,' he's fond of saying."

Colleen thought for a moment.

"I don't think there's anything wrong with logic," she said. "But I don't think it's the only thing that can guide us. Sometimes, my heart tells me something different than my head, you know?"

"Now you're sounding like a girl," said Frederick.

"No, not that way. I didn't mean emotions. It's more like... intuition. Sometimes I *sense* things about people. I can't explain it, really, it just *is*. Maybe the whole universe is like that – maybe there are things that we can't see and hear and touch, but are still real, and we still experience them somehow. They're magical."

"Like this place?" said Frederick.

"Maybe. I wonder what other passageways one might stumble through, and what magic those worlds hold? Maybe something totally, well, *different* from what we experience in our world, or even here. The legends back home do call the fairy people the *Others*," she said.

"Hopefully, they're not too much different from us," replied Frederick. "I wouldn't want to meet something with no head or covered in eyes."

"Better watch out." She laughed. "You just might."

Just then, Mrs. Wigglepox, Lily, and Rose walked from the tree, turned toward it, and stood silently for a moment. The tree trembled once, then slowly began to close its great opening. The sound of it was like a deep moan of sorrow.

Oracle appeared from behind the tree, placed his hands on a huge root, and closed his eyes. The tree seemed to sigh as the last bit of the doorway disappeared, and then all was still.

They stood for a long moment in silence before Mrs. Wigglepox said, "Let's be off, then. I suppose you children have enough food for a day or so?"

"We'll be fine," said Colleen. "We still have some berries, and I'm sure we can scavenge roots or something along the way. Let's ride Badger for a while."

Colleen mounted first and said, "Frederick, can you lift Oracle up to me?"

"If he's agreeable," said Frederick.

Oracle hobbled over and allowed himself to be hefted up, and Colleen sat him in front of her. Then Frederick handed her the Wigglepox family and she placed them in her pockets, then helped Frederick up behind her.

"Easy now," said Colleen to Badger. "Let's go, boy."

With that, the old horse stepped forward.

"Off at last," said Frederick.

Oracle chattered on quietly in his nonsensical way, talking to Badger, who seemed perfectly content to listen to the little hunchback.

Frederick reached into his pocket and pulled out a blackberry. "I think that I may never eat another berry pie again if I ever get back home," he said. "My stomach aches already from eating so many!"

"At least we have food to eat. We ought to be thankful for that," said Colleen. "Better a stomach full of nuts and roots and berries than an empty one."

"I suppose so," said Frederick.

On they went, always southward, and passed by an occasional meadow or glen in which birds sang and rabbits and squirrels scampered. Each of these had a flowing spring in it, but these were few and far between, and all the trees in the forest were bare, save a few of the old giants that held sleepy green leaves near their tops, and these also, as Frederick pointed out, had springs nearby.

There was a thickness in the air most of the time that made them drowsy, and after riding for some hours, Frederick said, "Can we stop and take a rest? I feel as though I could fall asleep sitting here."

"Lily and Rose are already asleep," said Mrs. Wigglepox with a yawn.

"We better reach the House of Mysteries soon," said Colleen. "It's getting late, and I feel so very sleepy."

Mrs. Wigglepox looked worried and said, "We better quicken our pace a bit. We need to reach that house before sundown."

Colleen urged Badger along a bit quicker, but kept having to do so, as he slowed down every few minutes.

The afternoon lagged on, and the ground began to rise and fall. Finally, they came to a deep forest glen that was wild and lonely, the bottom of which was filled with broken rock fallen from the cliffs that surrounded its shady depths.

They were about to pass by when Colleen thought she saw someone down in the gully, leaning against a large tree.

"Oh my!" she said, and backed Badger away from the cliff.

"What is it?" asked Frederick.

"I thought I saw someone down there," she whispered.

"Not one of those black things, I hope," said Frederick.

"I don't know – it looked as though it was resting against that large tree," she said, pointing to an aged giant whose top protruded from the ravine. "Come on, let's have a look."

Dismounting and putting Oracle and the Wigglepox family on the ground, she crawled to the edge of the cliff and peered over the edge. Frederick slid off of Badger, flattened himself on the ground beside her, and squinted into the deepening gloom.

"I don't see... wait, yeah, there is somebody down there. He's got his head on his chin, and he's got a long gray beard. But he's got no legs, or else he's sticking right up out of the ground," he said.

"Do you think he's dead?" asked Colleen.

"Could be," said Frederick. "He doesn't look too alive, that's for sure."

"Oh, dear," said Mrs. Wigglepox, coming up behind them. "What is he wearing? Is it a black robe?"

"No," said Frederick. "He looks more like a man than a goblin, if you ask me. He's got a long gray beard, anyway."

"Well, he's not a goblin, then," said Mrs. Wigglepox. "They haven't got beards."

"I suppose we better go down and see if he needs help," said Colleen.

"But what if it's a trap of some sort – you know, an illusion or something set by the Witch?" said Frederick.

Colleen thought for a moment and then said, "Trap or not, if that fellow is in trouble, we can't just leave him lying there. He could be hurt, or worse."

"See here, Colleen," said Frederick. "It's none of our business who he is or what he's doing down there. What if it *is* a trap set by those goblins? They could be waiting right in those shadows, ready to jump out at anyone passing by. This poor fellow could just be a bit of bait, and then where would we be? I say we leave well enough alone."

"No, Frederick. I'm going down there. Come if you like or stay. But it's just not right to leave someone lying by the side of the road if you can help it."

"Good for you, child," said Mrs. Wigglepox. "Good for you."

She rose and went back to Badger, where Oracle sat leaning against one his legs.

"Let's go, boy," she said. "Oracle, are you coming?"

She took the reins and led the horse along a thin rabbit trail that went down into the ravine.

"Come along, Frederick," said Lily. "Pick us up and carry us down there."

Frederick sighed and did so, then followed Colleen, with Oracle trailing along behind.

Down the slippery path she led them, watching the figure that lay against the tree to see if it stirred and watching even more carefully the shadows along the cliffs that now began to surround them.

"It's scary down here," said Rose.

"And the air is so heavy!" whispered Lily, with a yawn.

When at last they reached the bottom, Colleen could now clearly see the figure lying against the tree. It was a small man whose aged face was covered with stringy gray hair and whose gray and white beard covered his chest. Fallen leaves lay on his broad shoulders, and one sat unceremoniously on his head. He appeared to be half buried, but in a moment, Colleen realized that he was simply covered in leaves up to his waist.

She quietly inched her way forward, watching the gathering shadows, until she stood right before him. Frederick tiptoed up behind her and peered over her shoulder.

The man wore an old tattered leather brown coat that was quite weathered, and a dirty tan shirt beneath that. But the oddest thing was a jumble of sticks and grass that lay intertwined in the beard on his chest.

"He looks dead," hissed Frederick. "Look, there's a bird nest right in his beard!"

They stood absolutely still for a moment, until Colleen got up her courage, cleared her throat, and said, "Sir, are you all right?"

The man lay there, making no sound, not stirring in the least. His face wore a stern, troubled expression.

"Sir?" she said a little louder, but still he did not move.

"He's dead," said Frederick. "Now let's get out of here."

But Colleen went closer, bent down, and very gently touched his face.

"He's warm," she said and, even as she said it, his chest rose and fell with a single breath.

"Oh!" said Colleen. "He's alive!"

She began to brush the leaves from on top of him, and found that they lay at least a foot deep over his short legs.

"He is a small fellow, isn't he?" said Frederick, who had gotten up the nerve to help her.

"But he's in some sort of trance or something – this sleeping wood has gotten the best of him," he said. "And just look at him – he's not very happy, even in his sleep."

"You've nailed it on the head there," said Mrs. Wigglepox. "It's this cursed Spell of the Witch. Some who succumb to it sleep on and on, but they get no rest. Even their dreams are full of trouble, or so it's said. You can see that plain enough by the look on this dwarf's face."

"A dwarf?" asked Colleen. "You mean a *real* dwarf?"

"I'm fairly certain of it," said Mrs. Wigglepox.

Colleen paused, looking at the old face of the dwarf, his grim frown, the lines and creases in his forehead and behind his eyes. Then she moved to dig him out again.

"Come on, Frederick, help me get him uncovered. Who knows how long he's been sleeping here. He'll catch his death of cold if we don't get him to some shelter," said Colleen.

Frederick began brushing leaves aside, but then stopped and stared at the dwarf.

"Colleen, wait," he said.

She stopped again and looked at him.

"Wait. I think we'd better cover him back up," he said.

"Cover him back up! Why?" she said.

"Look at him, Colleen. Look at his hair and beard... Colleen, he's got a *bird nest* in his beard! He's been sleeping here for a really long time, I think. What are we going to do with him anyway? It's pretty obvious that *we're* not going to wake him up if he's slept through years of everything that Mother Nature has thrown at him."

Colleen stared at the old dwarf and then gently shook his shoulders. She called to him, shook him harder, and even tried shouting, at which Mrs. Wigglepox reminded them to keep still for fear of attracting attention to themselves from unwanted eyes.

But the dwarf slept on, a crooked frown on his hard, old face.

"No," said Colleen. "It wouldn't be right to just leave him."

She dug on. Frederick shook his head, and then went on helping her. At last, after much heaving and hauling, they managed to pull him out of the deep pile of leaves and twigs and branches that had covered him, and gently laid his head on the ground.

"I wonder how many years he's been sleeping," said Frederick.

Oracle climbed up on his chest and poked him with his cane.

"It's been many, many years since there were dwarves in these woods," said Mrs. Wigglepox. "And I do mean *many* years. I must say that this dwarf is under more than one enchantment. He sleeps under the Spell of the Witch, but he *lives* under some other magic."

"And now that we've got him out of that living grave, what are we going to do with him? We can't put him on Badger – he's much too heavy for us to pick up, and he'd fall right off anyway," said Frederick.

"We'll have to make a litter for Badger to pull," said Colleen. "Go find a couple of long, strong branches. We'll have to use Badger's blanket for the litter."

After they had found two sturdy limbs and laid the blanket across them, then tied them to the branches with a bit of rope that was in Badger's saddle bag, they carefully hauled the dwarf atop it and, with great difficulty, managed to lash the ends of the poles to the horse's saddle.

"There's no way I can ride now," said Frederick. "I don't think the old boy could carry us all and pull this contraption behind at the same time. I'll just walk."

"Me too," said Colleen. "I need to lead Badger and carry the Wigglepoxes anyway."

Oracle, however, climbed up on and sat perched on the bird nest that the dwarf's beard still sported. This made Lily and Rose laugh until Mrs. Wigglepox shushed them.

Slowly, they pulled the litter out of the gully, with Frederick on the downhill side, steadying the dwarf as he threatened to roll off.

But, at long last, they made it to the top and, with a great sigh of relief, started south again, the litter bumping along behind them.

Twice the dwarf would have slid off had it not been for Oracle's warning cry of something unintelligible, and so finally, Frederick lashed the last bit of rope under the sleeping dwarf's arms and to either pole to keep him from slipping.

Before long, the sun was low in the west, and the trees cast long shadows across the brown forest floor. Colleen looked back at the strange little man behind her. She wondered again how long he had been sleeping under that tree and what dreams he must dream in his long, deep, and troubled sleep. What magic or curse was this world under that could preserve life and yet condemn it to eternal nightmares? How could such a world even continue to exist?

But as she looked around, she realized that this was a dying land. Everything was slipping away into an eternal night, withering beneath the unrelenting power of the Spell. The whole world had nearly given up, succumbing to its dreadful weight. Colleen suddenly felt as though she was sloshing through thick muck, as if the very air were resisting her movements. She looked back at the others, and saw that Frederick's head was bowed, as if he were walking against a great wind. She turned and pushed on.

"Badger is really getting tired," she said after they had walked in silence for some time. "How much farther do you think it is?"

But even as she said it, Frederick stopped, rubbed his eyes, and stood blinking stupidly. After a moment, he seemed to come to himself.

"Look, there, just up the next rise. What's that?" he said thickly.

The ground rose sharply before them and, at the crest of the hill, they could see an old stone building looming through the trees.

"That must be it," said Colleen. "Come on, one more go and we'll be there."

She led Badger up the hill, which seemed to go on and on, higher and longer than seemed reasonable.

"I don't think we're getting any closer," said Frederick after a time. "It looks just the same as before."

"Hold on," said Colleen. "We've not been walking up this hill at all – we've just been going round and round it. See here, I remember this old tree stump. In fact, I've seen it twice, now that I think about it. Something strange is going on."

She strained her eyes, looking up at the distant structure, then saw it – a thin trail that she had missed before. But as soon as she looked straight at it, it disappeared.

"The trail is hidden, Frederick. Don't look straight at it. Just sort of narrow your eyes and look to one side."

Frederick squinted as well.

"Say, yeah, I see it now," he said.

Colleen turned and followed the trail up, not looking directly at it, and as soon as she did, it opened up before them, a clear path curving upward toward the summit.

The building loomed larger and larger as they approached, until they passed through the remnants of a stone wall and stood before massive stone pillars that supported the slate tiled roof of a large front porch, behind which was the most massive house that Colleen had ever seen.

"It looks like a castle," whispered Frederick. "Do you think anyone still lives here?"

Colleen said nothing, but craned her neck to gaze up at the towering walls and ornately carved but weathered windows that faced them. Marble steps led up to the porch, and a pair of dark ironbound doors stood tightly shut, with many of the now-familiar runes and symbols carved on them. They were the biggest doors Colleen had ever seen, at least thirty feet high.

"It looks spooky," whispered Colleen.

"Do you think the door is locked?" said Frederick.

"Only one way to find out," said Mrs. Wigglepox. "Let's try it."

Colleen tied Badger to a post and started walking up the steps to the huge front door.

But as soon as her feet touched the bottom step, there was a rumbling sound, as if deep under the ground something massive was moving.

She took her foot off the step and backed away, and as she did, the rumbling quieted and stopped.

"What was that?" hissed Frederick.

Colleen put her foot back on the first step, then on the second. The rumbling under the ground began again, deeper this time.

"Something doesn't want us to go in there," said Colleen. "First that hidden trail, now this."

Frederick glanced nervously about. Out of the corner of his eye, he thought he glimpsed a dark shape run behind a tree.

"Colleen, there's something in the woods..." he said, his voice cracking with fear.

Colleen stepped down again and the ground ceased its trembling. The wood grew still and nothing moved. She was about to turn around again when she also saw something. Her sharp eyes could see a black-hooded head peeking out from behind a tree, still as a stone, but there all the same, a darkness against the shadows.

"Maybe I was just imagining it," said Frederick.

"Hush!" she breathed. "I see it now. We've got to get in this house and shut the door behind us. When I say 'run,' we all run up these steps and push open that door!"

The shadow moved.

"Run!" she said, and they bolted up the steps, dragging Badger behind them.

"Ho!" called Oracle, who tumbled off the sleeping dwarf and began to roll away.

"Stupid leprechaun!" Frederick cried, but ran down the steps, grabbed the leprechaun unceremoniously by the belt, and then ran back up again.

The ground began to shake fiercely. The forest around them, and the whole house shook. Colleen watched as Frederick nearly lost his balance, stumbling to one side. The deep rumbling became an audible grinding of stone on stone.

"It's an earthquake!" shouted Frederick as he mounted the porch and put Oracle down.

Colleen turned to the doors. "There's no doorknob!" she said desperately, and reached out and gave them a push. Nothing happened. "There must be a latch or something," she yelled above the rumble that was now becoming like thunder.

"I don't see a key hole," yelled Frederick. "It must be hidden somewhere. All doors have locks."

He gave the doors a shove, then leaned his shoulder against one of them and pushed with all his might. But the doors held fast.

Then suddenly, Mrs. Wigglepox yelled, "Look out – it's a goblin!"

They all turned and could clearly see now a black-hooded figure stumbling toward them across the shaking ground. It seemed to *flicker* from reality to shadow and back again.

Colleen turned back to the doors, desperate and more than a little scared.

"You've got to OPEN!" she yelled.

Oracle poked the doors with his cane and, immediately, there was a clicking sound and they swung silently open, revealing a dark hall within.

For a brief moment, they all stared in amazement, but before anyone could speak, Lily cried out from Frederick's pocket.

"Mother!" she called. "I saw a face in the upstairs window!"

They looked up at the window that she pointed to, but there was no face to be seen, only ancient curtains that hung trembling behind the rattling glass.

"No time!" said Frederick, and pointed. The goblin was trying to run toward them now, and making a good show of it.

A boulder went careening toward the creature, barely missing it as it rolled away.

Colleen looked at Frederick and he nodded. She ran into the dark house, pulling the horse with her, and Frederick followed closely behind.

As soon as they were all inside, the door swung shut, surrounding them in darkness.

All at once, the quaking ground grew still and all was silent.

"I think we're going to need a light," said Frederick, and even as he said it, yellow torches sprung to life on the walls.

Colleen looked around. They were standing on a great slab of white stone, and a long, wide tiled hall stretched before them, with numerous shut doors on either side. The ceiling soared upward to a high peak, and a balcony stretched out on either side where she could see more doors. Ancient dusty tapestries hung from the balcony, depicting various forest scenes with many little people in them.

At the far end of the long hall appeared to be a broad stairway that split to the left and right, and between the two stood a tall stone statue of a great forbidding centaur holding a spear in its right hand. Its onyx eyes stared coldly at them.

"What is this place?" whispered Frederick.

"No one knows for sure," said Mrs. Wigglepox. "But it's said that it was built by the wizards, or perhaps by dwarves, back before the Great War. Some say that an old wizard hermit lived here, and other stories speak of this being a place where Anastazi the Great himself came from time to time. The dwarves held this as someplace special, and there were other houses like this once, but this is the last one that still stands."

"Well, we'd best move on," said Colleen, and she took a step forward.

But as soon as she did, the tiled floor seemed to shift under her feet and she nearly fell.

Stepping back onto the door's landing, she watched in amazement as all of the tiles down the long hall shifted places with one another like some giant children's puzzle, and then grew still again.

"Now I know there's magic here," said Colleen in a whisper.

"Yes," said Mrs. Wigglepox, "and it's still active after all these years."

"It's easy enough to guess that someone doesn't want us here," said Frederick, and he touched his toe to the tiles.

Again, they shifted and slid about, then grew silent again.

Suddenly, a deep booming voice broke the silence. Both Colleen and Frederick backed against the door in fright.

"The path is always treacherous when you do not know the way," it said.

"Who said that?" whispered Colleen.

She turned to look at Frederick, and saw that his eyes were wide and staring down the long hall. She followed his gaze and gasped, for the stone centaur at the end of the hall seemed to come to life. It shook itself and stretched, as if it had just wakened from a long sleep.

Slowly at first, and then more quickly, and then at a gallop, it charged down the hall, its great spear held out before it.

Badger whinnied and reared, sensing the danger. Colleen gasped, and Frederick could say nothing but "Oi!"

As the stone creature approached, Colleen could see that it stood at least seven feet high at the haunches. Its great stone, muscled upper body of a man towered another four feet upward to a stern, rough face with dangling stone curls.

It charged forward on thunderous hooves that echoed loudly as stone met stone.

Badger reared again and kicked wildly at the air. Colleen screamed, "Stop!" as the terrible spear drew up, ready to pierce her horse through the chest.

She covered her eyes and turned away sobbing, knowing what was about to happen next.

But the awful moment never came. Instead, she heard Badger snort in defiance, and Frederick collapse to the floor beside her.

A dreadful thought seized her mind as she uncovered her face and saw him sitting hunched against the door behind him.

But he was staring up, unhurt, and Colleen turned and saw why.

The great stone beast had stopped abruptly, its shining silver spear tip inches from Badger's neck. It was staring down at them with great black eyes.

Then, it spoke again. Its voice was like thunder and stone grinding on stone.

"Why does the daughter of the daughter of the Great One not speak the Words of Passage!" it roared. "Speak them, for you shall not pass until they are uttered!"

It was staring at Colleen now, and she did not know what to say.

"Speak!" it demanded in its rocky voice.

"I... I... don't know them," said Colleen. "What words?"

"I think that was the wrong thing to say, Colleen," whispered Frederick in a trembling voice.

"What she means, sir," began Frederick, "is that... that..."

There was a grinding sound as the centaur turned its gaze on Frederick and its eyes narrowed to black slits.

"And you, son of the son of the Great One - will you speak the words of passage?" it asked.

Colleen looked at Frederick. He seemed uncertain as to what he should say to this terrifying thing before them. He glanced at the door, then at her, then back at the centaur.

"We have..." he began, but his voice broke and he had to start over. "We have traveled from the world of Men," he began, and he tried to compose himself and sound important. "... and are here to destroy... er...uh, to defeat the Witch and her goblins and set free the little people from her ... uh... dominion."

The centaur looked back and forth between them and said, "I shall give you a riddle. Answer it rightly, and live. Fail, and I shall know that you are false!"

"Right then," said Frederick, and he swallowed hard. "A riddle it is. But first, uh, can we ask you a riddle so that we know that you are, well, uh, the proper guardian of the, uh, thing."

Oracle, who had tumbled behind Frederick, peered out from behind him, a strange grin on his face.

Colleen took a deep breath and steadied herself. Frederick didn't seem to be handling the situation very well, and she knew that she had to do something quickly.

"Sir, we are here to help, although it would seem that we came by fortune or providence. I hear that the Witch has taken my own mother, and I must find her and rescue her if I can, or at least return home to my own land and bring back my brothers to help me."

"First, the riddle!" thundered the statue, and bent down, its face toward Frederick. "I have never been defeated by any riddling. Only the true son of the son of the Great One could surpass me. I will permit you to speak first. If your riddle foils me, then you may pass. But these others must guess my riddle or they shall die!"

"What are you doing, Frederick!" whispered Colleen.

"Don't worry, I've got one that nobody has ever guessed," he whispered back.

Frederick cleared his throat, then spoke.

"Motherless, fatherless, born without skin.
Speaks once and never speaks again."

The centaur frowned and creases formed in its stone forehead. It rubbed its chin and looked thoughtful for several moments.

"See," whispered Frederick, "that riddle's been passed down in my family. Nobody else knows the answer! Besides, a stone centaur would never guess it."

"What's that!" boomed the centaur. "A hint! What would a stone centaur not know about – something beyond its experience? Hmm."

For several minutes, the centaur mumbled loudly, guessing this or that to itself, until with a frustrated grinding of its stone teeth it conceded. "Very well, son of the son of the Great One. Your riddle has surpassed my knowledge! Never before has anyone out-riddled me! Therefore, you may pass. But now, I shall give you my riddle."

The centaur raised itself to its full height and began to chant.

"Source of grief and pain and fear,
Home of love and hate and tear.
Place from which the song doth flow,
Home of dragons, lies, and woe.
Yet amid its raging storms is found,
A quiet little knocking sound,
Of one who stands outside its door,
And longs to enter its depths once more. "

Then it glared down at them, waiting.

"A moment, please, if you will," said Colleen, and she looked at Frederick, who seemed to be rather absorbed and was quoting the whole riddle back to himself.

"What do you suppose it is?" Colleen asked him after a moment.

"One moment," he said, and he quoted back the riddle again in a whisper, thinking as he did.

"I thought for a moment it was something like the pits of the Witch that Mrs. Wigglepox was telling us about," he said, "but I don't think so."

Just then, Mrs. Wigglepox peered out from Colleen's pocket and stared up at the stone centaur, which now was standing still as a statue again, its great spear pointed down at them.

"I think the answer is something much deeper than any pit the goblins could dig and something with much more woe than they could ever bring and more joy than any gift a leprechaun could give," she said.

"What could it be then?" asked Frederick.

"I grow impatient!" thundered the centaur. "But since you gave me a hint, I too shall give you one. This too is something that is beyond a stone centaur's experience."

A sudden thought struck Colleen and she said, "Mr. Centaur, may I touch you?"

"Touch me?" he said, and then looked thoughtful. "It is permitted."

Colleen took a slow step forward and put her hand on the great creature's side, closed her eyes, and began to hum.

For a moment, Frederick thought that his vision had blurred, for Colleen appeared to turn to the same gray stone as the centaur. He rubbed his eyes and looked again, but Colleen had removed her hand, and she appeared normal again.

"The answer is *heart*!" she said. "A stone centaur has no heart!"

And as soon as she said *heart*, the great centaur bowed once, turned, galloped down the hall, and stood back in his place at the base of the stairs.

"That was scary," said Lily from inside Frederick's pocket. "What do you think would have happened if we got the riddle wrong?"

"Who knows?" Colleen replied. "Let's just get past this place. We'll need to find a room that we can all stay for the night – someplace that's big enough for Badger too," she said.

"Frederick," said Lily, "what was the answer to your riddle?"

He blushed slightly and said, "Well, I don't think it's proper to say it in front of ladies."

"Come now, Frederick," said Mrs. Wigglepox. "Is it that bad?"

"Well, not really, but let's just say it rhymes with the answer to the centaur's riddle," he said.

"It rhymes with *heart*?" asked Colleen.

"Yes," he said.

Lily and Rose looked at one another and giggled. Mrs. Wigglepox looked perplexed, and Colleen put her hand over her mouth to hide her smile. Oracle only thumped down the hall, although Frederick thought he saw a twinkle in his eyes.

"Right, then, best get going," he said, trying to change the subject, and he followed after Oracle.

150

At the first door, Colleen stopped. It was like the big entry doors to the house – with no keyhole and no doorknob, and no amount of pushing would open it.

"Remember what you did outside, Colleen? Try saying 'open' and see what happens," said Frederick.

She stood in front of the door, and said, "Open!" Her voice echoed down the hall.

All at once, every door in the hall clicked and swung open, both downstairs and on the balcony upstairs. Some doors were small, not more than three feet high, and some were gigantic, nearly forty feet tall.

"Sheeeww," said Frederick. "You've really got a talent there! If there are any closed doors left in this house, let me give it a try!"

Colleen grinned at him and said, "Right. Now let's see what's been opened for us."

Chapter 20 – A Doctor of Stone

Frederick peered into the room. Torches with bright blue flames sprang to life on the walls, casting an odd light about the room. Tapestries depicting wizards and armies and princesses and a black dragon hung about the place, dusty, but not moth eaten or rotted with age. Against the walls stood suits of silver armor that gleamed dully in the blue light.

In the center of the room was a round table with a dozen seats around it, and above the table hung a fabulous crystal chandelier, the crystals of which glowed with a white light that radiated downward to illumine the table, and outward to mingle with the blue light of the torches on the walls.

"Amazing!" said Frederick.

"It's beautiful!" said Rose.

"It looks like some sort of meeting room," whispered Colleen, "but I don't think anyone has been here in ages."

Dust and spider webs covered everything, and it appeared that the room had not been disturbed for many years.

Frederick walked about the room, examining the armor and weapons lining the walls. They seemed just about his size, or smaller.

"They must have been small folk to fit into these things," he said, and he lifted a coat of silver ring mail that had an attached ring hood from its hanger on the wall.

"Why, this is amazingly light!" he said and, dusting it off, slipped it over his own shirt.

"And it fits too!" he said, smiling broadly.

There was a belt and short sword as well, and he buckled it around his waist and pulled the sword from its sheath. He held it up and it sparkled in the blue light of the torches.

Colleen giggled and said, "Hail, Sir Frederick the Knight!" She curtsied.

He laughed, swung the sword over his head with a flourish, and bowed in return.

"You might as well borrow it," said Colleen, growing serious. "I think the owners are long dead by now."

"Yeah, I guess so," he said. "But I wonder who made these things. They're marvelous!"

"Elves, likely, or dwarves," said Mrs. Wigglepox. "Not men, I think. They're too small."

Frederick saw that there was also a pair of blue boots and leggings, and these, he found, fit as well, and the boots were far more comfortable than his hard black shoes that he had been wearing.

There was a blue cape as well, and soon he had dressed himself completely in the outfit, and spread his arms wide, saying, "Well, what do you think, Colleen?"

Colleen stared at him for a moment.

"You look... royal!" she said admiringly.

He blushed slightly and he looked down at the outfit.

"Maybe I ought not to wear it, then," he muttered. "It doesn't really suit me too well."

"Nonsense," said Colleen. "I think they're better traveling clothes than what you had on before. See, there's a mirror over there. Go have a look while I do a bit of exploring."

Frederick walked over to the mirror and blew dust off its surface. At first, he looked at the outfit, which fit him remarkably well and was in perfect condition. *I do look rather royal,* he thought to himself, turning around and looking over his shoulder at the cloak.

But then he caught his own eye and turned again, looking harder. His dark hair was unkempt, and his face was dirty. The eyes that stared back at him did not seem royal to him, but were just a fourteen-year-old boy's eyes, not yet lined with too many cares, but filled with uncertainty. He knew that he was anxious, even frightened, not any sort of warrior at all.

I want to be, though, he thought. *I really do want to help Colleen find her mom.*

He stared a moment longer and then said aloud, "I suppose that's at least a start. Maybe if I just wear the armor and sword and cloak and boots, my heart will follow."

"What's that?" called Colleen from across the room.

"Nothing," he said, and turned away from the mirror. "I was just thinking about the centaur's riddle and... and other stuff. Let's go."

He left the room and Colleen followed. They continued down the hall, looking in each open door. Six more rooms were nearly identical to the first with the exception of their size, and the torches that sprang to life on the walls in each one were of different colors. The suits of armor were of various sizes, some quite large, even larger than Colleen's father could wear, and he was the biggest man Frederick had ever seen.

When they came to the smallest of the doorways, Oracle happily walked in through the three-foot high passage and began to bang his stick on the little suits of armor that lined the walls.

"What's he doing now?" said Frederick, poking his head through the door.

"Let us down for a moment," said Mrs. Wigglepox. "I want to see this room more closely."

She and Lily and Rose went in, and Frederick and Colleen followed.

"We'll get a neck ache in here," said Frederick as he crouched down to avoid bumping his head on the low ceiling. "But have a look at that – those suits of armor are just the right size for Oracle. There must have been a load of leprechauns his size once upon a time."

Oracle had now found a small table in the center of the room with low seats. He plopped himself down in one, banged his cane on the table, and shouted, "Order!" Then he snickered and got up and went on rummaging about the room.

Lily and Rose found a row of tiny silken dresses, which appeared to have slits in the backs.

"Those are fairy dresses, children," said Mrs. Wigglepox, "woven long, long ago from the finest silk. They've not been made in the Valley of Fairies for centuries!"

There were also leprechaun clothes, all much too big for the Wigglepoxes, but would just about fit Oracle. He fingered a fine bright green coat, looked at his own rather faded clothes, said "humph!" and walked by.

However, when he came to a shelf that contained four pots that were black as onyx, he paused, caressed them carefully, looked at the Wigglepox family, and smiled a knowing smile. But he left them on the shelf and walked on, hitting chairs and walls and most everything else with his cane as he went.

At last, he seemed to grow bored and left the room, followed by Mrs. Wigglepox, Lily, and Rose, and Frederick and Colleen came silently behind.

The seventh room, while looking much the same, was vastly different in size. The table and chairs were absolutely huge, and the ceiling stretched upward over forty feet to a massive chandelier.

They all stood in silence for several long moments, staring at the mammoth furniture, when Frederick noticed the tapestries.

"Look," he said, pointing to one of them. "Those are *giants* pictured there!"

Indeed, the scene showed a huge figure, and to its right stood a human man, less than a quarter its height, and on the right side of the man was a tinier figure that barely reached his knee.

"Oh my," said Mrs. Wigglepox. "So they are."

"This must have been a room where giants came," said Colleen.

"Yes," said Mrs. Wigglepox. "In fact, I think that these seven rooms we have just seen were meant for each of the other seven races – the elves, dwarves, goblins, trolls, men, giants, and little people."

"But what about a room for the Orogim?" asked Rose.

Oracle seemed to shiver at the mention of the name and drew his cloak close, and Mrs. Wigglepox said, "We rarely speak of them, dear. They were never allowed into the councils of the wise."

"Well, I've heard of little people and elves and dwarves and goblins and trolls, and of course men, but what are the *Orogim*," asked Frederick.

Mrs. Wigglepox gave a little shudder and said in a hushed voice, "A terrible people. Though they were not always so terrible, or so it's said. But they are the most feared of all the races. Pray that we never meet one of *them*!"

"What makes them so terrible?" asked Colleen.

"It is best not to speak of them," she said. "But suffice to say that few who have met them have survived to tell of it. Perhaps in another time and place, I will tell you the tales that I know."

Leaving the giants' room, Frederick poked his head into several more doorways, which proved to be storage closets.

"Look here, Colleen," he said, lifting a green robe and cloak from a hook and handing them to her. "This just might fit you, and here's a decent walking stick as well, and a pair of boots."

"I don't need those things," she said, looking at the clothes.

"Now whose turn is it? You made me put on this fancy stuff. What if we hit a rainstorm or something – you'll be needing a cloak and some decent shoes. Come on now, have a go – see if these things fit. Here, you can use this closet to change."

Colleen began to protest, but Mrs. Wigglepox said, "He's quite right, my dear. Besides, the owner of these things has been dead and gone for a long, long time. These things were left here for a reason – for someone like you who needs them to come along one day. Go on, then, try them on."

"All right, then," she said, and took the whole lot from Frederick and went into the closet.

A few moments later, she opened the door and emerged. Her golden hair streamed down the back of the dark green cloak. She spun around and smiled. Frederick's jaw dropped open.

"How do I look?" she said.

"Actually, rather, uh, well, pretty good," he said awkwardly, but inside he felt a rather queer knot in his stomach.

"But your nose is dirty," he added hastily, at which Colleen smiled broadly and scrubbed her nose with her old dress, which she then threw into the closet.

"Won't need that old thing," she said, and led Badger down the hall.

"S'pose not," said Frederick,

Now the stone centaur loomed before them, staring fixedly ahead with unblinking eyes.

"You don't mind if we pass, do you?" said Frederick to the centaur.

It said nothing, but remained motionless and silent.

"I think it's gone back to being just stone," whispered Colleen. "Let's get past it while we can."

Behind the statue was a pair of great stone doors nearly twenty feet tall, standing open, and beyond these was a large landing with broad steps leading upward. High white railings lined the upper balconies on either side of them.

Colleen led the way through the doors and Frederick followed with many a glance toward the centaur, hoping that it wouldn't change its mind and come to life again.

Colleen looked up at the high staircase that led upward before them, then patted Badger on the nose and sighed.

"Might as well go up," she said, "but I don't think Badger can make it up those steps, especially with the dwarf."

She tied him to the banister, and said, "Stay here, boy. We'll be back soon."

Badger snorted and stamped a foot, and Colleen rubbed his nose.

"Stay," she said, and started up the stairs.

Frederick followed Colleen up the short stubby steps, past a landing and to the left, where the stair split to either side of the hall, and onto a second landing at the top.

Torches flickered on in succession as they walked along the balcony above the downstairs hall, and they peered into the rooms as they passed them.

These proved to be bedrooms or sitting rooms, all filled with dust and cobwebs. But when they reached the middle of the hall, another hall turned to their right, and this they followed for a short ways when, suddenly, Colleen stopped and put her finger to her lips.

"Look!" she whispered. "Look at the floor!"

They all looked down at their feet.

"I don't know why I didn't notice it before," she said, "but the dust out here is all disturbed, like someone has been using this hallway all along, but has never cleaned it."

Dust lined the hall in front of and behind them, but it was not settled as it had been in the rooms behind the closed doors, but clumped and bunched together against the walls.

"There *is* someone here," hissed Frederick.

"I knew I saw someone!" whispered Lily.

"Best take care," said Mrs. Wigglepox. "Whoever it is knows we're here, and they haven't harmed us yet. It may be that this is Lily's old man after all, and perhaps he's friendly, but our welcome so far has not been a very good one. There may be more tricks in store for us. Frederick, you just keep that sword ready."

Frederick looked surprised, but nervously put his hand on the sword hilt.

Slowly, they walked down the hall, Colleen and Frederick side by side and Oracle following behind, his cane tap-tap-tapping as they went. They reached a corner and Frederick peered around.

"Take a look," he whispered. "The disturbed dust stops at that door down there."

Colleen leaned forward to see.

"He must have gone in there," she whispered.

They all stood motionless for a few moments, and Frederick began to wonder what sort of person would live in a place like this. Was it a goblin? An evil wizard? A madman? Who would have lived here for so long and escaped from the Witch and her spies? Or was he one of her spies?

But it was little Rose who broke the silence and said, "Why don't we just knock on the door?"

"I think that is an excellent idea," said Mrs. Wigglepox. "We're here for the night, and we might as well meet our host. After all, he already knows that we are here."

They slowly made their way down the hall and stood in front of the door.

"Frederick, would you do the honors?" asked Mrs. Wigglepox.

Frederick swallowed hard and then stepped forward and knocked. There was no answer.

"You'll have to do better than that, I think," said Colleen, and she took her staff and rapped on the door. The sound echoed down the empty hall, and she immediately regretted knocking so loudly. But there was no answer from inside.

"Do you think he's in there? Maybe he ran out through a back door or something. Or maybe he's not in there at all," said Frederick.

"Well, let's go in, then," said Mrs. Wigglepox, "Frederick?"

"What? Oh, right, well, then...OPEN!" he said.

His face fell when nothing at all happened.

Frustrated, he pushed hard on the door. It moved slightly and then stopped. "It's locked from the inside," he said, "with a regular lock this time."

Colleen rapped on the door again and said loudly, "Hello? We mean no harm. We only wish to be friends and spend the night here. Please, do come and open the door."

There was no answer for a moment. They were all wondering what they might do next when there came a loud *thunk* on the other side of the door and it opened just a sliver.

They all stepped back and saw an eye peering through the crack at them.

Then an old scraggly voice said, "How did you get in here? Go away!" The door slammed shut.

"Please, sir," said Colleen loudly. "We need to talk with you. Why won't you come out and see us? We have someone with us who needs help."

The door cracked open once again, and the eye peeked out at them.

"Who are you?" the old voice demanded. "Are you with the Witch?"

"Heavens no," said Mrs. Wigglepox. "We are on our way to see the Lady Danu. But we have a long way to go and need shelter for the night. Now come out here and speak to us properly!"

At that, there was a good deal of huffing and grumbling, and the eye looked back and forth at them, and then the door slammed shut again. They could hear a whole series of locks and chains clicking and dragging, until finally, the door was slowly swung open and the head of a very old, very short man of about four feet tall with a long gray beard peered at them from behind the door. He was quite obviously another dwarf and was wearing tattered brown pants with black suspenders.

They all stared at him, not knowing what to say.

"Well..." he said in his old voice. "You had better come in and not stand there in the hall."

He motioned with a bony old hand for them to enter, and they slowly filed in. Frederick came first, carrying Lily, followed by Colleen, who was carrying Mrs. Wigglepox and Rose, and lastly Oracle, who thumped in and gave the door a whack with his cane.

The dwarf quickly shut the door behind them and began locking dozens of locks and bolts and chains. This process took nearly a minute to complete, and he then hefted a large ironclad oaken bar across it.

"There now," he creaked. "The nasties won't get past that! And I hope you shut the front door behind you."

He grinned broadly, and Frederick noticed that quite a few of his teeth were missing.

"But see here," he said, looking at them in a sidelong manner, "you say you youngsters are going to see the Lady? Well, that's no easy task. And how did you get here in the first place? And, blimey! A tall leprechaun like olden times! Bless my soul!"

"First," said Mrs. Wigglepox, "we must have introductions. May we ask who you are?"

The dwarf looked at them for another long moment, considering, and then shrugged his shoulders and said, "A name is not an easy thing to entrust to strangers. But you may call me Doc. Yes, Doc the Dwarf at your service."

He gave a bow so that his long beard brushed the floor.

"I'm Colleen McGunnegal," said Colleen. "And this is my cousin, Frederick Buttersmouth."

"And I am Edna Wigglepox, and these are my daughters, Lily and Rose," said Mrs. Wigglepox.

Lily and Rose waved from their pockets. Oracle said nothing, but stared at the dwarf with squinted eyes.

"We call him Oracle," said Frederick. "We're not sure what his real name is. He's a bit mad."

Doc looked at each of them thoughtfully, and he said, seemingly to himself, "Leeeprechauuuuns!" His gravelly voice drew out the word. "Well, bless my soul."

Then he said, more to them, "I haven't seen your like around the mansion for... for... well, it's been a long time. And going to see the Lady! And traveling with a young..." He paused for a moment, looking hard at Colleen, then continued. "Say, girl, you're elvish, aren't you? And here we have a boy. A human boy! It's been a mighty long time since I've seen your lot."

"Colleen and Frederick are both humans, and they have come to our land through the Mirror in the Wood," said Mrs. Wigglepox.

"Ooohhhh!" creaked the dwarf. "Through the mirror! Why no one has come through that in ages... not since... since the cursed Pirate,

161

I should think! It was him that stole away our beautiful sleeping princess and brought the Witch back, he did. Stole the gold and treasure too."

Doc grumbled a bit under his breath, then seemed to come to himself and went over to Colleen, eying her up and down and said, "Are you sure you're human?" he asked.

Colleen was not sure what to say at first, but finally replied, "My mother is Ellie McGunnegal, who came here through the mirror from our land accidentally, and who the goblins have captured. My father is Adol McGunnegal, strongest man in all Ireland."

Doc snorted at this and mumbled something about humans and elves and pixies and then stepped over to Frederick, peering into his eyes.

Frederick stared nervously back. The old dwarf's eyes were sunken and gray, and wrinkles covered his aged face. In fact, Frederick could not remember ever seeing so many wrinkles on a face before. It was as if his skin had cracked over and over a hundred times, leaving not the tiniest spot unwrinkled.

"Human he is, at least mostly," the dwarf said at length. "Although there's something else deep in his blood. Something... I would have said 'dwarvish,' but that's not it. Something ... *regal*, though."

Frederick did not know what to say, so he just continued to stare back.

Doc glanced at Lily and Rose and Mrs. Wigglepox. "And it's obvious enough that you three are leprechauns."

Then he went over to Oracle, grunted as he bent low, and looked into his face. He stared for a long moment, and then a strange look came over him, as if he recognized something, and his eyes grew wide and he drew back.

But Oracle took his cane, jabbed the dwarf on his foot, and said, "Swigian!"

"Ouch!" said Doc, and hopped on one foot. "What was that for? He *is* a bit mad, isn't he? For a moment, I thought I recognized him, but I must be mistaken. Well, anyway, my eyesight isn't what it used to be. But I can see well enough that you're not with the

Witch's people. They all have *her* look, if you know what I mean," he said.

"Of course we are not with the Witch," said Mrs. Wigglepox. "As we said, we are going to see the Lady. Colleen's mother has been captured by the goblins and so has my own husband. We're going to see what can be done about it."

"Humph!" said the dwarf. "Little enough, it would seem... But look here! Come in and sit. But say, didn't you bring a horse with you? I saw one from the window."

"It was you!" said Lily. "I knew I saw someone looking at us from the window!"

"Yes, that was me. Forgive my earlier rudeness. It's a hard thing to live alone in these woods, what with the Witch's spies about and all. How was I to know that you were *against* her? That's a rare thing nowadays."

He motioned to two chairs for Colleen and Frederick, and pulled up a low footstool for Oracle. Then he excused himself, leaving through a side door, from which they could hear a good deal of rustling and banging, until the dwarf returned a few moments later with a tray bearing cups, bowls, a jug of drink, and a covered dish.

"See here, I haven't forgotten my manners completely." He sat the tray down and poured four cups of something from the jug, handed out the plates to Colleen and Frederick and Oracle, and from the dish scooped out helpings of stuffed mushrooms, which smelled delicious.

He paused for a moment, thinking, and then, realizing that he had nothing to serve the Wigglepoxes, scurried off grumbling to the side room again, where there was additional grumbling and banging, until he once again returned.

"It's the best I can do," he replied, and laid out three thimbles and a small teacup saucer. The thimbles he carefully filled with drink and he placed a single mushroom on the saucer and cut it into tiny pieces with a knife.

"Best give thanks," said the dwarf, and he mumbled a blessing of the dwarvish sort, which managed to stretch on a bit and included something about rocks and earth and mines as well as the food, though Frederick could not quite make it all out, so quiet and gruff was the dwarf's voice.

But when he was finished with his blessing, he grinned expansively and said, "Eat! And tell me your tale! It's been a long time since I've had company. A *long* time."

They ate, and Frederick thought that these were the best mushrooms that he had ever tasted.

"Where did you get these mushrooms, and what are they stuffed with?" he asked with a mouth full as he reached for seconds. "I've never tasted anything like them!"

"Ah!" said the dwarf, taking a long draft from his mug, his drink spilling down his beard.

"I grew them me-self! Down in the mines, you know. I know the old ways, I do, and there are places beneath the ground here where no goblin or witch has ever been. And the secret ingredient? Fish! Fish from the river beneath the mines. Deep and swift are its waters, and pure. The old Witch doesn't know about it, I'll wager, or she would have poisoned it long ago."

He giggled with glee at the thought, and then grew serious.

"And she must never know," he said. "These waters touch the Lady's lake, and feed the springs of the Forest, keeping the Spell at bay."

"I have often wondered," said Mrs. Wigglepox, "why it is that near the springs, the meadows and trees are not so much under her spell? I think now our own spring next to the Wigglepox Tree is the only thing that has kept it awake."

"Aye, could be, could be," said the dwarf. "I knew there were some of the old trees left still green, but I didn't know of any of the little people left in them. I thought they had all gone to the Lady or been captured by the goblins... Whoa, there, little man! Slow down on those mushrooms! Too much of a good thing will make you wish you'd had none at all!" he said as Frederick reached for thirds.

They ate on in silence for a few minutes, savoring the extraordinary flavor of Doc's food, and indeed Frederick began to wish he had not taken thirds, for his stuffed stomach began to feel a bit upset.

He put his hands on his belly, leaned back, and said, "That was really good."

Then a thought struck him.

"Mr. Doc," he began, but the dwarf held up a hand.

"Just Doc, lad!"

"Very well, Doc," Frederick said. "You said that the river runs to the south, to the Lady's Lake. How do you know that? Is there a passageway that follows the river that far?"

"A good question, lad," said the dwarf. "Yes, there is a passage, or there used to be. Long ago, when my people lived here in greater numbers, we made a passageway along the river that ran all the way beneath the Great Hills in the south and came out on the other side. In my younger days, my brothers and I would walk the River Path far to the north and south, opening new passages east and west in search of gems and gold. The little people would trade wishes for such treasure, and both our peoples prospered greatly. But I've not ventured so far as the Lake in many, many years. Last time I tried, the course of the river had changed, and there had been cave-ins."

"But if the passage is still there, could we follow it to the Lady's Lake?" asked Frederick.

"Too dangerous," said the Dwarf. "The old way is too unstable now. You might be able to belly-crawl through the blocked passages, but it would take you three times as long, and that horse would never make it."

"Are there any other ways down to the river between here and the Lake, Doc?" asked Colleen.

"No, lassie," he said. "This is the only place in this wood that I know of, and the only reason there is one here is because of this house."

"What's so special about this house?" asked Colleen.

"The wizards met here," said Doc. "Sages from all the races would meet and discuss their craft, even the Wise Ones of the Dwarves, and here we mined down, down, and we found many, many gems. When we broke through to the river, we found gold enough to buy all the kingdoms of the world!"

Doc's eyes shone in his old face at the memory, but then the light left them and his face grew hard.

"But now they are gone. All gone." He nodded and looked down at his plate.

"What happened to it all?" asked Frederick.

"Stolen! Stolen by the cursed Pirate!" Then he breathed a great sigh and said, "Well, anyway, it wasn't all him. But he took what was left after the War. And even when he returned it all, the goblins came and carried loads of it away."

"Doc," said Mrs. Wigglepox. "You said that the Wise Ones of the dwarves met here with the sages of the other races. Were you... were you one of the Wise Ones?"

Doc looked down again and was quiet for a long moment before he replied, "How long ago it was, I can't remember. The years have rolled by far too long. But yes, there were seven of us once, seven of us from the royal family who were once called the Wise Ones. We were the ones who discovered this hill and directed the building of this house. Now those were the days! There were elves and dwarves and men and giants and little people – the wisest of the wise from all the races. And even the Great Wizard came, and everyone prospered. But that was before the dark days – before the Witch and the goblins."

He was silent for a time and then spoke again, "I think I will trust you all. Yes, I was one of those that met. My full name is Doctor Eitri Sindri. But, as I said, you may call me Doc."

"You are a magician, then?" asked Lily.

Doc laughed a crackling laugh and said, "Ha! After the manner of our folk, you might say so. But our magic, if that's what you want to call it, isn't like elvish or wizard or giant magic. Our wisdom is that of stone and rock, of gems and gold, of building and tunneling, of shaping and carving and gathering and making things. We're children of the stone, and so our *magic* is of the stone too. And I was a Doctor of Stone. I was sent as a representative of my people, to give what help and wisdom we could and to receive in return what I could learn from the others. Aye, my brothers and I made many a magic thing for many folk."

He sighed and then continued. "But all magics fade under this accursed Spell of the Witch. Long it's been since I've mounted a bright gem in a shining ax whose blade will not dull, or carved a pillar of stone that will never break, or shaped a suit of armor that can't be pierced, or mounted a hammerhead that would fly like lightning when thrown. Once I did all these things, but no more."

He then eyed Frederick's armor and said, "But well, now, I do see that you have some fine armor on! May I see it?"

Frederick nodded, removed the cloak, pulled the mail shirt over his head, and handed it to the dwarf.

"Where did you get this, may I ask?" asked Doc.

"Well," said Frederick, looking at the ground, "it was downstairs in one of the rooms. I thought the original owners were long dead by now and wouldn't mind if I borrowed it, you know, seeing that we're going to face the Witch and all that."

"Downstairs!" he creaked. "You got into the rooms downstairs? But how? Those doors have been locked for ages. Even I haven't opened them in many a year."

"I did it, Doc," said Colleen. "I'm sorry... I just asked the doors to open and they did. I didn't mean any harm, honest."

The dwarf looked hard at her, as if trying to decide something. Then he sighed. "Ah, well, strange things are happening these days. Now here's a human child who has power in her voice to loose what's been bound." Then he muttered something under his breath about elves.

"But see here, Frederick. You just keep this armor and wear it well. That's no ordinary suit that you have there, lad," he creaked. "It was made in the Good Days, when there were no evil goblins and no Witch. These suits of armor were made through the combined skill of all the races. Why, I had a part in their making as well!"

"You did?" said Mrs. Wigglepox incredulously. "But I thought you said that armor was made in the Good Days, before there were evil goblins and such? Why, that would make you..."

But Doc cut her off and said, "Well, yes, then. It would make me quite an old dwarf. But such skill was once not beyond me. Now, though, with the Spell and all, and no one to help, I've not fashioned such armor in many, many a year."

Again, he sighed, and then his expression became shrewd and he lowered his voice to a whisper. "But! I still can do a thing or two – as you saw when you tried to come into this house and walk down the hall!"

"You did that?" asked Colleen.

"Aye, I didn't know that you weren't with the Witch. There was that goblin outside and all," he said.

"Yes!" said Colleen. "What ever happened to it?"

"Well, it got more than it bargained for. I sent a load of boulders rolling down the hill at it. It danced a jig like you've never seen, hopping about like a jack rabbit to avoid my rocks. Then when the door shut, it ran off into the woods. Aye, the stone still hears me now and then, especially in great need. And I've got a workshop far, far underground, down by the river where the Witch's spell is not so strong! There, where the river runs deep, and the power of the Lady still holds sway – there I can still do a thing or two, and there I have a few things that the Pirate missed and that the goblins know nothing of. This may be the very chance I have waited for! You must come with me to my workshop and see what I have kept. It may be that these things will help you on your journey."

The old dwarf's face beamed with excitement, and then he glanced out the window and said, "But see here, it is getting dark outside, and we must be getting into the tunnels. Can't have the Witch's people seeing any lights on in here. She doesn't know that I'm still here, you know. Come, come, and follow me now."

"But what about Badger?" said Colleen.

"Badger?" asked the dwarf.

"Yes, my horse!" said Colleen. "He's tied up at the bottom of the steps. And, oh! How could we have forgotten, we have another dwarf with us. He's sleeping on a litter that we made for him. We found him in a gorge sleeping fast and nearly buried under leaves and sticks."

Chapter 21 – Brother Dvalenn

"My brother, Dvalenn, once so keen,
Lost yourself, where have you been?
Sleeping long beneath the Spell,
What sad tales you could tell.
Once so sharp and keen and bright,
Your eyes now close to heaven's light.
Once you made the tools of gods,
Now your sleepy head just nods.
Even when you seemed to rise,
On useless things you kept your eyes.
You gathered gravel and stones you found,
That only weighed your pockets down.
I hope one day you let them go,
And look for treasures deep below,
Down, down you must descend,
To mine for treasures that will not end."

— The Lament of Sindri for his brother Dvalenn

Doc's eyes opened so wide that Colleen thought they might pop out. He leaped to his feet, spilling his drink and knocking his chair over.

"A dwarf!" he cried. "Take me to him!" And he ran to the door and began unbolting its many locks.

"You go with him," said Mrs. Wigglepox. "We'll be fine right here."

Colleen and Frederick ran after the dwarf, who was already out into the hallway, and Oracle thumped his cane behind them, trying to keep up.

"He's at the bottom of the landing," called Colleen, amazed to see how quickly the old dwarf could run.

Down the stairs they sped, and Doc darted past the horse and fell on his knees beside the sleeping dwarf.

He brushed the long stringy hair back and looked deeply into his face, then began to weep.

"He's my brother, Dvalenn!" he cried, and nearly fell on top of him for joy and sorrow.

Badger whinnied and Colleen soothed him.

After a moment, Colleen said, "I suppose we should take him upstairs if we can."

"How long ago did you find him like this, and where was he?" asked the dwarf, choking and wiping tears from his face.

"It was about an hour or so before we got here, in a deep gorge to the north. He was nearly buried in leaves beside a tree, and we nearly passed him by," said Colleen.

"Bless your sharp eyes, child," said Doc. "Dvalenn disappeared *years* ago. I searched long for him, but never did find him. In the gorge! Why I'd been by there many a time, but never saw him. How strange."

The dwarf looked again at his brother lying on the litter and shook his head.

"I thought the Witch had taken him, just like all the others," he said.

Then his eyes narrowed and he looked deep in thought. "It's been twenty years or more since I've been by that gorge. I'll bet my golden ax that he was captured, and escaped, and made it all the way to the gorge, but was overcome by the Spell and fell into the Black Sleep."

He sighed, then wiped his eyes on his sleeve.

"Speaking of the little folk, you best go and get Mrs. Wigglepox and her lasses. We've got to get Dvalenn down into the mines," he said.

Frederick ran up the stairs and returned shortly carrying the three little people in his pockets, and munching another mushroom. Oracle came sliding down the stairs on his behind, looking rather gleeful. Frederick shook his head as he passed the little man.

"Now, if you would all please step back a pace, I'll open the door," said Doc, and he motioned for them all to move away from the steps.

They all stepped back, and the dwarf turned to face the stair. Then he did what Colleen thought was a very funny jig. And as he danced, he moved back and forth in front of the stairs, and ended in a flourish of floor stamping and one final leap in which he landed with his arms spread wide. He turned, a sheepish grin on his face, and winked at Colleen. Just as she was about to giggle at the sight, a whole section of the stairs opened inward, leaving a large doorway from which a yellow light glowed.

"Amazing!" cried Colleen, and ran forward to give the old dwarf a hug. "Doc, you would do marvelously well in an Irish pub! My people love to dance!"

"Indeed!" said the dwarf, the grin on his face growing even wider.

"But why did you do that?" asked Frederick.

"Ha!" said Doc. "It's a *secret* door, you know. One has to know the password for secret doors. And this one's password is a *dance*. It was one of my other brothers, Avliss, who came up with the idea. Now he was a merry fellow. Loved to dance, he did."

Oracle hitched a ride by climbing up onto Dvalenn's chest and planted himself where the remains of the bird nest were still intertwined in his beard.

Doc led them into a passageway that sloped downward almost immediately, and they had not gone far when the door in the stair swung shut behind them, leaving nothing but a stone wall where it had once been.

"No one knew about that door except the dwarves, I think," said Doc. "We made it as an emergency exit from the building."

"But I thought this place was built during a time of peace, when all the races were friendly toward one another," said Mrs. Wigglepox. "Why would you need secret doors and... and suits of armor?"

"I suppose that's true. But we dwarves are a careful lot when it comes to building things. And we always have a back door that's secret, you know," he said. "And there were the Orogim. We sensed a tension in the very rock – as if something evil were brewing. We prepared for it." He fell silent for a moment, as if remembering some old pain.

"But see here," he said. "It's a long walk ahead of us. Let me tell you a tale or two, and perhaps you might tell me one as well."

He cleared his throat, thought for a moment, and said, "Long, long ago, before the War between the wizards and the Witch, all the peoples of all the lands were good and noble. Why, even the goblins and trolls were once decent folk, and aye, even the Orogim. But none of the races knew of the others, except maybe the fairies – and they kept their secrets, until Anastazi the Great Wizard opened the Gates, and all of them opened into the Timeless Hall, where the peoples freely came and went."

"What is the *Timeless Hall*?" asked Frederick.

"Ah! It's a place *between* the worlds, or so they say. The Great Wizard either found or created it, and there he built the Gates. And as long as you stay there, you never age! In fact, no time passes at all."

"You mean I could go in, sit for a year, and come out and no time would have passed?" asked Frederick, his curiosity growing.

"That's right, my boy! Least ways not for you," said the dwarf. "That's why it's called *timeless*! Oh, time for the *worlds* still passes, but as long as you're in there, you never age, or at least not enough to notice."

Then a sly look crept over his face, and he lowered his voice and said, "The Gate to this world was lost after the Cataclysm, and the Witch doesn't know where it is, or she would surely have tried to open it by now... but there *are* some people who know where it is!"

"And what was the Cataclysm?" interrupted Frederick again.

"That was the terrible destruction that was unleashed at the last battle between the Witch and the wizards that I told you about," said Mrs. Wigglepox.

"Yes!" said the dwarf. "Everything was changed. The sea, the land, the hills, the desert, even the forest above us, and the magic not only destroyed things, but *rearranged* them – that's the best way I can put it. It was like the whole world got *shifted around.* So that's why the Witch could never find the Gate once she came back. And that's why the sacred places of the little people got lost too."

"But I thought that these wizards were really powerful, and all the legends back home of the little people say that they can grant wishes and do all sorts of magic too. If this land was *filled* with little people, how could just one old witch and a few goblins take over?" said Frederick.

"That's the sad part of the tale," said Mrs. Wigglepox. "There was betrayal."

"Betrayal?" asked Colleen, shocked.

Mrs. Wigglepox shook her head sadly. "Yes, one of our own people betrayed us. One of the grandsons of the Elders, Lugh himself. He gave himself over to the Witch and taught her our magic. And it's said that he even surrendered his own pot of gold to her."

"But why would he do such a thing, Mother?" asked Lily.

"Greed for power, my dear. Greed for power," she said. "The Witch promised to give him power over people – to make him a god. Can you imagine that? A little leprechaun pretending to be a god? Why, how absurd it would be, to see the smallest of the peoples sitting on his tiny throne with giants and goblins and men and trolls and elves and all the great spirits bowing to such a little thing? But, Lugh didn't see it that way. The Witch wove such lies in his mind that he began to believe such nonsense, and he gave all his power to her. He spent all of his wishes and wasted all of his magic gold and gems on her, and what did he get in return? He was lost, that's what he got, and he was cast down from his self-proclaimed greatness by one who was truly great."

"Yes," said the dwarf. "'Tis a sad tale. Lugh did have much power in this world, and you might as well say that he traded his pot of gold for a pot of beans – and bad beans at that. Sad, sad. The little people were taken by surprise again and again, because the Witch seemed to know everything about them – where their pots of gold were hidden, where their trees were, how many of them she would face – all because Lugh was feeding her information while pretending to oppose her. By the time Lugh's betrayal was discovered, the Witch had gained much power and the little people had lost just as much. Many people think that Lugh used his Last Wish in the Cataclysm."

"Hush!" said Mrs. Wigglepox sternly to the dwarf. "You mustn't speak of such things!"

"Ah, come now, Mrs. Wigglepox. You know it's true," said the dwarf.

"Yes, but the Last Wish is a sacred thing to the little people. We do not speak of it openly!" she replied, crossing her arms.

"But why? What's a last wish?" asked Frederick.

Mrs. Wigglepox began to speak, but the dwarf put a finger to his lips and said, "Perhaps another time we shall speak of this. Come along, we're almost there."

"Doc," said Colleen, "you said a moment ago that some people know where the Gate of Anastazi the Great is. If the Gate is not at the castle anymore, who can we talk to, to find out where it is?"

The old dwarf positively cackled with glee at Colleen's question, and continued to do so until Frederick whispered in Colleen's ear, "Do you think he's gone a bit mad, like Oracle back there?"

Doc suddenly stopped laughing and turned to face them. "*Mad?*" he said. "*Mad?* Well, lad, it may be so! But it was not *madness* that made me laugh, *no!*" And again, a fit of cackling took him.

Then he stopped laughing and a mixture of seriousness and wonder and delight all at once filled his aged face.

"I must warn you all," he said. "At your peril, do not stare for more than a moment at what you are about to see!"

Chapter 22 – Fight at the Inn

The next night at the Five Springs Inn, so many people turned out from the town and the surrounding land that there was standing room only when the McGunnegal children took their place in the middle of the dining hall and began to sing.

The cook gave Aonghus a large hat to place on the floor and, as they sang, coins began to fill it. At first, they thought this was a grand thing, but while Bib and Abbe were singing a duet about the sea, their sweet voices carrying across the hall and charming their listeners, Henny tugged on Aonghus' sleeve. He bent down and she whispered in his ear.

"There's a funny-looking man over at that big table," she said. "He keeps staring at me. I think he wants to take me away."

Aonghus looked briefly at the table where Henny indicated and there was indeed a fellow with an untrustworthy look about him. His shifty eyes kept darting between Henny, Abbe, and Bib, and more than once to the hat that was filling with coins. But his eyes kept coming back to stare at Henny.

Aonghus looked into Henny's frightened eyes and said, "Don't you worry, Pumpkin. I'll take care of you."

He lifted her in his great arms and glared at the man. The man met Aonghus' eyes once and then they flitted away to the hat, then back to the girls.

The evening proceeded uneventfully, and their hat was filled to overflowing, not only with copper and silver, but with gold as well.

But during their last song, Aonghus noticed that the shifty-eyed man rose from his seat, nodded to a fellow across the room, and both of them left. The first slipped into the hall that led to the stairs, and the other left through the front door.

As the girls sang a verse on their own, Aonghus whispered to Bran, "There's likely going to be some trouble tonight," he said. "Two shady-looking characters just slipped out of separate doors. I'll bet that hat of coins there's more of them too."

"Do you think they're after the money?" whispered Bran.

"That and the girls, I think, especially Henny. Keep your eyes open," he said.

Just then, the girls finished their verse and Aonghus and Bran joined in the final chorus in perfect harmony and the song ended to a roar of applause and a shower of coins.

The children could not help but notice Mabel sitting at a front-row table, smiling broadly and eying the money.

With a flourish of bows, the evening ended and the children collected the coins that had been thrown about them. They would not all fit in the hat, and so they stuffed their pockets full and headed for the kitchen.

Aonghus came through the door just in time to see a dark figure slip out of sight. He motioned for his brother and sisters to come close and he whispered, "Something's going on here. There are shady folk about, and I just saw one leave through the back door. Stay close, but don't look too suspicious."

But as they made their way to their rooms, nothing further happened.

"Come on, Bran," Aonghus whispered. "Let's help the girls count the coins."

In the girls' room, they emptied the hat and their pockets onto the bed and began to count.

"There's twelve pence to a shilling and twenty shillings to a pound," said Bib.

"Look at this one!" said Bran, holding up a gold coin.

"Let me see that," said Bib, taking it from him.

She inspected it for a moment and then said, "This one's a British India coin. It's got Queen Victoria on it."

"And what's this?" said Henny, holding up another.

"That's a crown. It's worth five shillings," she replied.

"I've never seen so many coins in one place," said Abbe, looking at the pile.

"Well, to figure out how much it is, we've got to remember that a florin is worth two shillings, a crown is five, a half-crown is two and a half, a tuppence is worth two pence, and a thrupence is three pence. If you find a guinea – that's a gold one – it's worth one pound and one shilling."

"That's too confusing," said Bran. "I've not held more than a shilling in my hand before today."

"There's more," said Bib. "A groat is worth four pence, a tanner is six, a ha'penny is worth half a penny, a farthing is a quarter penny, and a mite is worth one eighth of a penny."

Bran shook his head.

"What'll we do with it all?" said Abbe.

"We pay the taxes on the farm, that's what," said Aonghus. "No more worries about that. But see here, let's not get all worked up over this stuff. I wouldn't want greed taking hold of us. Just our daily bread – that's what we need, and enough to pay Caesar his due. I'm thinking the rest of it ought to go to help our neighbors. There's plenty of food here, and almost none back home. I say we buy a shipment of food and send it back home, first thing tomorrow."

"Skibbereen needs it most," said Bib. "The famine is worst there."

"Aye," said Aonghus. "Now let's finish counting."

They divided up the coins by type and Bib did the final count.

"It comes to fifty-eight pounds, six shillings, and three pence," she said.

"Not bad!" said Bran.

Suddenly, there was a knock at the door. Aonghus tossed a blanket over the pile of money and went and opened it to the round form of Ted.

"I've come to wish you good night, but if you care to listen, there's a late night speaker down in the common room. The Five Springs sometimes hosts political figures, or scientists, or adventurers. Tonight, it's a fellow named John Michaels. I hear he's quite passionate about helping Ireland through the famine. Thought you might be interested."

"Thanks, Ted, yes, I'd like to hear what he has to say."

"Well, he'll be starting soon. There aren't any seats left, but you might be able to hear from the stairs. Good night to you all," said the cook, and he turned and left.

"I'd like to hear this," said Bib.

"And me too," said Bran.

"Come on, then," said Aonghus.

They left the room together and Aonghus locked the door, then they sat lined up on the stairway that overlooked the common room. In the middle, where they had sung that night, stood a young man, perhaps in his late twenties, with dark hair and a kind face. The Master of the Inn had just introduced him, and the room grew quiet as he began to speak.

"Friends," he said, "tonight, less than a hundred miles away, children are hungry. They are hungry, not only from lack of available food, but because of ill-conceived policies and greed. I am newly come from the shores of Ireland, and have seen horrors beginning that no human being ought to endure. Disease is taking hold. Decent folk are run from their homes. And landlords plunder the mean hovels of the impoverished and destitute so that they might graze their fat cattle and build bigger barns on the backs of the poor.

"I would call us tonight to consider Ireland as Lazarus, and we as the Rich Man of the parable. Lazarus sits at our door. Dare we sit by day by day and watch the dogs of famine and pestilence lick his wounds? Nay, we must act now, before we are called to account for his inevitable death. And more than one beggar is he, for he is millions.

"This famine in Ireland is no small thing to be trifled with. Our government must be made aware that multitudes of our neighbors, yes, even members of our own empire, will soon have nothing to eat. These poor folk watch as the grand policies of the Market are enacted and they sink beneath the weight of its injustice. Let me read to you hard words that are being spoken by those suffering under this scourge."

Aonghus looked out at the crowd as the young man pulled a piece of paper from his coat pocket. A woman in a satin dress pulled a fan from her bag and began to fan herself with it. Others fidgeted, looking uncomfortable as the speaker went on.

"We are expecting famine day by day. And we attribute it collectively, not to the rule of heaven, but to the greedy and cruel policy of England."

At these words, a murmur went up from the crowd, and their faces grew dark and angry.

"Let me read on," said Michaels more loudly, and, clearing his throat, he continued.

"Our starving children cannot sit down to their scanty meal, but they see the harpy claw of England in their dish. They watch as their food melts in rottenness on the face of the Earth, all the while watching heavy-laden ships, freighted with the yellow corn that their own hands have sown and reaped, spreading all sail for England."

Michaels paused, surveying the crowd. Some met his gaze with dark glares, while others looked away. He went on.

"I do not bring these words to our shores lightly, nor do I wish to accuse. I only wish to inform and plead with the good people of Britain to send aid, and to petition our government to act swiftly, and not send analysts and bureaucrats, but food and medicine to the Irish. Stop the export of food from Ireland and feed it to the people, stop the destruction of homes and give the homeless shelter, stop the burden of heavy taxes and let the people work the land, and give relief to Lazarus before he dies, and the soul of our people is called to account for failing to see him lying at our gate."

Michaels went on for some time, describing the terrible sights that the McGunnegal children were all too familiar with. An hour passed, and then he closed his speech.

"Friends, I know you are a good and generous people. Will you not help? I watched as you tossed good coin to Irish singers tonight for their magical voices. I tell you, a whole nation like them awaits you now. Will you not send them aid? Not only a few pence or even a few pounds, but your voice and influence as well? Write to the House of Commons and the House of Lords. Visit the Parliament, and speak for the needy. I will be here for another hour if any of you would like to discuss these things further. Thank you for your time and consideration."

The crowd began to rise from their seats and mingle, forming little groups, and more food and drinks were served.

Ted came halfway up the stairs and said to Aonghus, "They'll be going on for quite a while now, discussing the speech. All sorts of politics will get bantered about tonight, I reckon. I'm in for a long one. Well, good night to you all."

"Night," they said, and rose to return to their room.

"I think we ought to sleep on the floor of the girl's room tonight," said Aonghus to Bran.

"Right," he said. "I was thinking the same thing. I haven't forgotten that shifty-eyed fellow."

They all settled in, and Aonghus and Bran made themselves as comfortable as they could on the floor behind a room divider.

"It seems that there are some folk here in Britain who care about Ireland," said Abbe.

"I hope they care enough to listen to that Michaels fellow," said Bran. "I don't think the folk here know how bad it's getting."

"Let's pray they listen and do something. Well, let's get some rest," said Aonghus.

"Night," the others replied, and soon Aonghus could hear their breathing change to the slow, steady rhythm of sleep.

But he could not rest. John Michaels' words kept repeating in his head. Was the British government really that oblivious to their plight? Didn't they see what was happening?

He lay thinking about this for some time, and finally dozed off. The Inn had grown quiet, and all the guests finally retired for the evening or left, when something brought him wide awake. It had been a little sound – just a creaking floorboard in the hall.

Bran opened his eyes and whispered, "What is it?"

"Shh. Listen," he whispered.

Another creak, then a third.

They quickly roused the girls and held fingers to their lips, and Aonghus lifted Henny, who was still asleep, and placed her behind the room divider.

"Watch her," he whispered to the girls, then he and Bran stood on either side of the door and waited.

A few moments later, there was the sound of a key being placed in the lock, then a quiet *click*, and the slow turn of the doorknob. The door swung open ever so slowly, and a black clad figure slipped in through the door and tiptoed toward the now empty beds.

A second, then a third came in, and when they were all slinking forward, Bran closed the door behind them.

All three turned around, and the last thing that the third man who had come in saw that night was Aonghus' fist punching him square in the nose. He fell with a resounding crash and did not stir.

The other two men, barely able to see anything in the dark other than Aonghus' huge shadow, rushed forward together and attempted to grapple with him.

One tripped over something, which turned out to be a broomstick, which Bib had stuck out from behind the divider.

Bran picked up a large spittoon and forced it down over the other man's head. He went whirling this way and that, tripped backward over one of the beds, and lay still on the other side.

The man whom Bib had tripped was on his feet in a moment, but tripped over his unconscious partner and fell flat on his face.

"Get the lights, Abbe," said Aonghus, and a moment later, an oil lamp was lit.

Aonghus strode forward and picked up the tripped man by his black shirt. He wore a black mask, which Aonghus ripped from his face. It was the man with shifty eyes that he had seen earlier that evening.

"Who are you and what do you want with us?" demanded Aonghus.

Before he could answer, there was a scuffling of feet outside the door, a loud yell, and a bang, as if a gong had been struck, and then the door opened and the round face of the cook peered in, his bald head covered in sweat and a large iron frying pan in his meaty hand.

He took in the scene with a glance. "Well, I see you have things well in hand here, Aonghus. There's a third... oh, rather a fourth one out cold in the hall," he said, spying the unconscious figure with the spittoon on his head lying across the girls' bed with his feet in the air.

Aonghus smiled and then turned back to the man whose feet were now dangling off the floor.

"As I asked," he said to the man, who was now struggling to breathe. "Who are you?"

When the man did not answer, the cook said, "I can tell you who he is. His name is Dranshot, Fred Dranshot. He's been in and out of prison half a dozen times that I'm aware of. And that fellow there with the broken nose is Ernie Stripjaw – another bad potato."

Bran walked over to the third man, hefted him over the bed and onto the floor, and with a yank, removed the spittoon, which came off with a pop.

"I might have guessed," said the cook. "Dortus Crumpleshoe – another fly in the stew."

Just then, a voice from the hall called for lights and the voice of the Master of the House could be heard.

"What's going on here!" he said in a hushed voice. "You'll wake all the gue..."

But he went silent when he saw the unconscious black figure in the hallway, peered into the room past the cook's considerable girth, and narrowed his eyes.

"What is this?" he said. "Who are these people?"

The cook moved aside to allow the Master in and said, "Looks like

183

some shady characters tried to do a bit of kidnapping, sir. Lucky that these young lads were watching out tonight. I was up, well, taking care of some business, when I thought I heard someone walking in the hall. I peered out from my room and, sure enough, this fellow in the hall was standing by the door here, keeping guard like. When he heard the ruckus going on inside the room, he turned to open the door. That's when I came right up behind him and knocked him in the head."

"Kidnappers? In my establishment? This is outrageous!" the Master hissed. "If word of this gets out, I'll have no further business! Quickly now, bring that man in the hallway in here."

The cook dragged the unconscious man in.

The man still in Aonghus' powerful grip was struggling frantically now to free himself, and was turning purple in the face.

"Better let him down, Aonghus," said Bran. "I don't think he can talk too well, hanging in the air like that."

Slowly, Aonghus lowered the man to the floor and allowed him to breathe.

"Why were you trying to kidnap my sisters!" he demanded, his face terrible with anger.

The man cowered, trying to pull free, but could do nothing to escape the iron grip that held him in place.

"We... we were paid..." he stammered.

"By who!" demanded the Master of the House.

"I... I... d...don't know!" he whimpered.

Aonghus tightened his grip and looked even more threatening.

"It w...was a m...man in a dark r...red cape! He gave us three pounds each." The man's tongue seemed to loosen the more he talked, and now he spit out the whole story in a rush.

"He was at the dinner last evening, and heard them sing. He promised us seven more pounds once we delivered the girls to him," he said in a rush.

"Where?" said Aonghus simply. "Where were you going to deliver the girls?"

"Around back, by the stables," he pleaded.

"Tie these blokes up, Bran, Ted, if you could please help," said Aonghus.

"Gladly," said the cook and, taking the man from Aonghus, took his great frying pan and soundly knocked him cold. "Let me get some rope," he said, and waddled out the door, returning a few moments later with rope and rags, which he unceremoniously stuffed into their mouths, and tied them up.

As soon as they had been bound, Aonghus slipped from the room and quietly went out the back door. The barn stood a short distance off from the Inn, and he stole silently across the yard, slipping into the shadows and around the side of the barn.

His sharp ears could hear hushed voices coming from the other side of the barn.

"They'll steal a pretty price once we gets them to the proper place," a grizzly voice said.

"Aye, a few hundred gold pounds each, I'd say!" said another.

"Or maybe none at all," said Aonghus as he banged their heads together and they fell senseless.

Going back to the room, he found the four kidnappers tied hand and foot and gagged, with the cook and Master standing discussing what to do with them.

"If you young men wouldn't mind," said the Master, "I'd like to take these worthless... gentlemen to the jail this very hour, rather than make a disturbance for my guests in the morning."

Both Aonghus and Bran frowned, but agreed.

"There are two more out behind the barn," said Aonghus. "They have a cart that should serve nicely."

Aonghus carried one man, Bran another, and the cook and Master huffed and puffed their way down the steps, carrying a third. The girls kept watch over the unconscious fourth one until Aonghus came back and, tossing him over his shoulder, carried him out as well.

When they had all six of the men bound in the back of the cart, they threw a tarp over them. "We'll take care of them from here," said the Master. "You two go back up with your sisters and care for them."

Off they went then, and Aonghus and Bran returned to the girls' room and found that Henny had finally woken. She had slept through the whole thing.

"Well, there, little one!" said Aonghus. "We're all safe and sound now."

"What happened?" she asked, her little girl's eyes wide with wonder and fear.

"Never mind that," said Aonghus. "But we'll be leaving in the morning at any rate. No more staying here for us, no matter what Cousin Mabel says."

"That's for sure," said Bib.

And so they tried to get back to sleep, but only Henny dozed off, and the rest of them talked until morning.

When breakfast time came, there was a knock on the door. Aonghus rose and opened it to find the cook, who bustled in and shut the door behind him.

"Good morning, ladies, gents," he said. "Hope you were able to rest a bit after all the excitement last night."

He looked at their faces and realized that they had not slept at all.

"Well, at any rate, those blokes who broke in last night are in the local prison. The police will want to speak to you today. I expect they'll be here by mid-morning," he said.

"We're planning to leave as soon as possible," said Aonghus.

"Of course," said the cook. "And I don't blame you. Only you'll want to give testimony to the break-in and identify them so that they get what's coming to them."

He paused and then removed a large pouch from his hip.

"And I brought you this," he said, handing Aonghus the pouch. "It's your money from a few nights back. I haven't counted it or anything, but it's a fair amount. Probably not as much as you got last night, though."

Aonghus accepted the pouch and thanked him, extending his hand.

"You've been a good friend to us, Ted. We're in your debt. If you ever need a strong hand, you've got mine."

"Friends, then," said the cook, shaking his hand.

"Friends," said Aonghus, and proceeded to give the large man a bear hug.

"Good Lord, man," said the cook, catching his breath. "In all my days, I've never met a lad like you. You don't know your own strength!"

Aonghus smiled, and the cook bid them all farewell, bidding them come down for breakfast as soon as they were ready.

And so they busied themselves getting ready to depart, and Bib counted the money in the bag.

"Look here, all," she said excitedly. "We have nearly sixty-five pounds now."

"We've got to get that to Father," said Abbe.

"Yeah," said Bran. "But how?"

"Can't we send it to him?" asked Henny.

"Not the way the mail is," said Bib. "You can't send cash. It would sure as anything be stolen. One of us will have to take it back to him."

"I'll do it," said Bran.

They all looked at him.

"It just makes sense," he said. "See here, we can't send one of the girls, not with what happened last night. And you need to watch over them, Aonghus. That leaves me. I can take care of myself."

"No," said Aonghus.

"Now see here..." began Bran, but Aonghus cut him off.

"We'll all go," he said.

"All of us? But we've just gotten here. Father said..." began Abbe.

"Father told us to stick together, Ab," he cut in.

"But we'll need to get on a ship," said Bib.

"That shouldn't be hard. We have the money for passage now," said Abbe.

"But what about Colleen? We should wait until she arrives so she can go back with us," said Bran.

"If we leave now – right now, I mean, we might be able catch a ship back before she even leaves," said Aonghus. "See here, we'll talk to Ted the Cook about the idea. He might know if there are any ships sailing back to our port in Ireland in a day or two."

They went down to breakfast together and found Mabel busily consuming a large plate of eggs, cakes, and sausage.

Ted the Cook spotted them and motioned for them to sit at a table. He served them all the same, along with fruits and milk.

"They sure eat well here in Britain," said Bib.

"You mean you don't eat like this in Ireland?" said Ted.

"No, sir," said Bib. "What with the famine and all, folk are beginning to starve. It's been a hard year for us."

"So what that fellow said last night is true, then?" asked Ted.

"Yes. We only hope that the crop is better this year," said Aonghus. "A good many people are getting sick too, and more can't pay their rent, and so are getting evicted. Who knows where they'll go."

Ted looked shocked. "I'd not heard it, no I hadn't, although folk around these parts are often unkind to your countrymen and don't speak well of them. But I say you're decent men and women, and I'll put an iron pot to the head of anyone who says otherwise. Just 'cause a man's accent is different doesn't make him less of a man.'"

The cook shook his head. "Well, you all enjoy your breakfast. It's on me today," he said, and bustled off to the kitchen.

After finishing their meal, Aonghus said, "They truly do eat well here. I'm stuffed."

"Aye, at least at this Inn they do," said Bran. "But I'm not so sure I'd want to eat like this all the time. Might end up like Cousin Mabel over there."

He nodded toward Mabel, who had just finished cleaning her third plate with a biscuit and was leaning her great bulk back to make room for her belly, but eying the table for some last sweet to complete her significant meal.

"Bran!" said Abbe, scolding him. "You shouldn't say such things!"

"He's right about one thing," said Aonghus. "Seems to me that too much pleasure turns one jaded."

"What's 'jaded'?" asked Henny.

Aonghus leaned over to her and said, "It's sort of like putting too much honey in your tea," he said. "At first, it's really sweet. If you down it anyway, it makes your stomach upset. If you just keep putting too much honey in your tea, pretty soon that's the only way you can drink it, even though it makes you feel sick after you do. Seems to me that most sorts of pleasures are like that. A little makes life sweet. Too much just makes you bored and restless and not satisfied with much of anything."

Henny nodded with understanding, having, on occasion, put too much honey in her tea.

While they were eating, Aonghus beckoned to the cook and he came over.

"Ted, we've decided that we're going to return to Ireland as soon as possible. We've earned enough money in the past two nights to do it," he said.

The cook looked surprised. "Why, I thought that you lot were off to school or something."

"Well, we were," said Aonghus. "But that's changed now. Can you find out what ships are sailing back in the next few days? It would have to be soon. We need to meet our sister there."

The cook looked at them and said, "Well, that's a good school you were heading to. Shame to miss the chance, I'd say. But," and he sighed, "I'll check for you. Shouldn't take more than an hour or so. I'll send my lad Teddy."

With that, he bustled off, shaking his head.

"Well, we'll have to delay Mabel until we get word," said Bran. "Might as well go and unpack..."

The girls grinned and raced up the steps to their room, where they busied themselves with undoing their morning packing.

Aonghus and Bran began to follow, not wanting to leave the girls, but Mabel called them over to her table.

"Be ready to leave within the hour, boys," she crooned. "Our coach will be wanting to depart soon."

"I suppose we better go pack our things," said Bran.

An hour later, there was a knock on the door and Bran opened it to a shy serving girl. She blushed when she saw him and timidly said, "Your Cousin Mabel bids you come down with your belongings – the coach is ready."

"Thank you... what is your name?" he asked her.

"Lizzy," she said.

"Thanks, Lizzy," he said, and smiled broadly at her.

She blushed and hurried down the hall, glancing back at him once before disappearing around the corner.

"What do we do?" asked Bran. "Teddy doesn't seem to have come back yet."

"Let's take our things down one at a time. I'll do it. You lot stay put," said Aonghus and, with that, he took one bag in his arms and carried it down to the waiting coach.

He fussed with it for several moments, positioning it this way and that on top of the coach until Mabel shouted from inside, "What are you doing up there?"

"Well, we don't want to make the coach imbalanced, cousin," he said. "We wouldn't want to tip over."

"Well, hurry along!" she said irritably.

Aonghus went back to the Inn and found the cook and his boy Teddy in the room with the others.

"Teddy here just arrived," said the cook, "and I'm afraid his news will be disappointing to you."

He was a thin boy, quite unlike his portly father, and a few years younger than Bran. Looking into his large brown eyes, Aonghus could see that he was a fine young man and trustworthy.

"Right," said Teddy. "The dock master says that there won't be any ships leaving for the whole east coast of Ireland for nine days."

"Nine days!" said Abbe. "But that's too late!"

"They say the government is planning things out and making sure shipments get done properly," he replied.

They were all silent for several moments and then Aonghus said, "Thanks, Ted, Teddy. We really appreciate it."

"Not a problem, Aonghus," said the cook. "Sorry it didn't work out for you."

"Well, we'll get along okay," he said. "Could you do one more favor for us?"

"Name it," said Ted.

"Take this money and buy a load of food with it, and send it to the town of Skibbereen in Ireland. It's down south, in County Cork."

"Won't you be needing that?" asked the cook.

"We've saved enough out for the trip back and to pay the taxes," he replied.

They shook hands again, and Aonghus said, "Might as well get your things, everyone. No sense in delaying now."

191

So they all gathered up their belongings and trudged down to the waiting coach where Mabel scolded them for being so slow.

"We'll miss our train if you don't hurry along!" she called from inside the coach.

"A train!" said Henny. "I've never been on a train before!"

Soon they had their bags stowed in the carriage and away they went, with Aonghus and Bran hanging on the back at times and trotting beside the horses.

It was not long before they rounded a bend, and the deep sound of a steam whistle reached their ears. The horses snorted in response, and the driver whipped the reins for them to gallop.

"Best hurry," he shouted. "That's the warning whistle. They're boarding now."

Chapter 23 – The Gate of Anastazi the Great

Doc led Colleen, Frederick, and the Wigglepox family down to the end of the passageway and stopped at what appeared to be a bare wall.

He placed his hands on this and a door swung silently open. A wide hall opened before them.

As they entered, the dwarf cried out in a loud voice, "Behold the Gate of Anastazi the Great!"

Colleen gazed in wonder at an enormous door that was set in the wall opposite them. Shining like the moon, its silver radiance pierced the darkness like a song. Frederick let out a low whistle, the little people all gasped, and even Badger whinnied and shook his mane. Oracle slid from Dvalenn's beard and came around to gaze at the sight. But Colleen simply stared at its incredible beauty.

Standing at least forty feet tall and twenty feet wide at the base, its double doors rose upward to a peak. A golden frame surrounded the massive gates, carved and inlaid with intricate scroll work and figures of little people, elves, dwarves, men, giants, and others that Colleen guessed were peoples she had never heard of. But there were no evil creatures on these gates – all were bright eyed and happy, and the golden frame of the doors seemed to be some sort of history, telling some tale of long, long ago.

For a long moment, Colleen stood transfixed, her mind filled with visions of antiquity – of heroes and wizards and princes and princesses – of all the legends and fairy tales that she had ever heard and, as she stared, it seemed that they all might be true in some way – that beyond those gates might lie worlds without end, where any dream might become a reality.

She did not hear Doc's voice saying, "Do not stare at it for long!" for once again, something seemed to awaken within her in that moment. It was a bit like the way she felt when she was standing on the Hill back on the farm, singing that night with her family all around. How long ago was that? Was it a day? Or a week? She could not remember. But this feeling was even deeper, as if she were suddenly roused from a deep sleep, awakened from a dream that she had been dreaming her whole life long. The runes and images on the door grew sharp and clear to her eyes and mind, and she *read* them – *understood* what they said, and knew that they were indeed a history, and that somehow she was a part of it.

She stretched out her hand toward the Gate, dropping Badger's reins, and began to walk forward, enthralled by the sight. One step, two, and then she was hurrying forward.

Distantly, she heard everyone shouting warnings to her, but the Gate held her gaze, its power and beauty capturing her mind.

Then suddenly, Frederick's face loomed in front of her, blocking her view of the shining doors, and strong hands gripped her shoulders from behind.

His voice, loud in the echoing chamber, snapped her mind into focus.

"... got to stop, Colleen!" Frederick was saying. "There's a rushing river right in front of you! You've got to..."

She blinked and stared at him.

"What?" she said.

"You're going to ... or, it looked as though you were in some sort of trance or something, Colleen. Colleen? Are you all right?" he asked, worry written on his face. "Colleen? Don't look at the Gate, Colleen, look at the floor!"

She looked down then, and just a few feet behind Frederick was a rushing river, the sound of which now filled her ears. The cavern, Frederick, Doc's old hands on her shoulders, and a worried Lily peering out of Frederick's pocket all came rushing back to her.

She rubbed her eyes and then peered around him at the still shining Gate, then back at Frederick.

"What happened?" she asked. "I feel as if I've just woken from a long sleep."

"Perhaps you have," said the dwarf. "Such is the power of the Gate to those with eyes to see."

"See what?" asked Frederick, looking at the dwarf. "Can we move away from this river's bank? It makes me nervous."

"Yes, please do," said Lily.

They moved back and sat down against the wall behind them, and the dwarf bade them not stare directly at the silver doors that Colleen now realized were on the other side of the wide river. Now she knew that she had very nearly tumbled right into the swift current that cut across the massive hall.

"How... how did the Gate get all the way down here?" asked Colleen after a moment.

"As I said, young lady, things got *shifted.* Whether the Gate moved or the land moved around the Gate, who can say? But here is where I found it, long after that terrible day. Deep beneath the ground right across the river from my tunnel. So, either by chance or by Providence, I became the Keeper of the Gate. And here's what's more – I've been here alive and well ever since that day so many thousands of years ago."

"Thousands? How is that possible?" asked Frederick, disbelief in his voice.

"Well, dwarves are a long-lived people, although not usually this long. Personally, I think the Gate was damaged in the Cataclysm, and is *leaking,"* said Doc.

"Leaking?" asked Colleen. "Leaking what?"

"*Timelessness!*" said the dwarf. "Or *agelessness.* When I'm down here, I just don't seem to age much at all. And even when I'm up in the house, it seems nearly the same. It's as if the magic of the Timeless Hall is leaking out of that Gate and filling this whole area. Now that I think of it, it could be how Dvalenn survived out there all those years."

The thought suddenly struck Colleen that she was in a place that time had forgotten – with a dwarf who was thousands of years old. And now she was no longer aging either – that the power of the Gate of Anastazi the Great was flowing all around her and in her and through her, making her ageless in this strange underground world.

"But wait a second," said Frederick, interrupting her thoughts.

"You grow mushrooms down here. *They* certainly must age or they wouldn't grow."

"A very good point, young man," said Mrs. Wigglepox.

"Indeed," said the dwarf. "The magic only seems to affect creatures like you and me, but not fish or plants or insects that I've encountered. I don't know how it might affect your horse, Badger."

Colleen pondered this for a moment and then a dreadful image came to mind.

"Frederick," she whispered. "Outside, the Spell of the Witch is creeping through the forest, putting everyone into a dreadful sleep. This door is leaking timelessness into that same forest. Do you suppose the two magics are mixing together, and the little people out there go on sleeping forever in some dreadful unending life of nightmares? What kind of world is this?"

"I hadn't thought of it that way," he said, frowning. "What an existence that must be! Do you think they even know it? I mean, are they just lying there, dreaming away, and not even aware that they are sleeping on and on, their whole life one big fantasy? Do they even know anymore that there's a real world that they could awaken to?"

Colleen shook her head.

"I don't know, but it's all the more reason for us to try to help them. And now's our chance, Frederick. This is the Gate of Anastazi, right in front of us. It's time for us to go through it and get home and bring back some real help."

"Lass, it's not going to be that easy," said Doc. "That door has been locked for thousands of years. I've tried a hundred times to open it, and failed every time. I'd have gone home long ago and brought an army of dwarves here if I could have, but Anastazi the Great himself locked it. It would take a magic greater than his to unlock it – unless you had the key."

"I've got to try," said Colleen. "Can you get me over there?"

"Aye, but first things first. Let's get Dvalenn to my workshop," he said.

196

Colleen looked back longingly at the Gate as Doc led them away. Could she open this door like she had the others up in the house? And if not, what would they do now? Hope and despair mingled in her heart as they turned a corner and the shining light disappeared.

Doc led them on for some distance until they came to another blank wall. Once again, he touched the rock and a door swung silently open. Through this, they entered another tunnel that was illuminated with bright glowing gems that twinkled as they passed. The floor was smooth, but not slick, and was made of great slabs of green and brown agate. The walls were swirls of orange and yellow and red and white that seemed to take in the light of the gems and hold it, making the passage warm and beautiful to behold.

"Did you make this passageway?" asked Colleen.

"Aye. It's taken me many years, and I'm still working on it, but aye, I made it."

"But it's incredible!" said Frederick. "How could one person do it all alone?"

The old dwarf smiled and actually seemed to blush. "We dwarves know a thing or two about stone craft, as I've told you. It's in our blood. Kind of what gives us meaning in life, you know."

"To cut stone gives you meaning in life?" asked Frederick.

"No, no, boy," said the dwarf. "It's more than cutting stone. You see, we believe that when the dwarves were made, we were given a great task – to build great halls and rich tunnels and grand caverns. Not just for our own glory, mind you, but for the Creator who made us, and to share these with everyone else. If we don't try to accomplish the very thing we were made to do, then there wouldn't be much meaning in life. Why, what good would it do, in the long run, just to *exist* without *doing* what you were made to do and *being* what you were made to be, and then sharing it with others? And *that* is another reason that I am quite pleased to see you. At long last, I have someone that I can share all of this with. And wait 'til I show you the Crystal Cavern."

"The Crystal Cavern!" said Rose excitedly. "What's that?"

Doc grinned a toothy grin, winked at her, and continued down the hall.

Chapter 24 – Leprechaun Gold

The passageway twisted and turned as Doc led them on. Frederick watched the eerie light of glowing crystals rise and fall as they passed by, and Badger's hooves echoed *clippity-clop* with every step. The echoes, the lights, and the growing sense of moving steadily deeper and deeper underground was beginning to weigh on him. Minutes ticked by, and Oracle began to hum a tune in time with the horse's footfalls.

"Are we there yet?" Frederick said at last.

"Just around the bend," said Doc, and a moment later they came to a dead end.

"Another secret door?" asked Colleen.

Doc smiled and said, "Step back a bit. That's it – just a bit more."

As they backed up, the dwarf cupped his hands against the wall and whispered something that they could not make out. Without warning, the floor under Doc's feet began to sink.

He lightly stepped aside as a large, perfectly round hole appeared, the white stone sliding silently away, and they could see a green ramp descending into darkness.

"I'm afraid your horse will have to stay here, Colleen," said Doc. "He could go down the ramp, but not beyond the next chamber."

"But what if he wanders back to the river? He might fall in and drown!" she said.

"Now don't you worry about that," he said. "I have just the place we can keep him."

He cupped his hands once again against the wall to their right, whispered something, and this time, the wall itself slid aside, leaving an opening large enough for Badger to walk through.

"Bring him along," said Doc as he entered.

Frederick followed as Colleen led Badger through the open wall. He found himself in a chamber that had a distinct earthy smell, and, looking about, saw a great many mushrooms growing on shelves and in buckets and on decaying logs.

"It's your mushroom garden, isn't it?" said Frederick.

"Yes!" said the dwarf. "And I have just the place for this fine horse. I had a horse a long time ago. A long time ago."

He paused, remembering, then shook his head and led them to the far side of the room, where there was a stone rail and wall that surrounded a stall, of sorts, the floor of which was covered with pine needles.

"There are certain kinds of mushrooms that need a bit of acid in their soil, so I keep a bin of pine needles for just that purpose. It's a bit low right now, and would make a nice soft bed for your horse, and we can tie him to the rail."

"Wonderful!" said Colleen. "But I wouldn't want to leave him for long."

"He'll be fine," said Doc. "I've even got a bit of something that he might like."

He went to an adjacent bin and brought out an armload of brown dried grass.

"You use that to grow mushrooms too?" asked Frederick.

"Of course, and many other things as well. You can flavor your mushrooms by the humus that you create for them to grow in," he said. "But come along now. I want to show you my workshop. Please, help me with my brother."

Frederick and Colleen untied the litter from Badger and gently lowered it to the floor.

Colleen patted Badger and whispered in his ear that she would be back soon, and led him into the stall. The old horse began to munch happily on the grass and seemed content to stay put.

"Come now, help me with Dvalenn," said Doc. "Let's get him down to my workshop."

With Doc on one end and Colleen and Frederick on the other, they picked up the litter and carried it out to the ramp.

"Your brother is heavier than he looks," panted Frederick as they reached the ramp.

"Dwarves are a sturdy folk," said Doc. "Dense bones, you know. Now watch yourself – don't drop him, especially when we get to the bottom."

"Why?" asked Frederick as they descended. "What's at the bot..."

But he did not finish his question, for as they reached the base of the ramp and walked through yet another door, a cascade of colors suddenly met Frederick's eyes and he stopped dead. His mouth dropped open, and he stood speechless, staring. Then they all lowered Dvalenn to the floor and slowly walked forward, and the wall slid silently closed behind them.

A dazzling kaleidoscope of rainbows and shining gold washed over both of them and they stared up in wonder.

"It's gold," whispered Frederick, more to himself than anyone else. "And gems and crystals. There must be a million of them!"

For several long moments, they stood in awe, gawking at the gigantic room they had entered, whose golden walls arched upward to form a great red-gold domed ceiling that was crammed with crystals of every color, some as thin as hair, and others huge and jutting from the ceiling like great spikes. All were shining, radiating brilliant light that filled the cavern with a multitude of rainbows. The floor was gold as well, and every inch of the room was so perfectly polished that it reflected everything around them as if they were surrounded by mirrors, or perhaps were inside a mirror. The effect was to make everything seem to stretch outward forever and ever, the light and gold and rainbows going on and on until it went beyond their vision.

"Behold the Crystal Cavern – the Hall of Sindri!" he cried.

Mrs. Wigglepox let out a gasp and put her hand to her heart, then both hands over her mouth, and stared. Oracle squeaked with delight, and Lily and Rose both said, "Oh!"

"What's wrong, Mrs. Wigglepox?" asked Colleen. "Are you all right?"

For a moment, she did not answer, but then seemed to come to herself and said, "I don't believe it!"

Doc grinned expansively and danced a little jig across the polished gold floor. Reflections of himself jigged around the walls and floor and ceiling, casting the illusion that a dozen other dwarves danced with him.

"I told you I saved a few things from that pirate and the Witch!" He laughed, then danced about again.

"Not in all my years..." began Mrs. Wigglepox, and then she repeated "Not in all my years..."

"Mother," said Lily, "are we inside a pot of gold?"

"Yes!" shouted Doc with glee. "Yes, indeed you are, youngster, and it's the biggest pot of gold in the world, made from leprechaun gold and gems and dwarvish magic!" And once again, he just could not help himself and stamped his feet and danced about.

"But... but how?" asked Colleen. "Where did you get so much gold and so many gems?"

"And leprechaun gold at that!" said Mrs. Wigglepox.

"I can see myself everywhere," said Frederick, turning around and around, and watching hundreds of golden reflections of himself turn with him.

"Yes," said Doc in a serious tone. "You truly *can* see yourself in here. *Every bit* of yourself."

"I suppose so, with so many reflections," said Frederick.

"No, he doesn't mean that," said Colleen, gazing at herself in the nearest wall. I can see..." She paused, tilted her head sideways, and then frowned and looked down.

"What's wrong?" said Frederick.

"That's a side of myself I don't like to look at," she said quietly.

"You look all right to me," said Frederick. "I mean, you don't have any zits or anything."

"No, boy," said Doc. "Look closer in the mirror. Look at any one of your reflections in this room and it will show you a bit about yourself. It reveals one little aspect of who you *really* are."

"I don't get it," said Frederick.

Doc sighed.

"You see how these crystals refract the light, taking in normal white light and breaking it up into all the colors of the rainbow?"

"Sure," said Frederick, looking at the ceiling.

"Well, this room – these walls and floor and ceiling – do that to your image. They refract the image of *you* into all its pieces, and show you each color of your heart and soul and mind and body – the whole *you*. All you have to do is look carefully enough and you'll see."

Frederick paused, looking at the image of himself before him. He stared for a moment, and suddenly it was no longer just a reflection of his body, but a darker image. Its greedy eyes darted back and forth to the gems around it. It smiled malevolently, reaching out to grab one of the glowing stones. Frederick shut his eyes.

"You see?" asked Doc.

"I don't like looking at myself like that. I'd rather not even see that stuff," said Frederick.

"None of us do," replied Doc. "But the real power of the room can only be experienced once you face who you truly are. If one just dares to stand and face himself, then the power becomes available to do something about it. Until then, the room holds no power for that person."

"And what is that power?" said Frederick.

"It's the power of the Wish," said Mrs. Wigglepox. "One of the most potent powers in the universe."

"You mean I could make a wish in here?" asked Frederick.

"You could," said Doc. "But you must not! Not while there are so many of you dancing about the walls. You never know what might come about with so many Fredericks making a wish. It might turn out to proceed from a rather ugly part of you, and the wish would surely turn sour. You first must clean every image within you and, having done that, unify them all into one grand, bright image."

"How does one do that?" asked Colleen, looking at the half dozen images of herself that stared back at her.

"It can be a lifetime of work. You need a guide, and all the good powers of Heaven and Earth helping you. The Hall of Sindri only shows you how far you have to go. It doesn't give you solutions. But, for starters, just being honest enough to stare your ugly self in the mirror goes a long way. Once you've gotten yourself together, you'll look in the mirror and see a single image – your true self – the person you were made to be in the first place. When that person walks into this hall and makes a wish, it will never go astray. Now leprechauns, they're natural wishers, and except for those that got turned into gremlins and such by siding with the witch, they should be able to look at themselves in these mirrored walls and see just who they are."

Oracle hobbled over to one wall and banged his reflection with his cane. A single reflection of himself stared back.

"Put us down, please," said Mrs. Wigglepox.

As soon as they were on the floor, the three little leprechauns joined Oracle and stared at themselves in the walls. Three Mrs. Wigglepoxes stared back from various places around her, and for Lily and Rose, there were only two.

"See!" said the dwarf. "Not as much work to be done with these good folk. They've fought a good fight against the Witch and her spells."

"That's too much to think about," replied Frederick, feeling a bit embarrassed that so many Fredericks stared back at him all around.

"But I can see that if word got out about this place, there might be an all-out war to get it. Can you imagine being in control of a place where you can wish for anything? I mean, I know some people that would do just about anything to have this place. By the way, where did all this gold and these gems come from?"

"Well, to answer the first question, I suppose you can actually *thank* the Pirate for that," said Doc. "It was strange... after stealing so much from the little people, one day he showed up with the *whole lot* of it, and left it right there in front of the house. Just left it there and disappeared and never returned. It took me all day long to get a load of it into the house and many days more to haul it all down here, and *years* to build this room. But before I could get it all hidden, a whole troop of those goblins showed up and took the lion's share of it away. I stowed what I had saved down in these tunnels and, over the years, assembled it all in this – the Crystal Cavern!"

He waved his arms about the room, still grinning, and then continued. "And here's my plan. You see, the Witch probably thinks that *she* has all the leprechaun gold. Sadly, she does have most of it. But, as you can see, she hasn't gotten it all. I figure if we can get enough good little people down here in this room, maybe they can plumb *wish* away the old Witch and all her goblins, or something near to it. But I'm real cautious about it, mind you, what with the Betrayal and all that. You never know which of the little people, begging your pardon, Oracle, Mrs. Wigglepox, Lily, Rose... which of the little people are *safe* to let in on the secret. But the Hall is a revealer of hearts, see. I'll bet if a black leprechaun came in here, the whole room would go dark with the reflections it would give off."

Mrs. Wigglepox looked sad.

"What is it?" asked Frederick, who could see her face sticking out of Colleen's pocket. "What's wrong?"

She sighed and then said, "Well, it's not even as easy as that. You see, a leprechaun can't use just *any* gold. Not even another leprechaun's gold. Each piece must be found and blessed with leprechaun blessings and placed in the pot just so, and buried in a certain way and a rainbow called down on it, and other secret things as well. It could take *years* to make a decent pot of gold that's any good for granting wishes. And even then, wishes are tricky things. You might wish for something that you think is good, and something even worse comes of it. Why, you might wish that the Witch were gone from our land forever, only to find that some evil giant has appeared, smashed the Witch flat, and is now wandering about smashing everything else in sight too. And there are limits to wishes. So, you have to be very careful what you wish for. The safest wishes are for the good of people, not for their hurt. That's why the little people were given the power to grant wishes in the first place – to help others. Wishing for bad things almost always turns into something bad for the wisher."

Now it was Doc's turn to look downcast. "Do you mean," he said quietly, "that all my work here was for naught?"

"Oh, no!" said Mrs. Wigglepox. "I can see that this indeed *is* leprechaun gold, and most of these gems were from leprechaun pots as well. There is a *great* deal of leprechaun magic in this room, Doc, and a great many leprechaun blessings as well. And just look at these rainbows! But I really don't know what would happen if I tried to use it. It is *very* powerful. I have never felt so much magic in one place. But if I made a wish here, with the gold of hundreds and hundreds of leprechauns all mixed together, why, the wish might go astray, or go too far, and do some great harm. I think that the only way to use this room would be for at least *three* experienced leprechauns to focus all their powers together to control the wish. And a new pot of gold is best if it has the blessing of a leprechaun Elder as well – one in direct descent from the First Elder. Alas, the last Elder of our neck of the wood disappeared many years ago."

"Mrs. Wigglepox," said Colleen, "there are *four* leprechauns here. You and your children and Oracle!"

"Alas," she replied, looking sadly at her two daughters. "Lily and Rose have not even made their *first* wishing. There's been no chance even to look for gold since the times have been so hard. If only they could find a bit of gold for themselves, then I could begin to teach them."

Doc, who had begun pulling on his long white beard, suddenly brightened and said, "You all wait here and enjoy these rainbows. I'll be right back."

Then he stood in the middle of the room, did another dance, and the floor beneath him began to lower him down, down in a circle about three feet across, until he and Dvalenn completely disappeared from their sight. When he was gone for several minutes, Mrs. Wigglepox led her children around the room, pointing out various kinds of gems and the pure quality of the gold.

"It really is amazing," she said. "But to think that I have so many tainted reflections of myself. I've got work to do before I start wishing again."

A moment later, Doc rose out of the floor, the stone circle lifting him upward until the floor was as whole and smooth as ever.

"I left Dvalenn in the workshop," he said. "Come now, gather close around me. And hold on to one another. I wouldn't want you falling off before we reach the bottom."

They gathered around him and the little people were carefully placed back in the pockets of Colleen and Frederick, and Doc did his dance. All at once, Frederick felt his stomach lurch inside him as the floor dropped downward. Colleen grabbed his hand and held it tight, and he noticed how rough her hand was, calloused by hard work on their farm, he supposed.

She smiled at him as they descended.

"Don't let me fall, now," she said.

"Ha, I'm the one who's likely to go tumbling off this thing," he said.

She laughed, and he suddenly felt glad that he was here with her. He hoped his hand wasn't sweating. That would be just like him, he thought, to ruin a perfectly good moment of kindness by getting nervous.

Suddenly, he noticed that Oracle was not on the platform with them, but had walked over to the golden wall of the room and had both hands stretched out on it and his head bowed.

He mumbled something that was indecipherable, and just as Frederick dipped below the floor and lost sight of the bent leprechaun, there was a change in the room above, as though the air had suddenly become charged and brighter, and the rainbows grew crisp and clear. Energy seemed to fill the room, and Frederick was wondering what was happening when the face of Oracle appeared, peering down the hole at him.

"Fredersmouth!" he called, and jumped.

"Whoa!" Frederick cried as the leprechaun came falling down at him. He let go of Colleen's hand and barely caught the little fellow and put him on the floor, saying, "Are you out of your mind? What if I had missed catching you?"

But Oracle said nothing and only giggled his coarse laugh.

Colleen grabbed Frederick's hand again and took Oracle's with her other.

They descended in a shaft of golden light for a moment until even it faded away and darkness took hold.

"Nobody move," said Doc. "You wouldn't want to fall now."

Frederick watched as the bright hole in the ceiling became smaller and smaller, until it was a tiny circle – a star in the black void that surrounded them. He was beginning to wonder how far down they would go when the stone slab stopped with a quiet *thump*.

"Keep together," said Doc, "and follow me."

"Where are you?" said Colleen.

"Here," he said from the darkness in front of them. "Step forward."

They did and, a moment later, there was a *SWOOSH* behind them. Frederick looked back, but could see nothing. He looked up, and the tiny circle of light far above winked out.

"Doc?" said Frederick.

"A moment," said the dwarf from some distance away. "I'll get the lights."

Chapter 25 – Doc's Workshop

Colleen stood in the darkness, holding two hands – Frederick's with her right and Oracle's with her left. She was struck by the difference between the two – Frederick's was warm and soft. He'd not done much manual labor, she decided. Oracle's, was small, like a child's, but as calloused and bony as her grandfather's. Somehow, the old leprechaun reminded her of him, and she realized how much she missed the old man. Had he come here too? Or was he off to some other world, finding his *true self,* as he had said that night he disappeared? And what of herself and Frederick? Would they do the same in this strange land? Would she discover why she felt both deeply at home and strangely out of place back in Ireland? Were all her reflections in the Hall of Sindri truly pieces of herself that she needed to reconcile and bring together to find out who she really was? And this strange little man standing next to her had only a single reflection. What could that mean? He seemed almost crazy at times.

She shut her eyes in the darkness and focused on him, trying to read him, understand him, feel what he felt. There was something hidden beneath his old cloak – something more... She reached out with her heart and mind for it. But just as she did, lamps sprang to life all around them, and the little leprechaun let go of her hand and banged his cane on Frederick's foot.

"Ouch!" he said, releasing Colleen's hand and hopping on one foot. "What was that for?"

"Careful!" cried Lily from Frederick's pocket.

"Oh, sorry!" he said. "I forgot you were there."

Oracle only grinned.

Colleen looked around. The room in which they were standing was carved from gray stone that ran in a high shaft far above them into darkness.

"Over here," called Doc, waving to them.

They went to where he stood and, as they did, a stone door swung silently open before them.

"Welcome to my workshop!" he said, and led them all inside.

The room was illumined by large, radiant crystals mounted on the walls, and they could see many stone tables and chairs laid about, and on these tables were various hammers and chisels and saws, and many, many uncut or partially cut stones and gems. Along one wall ran a small shallow stream. Its waters gurgled softly as it slowly ran along the entire length of the room, appearing out of one wall and disappearing through a hole at the other end. In one corner was a cot of sorts with some old blankets and a hay-stuffed mattress and pillow on which Dvalenn lay sleeping.

The walls and floor, though smooth, were plain and gray.

"Why haven't you made your workshop as beautiful as the halls and caverns outside?" asked Frederick.

"What's that?" said the dwarf. "Oh! Well, why would I?"

"My father has all sorts of things in his study back home – rare paintings and statues and tea cups and swords. It's like his own personal treasure chest," said Frederick.

"We dwarves aren't like that, you know. Our workshops are just that – workshops. All the beautiful things are to be shared and enjoyed by all. It's our joy to make them and share them," he said. "One day, I hope that I will be able to open up these tunnels as the grand Road to the Gate of Anastazi."

"All the stories I've heard about dwarves," said Frederick, "are that they love to hoard gold and gems and fight anyone who tries to take it away from them."

Doc looked grave and said, "I've been away from my homeland for a very long time. It would be sad if such a thing has befallen my people. That's not our *natural* way, if you take my meaning. It would be most *unnatural* for a true dwarf to hoard gold and such in his workshop for himself. And besides, it wouldn't mean much in the end, would it?"

"No, I suppose not. In our world, it seems like some folk collect wealth just for the sake of collecting it," said Colleen. "The more they get, the happier and more miserable they seem, all at the same time."

"Yes, and just think about this too," he replied. "If I go and hoard all this leprechaun gold and all these gems and rainbows and such for myself, I'd be no better than the Pirate or the Witch, now would I? She'd like that, you can be sure, if I kept it all to myself."

"She would *like it?*" said Frederick skeptically. "I thought she wanted it all for herself?"

"Of course she would like to have it," Doc replied. "But, more than that, she wants *power* - power over people. If I give my heart over to living like her, then she's truly defeated me. She might one day break in here and steal my life's work away. But if she doesn't steal my heart, then she hasn't won anything more than a pile of rocks in the end."

"But look here," he said, brightening a bit. "I have a job for these little people. How about hopping down and coming over here to my little stream."

Colleen and Frederick put them down and they all went over to the slowly flowing brook.

"I've been meaning to do some panning for gold in this here stream, and, what with all my other labors, I've not had a chance to do it yet. Now how about you all take these," he handed them three tiny pots, "and do some panning for me. And I'll tell you what, you just keep the first load that you find. And, Oracle, here's one for you as well."

Oracle took the pot, turned it over a few times, and then handed it back to Doc, shaking his head.

"Suit yourself," said Doc with a frown.

Mrs. Wigglepox looked at the pot she was holding and turned it over and over in her hands.

"This is a leprechaun pot!" she said.

"Straight from the Pirate's treasure!" he replied. "And there's a load more where that came from."

He strode over to one wall, opened a cabinet door, and waved his hand. Inside the shelves were lined with scores and scores of tiny pots.

Tears filled Mrs. Wigglepox's eyes, but she wiped them and turned to Lily and Rose. "Come, children, let's see what gold we can find."

Oracle followed the Wigglepox family as they walked to the edge of the stream. He seemed most curious to watch what they did.

"And you youngsters, come with me," said Doc, and led them to the other side of the room.

"You're not s'pose to watch or see when or where leprechauns get their gold from," he said. "So how about you make yourselves comfortable for a bit. Here, Colleen, you take this old bed next to Dvalenn. Kick off your shoes and rest. And Frederick, here I have a hammock set up that you can rest in."

"Thank you, Doc," said Colleen. "I am rather tired."

She lay down, and Frederick climbed into the hammock. Within moments, she noticed that Frederick had closed his eyes and seemed to be asleep.

Poor thing, she thought. *Trudging all this way with me. He must be exhausted. He's not such a bad chap, after all.*

Soon she too drifted off to sleep.

* * *

But Frederick's mind would not let him rest. He lay there thinking of all that he had seen and heard that day – of pirate gold and treasure and magic. How much had the Pirate stolen and then returned? And why did he return it? His father had been right – there was a huge treasure to be had, only now it was in the hands of a Witch that everyone seemed to think was terribly evil and powerful.

But this dwarf had a load of treasure too, and probably more in his vast halls. Why, just one of those glowing crystals in that chamber out there would sell for a king's ransom back home. If he could only take one of them back, his father would be so proud of him. *No*, he thought, *they are not mine to take. Maybe if I found one lying about, that would be different.*

His thoughts trailed off and sleep finally took him, and as he slept, he dreamed of finding a great treasure chamber, and stuffing his pockets with gold, returning home to rescue all of Ireland from the famine, and making his family rich beyond their wildest dreams. But through his dreams, the aged voice of Doc kept interrupting and saying something about guarding his heart. Sometime in the night, he woke with a start, looked about him, and saw the old dwarf sitting on a low stool with his chin in his hand and mumbling something he could not hear. So he shut his eyes and dreamed no more until morning.

Chapter 26 - The School

As they neared the train station, Aonghus could see the smoke of a steam engine billowing up over the houses and the distinct clang of a bell ringing.

"Best hurry, Miss Mabel," said the voice of the coach driver. "That would be the boarding call."

He cracked the whip and the horses surged forward. A moment later, the coach rounded a corner and pulled up in front of a large black steam engine with the words "Southern Railway" painted in yellow letters across the side. The driver leaped from the coach and ran to the ticket collector, who was just boarding a passenger car, and spoke to him. The man stepped quickly over to the coach and said, "You just made it, folks. Come quickly now, get your things and get aboard. Follow me, please."

Aonghus and Bran unloaded Mabel's things, including her heavy trunk, and carried them aboard the train car along with their own things. The girls carried their own luggage, as well as Colleen's small bag that she had left on the ship and which they had been toting along with them.

After being shown to Mabel's cabin, where they placed her belongings, they were shown to a second cabin, significantly more cramped, where they would be spending the journey. It would not be a long trip – just a few hours – so no sleeping quarters were provided, except for Mabel.

"I do believe it is time for a bite to eat," she said to the ticket collector as soon as she was settled. "Would you be so kind as to show me to the dining car?"

A moment after she had gone, there was a lurch of movement and a loud whistle, and the train began to roll.

"Now's our chance," said Bib.

"Right," said Aonghus.

He led them to Mabel's cabin, but when they arrived, the door was locked.

"Not a problem," said Bib, and she pulled a hairpin from her mop

214

of red hair and quickly opened the door.

Aonghus led the way in and shut the door behind them, then opened the trunk. He found four large bags of rocks within, pulled them out, and handed them to the others. Then they quietly left the cabin, locking the door behind them.

As they entered their own cabin, Henny said, "Oughtn't we to have asked Cousin Mabel if we could take those rocks?"

"It's not as though we're stealing them," said Bran. "They took them from *our farm*. They stole them from us. You can't steal what's your own."

"Henny, you would be right in any other situation," said Aonghus. "Any time you take something that isn't yours without the owner's permission, it's stealing, no matter how small it is. But in this case, our cousins actually took something from us without *our* permission. Dad told Rufus that he could take a few of these stones, not whole bagful's of them. It's really ours, see, so it's not stealing to take it back."

She nodded, but her face still looked troubled.

"Tell you what, Henny. When we see Dad again, you can ask him. If he thinks we should give these rocks back to the Buttersmouths, we'll do it."

She smiled then, and they proceeded to pick rocks from the bags and look at them. Each one had some emblem or writing engraved on it.

"See there," said Abbe, "these things must be worth money, or Rufus wouldn't have taken them. These sorts of symbols are carved all around the farm. I wonder what they mean?"

"First chance I get, I'm going to do some research. Maybe the school will have a library that will help," said Bib. "Or a teacher who can read this language."

She ran her finger across one of the symbols and looked thoughtful.

"This language must predate even the Celtic Tree Alphabet, and that dates back to around the fifth century A.D.," she said.

215

"How do you know that?" said Bran.

"Haven't you ever read about the Ogham inscriptions, Bran?" she asked.

"Well..." he replied.

"Come now," she said. "There are hundreds of Ogham stones all around the Irish Sea. They're inscribed with Ogham, or the Celtic Tree Alphabet. But these carvings don't look anything like that. It's a much more complex language, it seems to me."

"We best hide these bags among our own, and once we get to the school, we can investigate them further," said Aonghus.

After hiding the bags, they talked on about the stones, wondering what ancient civilization might have existed thousands of years before their time – who they were, and what they might have been like. But before they knew it, the hours had rolled by. The whistle sounded, a bell clanged, and the train pulled into a station.

"Let's help Mabel with her things," said Aonghus to Bran. "Ladies, can you handle our things? They're a bit heavy."

"No problem," said Abbe, and she went to pick up two bags of rocks. But she quickly put them down again.

"Maybe they are a bit heavy," she said sheepishly.

"All right, then. You all stay here while Bran and I unload Mabel's things, and we'll be right back.

Aonghus and Bran went to Mabel's cabin, took the chest from the train, and then returned for their sisters. When they were all outside, Mabel looked them over and shook her head.

"Well, then, children, here we are," she said in her most drawling voice. "The school is outside of town, down by the seashore. You can see it from here."

They turned and looked where she pointed, and they could see about a half mile from the train station, down a long hill, a series of brick and stone buildings surrounded by green gardens.

"Professor McPherson is the headmaster of the school. He is expecting you. I wired ahead and told him that you five would be arriving shortly."

"Aren't you coming with us, Cousin Mabel?" asked Bib.

She chortled a rather false laugh and then said, "Heavens, no, child. You have to *walk* down there. I shall be going to London on the next train, which, I believe, leaves in twenty minutes. I have some... some business there. You children will walk down to the large stone building in the center of the campus and go in the front door. Tell the receptionist that you are the McGunnegal children, sent by Rufus Buttersmouth, and that Professor McPherson is expecting you."

She looked at them all gravely and then said, "Well, hurry along now. Just follow that path down." She indicated a dirt path that led down the hill toward the school.

"All right, then," said Aonghus. "You take care of yourself, Mabel. Will you be contacting us?"

"Contacting you? Oh, I suppose, now and then. We'll have to see. But off you go then," she said, and waved her hand for them to be on their way. Then she turned and made her way into the train station without a backward glance.

"Would you get a load of that!" said Bib. "Dumps us off in the middle of Wales, with hardly a good day, just like that!"

"Come on," said Bran. "Let's just get down to the school."

Aonghus glanced one more time at Mabel, shrugged, and picked up three bags of the rocks as well as his own bag, and started down the dirt path toward the collection of buildings that Mabel said was the Ismere Boarding School. Bran took the last sack, and they all followed behind.

The path, although dusty, was not at all bad, and soon they were walking past brick buildings that appeared to be apartments of sorts and a large stone building with the word "Ismere" carved into a stone arch above two large, bright red wooden doors.

Aonghus led them up a flight of steps to a wide porch, opened the door, and held it as his brother and sisters filed in. As he followed behind and closed the door, he found himself in a great hall with green marble floors and ornately carved pillars. Red draperies framed the windows, and there was a bronze statue of a man in a robe with a plaque on its marble base that read "Professor Evan Ismere, founder and philanthropist."

Several boys who were standing in the hall stopped in mid-conversation and stared at them. They were dressed in black knickers and white shirts and wore smart-looking red jackets.

"Can I help you?" said one of them after a moment. "We don't accept solicitations here."

They looked the McGunnegals up and down and turned up their noses.

Aonghus started to say something, but Bib elbowed him in the ribs and walked over to the boys.

"We're not here to buy or sell anything," she said, putting on a beautiful smile, showing her perfect white teeth. "We're here to enroll in school. Could you boys help out a lady and show us where to go?"

They blinked, and one of the boys shut his mouth, which had been hanging open. Somehow, Bib had gone from being the brains of the family to an amazingly attractive young lady.

"Yes, of course!" said the older of the two, who appeared to be about sixteen, and who was now speaking a bit too loudly. "My name is John. Follow me, I'll show you to the secretary!"

He turned to lead her to the other end of the hall, but managed to bump into the other boy, who was standing and staring at Bib.

John punched the other boy in the arm. "And that's David," he said, and pushed past him.

Bran turned to Aonghus and whispered, "Did you see that? She's got those boys practically falling over each other. Where'd she learn that?"

"Don't try to understand girls, Bran," said Aonghus as he picked up his bags.

They followed the boys, who were now giving Bib a guided tour of the expansive hall, explaining its ornate architecture and massive pillars. Bib appeared to be listening intently, with wide eyes and many a "you don't say" as they led on. But she turned and winked at her brothers and sisters as they followed.

The boys just shook their heads as they passed through a set of wide doors that had carvings of grape vines around them and entered a somewhat smaller hall. There, a gray-haired woman wearing small spectacles low on her nose sat at a large desk.

She looked over her reading glasses as they entered and said in a very proper English voice, "Ah, you are the McGunnegal children. I am Miss Fenny, the school secretary."

Miss Fenny wore a beehive hairdo and a heavily starched white blouse with a red tie and jacket and checkered skirt. The McGunnegal children had never seen a woman dressed like this before.

She paused, looking at them for a long moment, and then said, "And where is your sister?"

"She'll be coming along on the next ship, ma'am," said Abbe, when no one else spoke.

"And when will that be?" the woman inquired.

"In about two weeks," said Aonghus, stepping forward to the desk.

He towered over the small woman even though she stood from her seat and straightened herself to her full height.

"Well, young man," she said, looking up at him and placing her hands on her hips. "I certainly hope so. The semester begins in just under three weeks. Now let me see..."

She paused, picking up a piece of paper and examining it.

"You must be Aonghus? And Bran, Abbe, Bib, and Henny," she said, pointing to each of them in turn. "That means that Colleen is the one coming later? Fine, then. John! David! You may stop goggling and be excused now. I will ring the bell when I need you."

The two boys seemed to awaken from a trance and shook themselves, then quickly left the room through the doors they had entered.

"You best watch that talent of yours," whispered Bran to Bib. "You'll have all the boys in the school drooling all over their desks if those two fellows are any example of what the lads are like around here."

Bib gave him a quizzical look as if she was not sure what he was saying.

But Miss Fenny was speaking again and he could not respond. "... Segregation of genders, and that means that there are two strictly separate halves of the campus, with this building being the sole place that boys and girls may interact. If we find any young ladies on the boys' side of the campus or any young men on the girls' side, there will be *serious* consequences."

"Do you mean we can't visit our big brothers?" asked Henny.

Miss Fenny seemed thrown off guard for a moment and, looking at Henny's big, innocent eyes, she seemed to soften. "That is correct, child," she said. "However, for someone your age, and seeing that you certainly *should* see your brothers, we can arrange times for you to meet here."

She gave a faint smile, and then returned to her business self.

"Well then, I shall show you around the building," she said, stepping around her desk. "Follow me, please."

Aonghus listened with detached interest, and noticed that the others did not seem to be paying attention much either, except for Bib, who seemed genuinely fascinated as Miss Fenny described the thirty-eight classrooms on two levels, the history of the school, and various "departments," which included History and Archeology, Religion, Classical Literature, Science, Athletics, Mathematics, Agriculture, and "Foundations," which Miss Fenny described as the most important elements of education, and included reading, writing, and arithmetic.

"You shall have some exposure to all of these departments for the first two months of your time here and, after that, you shall choose a main discipline in one department. Choose your discipline well, since it will occupy most of your time here at the school. After you choose a discipline, you will join that department's "house," and you will move to that house's dorms and live with other house members who have also chosen that same main discipline."

On and on she went, describing the various houses and walking about the building, showing them each of the thirty-eight classrooms, fire escapes, bathrooms, and other places, until she came at last to the center of the building where a large oak door stood shut before them.

"This door leads to the Dean's personal studies and offices in the Tower. You are never to walk beyond this door without permission of the Dean, Professor McPherson. He is a private man and does not take kindly to children snooping around his private quarters. You will note that the door is locked," she said, giving it a slight shove.

"Professor McPherson!" whispered Aonghus to Bran. "We've got to see him!"

"Excuse me, ma'am," said Aonghus. "Will we be meeting the Professor today?"

"Oh, no, he is a very busy man and cannot individually meet every new student. You will meet him on the first day of the semester at the General Assembly in the Great Hall. In fact, I was just about to take you there. It is in the basement. Please follow me," she said, and walked briskly down the hall and led them down a long flight of stairs and showed them a large auditorium that looked to seat at least four hundred people.

Finally, their tour ended and Miss Fenny, finding her assistant – an older student named Jane – asked her to show the girls to their rooms. She then picked up a small bell from her desk and rang it.

John and David nearly fell in through the door and came hurrying up to Miss Fenny's desk.

"But where will our sisters be staying?" asked Aonghus.

"Never you mind, young man. It's not for the boys to know where the girls stay," she replied firmly.

Aonghus frowned and said in a kind but firm voice, "Miss Fenny. I promised my father that I would look after my sisters while we were here. I wouldn't take kindly to anything bad happening to them. Please, at least let us know what building they are in so that we can send them a message if we hear from home or there's an emergency."

Miss Fenny looked him up and down, as if considering his massive form, and frowned, a hard look crossing her face.

She began to speak when Henny said in a quiet voice, "Please, Miss Fenny?"

For a moment, she seemed flustered, and her hard look softened. She stood as if dumbfounded, and then said, "Building Three-G."

"And where will Aonghus and Bran be, ma'am?" asked Henny.

She paused again and said, "Four-B. Now, off you go. John, show these boys to their rooms. Jane, you take the girls."

Having said this, she sat down in her chair, picked up a pile of papers, and began to shuffle through them.

"Come on, follow me," said John.

Aonghus paused for a moment, picked up Henny, and gave her a hug.

"Now don't you worry, little one. Bran and I aren't far away, and Bib and Abbe will watch out for you," he said.

Henny waved goodbye and headed off behind Abbe and Bib, looking back with a sad face, and Aonghus and Bran followed after John.

"That little sister of yours could melt a witch's heart, I think," said John after they had left the room and gone some distance, well out of Miss Fenny's hearing. "I've been here for five years and I've *never* seen Old Fenny soften up like she did for her. She actually *told* you what building the girls would be in. That's just unheard of!"

The boys said nothing, but walked on behind John as he led them outside and across the campus grounds. Aonghus, however, determined that he would most definitely be finding out just where Building Three-G was.

Chapter 27 – Four-B

Aonghus followed behind Bran as John led them to an aging stone building with broad battlements around its top. It loomed tall and silent before them, with two large windows on either side of a wide, green door. Aonghus felt as though he were approaching some great crowned head with closed eyes stuck in the ground. The letters "4B" were engraved on an archway over the door.

"Here we are," said John. "You two will be on the fourth floor, and you've got a good room that overlooks the old lake out back."

He pushed open the door and walked in. An image of the great head swallowing John flashed through Aonghus' mind and he smiled to himself. A stone entry hall with dark wooden flooring greeted them as they walked in. The floorboards creaked under their weight as they passed aging oil paintings of stern-looking men and women dressed in rich clothing.

"It feels... *old* in here," said Aonghus. "The very floors have voices. How many years, I wonder, have these old boards spoken to those who walk on them, and what stories might they tell?"

John glanced at him, but said nothing until they reached the bottom of a polished oak staircase.

"You be careful about saying thing like that, Aonghus," said John in a serious whisper.

"Why, what do you mean?" said Aonghus.

"That talk of the floors having voices," he said, lowering his voice even more. "Some of the boys here say that they do – that some nights they creak all on their own, and when you go to look, no one's there."

Aonghus and Bran looked at each other, but John was going on.

"And that lake out back – you watch yourself out there too. They say that years ago, some kid went swimming in there. He came back all crazy in the head, saying he had seen strange things down in some underwater caves, like a dead man lying on a rock and all sorts of weird creatures that guarded the body and wouldn't let him near it."

"Do you think it was true?" asked Bran as they began to climb.

"Maybe just a story to scare us away from swimming there," he replied. "But who knows? It's a weird lake, anyway."

"How so?" asked Aonghus.

"You just look out your window at night when the moon is full and shining down on it and you'll see what I mean," he said. "The shadows in that water are sort of eerie. I mean, they, well, *dance*. That's the best way I can put it."

Four flights of stairs later, with John huffing and puffing, but Aonghus and Bran not even breaking a sweat, they pushed through an oaken door that sported a large brass knocker that looked like the bust of a man with a long beard.

They entered a cozy hall with stone walls covered with tapestries. Aonghus reached up and ran his fingers along one that held a golden lion on one side and a red dragon on the other.

"Beautiful," he said.

"It's the coat of arms of one of the school benefactors. Must not be a recent one, though, to end up here. Anyway, this is the lounge for the fourth floor. It's where you can just hang out with the other Undesignateds, like these blokes here," he said, waving a hand at a few teenage boys who sat about the room.

Aonghus walked over to one of them and held out his hand. The boy rose, spilling several books and a stack of papers to the floor. He was thin and wiry, and only came up to Aonghus' chin.

"I'm Aonghus McGunnegal," he said, "and this is my brother Bran."

"Pleased to meet you, Aonghus, Bran," said the boy, taking his hand. "David's the name. David Rhigy. And this is Afan Ceredig, Aaron Malo, and Govan Bell. Pull up a seat and chat for a spell. We've been debating what discipline we want to take."

"Let me show them their room first," said John. "Then I'll leave them to you. Come on, then, here you go."

"What are 'Undesignateds'?" asked Aonghus as John led them through a door with a number seven on it.

"You're an Undesignated until you decide what your main discipline is going to be."

"Are there many Undesignateds?" asked Bran.

"Sure, plenty," said John. "Probably about thirty right now. They're probably out by the lake or something. You've got a while before you have to decide what main discipline you want."

"What's yours?" asked Bran.

"Athletics," said John. "Say, Aonghus, with your muscles, I'll bet you'd be great at rugby and the pole toss. And Bran, I bet you can run pretty well with those long legs. How about you guys come down to the athletic field tomorrow afternoon after lunch? We're having some tryouts for the school teams and you might enjoy it. Plus, the girls are allowed down there too – that's the other place we can meet with them. I'll bet old Fenny didn't tell you that, did she? She doesn't approve, but McPherson says that it's okay."

Aonghus looked at his brother and they smiled at each other. Neither of them had ever been outdone by any human being of their age, except each other, in any athletic contest in which they had ever competed.

"Take a look out over the lake," said John, leading them across the room to a large window.

Aonghus looked down and, a few hundred yards away, there was a beautiful lake shining in the sun, which covered several acres. Its shores were lined with trees and gardens, and he could see a number of students lounging in the shade.

"Doesn't look eerie at all to me, especially when you've been in the old bog back where we live. This looks like a garden paradise," said Aonghus.

"You just wait until night and a good full moon, then let me know what you think. Anyway, here's where you'll be living for a while," John said, gesturing at the big room.

Two spacious bunks, a bookshelf, oil portraits of British nobility, several cushioned chairs, a washroom, and a bowl of apples sitting on a good-sized table that had four chairs around it met their gaze. There were also various decorations and tapestries along its long walls, including several suits of armor and oil paintings of ships and lighthouses and coasts along the sea.

"This room is for just the two of us?" asked Bran.

"I know it's not much," said John ruefully. "But you'll have to make do until you choose a discipline."

"Not much?" said Bran incredulously.

"Shabby, I know," said John. "But the Undesignateds get the old stuff that the other houses don't want."

Aonghus wondered what the other house living quarters must look like if all of this was just leftover and rejected furniture and decorations.

"This is... fine," said Aonghus, dropping his bags on the floor and sitting in one of the big chairs.

He sank deeply into its ornate cushions and whistled. He had never sat in a chair quite so soft and comfortable.

"I could get used to this," he said.

"And grow fat doing it," said Bran, laughing.

"Well, I'll leave you to your room. Dinner will be served at six in the dining room of the Great Common Hall, just beside the room where you met Old Fenny," he said, pointing to a large grandfather clock that adorned one corner. "Nothing special, mind you, since school hasn't started yet. You've got about an hour to wash up. I'll see you then."

Aonghus and Bran just looked around the room and then at each other.

"Did you ever imagine in your wildest dreams of being in a place like this?" said Bran. "And check out the beds..."

He flopped himself on one of the lower bunks, which was twice as wide as his bed at home. The mattress was stuffed with goose down, and he sunk down deep into it.

"Oh, man, I don't think I could sleep on this," he said after a moment. "I might never wake up. It's too comfortable."

Aonghus lay on his own bed and said, "I'm with you there. I think I might try it tonight, but I might end up on the floor instead."

"Well, might as well get washed up," said Bran.

"Right," said Aonghus, going to the washbasin and splashing himself with water.

As they made their way back into the lounge, Aonghus called to the boy they had spoken with earlier.

"Tell me, David, what are you thinking of for your discipline?"

"Dunno. Maybe Religion. Or Sciences. We all think that Aaron, over there, is going to be a hermit," he said, indicating a boy whose face was hidden behind a large book. "This is just about as social as he gets. We're lucky he's emerged from his room today."

Aaron peered at them over the top of his book and then sank behind it once again. Aonghus could see that it was entitled *Inferno*.

"What's that you're reading, Aaron?" said Bran.

Aaron's eyes appeared again and he mumbled something about Hell, then sunk back behind his book.

"He's always reading stuff like that," said David. "Last week, it was something from Plato – something about a myth. Anyway, we don't know what we want to do, really. Miss Fenny keeps scolding us for having *lack of vision*. But we have a whole year to figure it out."

Aonghus and Bran took seats and talked for some time about the school and the students and teachers, until Aaron silently stood and left the room. A bell rang somewhere in the distance.

"That's the five-minute dinner warning," said David. "Aaron always knows when it's going to ring even without looking at a clock. Best get down to the Great Common Hall."

"Right," said Aonghus as they rose and followed Aaron out the door.

In the Great Common Hall, Aonghus and Bran found their sisters and joined them. Dinner was, by their standards, quite sumptuous, though it was really a simple meal of meat, vegetables, cheese, and bread, with water to drink.

"Aonghus!" said Henny as they ate. "Is your room as big as ours? We have giant soft mattresses and great red curtains and paintings and all sorts of mirrors and decorations. It's like a museum!"

They all smiled, and Aonghus said, "Yes, Henny. I think we'll be seeing a whole different world here at this school, with lots of stuff that we don't have back home. But don't lose yourself in it– it's just *things,* after all."

After dinner, a dark-haired girl with equally dark eyes came up to them and said, "You must be the new lot. My name's Jenny. I'm off to the library. Want to come?"

"We do indeed," said Bib.

"Nice how she speaks for the rest of us," said Aonghus with a wry grin.

"Come on, Aonghus," said Abbe. "You might as well find out where it is. You can't spend all of your time running around on the athletic field, you know."

Jenny looked at Aonghus, went over to him, and touched him lightly on the arm. "Aonghus, is it? And might a lady walk with a gentleman such as yourself?"

"Oh, of course," said Aonghus.

Jenny took his arm, smiled at him, led him out of the dining room, and said, "The library is just down the hall."

"Get a load of that," said Bran to Bib. "First you, now Aonghus."

Bib punched him in the arm, then followed after the pair, and the rest of them came behind.

"The library is quite grand," said Jenny as they passed through a pair of ornately carved wooden doors. "See?"

Aonghus stopped and gawked. They had walked out onto a high balcony that looked down upon a massive room filled with thousands upon thousands of books. Shelves lined the walls and floor and, all around the balcony, which spanned the entire room, a second story of the collection met their eyes.

Bib let out a squeal of delight and grinned. "I'll see you all later," she said, and headed for the stairs that led down to the first level.

"Closing time is nine o'clock," said Jenny after her.

Bib waved and was gone.

"Come on, Henny," said Abbe. "Let's see what books we can find for you."

"And how about you, Aonghus?" said Jenny, still holding his arm. "What will you be studying here at school?"

"Agriculture," he said.

"Truly? So am I," she said. "Let me show you that section."

Aonghus turned and raised an eyebrow at Bran as Jenny led him away.

"How do you like that?" said Bran aloud to himself. "They've all left me. Well, might as well do a bit of exploring. It's the lake and the woods for me."

With that, he turned and left and headed outside.

* * *

The next few days were uneventful, and Aonghus found himself spending more and more time on the athletic field with Bran. The other boys were amazed at his incredible strength and Bran's speed, and the sidelines began to be frequented by more and more girls who came to see the new boys that had come to school and whose reputation was spreading.

One day, as they were on the field practicing rugby, Aonghus noticed a new, rather big fellow, walking onto the field.

Will Green, a friendly blond-haired boy with long lanky legs and arms, nudged Bran and said, "Look out, chaps, here comes trouble."

"Who's he?" asked Bran.

"That would be Ed Choke. He sort of rules the roost here, him and his cronies. And look – there's Fred Hinder right behind him. Watch out for that lot," said Will.

Choke was a tall boy, as tall as Bran, and well-muscled. He strode toward them with an arrogant look on his face. Hinder, on the other hand, was short and stocky, tough looking, and rolled onto the field like a boulder ready to smash anything in his path.

"Great, and here comes Slick and Bigs too," said Will, indicating a greasy-haired boy with shifty eyes and a very short, thin boy with a sour expression, pushing through the crowd. "Their real names are Hank Slips and Billy Sour."

Slick and Bigs jogged up behind Ed and Fred as they approached, and Aonghus saw right off that they wanted trouble.

The rugby game came to a stop. The other players backed up a few steps, leaving Aonghus, Bran, and Will standing alone.

"Hello, Ed," said Will, wiping sweat from his face. "Back for the season, I see."

Ed looked at him condescendingly, and then eyed Aonghus and Bran, sizing them up.

"Bran McGunnegal," said Bran, introducing himself. "And this is my brother, Aonghus."

Bran held out his hand, which Ed looked at, but didn't take.

Bigs stepped forward and said, "I hear that these fellows think they're something special, Ed. I've been keeping an eye on them, see, and on your girl Mary. She's been visiting the field here ever since they showed up. I think she's got eyes for this one."

Ed pushed Bigs aside and came nose to nose with Bran, a sneer on his face. He was just as tall, but broader than Bran, and now the crowd was gathering in a circle, anticipating a fight.

"So, been moving in on my girl, eh?" snarled Ed.

"Now see here, Ed," said Bran. "I have no intentions of moving in on your girl. I don't even know who she is. What's this all about?"

Just then, a pretty raven-haired girl pushed through the crowd and wedged herself between them. She was tall and shapely and had rose-red lips. Her eyes were dark and, in that moment, Bran thought she was the most beautiful girl he had ever seen. He could not help but stare.

"Leave him alone, Ed," she said. "He's not done anything."

"So, Mary, you're taking up for this Irishman?" said Ed with a sneer.

Ed noticed Bran's gaze at her, narrowed his eyes, and pushed Mary away. She stumbled and fell, her face heading straight for the ground.

Bran moved so quickly that for a moment he seemed to have vanished. But before Mary hit the ground, Bran had caught her around the waist and gently set her back on her feet. They came face to face with Bran's arm around her.

"Are you all right?" he asked gently.

"I'm fine," she said, glaring up at Ed. "Thanks."

Then Bran felt a hand grip his shoulder and spin him around and, an instant later, saw Choke's fist coming for his nose.

He ducked, stepping in under Ed's left arm that gripped his shirt and ended up behind him. He pushed him from behind just as Ed's punch swooshed in the empty air. Ed stumbled and fell face first into the mud.

The crowd laughed and then began to chant, "Fight! Fight!" and the circle tightened around them.

Ed jumped to his feet and dove for Bran. But he simply stepped to the side, and Ed slid in the mud, dirtier than ever.

Suddenly, Bran felt both of his arms gripped from behind, as Slick and Hinder grabbed him and tried to hold him for Choke to pound.

But just as quickly, he was released, as Aonghus hefted one in each hand in the air and said, "None of that, now, chaps. Let the man fight his own battles."

Slick and Hinder thrashed about for a moment in the air, their feet dangling, and then went limp, realizing that this big Irishman was too much for both of them.

"Thanks, Aonghus," said Bran as Ed slid in the mud next to him in another futile attempt at a tackle.

"Goodness, Bran," laughed Aonghus, "this is the second fight you've been in this week. Whatever has gotten into you?"

Ed was getting up again and, this time, his fists were up like a boxer's, and he approached more carefully.

"Now see here, Ed," said Bran. "I've got nothing against you... yet, and I'm not trying to steal away your girl. Why, just now is the first time I've met her, thanks to you. Although I must say, you're a lucky man if she'll have you. Why don't we end this silliness here and now? How about we shake and call it a draw?"

Bran held out his hand to Ed.

"I intend to end it here and now," said Ed, and dropped his fists. Then he grasped Bran's hand. But instead of shaking, he squeezed as hard has he could, making Bran wince with pain, then pulled him close and brought his other fist in hard, driving it toward Bran's ribs.

But Bran saw it coming and once again danced aside, then pushed forward under Ed's right hand that he was clasping, and spun around, bringing Ed's arm up and behind his back.

"Right, then," said Bran. "You're obviously the sneaky sort and don't like to fight fair. I'll bet you've bullied everyone here at one time or another. I think that's about to change, though. I think it's time you became a bit more polite to people."

Ed struggled mightily, but Bran held his arm firmly behind his back. The crowd around them looked on in silence now, seeing Ed, who had indeed been the school bully, so humbled, and his two sidekicks still dangling in the air in the powerful arms of Aonghus.

But suddenly, the crowd parted, and onto the field strode Miss Fenny, followed behind by Bigs.

"You see, Miss Fenny," Bigs was saying, "just like I told you. Those two new kids are starting fights."

Fenny looked at the scene, opened her mouth once, then pursed her lips and narrowed her eyes.

"Mr. McGunnegal!" she said to Aonghus. "Put those boys down this instant!"

Aonghus let them go and Slick and Hinder dropped in a heap at his feet.

"And you, Mr. McGunnegal!" she shot at Bran. "You let Edward go. All five of you, to my office, now!"

She turned and walked away, expecting immediate obedience.

Aonghus and Bran looked at each other and shrugged and followed along.

"This isn't over, McGunnegal," hissed Choke. "Not by a long shot."

Bran ignored him and walked on.

"Guess we're in for it now," whispered Aonghus, and turned to see Choke, Slick, Hinder, and Bigs all following them in a huddle, whispering to each other. Behind them came Mary, a worried and angry look on her face.

When they reached the door of the hall, they were greeted by a tall, thin man with short blond hair who appeared to be middle aged. There was a distinct scar on his left cheek that gave him an embattled look, but his eyes were deep and wise.

"Ah! Professor McPherson!" said Miss Fenny. "These boys were fighting. Fighting! Out on the field! Mr. Sour here says that these McGunnegal boys started the whole thing."

"That's not true," said a voice from behind, and Mary shyly pushed her way forward. "That's not true, sir," she said.

She looked sidelong at Choke, straightened, and then said, "Ed started it, sir. Bran and Aonghus were just playing rugby and Ed stepped onto the field and started trouble... like always."

"That's a lie!" spat Choke. "You're only saying that because you've got eyes for this Irish..."

But Professor McPherson cut him off and said, "It so happens that I was watching from my window, Edward. Would you care to elaborate on exactly what happened?"

Choke looked down and said, "No... sir."

"Then I suggest that it might be useful for you to do a fifteen-page report on the merits of civilized behavior. It will be due in three days. You are dismissed," said the professor.

Choke gave Bran one last menacing look and then stomped away.

"Ms. Fenny, I'm sure these two gentlemen would be more than happy to do some extra cleaning in the hall for a day or two," he said, indicating Slick and Hinder. "And if you would, please send for the McGunnegal sisters. I might as well meet them all."

"Now, Aonghus and Bran are your names, right? Good. Please, do come with me to my office," he said.

As they turned to go, Mary piped up and said, "Professor, they really didn't do anything to start that. And Bran could have really bashed Ed, I think, but he never hit him at all."

"Thank you, Miss Nottingham. You may go now," said the professor.

Then he turned and strode through a door to one side that led up a flight of steps.

Aonghus and Bran followed after him and, just before they turned a corner, Bran looked back and noticed Mary still at the bottom of the steps, looking up after them, concern written on her face.

"Come, gentlemen," said the professor as he entered through a large wooden door on the right. "Have a seat."

Professor McPherson sat down behind a large, ornately carved wooden desk. Behind him on the wall were many strange pictures, carvings, masks, and odd ornaments. Shelves lined the other walls of the office, and these were filled with books of all sizes and shapes. To one side was another door that was marked "Private – Do No Enter."

The professor looked at Aonghus and Bran with his deep, penetrating eyes and said, "Well, while we wait for your sisters to come, how about you tell me about yourselves?"

"Professor," said Bran, "I'm really sorry about the fight."

234

"Never mind that, Bran," he said. "You handled yourself like a true gentleman. However, I suggest that you watch yourself around Edward. Please, tell me about yourselves."

A thought struck Aonghus and he said, "Professor, may I please run back to my room for a few minutes. I have something that we need to show you."

"Certainly," he said. "Bran and I will chat until you return."

Aonghus thanked him, dashed out the door, and ran all the way back to his room. There he grabbed a bag of the rocks from home and ran back to the professor's room, just in time to meet the girls as they were coming up the steps.

"Now's our chance," he said to them. "We're going to tell Professor McPherson the whole tale."

Chapter 28 – Traveling Plans

Frederick awoke with a start. Someone was shaking his shoulder. For a moment, he was disoriented, and then he realized that the old cracked face of the dwarf was leaning close to his.

"Ho!" Frederick said. "You startled me!"

"Sorry, young'un," creaked Doc. "Them there leprechauns is done with their gold-gatherin'. It's time to be makin' plans, it is."

"How long have I been sleeping?" he groaned, rubbing his eyes.

"All night," said Colleen, who was already awake and sitting at a table, her long hair spilling over the shoulders of her green cape.

"No one should look so nice after waking up," he grumbled, and brushed down his own mat of dark hair, knowing it to be a mess.

He made his way to the table and sat down. Doc offered him a cup of something steaming.

"Drink!" said the dwarf. "It'll give you strength."

Frederick sniffed the cup. It smelled of an odd cross between mushrooms and lemons. He took a sip, and the hot liquid tingled in his mouth and throat. Heat seemed to spread across his face and down his arms.

"Wow!" he said. "What is that?"

"Ha! My own secret recipe," said Doc. "An old family tradition. Nothing bad, mind you. A mug of that will keep you going all day long. In fact, I've got a small keg of it for the journey."

The journey?" asked Colleen. "Do you mean that you'll be going with us?"

"Well, I've been thinking about that," he said. "I'm truly torn. At first, I was inclined to stay put and guard the Gate and all. But now that Dvalenn has showed up, and won't wake up, I feel that I've got to get him to the Lady. If anyone can wake him from this dreadful sleep, it's her. But the Gate... someone has to guard it, you know. If the Witch ever got hold of it, well, it would be mighty bad."

"It would be wonderful if you could come with us, though," said

Colleen.

Doc was silent for a long time, staring at his brother. Then, he quietly said, "Would you take him to the Lady for me?"

"But how will we get him there? We can't have Badger drag a litter all that way – we would wear him out," said Colleen.

Well," said Doc. "I've got a cart, of sorts, that I use to haul rock and such through these tunnels. It's just about big enough for Dvalenn to sleep in. We could harness it to your horse."

"I suppose we could try," said Colleen. "But I do wish you would go with us. It's terribly scary, you know, traveling by ourselves."

The old dwarf looked at the two children and nodded his head.

"You're right, it is a frightful thing to go about these woods alone. But, you do have these Wigglepoxes with you, and that Oracle fellow, for what he's worth. Although I wouldn't discount him too much – he's an odd bird, he is, but there's something about him that makes me glad he's with you."

Frederick looked skeptical. He really didn't think the little people would be much help if goblins or the Witch showed up.

"Right then," he said. "So, what's the plan?"

"First, we've got to make sure we have enough food," said Colleen.

"No problem there," said Doc. "I've got dried fish and mushrooms aplenty, and my special recipe." He tapped the side of his mug. "And I've also got a sack of tubers and a bit of nuts and dried fruits. That ought to last you for weeks."

Colleen smiled.

"Thank you, Doc," she said. "At least we won't starve to death or be eating berries the whole way."

Suddenly, there was a noise from the bed where Dvalenn was sleeping. They all turned their heads to look, and the dwarf was yawning widely. He rubbed his eyes once, blinked, then shut them again and began to snore.

Doc ran over to him and shook him.

"Dvalenn!" he shouted, "Dvalenn! Wake up! You've got to come out of this sleep! Dvalenn!"

But the dwarf only smacked his lips, turned over, and snored on, a frown on his face.

Doc turned to the others. "You see, the Spell is not so strong down here. But the trouble is that once you give in to it, it sort of sinks into your bones. I think you carry it with you wherever you go after that. Almost becomes a part of you, it does, and on your own you can't seem to shake it, although you have to be willing to try."

He paused for a moment, staring at his brother.

"Dvalenn!" he whispered, a tear falling from his eye.

"I've got to get my brother to the Lady. I hear that she's broken the Spell from loads of the little people, least ways that's the rumor that I hear in the rocks," he said, almost to himself.

"But then I... I can't..."

He sighed and returned to the table.

"I'm guessin' we'd best be finishing up our plans and then get you on your way," he said.

"That's true," said Mrs. Wigglepox.

"But how will we know where to go?" asked Colleen.

"Ah!" said the old dwarf. "Let me show you something."

He went to a closet and began to rummage around among a load of buckets and brooms and stacks of paper until he found a rolled scroll of sorts. He brought it over to them and carefully unrolled it on the table.

"Now this here is a map of the lands after the Cataclysm, but before the Pirate came and brought the Witch back. My brothers and I made this, and I don't think that the land has changed all that much, although it's been about fifteen hundred years," he said.

"This map is 1500 years old?" asked Frederick.

"No, this here is a copy of one we made back then. We dwarves are masters with maps, and we don't make mistakes with 'em. Now see here," he said, pointing his finger at a lake drawn on the map.

"That's the Lady's Lake. It's about three days away from here, I would say, assuming that you find a decent path and the forest hasn't closed in after all these years. There used to be the Great Road that led from the Seven Houses all the way north to the Gray Sands and the Ices and all the way south to the White Sea. But it's long overgrown now, far as I know, but you can see bits of it now and then still sticking up through the brush and forest floor. That would be the path to follow. It passes by the Lady's Lake, or used to."

"What are the Seven Houses?" asked Colleen.

"This is one of 'em! They're the houses that my brothers and I built and looked after. Each had a watchtower, and each of us watched the lands around our house."

"Watched for what?" asked Lily.

"Why, at first, we watched for friends. From those towers you can see mighty far, farther than with your natural eyes, mind you. It's a special thing when you ascend into the watchtower and take note of all the land. But when the Witch came, we watched for her and her lot as well. And that takes a bit of doing. The goblins are sneaky, you know, and can slink through the forest like a shadow, and it takes a careful eye to pick 'em out and make a defense against 'em," he said.

He sighed then and said, "Ah, but six of our houses are fallen, fallen along with my brothers."

"Was that pile of ruins that we climbed once a house like this?" asked Frederick. "The one that Mrs. Wigglepox showed us – where we found Oracle?"

"Off to the north? Aye, it was. That was Dvalenn's house, poor thing. After he disappeared, his house slowly crumbled and went to ruin. I couldn't maintain both his and mine. Without him there, it got ransacked by the goblins and, over time, just fell to pieces," said Doc. "But I did manage to hide the secret passages under his house. There are more than a few magic things buried there."

He paused, looking sad, glanced at his brother, then looked down at the map and continued, "Now look here – another few days' walk from the Lake brings you to the Great Hills. The road used to run right through them to the Burning Sands, and that," he pointed his finger to a picture of a castle on the map, "that is the old Wizard's Castle. It's in the middle of the desert, about three days walk from the Great Hills, if my memory serves me right. That's where we found *her*, you know."

"Found who?" asked Colleen.

"The sleeping lass. She was a beauty, she was. Found her in a glass room of sorts in a tower, sleepin' like a baby. Sleepin' like Dvalenn over there, though her sleep was a peaceful one. Her hair was golden red – rather like yours, Colleen."

Suddenly, the dwarf stopped and looked hard at Colleen, his old eyes wider than she had seen them yet. He opened his mouth and was about to say something, then shut it and shook his head and looked down.

"What is it, Doc?" Colleen asked.

"Oh, nothing... nothing at all. Just an old dwarf's imagination," he sighed.

"Please, Doc, what's wrong?" she asked.

"It's just... just that ... well, it's been a very long time you know, since I've seen her," he replied slowly. "But you... you remind me of her in a way. Your hair and your eyes... why... why... it's rather uncanny..."

He paused, staring into Colleen's eyes for a moment more, and then added quickly, "But never mind all that. Come now, let's get back to our planning. Now, where was I?"

"You were telling us about the Wizard's Castle," said Frederick.

"Right. Now, there's water there, or there used to be. This river used to run right under it, and there was a well that the wizards sank down to it that supplied the whole castle. My brothers and I used it for years. That's where you'll have to re-fill your water sacks. But, mind you, back then, it was a *wishing well*. The leprechauns helped us make that, they did. Take care what you say around it. If you throw a piece of leprechaun gold in and make a wish, it's as good as a leprechaun granting you that wish!" he said.

"Does anyone live there?" asked Lily, who had walked out onto the map with Rose and had seated herself next to the picture of the castle.

"Who knows these days?" said Doc. "We left there long, long ago. Somethin' strange happens there – the air itself shimmers and shifts and, at times, you have strange visions. We didn't think it was safe any longer after we lost the lass, so we left. But I don't hear any rumors of it, and the news from the rocks is rather sparse from so far away."

"Do you talk to the rocks?" asked Rose.

"You might say so," he said. "I've rather mastered the old dwarvish art of rock listening. No one else to talk to down here, you know, except the fish and the mushrooms, and they don't talk back. But the rocks, they have long memories, and their stories hold long and hard, just like them. A good dwarf can hear those stories if'n he listens careful enough. But it's a real faint whisper that comes from those parts, and it takes a long time to hear it."

"That's amazing," said Frederick. "I always thought rocks were just, well, stupid old things that just sat there and didn't *do* anything at all."

"Shame for you that you never took time to look closer and listen harder to the world around you, boy. Then again, I s'pose you are just human. My recollection of most humans is that they're rather like old Dvalenn over there, sleepin' away, eyes shut to a bigger world that's all around 'em, preferin' their troubled dreams to bein' waked up and really livin' like they could. Shame," he said, shaking his head.

"But maybe there's hope for you lot," he continued. "Here ya are on a trip to meet the Lady! She might do a thing or two for you all as well."

Frederick was not sure what to say, but his interest in meeting this Lady Danu was growing the more he heard about her.

"Now, see here," continued Doc. "After the Sands and the Castle – another two or three days to get out of it – and you come to the

Sea."

"It looks like your map ends at the Sea," said Lily, walking to the edge of the parchment.

"Aye, that it does," said Doc. "We aren't much of a sea-faring folk, you know. What lies beyond that, I don't rightly know."

"The Island of the Waking Tree is out there somewhere," said Mrs. Wigglepox.

"So it's said," said Doc. "And also the Witch's fortress. That's where she keeps her prisoners."

"Then that's where we need to go," said Colleen. "That's where my mother will be."

"You're likely to be right," said Doc, "although I don't know how you might expect to get her out. That Witch is powerful, and she's got loads of goblins in her army. I suspect there'll be quite a troop of 'em guarding that place, wherever it is. Them there wizards were *mighty* folk, and they plumb failed to do her in. You'll need plenty of help, I'd say."

"Wait a second, do you mean you don't know where her fortress is?" asked Frederick.

Doc looked a bit embarrassed. "No one knows, except those goblins," he said. "No one's ever escaped from her before."

All at once, the same thought struck them all, and they turned and looked at Dvalenn, who was still sound asleep on his bed.

"Dvalenn did!" said Colleen excitedly. "And he made his way here. That means he must know the way back!"

"For all the good that is," said Frederick. "Just look at him – snoring his life away when the world needs him most."

"All the more reason to get him to the Lady," said Doc. "And you're right. He's the first one I've ever heard of escaping from the Witch's lair. I'll bet he'll have a tale or two to tell."

Frederick turned back to the map and studied it for a moment. "Wait a second," he said. "There's something strange here."

"What?" asked Colleen.

"Well, my father has a map that looks an awful lot like this one," he said.

"Your father? But how could that be?" she said.

"I'm not really sure," he said. "But I've seen it before. It's actually three maps... or four now that he's got a copy of that one over your fireplace, Colleen."

"What four maps?" asked Mrs. Wigglepox.

"That's what my father has been searching for the past twenty years. He found three pieces of a map that someone made a very long time ago. The fourth piece was over the fireplace back in Ireland. It seems to me that when you put them all together, they look quite a bit like this map, except for that fourth part, which I think would be here," he said, pointing his finger at a section of the map where there was a small house.

"Why, that's just about where we are now, you know – that house is the one above us, and see here...." Doc pointed a short distance away. "... that is the Mirror Wall where you two came through."

"So," said Colleen, "that means that the maps back home *were* made by the Pirate – Atsolter the Pirate! And they're not maps of Ireland at all – they're maps of the Land of the Little People!"

"Aye, it may well be," said Doc. "He was here long enough to make such maps."

"But there's just one difference," said Frederick. "On those other maps," he pointed to the eastern side of the map, "the sea had two islands in it. The one in the east had a big tree on it, and the one in the west had a sort of castle on it."

"Then that spells it out for us," said Doc excitedly. "The Island of the Waking Tree is in the eastern part of the Southern Sea, and the Witch's fortress is in the west!"

"So we've got to find a ship or boat or something and head southwest and rescue my mother."

"The Sorrows shall be harrowed!" Oracle said suddenly, and he climbed up on a low stool, peeked over the edge of the table, and stabbed a finger at an empty spot on the map in the middle of the sea.

They were all silent for a moment, once again unsure of how to deal with Oracle's madness.

"Right," said Colleen at last. "We might as well go now. No time to waste."

Chapter 29 – Lily's Wish

Colleen listened as Doc hummed some dwarvish tune as he crammed a huge pack to the brim with all sorts of supplies – pots and pans and containers of mushrooms and dried fish and roots and blankets and clothes and tools and just about everything else he could fit into its nooks and crannies.

"What's all that for?" asked Frederick.

"I know, I know," said the dwarf. "It's a bit small, but I wasn't sure just how much you could carry."

"Small!" said Frederick, amazed. "You expect *me* to carry that thing?"

"It will just have to do," said Doc sadly.

Frederick's mouth dropped open.

"I... I can't carry that!" he objected.

Doc paused, looking confused, but he winked at Colleen.

"I'm just kidding with you, lad. See here, this one is for you."

He produced a smaller pack just large enough to hold two blankets, a pouch of food, a flask of water, and a few odds and ends.

"Shew!" sighed Frederick with relief.

"And one for you, young lady," he said, and produced a slightly smaller one for Colleen.

"Now, Oracle, here's a side satchel for you." He handed the hunchback a small bag with a shoulder strap. Oracle accepted it with a grin, slipped it over his head, and let it dangle down his back.

"Not that way," said Doc, and adjusted it for him.

Oracle grinned again.

"And for the Wigglepoxes," he said, and laid out three small cloths and tiny sticks, and several piles of finely chopped mushrooms and nuts and several extra cloths to serve as blankets.

"You'll have to wrap your own things," he said. "My old hands aren't nimble enough for that anymore."

He left the room and returned a few moments later with a large cart lined with dried grass.

"Now, help me with my brother," said Doc.

Together, they put the sleeping dwarf up in the cart, and Doc took hold of the cart poles and pulled it down the hall, back to the Crystal Cavern.

"Best go fetch Badger, Colleen," he said.

"Right," she replied, and went down the hall and found Badger happily standing in his stall, munching on the pile of grass.

"Come on, old boy," she said. "Time to get on with our adventure."

She led him down to the Crystal Cavern, where the others were gazing up at the rainbows that danced around the golden ceiling.

"Fixed up this cart last night so that your horse can pull Dvalenn along in it," said Doc.

"It's a shame that Badger is so old," said Frederick. "Then he could pull that cart and carry us as well."

Colleen looked at the old horse for a moment. He was a bony old thing, ribs showing, and head sagging.

"It is a shame," she said. "My mom used to say that when he was young, he could pull a plow all day long."

Suddenly, Lily, who had been gazing intently at the old horse, smiled broadly and disappeared into the depths of Frederick's pocket, only to re-emerge a moment later with her tiny pot in her hands. Its contents shone in the light of the Crystal Cavern, and a tiny rainbow descended from the ceiling and settled in the gold that she clutched in her arms.

Everyone stared at the little rainbow, its delicate, mesmerizing beauty.

"Now, dear, what are you doing...," began Mrs. Wigglepox.

But Lily's little voice broke in, "I wish Badger were a mighty stallion with the strength of ten horses, and that he could carry us all forever wherever we needed to go, and the wagon were grand and magical!"

"LILY, NO!" cried Mrs. Wigglepox.

But it was too late. Rainbows began to flash about the room, dancing wildly from floor to ceiling and all of them converging on Lily's little pot of gold. There was a blinding flash. Badger whinnied and reared up, Colleen gasped, Frederick yelled, and Doc cried, "Glory be!" Oracle raised his cane over his head and then was hidden from sight amid the wild spectacle of colors.

Lily collapsed into Frederick's pocket, and Mrs. Wigglepox cried out in fear. And then, as suddenly as it had begun, all was still, and the Crystal Chamber returned to its normal brilliant self, its array of rainbows lazily shining from one crystal to another.

They all turned to look at Frederick's pocket, worry on their faces.

"LILY!" called Frederick, opening his pocket wide. "Are you all right? LILY!"

But there was no response.

"LILY!" cried Mrs. Wigglepox. "My little Lily!"

With great care, Frederick reached into his pocket and pulled the little leprechaun out and laid her on the floor. The tiny figure was limp and still. They all gathered around and knelt beside her, worried looks on their faces. Then, a single rainbow seemed to appear, reaching from Lily's body and upward through the ceiling.

Mrs. Wigglepox leaped from Colleen's pocket to the floor and took her child in her arms.

"Lily!" Mrs. Wigglepox wailed again. "Come back, child!"

But she was still, and the rainbow began to fade.

Frederick knelt over her, and gently, ever so gently, he took Lily from the arms of Mrs. Wigglepox and laid her in his hand.

"Lily!" he whispered, tears in his eyes. "Come back!"

247

Oracle jumped in the air, waving his cane at the fading rainbow, muttering something indiscernible. For a moment, Lily lay still, then she took a deep, shuddering breath and opened her eyes. She smiled weakly up at Frederick. Then, pointing at Badger, she said, "Look!"

They all turned around, and their jaws dropped and their eyes grew wide.

In place of the old, graying horse stood the most magnificent stallion they had ever seen. Its muscles rippled and its long mane shone brilliantly in the Chamber's light. And he was *big*. In fact, he was the largest horse Colleen had ever seen. But his eyes were Badger's eyes, and he whinnied as Colleen carefully approached his massive head, and he leaned down to her and nuzzled against her cheek, nearly knocking her over with his newfound strength.

"Badger?" she whispered.

The horse whinnied quietly and nuzzled against her again.

"Badger!" she cried, "Look at you! You're ... grand!"

He tossed his mane and snorted.

"And look!" said Doc. "He's got on a new saddle!"

Indeed, on Badger's back was a new shiny saddle with new blankets and saddle bags, and a new harness with golden buckles, and his feet were shod with golden horseshoes.

Frederick whistled and said, "He looks like a war horse! That was some wish, Lily!"

The little leprechaun sat up slowly in his hand.

"Frederick," she said. "I heard you... you... you called my name and I heard you. I was... I was... And there was another voice too..."

"I thought you had left us, Lily," he said. "Somehow, I thought that if I just called your name, maybe you wouldn't... wouldn't..."

But he could not bring himself to say "die."

Mrs. Wigglepox was not staring at the magnificent horse that had suddenly appeared, but only at Frederick, tears of joy and wonder spilling down her cheeks.

"Frederick, forgive me for ever doubting you," she wept. "You saved my little girl."

"Saved her? I didn't do anything at all. I was just so scared that... well, I just didn't know what to do, so I just called her name," he replied, embarrassed. "I didn't do anything, really."

"You don't understand," she said. "I saw her going over the rainbow. You called her back!"

Oracle stared at them from behind, a mischievous smile on his face.

"Please, would you put Lily here with me?" said Mrs. Wigglepox.

Frederick gently put her back on the floor, and Mrs. Wigglepox held her close, tears of joy spilling down her face.

"Well," she said after several moments, "wonder of wonders." A concerned look crossed her face and she said, "Let me see your pot, my dear."

"It's still in Frederick's pocket," she said.

Frederick fished the tiny pot out and handed it to Mrs. Wigglepox. It was empty.

"Oh, dear," said Mrs. Wigglepox.

"What's wrong?" asked Colleen.

"She used up her gold with that wish," she said.

"What's that mean, Mother?" asked Rose.

"Well, I've never heard of it happening before – at least not on a First Wishing. It usually only happens on a leprechaun's Last Wish," she said gravely.

"Can't I just get some more gold from the river?" asked Lily.

"Perhaps," said Mrs. Wigglepox. "But usually after a leprechaun grants the Last Wish, he or she begins to ... to ... well, never you mind. It may be that this room, with all its leprechaun gold and these dwarvish gems and such did something that's never been done before. We'll just have to wait and see."

"Am I going to be all right, Mother?" asked Lily.

"I'm sure you will be just fine, dearest," she replied, although her face betrayed her worry. "Your gold seems to have been all used up, but your heart was pure in making that wish, and that means a whole lot."

She smiled at her daughter then, and gave her a hug.

"Well, you leprechauns are welcome to go and get more gold if you like," said Doc.

"It's not so easy as all that," said Mrs. Wigglepox. "You see, we can usually only receive gold from each place once in our lives, and we have to be offered it. Taking more from one place would be greedy, and that would turn our wishes sour. We'll just have to hope to find gold somewhere else, and see if Lily's pot will accept it."

"All right, then," said Doc, "you best be off. But I must say, I've not seen a wishing like that in many a long year. What a horse! And look at what's become of my old cart!"

In place of the old wooden cart stood a delicately carved wagon large enough for all of them to sit – two or three in the driver's seat and room for all of them and their packs in the back. Its wheels had spokes of brass and rims of gold. It was finer than the finest coach Colleen had ever seen.

"You really did do well, Lily," said Colleen. "Thank you."

They hooked up the wagon, which they found attached perfectly to the fittings on the saddle and bridle, to Badger, and they all climbed into the wagon, with Colleen and Frederick in the driver's seat and Doc and Dvalenn in the back. Colleen took the reins and said, "Let's go, boy!"

Effortlessly, the great horse pulled and the cart silently moved forward. Not a squeak or a grind did the great wheels make as they rolled up the ramp out of the Crystal Cavern.

"Now this is a day that I'll never forget!" said Frederick.

"That's for sure," said Colleen.

"Let's stop at the mushroom farm and get a few more supplies," said Doc. "This wagon can hold a bit more now."

They loaded it up with supplies until Colleen was fearful that even this new Badger would not be able to pull it.

But the horse easily pulled them all along the hall, and soon they came to the Gate of Anastazi.

"Do you still want to try and open it?" asked Doc.

"Yes," said Colleen. "I have to at least try."

"Then follow me. But I'm afraid your horse will have to wait here or swim the river," he said. "There's only a small tunnel through the ceiling, and I don't think he'll fit."

"Take me across then," said Colleen. "I'll come back for him whether the gate opens for me or not."

"I'm coming too," said Frederick.

"I need you to stay here with Badger, Frederick. Let's just see what happens," she said.

"No way," he said. "I saw what that thing did to you. I'm coming."

"We'll stay with Badger," said Mrs. Wigglepox. "Just set me up by his ears so that he can hear me."

"All right then, as long as Badger will let you," said Colleen.

"Of course he will," she replied and, sure enough, the big horse lowered his head, allowing Colleen to place Mrs. Wigglepox right between his ears.

Doc led Colleen and Frederick to a blank piece of wall and, with a wave of his hand, a door opened for them. Up a small flight of steps they went, through a passage and down again, to a second door that opened on the other side of the river.

"Don't stare at the gate," said Frederick. "Remember what happened last time."

"I wasn't ready for it then," she said. "Here we go. If something

251

goes wrong, promise you'll keep going, Frederick."

Frederick swallowed hard.

"I'll do my best," he said.

She walked in front of the gigantic doors and gazed up at them. Their strange radiance threatened to draw her mind into them. But she knew what to expect now, and she fully embraced their power. Placing both hands on the doors, she closed her eyes. A whirlwind of thoughts and images leaped into her mind, and thousands of years of history coursed through her in an instant. Her eyes shot wide open and she gasped. Then the power of the gate seemed to flow into her – the timeless magic that radiated from it like light from the sun. A strange vision of an eternity past and future swept through her. She felt small and insignificant, the miniscule thirteen years of her life less than a drop in the great ocean of time and timelessness. She knew that this gate – the Gate of Anastazi the Great – stood as a portal between those two vast realities and existed simultaneously in both of them. And it was locked – bound by the magic of both realms, shut fast by the twin locks of time and eternity.

But then she saw it – a tiny *bend* in the lock of time, allowing the Gates to open ever so slightly outward, into time. If she could cause that lock to bend just a bit more, the Gates might open wide. She focused all her thought on that bend, willing it to bend more.

"Open," she whispered.

In that moment, the door moved and with it, the very universe around her seemed to, ever so slightly, shift. There was a terrible grinding and bending, and Colleen suddenly had a flashback, as though she were remembering something. Images of the Cataclysm came to her mind – a piece of the vision she had seen when she first touched the door. The fabric of time and space had been rent and torn then. Had that caused this lock to bend? Was she about to do the same?

She was suddenly aware of a trembling in the ground under her feet and the voice of Frederick calling to her. She willed the door back to its place, the pressure on the locks ceased, and everything grew still.

Colleen pulled her hands from the door. Her breathing was ragged and she sank to her knees.

Frederick rushed to her side and put his arm around her.

"Are you all right?" he said.

She looked up at him and nodded. "I think so."

After a moment, her breathing calmed and she said, "I saw it, Frederick. "I saw how he did it."

"Did what?" he said.

"How he made the Gates and how they're locked," she said.

"Say nothing!" said Doc quickly. "Come, first we must go up to the house."

They returned to the other side of the river and Colleen took Mrs. Wigglepox from between Badger's ears.

"What happened, Colleen?" she asked. "For a moment, it looked as though the light of the gates flooded over you and you vanished. Then, a moment later, you were back and Frederick was helping you up."

"Let's get upstairs first," Colleen said.

As they left the Gate of Anastazi, Badger reared his head and gave a great neigh and stamped his gold-shod feet.

"Easy there, boy," said Colleen, and urged him forward.

She glanced back once before the brightness of the doors vanished behind them, giving way to the magical light of Doc's tunnel.

Badger pulled the wagon up the passage until they came to the dead end, then Doc opened the wall beneath the stairs and they went out into the House of Mysteries.

"Now tell us, Colleen, what happened down there at the Gates?" asked Frederick. "It seemed to me that you became part of the door or something. That's the best way I can explain it. I've seen you do that sort of thing before, like with the stone centaur."

"Honestly, I don't know what you mean by that, Frederick," she said. "I tried to unlock the Gates – or break the locks. But something terrible started to happen. I knew that I had to stop."

"The ground and air all started to tremble, Colleen. I'm glad you stopped whatever it was you were doing. What was going on?" he said.

"I'm not sure," she said. "But I experienced something that words can't explain. Something *other* than myself. Something much bigger. It made me feel very small. It was as though I glimpsed the edge of eternity, Frederick. It was another place... no, not a place... a *state?* I don't know how to describe it."

"Maybe it's best left unsaid, lass," said Doc. "Some things are best *tasted* rather than thought about and analyzed."

"Yes, perhaps you're right," she said.

They were all silent for a moment until Doc finally said, "Well, here's where we must part, I fear."

"Won't you *please* come with us, Doc?" begged Colleen. "I would be so much less afraid."

Doc hung his head and said, "I've thought it through, Colleen. My responsibility lies here, guarding this door. The Witch must never get it, and she must never get the Crystal Cavern either. There are other things I've hidden down there that those goblins would love to have. Why, if she and her goblins were to get hold of this house and find out its secrets, it well might be the end of not just this world, but your world and mine as well. That's all I dare say."

He paused, looking about the hall. "One moment, before you go," he said.

Getting down on his hands and knees, he pressed his ear to the floor and shut his eyes and became very still. For several minutes, he stayed like this, until Colleen and Frederick both began to wonder if he had fallen asleep.

But just as Colleen was about to get down herself and rouse him, he stood up and said, "The rocks say that the goblin that was here the other day seems to be gone from the area about the house. In fact, the strange thing is that there's no sign of it for miles around. It either left straight away or is no longer in contact with the ground."

"You mean it could be hiding in a tree or something?" asked Frederick.

"Aye, could be," said Doc. "You'll have to keep your eyes open today and keep watch tonight. Even if it left, it will have gone on southward to warn the Witch of your presence. Never sleep in the open. Find a tree or a cave or some shelter to hide in during the night."

He walked over to the doors and, with a flourish of his hands over the symbols surrounding them, opened them wide.

He stepped out onto the porch and took a deep breath of air.

"Ah, it's been some time since I've been outside and seen the sky and the wood. I think that I shall walk just a short way with you," he said.

"What about the steps?" asked Frederick. "I don't think this wagon can go down those very easily.

Badger shook his head and snorted as if in protest.

"Sounds like Badger disagrees with you, lad," said the dwarf. "We'll just have to take it slow.

Leading the great horse forward, they brought the wagon onto the front porch, which was easily large enough to hold it.

"Let's take it nice and easy, old boy," Colleen said to the horse.

To her surprise, he turned his head, looked her in the eyes, snorted, and began to pull. One step, two, three... down he went until the front wheels of the wagon were right at the edge of the porch, and then, with almost a human look, he turned his head, considered the situation for a moment, and then continued down the steps.

The wagon gave a "THUMP" as its front wheels rolled off the porch and on the top step. But Badger held his ground, and the wagon went no further. Then, he slowly went down the steps, and bump by slow bump the wagon made its way down, until at last they were on the ground.

"Do you see that opening over there?" said Doc, pointing to a wide gap in the trees.

"Yes," said Colleen.

"That's the Old Road. That's the way you should take as long as you're able," he said.

Off they went, with Colleen driving the wagon and Doc walking alongside. Frederick rode in the back with Dvalenn and Oracle and, as always, Mrs. Wigglepox and Rose rode in Colleen's pocket while Lily rode in Frederick's.

Doc looked back at the House of Mysteries and sighed.

"It's been a long time since I've left that house for any length of time. I've been waiting a very long, long time for this day. But I knew it would come eventually. Things would have to change – they generally do, you know. But I'm a right bit surprised at the way the change is coming," he said.

"What do you mean?" asked Colleen.

"I mean, who would have thought that two human children would come to this land so long ruled by the Goblin King and his Court Witch and seek to change the state of the whole world," he said.

"I didn't come to change the world," said Colleen. "I came here quite by accident."

"Accident?" said Doc. "Accident? Well, if there are such things as *accidents*, I don't believe you coming here was one of them."

"But it was," said Frederick. "I fell through the mirror quite by accident, and Colleen just fell in right after me."

"Sometimes, we don't see the purpose in things that happen," said Doc. "But, we just need the patience to wait and see what comes. I'm the last dwarf in this world, or I thought I was before you found my brother. I've been stranded here for a long, long time. But I trust that my time here has been important, and that gives me hope. Never be idle with the time you're given. You don't know how you're shaping the future, or even Eternity, by what you do today. You're here for a good reason, and not by accident."

For a moment, they were all quiet and only the sound of Badger's hoof-falls and the crunching of leaves under the wagon wheels could be heard. Ahead of them, the Old Road stretched into the forest, its broad path still visible through the ancient trees.

Colleen wondered where this adventure would take them, and what a strange adventure it was already in so few days. She glanced back at the sleeping dwarf behind her, at her cousin who was now whispering with Lily, then at Doc walking next to her, at Oracle, who had a foolish grin on his face, and then down at Mrs. Wigglepox and Rose riding in her pocket.

How very strange and wonderful and incredible, to be riding here in a wagon-load of fairy tales. In fact, living in a fairy tale! she thought to herself.

Her thoughts drifted away to all the strange and wild Irish stories that her mother and father had ever told her. She had always thought of them as great fun. But she had never *really* considered that some of them just *might* be true.

After some time, they came to the top of a rise, and there Doc called them to a halt.

"Here's where I stop," he said.

Colleen climbed down from the wagon and gave him a huge hug, at which he blushed.

"I will miss you, Doc," she said.

"Aye, and I'll miss you too, lass. You just stay on this road and it will lead you to the Lady. And remember what I told you. *Watch,*" he said. "Oh! I almost forgot. Take this." He reached into his pocket and pulled out a golden key. "The only lock this key has ever failed to open is that Gate down there. It's magic, see. Take good care of it. It's the last thing I have that my brother Fafnir made. Who knows when you might need it, especially if you ever make it to the dungeons of the Witch."

"Thank you, Doc," she replied, and slipped it into her pocket.

Frederick climbed down and extended his hand. The dwarf took it in his firm old grip, then led Frederick a few paces away.

"You watch after that girl, Frederick. I think your part in this adventure has not yet been seen. But it's important, mind you," he said.

"But what if the goblins come?" whispered Frederick.

Doc looked hard at him and then said, "I remember the valor of men long, long ago. You may be young, Frederick, but you are *human*. Seems to me that humans could dig deep somehow and find courage and loyalty and strength. It's just buried down deep in your heart. Pray that you find such virtues when the time comes for you to need them."

He nodded then and walked back to Colleen.

"Well, Oracle, Wigglepoxes, Colleen, Frederick, fare you well. Tell the Lady about me, and ask her to wake Dvalenn from his sleep," he said.

He then climbed up the side of the wagon and looked long at his brother.

"Farewell, Dvalenn, farewell. Shake the heavy sleep from your eyes, and remember our true home," he said.

Then he turned with a wave and trotted down the hill, whistling a tune. They watched him go and then Colleen sighed and said, "Well, then, let's go find the Lady Danu."

Chapter 30 – Gnomes

The hours rolled by, and the road wound its way around through deep glens and thick stands of huge trees, as though its makers did not wish to disturb the natural lay of the land or the forest.

Occasionally, they stopped at a stream or field to rest, until the sun began to sink in the west, and Mrs. Wigglepox said, "We had better find a place to sleep tonight. It will not do to be out after dark. Help me look for a large tree that is still showing a few leaves."

For another hour, they pushed on until finally, Colleen said, "How about that big old tree over there?" She pointed just to the east.

There a huge tree stood majestically above the others, its massive branches reaching outward and upward and still showing a scattering of green leaves in its high canopy.

"Let's have a look," said Mrs. Wigglepox. "I'll need to have a bit of a conversation with it."

They trotted through the fallen leaves and rode up to the massive trunk. Around the base of the tree, tiny yellow flowers grew in a green patch of grass.

"Ah, this is a Great Oak – one of the Ancients. It's still fighting the Spell. Colleen, put me down by its roots," she said.

Colleen dismounted and carefully put the little lady down at the base of the tree, where a tiny spring issued from the ground, then backed up a few steps while Mrs. Wigglepox walked to the tree trunk, cupped her hands against it, and began to sing.

They could not hear what she was singing, but in a few moments, she stopped and pressed her ear against the tree as if listening for it to say something in reply. Again, she sang to the tree, and listened again. Four or five times she did this, and with each pause in her singing, her face grew more and more excited, until with a creaking and a groan, a small door opened in the base of the tree and out walked three tiny people. All three of them wore what Colleen thought were very silly-looking red and white striped tights, green shorts, yellow shirts, and pointed slippers. They also each wore a pointed hat – one blue, one yellow, and one brown, and all had reddish-brown beards and mustaches.

Oracle, who had climbed into the front seat, chattered to himself in his unintelligible language, a grin on his face.

Mrs. Wigglepox clapped her hands and actually giggled, and walked over to the three little men and spoke with them in whispers, while the three of them looked nervously up at the towering children and the even more enormous horse and wagon. After a brief conversation, Mrs. Wigglepox turned and walked back over to Colleen and beckoned to the others.

"These fine gents are named Zelo, Nemon, and Humble. They are gnomes," she announced.

The three little men removed their hats, revealing bald heads, and bowed low. Colleen curtsied, and Frederick bowed in return. Oracle waved and looked gleeful.

"Hello," said Colleen. "My name is Colleen McGunnegal."

"And I'm Frederick Buttersmouth," said Frederick, bowing again.

"I'm Rose."

"And I'm Lily," said the Wigglepox girls in turn.

"And Frederick," Lily added. "Next time you bow, *please* remember that I'm in your pocket! I nearly fell out!"

Oracle said nothing, but just kept waving at the three little gnomes.

Zelo, Nemon, and Humble bowed again, and Zelo stepped forward and said, "Mrs. Wigglepox says that you are on your way south to free your mother and wake the Waking Tree."

"*That* is the best news we've had in years," said Nemon.

Zelo began to sing and dance about, kicking his knees high, Humble bowed low, and Nemon rubbed his chin, looking bright, but very thoughtful. Then Humble walked up to Colleen and waved for her to come near. She stooped down so that her face was quite near his.

In a rather shy voice, he said, "If you would honor us, please do spend the night under our tree. You do know that we live *under* it, don't you? You're much too big to fit in our little hole, but I think our tree might be able to help us out there. Our home is not much, and our garden is not grand, but we would be quite glad to have you stay."

The other two gnomes looked on for a moment, and Colleen looked over to Frederick, who just shrugged.

"The honor would be ours," said Colleen.

The gnomes threw their hats in the air and began to dance arm in arm in a circle, singing a happy tune. Colleen and Frederick backed up several steps, for as the gnomes whirled about, the great roots of the tree began to shift and move like great arms, and the earth began to open up with a grinding sound like stone against stone. A cloud of dust and debris rose about the tree and, for a moment, Colleen was afraid that something was terribly wrong, or that the tree had come to life and was angry. But a moment later, all grew still, the dust settled, and there before them was a large hole in the ground framed with thick roots, and a dirt ramp that led down into darkness.

"Welcome to our home!" all three said at once, picking up their hats and placing them back on their heads. "Please, come in!"

"Don't go in there!" said a voice suddenly from the west side of the road.

They all turned to see another gnome who wore a faded yellow jacket, red shorts, and a rather tattered blue hat. "It's no good under their tree," he said. "Come and stay with me in my thorn bushes. That's where the real safety is."

The gnome made his way out of a thick patch of thorns and walked over to them. "Rich is my name," he said. "I couldn't help overhear that you need a place for the night. It's much more comfortable in my thorns, and no goblin will get you there."

"No," said Zelo. "Your thorns do nothing but choke out anything good that you plant, and they're just a snare when the goblins come. It's hard to deal with the Witch's people when you're all caught up in a sticker bush."

Just as Colleen was about to speak, another voice sounded. "Don't listen to them," it said. "Come and stay in my rock garden."

They all turned again, and coming down the path was yet another gnome all dressed in gray and black.

"Rock is the safest place to be," he said. "You can't be hurt there."

"But your garden can't take root, Stony," said Nemon.

"Ah, we all get the same seeds, and mine shoot up plenty good. So what if they die off in the sun – who needs a garden anyway?" said the gnome. "Hard rock, that's what you need to be safe these days, not gardens."

"I disagree," said yet another voice.

"That's Path," said Humble. "He lives under the leaves beside the old road. Tries to grow his seeds right on the road, but the goblins keep trampling it."

"It's just too much trouble to worry about planting and tilling. Life is short, and you've got to try to enjoy every moment you can. Gardens are hard work – it's much easier to just toss the seeds along the way and see what comes of them. You can join me under my pile of leaves and be safe and sound," said Path. "You would be right by the road and could be on your way in no time. Now that huge wagon would have to be parked by the road, but who needs a big old wagon and horse anyway when you can just hide under the leaves whenever you want, then troubles won't find you."

"You'll be snatched away by the goblins one day, Path," said Zelo. "You ought to move in with us. We could teach you how to care for your garden properly."

"I'll keep my thorns any day over that tree and garden of yours," said Rich.

"Thorns, ha! Rocks are the only safe place," said Stony.

Soon they were all debating the merits of planting and living among thorns or rocks or by the roadside, and seemed to have forgotten the visitors.

Humble whispered something to Mrs. Wigglepox and she waved for Colleen to follow them down the ramp and under the tree.

Hesitantly, they all went in, Colleen leading Badger down the sloping ground and into a high tunnel. The wagon barely fit, and Badger snorted and blew nervously as Colleen urged him forward.

The darkness, however, lasted only a moment, for as they passed beneath the great trunk, they found that the entire passage was lined with the tree's roots, and these were covered with glowing green and orange lichens that dimly illuminated the path.

"It's sort of spooky," whispered Frederick. "Do these gnomes really live down here all the time?"

"Well, of course they don't live down here *all* of the time," said Mrs. Wigglepox. "This is their home, though, and you had better be on your best behavior, young man."

Frederick looked nervously about, remembering the Wigglepox Tree.

Soon they passed through the glowing hall of roots and rolled down into a rather large chamber. Colleen looked up and it seemed as though they were directly under the heart of the great tree. The gigantic roots spread outward to form what appeared to be pillars all around them, supporting the vast roof that was the base of the tree. Even brighter green and orange and blue glowing fungus grew in an ornamental fashion above them, and intertwined with the roots were white and green vines from which yellow and pink flowers hung in small bunches.

Frederick whistled. "Now *this* is pretty cool!" he said.

"I regret that we haven't got much in the way of accommodations, you understand. We've never had any of the big people under our tree before," said Humble, removing his brown hat. "Please forgive our poor little garden. Not much grows underground, you know, and what little we can put around our tree we must arrange to look natural so that we do not call attention to ourselves."

"Yes," said Zelo, whose hat was yellow, "but it is quite exciting to have visitors, especially from a distant land."

"Yes, quite curious," said Nemon, taking off his blue hat. "It has been so very long since the big people have come."

"Oh," said Zelo. "We have nowhere for you to sit. A moment,

please."

The three gnomes huddled together, linked arms once again, and seemed to hum a low tune. As they did, the roots along one side of the chamber shifted and moved about, shaping themselves into a good likeness of two armchairs.

"Amazing!" said Colleen as she climbed down from the wagon. "May I?"

"Please do, and Frederick as well," said Humble.

Frederick climbed down, and they sat in the chairs. To their surprise, they found them quite comfortable and, as Frederick leaned back, the roots shifted and leaned back with him, and others rose up under his feet, so that he was nearly lying down.

"I like this tree!" he said.

"This is quite comfortable," said Colleen, leaning her head back and closing her eyes. She began to hum an odd tune that seemed to suit the tree.

Frederick looked over at her and was going to say something about the song, but stopped. Where had she gone? In her seat was an odd old stump with four roots and old Spanish moss on top of it. He blinked, then shut his eyes and rubbed them. But when he opened them again, Colleen was rising out of the chair and complimenting the gnomes on their marvelous house.

"That's the third time..." he began, but then shook his head and said, "This is a weird land. But I like your tree."

The gnomes looked terribly pleased, and soon they were all talking about their adventures and the state of the forest, and how Colleen and Frederick had happened into their land. For some time, they spoke to one another, and the three gnomes, who turned out to be brothers, wanted to know everything there was to know about the land of the Big People, as they called it. Did they know of any gnomes there? Were there still fairies in that land? Did they have witches there too? And on and on with a hundred questions, until it was quite dark outside, and Mrs. Wigglepox said, "Do you think we should close the door for the night?"

"Oh my, yes," said Zelo, glancing out through the dark

passageway.

The three gnomes clapped their hands and did a dance again, singing a song to the tree and, a moment later, the roots of the tree drew together with a sound of moving and shifting earth.

A nervous thought of being trapped underground struck Frederick, but he pushed it away, reminding himself that he would have some grand tales to tell his brother when he got home.

So their conversations continued, and both Colleen and Frederick told them as many tales as they could remember that had anything to do with leprechauns or fairies or gnomes or sprites or pixies, or any other kind of little people that they could think of. The gnomes and leprechauns, and especially Oracle, listened on and on.

After a time, Frederick asked, "What about those other chaps outside – will they be safe? Why don't they come in and live with you?"

"We've invited them many times," said Humble, "but theirs is mostly a sad tale. Once we gnomes were the Forest Gardeners, you know. We kept the most beautiful flowers and vines and rocks and plants, and arranged for the berries to grow just right and the root harvest to be prosperous. But when the Spell came, all that changed. Now our people are divided into a confused lot. Rather than gardening, many just toss their seeds any which way, just like Rich and Stony and Path. They've lost their way in this world and have forgotten who they are. It's not natural for us to live like that, not caring for the forest and not planting properly. I fear they're on the road to becoming gremlins."

There was an uncomfortable silence for a moment until Mrs. Wigglepox spoke. "Well, we've had a very long day and simply *must* get some sleep. Thank you so much for helping us! I'm sure your garden will grow brighter for your kindness."

"We're forgetting our manners!" said Humble. "Please, rest now, and we will talk more in the morning when the sun is shining."

They said their goodnights, and Colleen and Frederick lay down in the wagon, one on either side of Dvalenn, and the gnomes led the three leprechauns through a small hole beneath a curved root, saying that they had plenty of apartments for visitors now that so few little people came by. Oracle climbed up into one of the root chairs, wrapped his gray cloak around himself, and lay down.

* * *

Once in the night, Frederick woke, hearing a commotion outside. The muffled sound of harsh voices and barks, and what he thought were squeals of terror reached his ears. The tree above him began to creak and groan, and the shouts grew louder. His breathing quickened as he listened, and he was about to wake Colleen, but then the sounds faded and seemed to slip away into the distance. The tree grew still. He lay back down, wondering what had happened, listening for any sound, but only hearing the pounding of his own heart.

How long he lay there, staring into the darkness, hardly daring to breathe, he could only guess. But at last, he closed his eyes against the night and fell back into a fitful sleep.

Chapter 31 – Shadows and Pixies

Someone was whispering. Three someones. Frederick could hear them going on and on, disturbing his sleep.

"It happened in the night," said one.

"And they're gone now?" asked another.

"Taken. All of them," said the third.

"They didn't watch," said the first.

"Never did," said the second.

"Do you think there's any hope for them?" said one.

"There's always hope," said another.

"And what of us? Will they come again?" said the third.

"Yes, now that they've found us," said the second.

"What about the boy? He is of the Old House," said the third.

"Yes, he could protect us," said the second.

"He's only a boy," said the first.

"Shh. He's awake."

Frederick opened one eye. The three gnomes were sitting in a circle a few inches from his nose on a wide root. They all turned and stared at him for a moment, then Humble rose and bowed.

"Forgive us," he said. "We did not mean to wake you."

Frederick yawned and sat up. Shafts of light streamed in through several open knotholes over his head, dimly illuminating the interior of the cavernous room.

"What were you all talking about just now?" he said. "And what was that noise in the night?"

"So you heard it, then?" said Zelo.

"I heard what sounded like distant shouts or something," said Frederick.

Colleen sat up and stretched. Her golden hair spilled down her shoulders as if she had just combed it.

"Good morning," she said, smiling.

"I'm afraid it isn't so good," said Neman.

"Why?" she said. "What's happened?"

The gnomes looked at each other.

"Come, we'll show you," he said.

Humble climbed from the root where he was sitting, walked to the far wall, and spread his arms wide. The great roots began to move with a noise of shifting soil and the smell of tilled earth. A wide tunnel opened before him, and suddenly a dazzling flood of sunlight burst through, hiding the little gnome in its blinding radiance and casting a long shadow behind him.

Frederick shielded his eyes against the light, but Colleen rose and walked into the radiant beam, lifting her face to feel its warmth.

"What's wrong?" she asked. "It looks to be a beautiful day."

"Come," said Humble, and he walked up the dirt ramp.

The other gnomes joined him, and Colleen and Frederick followed. Oracle peered over the wagon's edge, then climbed down and came behind.

When they had reached the top, Frederick stopped and stared. The ground all around the tree had been trampled, and the flower garden lay uprooted and ruined. But worse than this, where Rich's thorn bush had been was a broken jumble of half-burned thorns, and hanging among them was Rich's little cloak, tattered and ripped.

"His own thorns snared him, and he couldn't escape when the goblins came," said Humble.

They were silent for several long moments, until Colleen said, "What about the others – Stony and Path?"

Frederick walked a short distance away to where Stony's rock garden had been. It had been dug up, and its stones scattered. Its former occupant was nowhere to be seen. He walked on, and found that Path's house of leaves was nowhere to be found, and the forest floor was tossed here and there, as though rough hands had been digging and searching through the humus. Path too was gone.

"They're not here," called Frederick. "Their houses are a mess too."

"We'll be next," said Neman, bowing his head. "Tonight they will come and take us away too."

"Then there's nothing for it," said Colleen. "You're coming with us."

The three gnomes looked up at her hopefully.

"You would take us with you to see the Lady?" asked Humble.

"Of course we will," she replied. "Now you just go quickly and get whatever you can carry. We've no time to lose."

As the gnomes ran back into their tree, Frederick kicked at the strewn rocks of Stony's house. Colleen and Oracle made their way over to him and stared at the ruin.

"It's a wonder they lasted as long as they did," said Colleen. "They had no protection against the goblins out here."

"Yeah," said Frederick. "Did you hear all that commotion last night? I think the tree got downright angry and came to life and drove them off. I'm glad we didn't stay with Rich or Path or Stony. We'd probably have been caught too."

"I didn't hear a thing," she said. "I must have been out cold."

Oracle was silent. His usual grin was gone, replaced by a look of deep sadness. As Frederick and Colleen walked back to the tree, he sat down among the rocks of Stony's former garden and bowed his head.

It was not long before the gnomes were ready, and in fact only carried a small satchel each. Colleen went back into the tree and fetched Badger, leading him out into the sunshine.

"We must say farewell to our tree," said Humble. "Will you give us a few moments alone with it?"

269

"Of course," said Colleen, and she and Frederick led the great horse some distance away.

After a few moments, there was the familiar sound of earth and stone shifting and moving. The great tree's branches swayed, as if waving farewell, and then it grew still. Humble, Zelo, and Neman came walking slowly to the wagon, their faces sad.

When they were all loaded, with Oracle coming last, and looking sadly at the burned thorns of Rich's house, they finally started out.

"I do hope the old tree will be safe," said Neman.

"It will be," said Zelo. "The goblins want us. If we're gone, they'll leave the tree alone."

Frederick was not so sure of this, but said nothing. He had seen a number of huge trees that seemed twisted and bent, as if something terrible were happening to them – as though they were slowly writhing in some silent agony. He hoped the gnome tree fared better if the goblins returned.

For a good portion of the morning, as they rode along, the gnomes told stories of their part of the forest and how the goblins had often come and taken away the folk that lived there.

"Now, more to the south," said Nemon, "I remember there used to be a Pixie Tree. Who knows if it is still there? It would be eight or ten days' walk for us."

With that, he went off into a song about giants and horses and warriors that he seemed to be making up as he went along.

The afternoon passed, and they saw no sign of goblins, nor of the Pixie Tree that Nemon had spoken of. The sun was sinking in the western sky when Frederick said, "I'm beginning to feel terribly sleepy, and it must not be half past four yet. Something is different about this part of the woods."

"I feel it too," said Humble.

"Perhaps we could just take a nap before it gets too dark," yawned Colleen.

"No!" said Mrs. Wigglepox. "This is the Spell of the Witch. It seems to be getting stronger the farther south we go. We've got to keep moving and find the Pixie Tree. If we rest now, we might well end up like poor old Dvalenn."

"She's right," said Zelo. "Do you see them?"

"See who?" asked Frederick, looking around.

"The Shadows," whispered Zelo.

"The Shadows... what are they?" said Frederick, nervously looking about.

But Mrs. Wigglepox urged them to slap their cheeks and stamp their feet and rub their eyes.

"Zelo, what are these Shadows?" asked Colleen as they moved on. "I don't see anything except a few leaves blowing about."

"They are not easily seen. You must be watchful for them," he said. "But they carry within themselves the Spell of the Witch."

"You mean they're creatures of some sort?" she asked.

"Yes, of a sort," said Humble. "They are creatures of the air that have no home. They do the bidding of the Witch because she promises them dominions of their own when the entire world is under the Spell."

"That's terrible!" said Colleen, yawning, and rubbing her eyes to stay awake.

"Only to the very watchful eye can their movements be seen," said Nemon, "and the listening ear can hear them."

Colleen tilted her head to one side and listened. At first, she heard nothing, but then a very faint sound seemed to come. Yet it was not something she heard with her ears or even with her mind – it came from some other sense – something deeper and beyond them both.

"They are so sad – and angry!" she said. "And they are... cold."

She shivered involuntarily and, as though in a trance, she stared straight ahead and whispered, "I don't want to sing with them."

"Will they harm us?" asked Frederick, looking about.

"No, not directly, as such, or at least not usually," said Neman. "Their job is more subtle than that. They just take the power of the Spell and spread it about to all the living creatures they find. They even try to spread it over the rocks and trees of the forest. That's why we're so sleepy here. There are several of them in this area flitting about and spreading the Spell. That means there must be some of the little people still nearby."

Colleen roused herself and looked about, but she could see nothing except an occasional branch waving in the wind. Still, she felt so extraordinarily tired that she could not help but believe that what the gnomes said was true.

"There are ways to fight the Spell, you know," said Humble. "We've been fighting it for years and have discovered a few things."

At this, Oracle seemed to perk up and listened intently.

"Well, tell us," said Mrs. Wigglepox, yawning and stretching.

"First, you have to realize that you can't fight it on your own," said Humble. "You need to help each other."

"Then," said Zelo, "you have to *want* to fight it. You've got to know what you stand for, and what that old Witch stands for, and you've really got to fight to stay awake. Sometimes, it takes all you've got, and all your friends have got, but you've got to *want* to be awake like a gnome in the desert wants water."

"And you've got to remember," added Nemon. "Remember that the Witch is a *witch* – and that you are not *hers*. You've got to remember how your mam and pap taught you to live. You've got to remember what's right. You've got to remember that there's a better life than the tortured *sleep* that the old Witch wants to put on you. You've got to remember that you weren't made to sleep your life away, or consume your whole life with procrastination, but to be and become something more."

"And I might add," said Mrs. Wigglepox, "that you've got to be always on the watch, just like old Doc said. The Witch is sneaky at times, and will try to get you in all sorts of ways. Might be a goblin or a shadow today, and it might be someone who you think is a friend tomorrow. Always keep watch for her tricks, and always watch your thoughts. See, once the Spell starts to *stick* in you, then those shadows and the Witch herself can start to whisper things in your mind. That's sort of the nature of it, you know – once the dark magic starts sinking in, it's like a channel for her power to work on you. You can actually start thinking that what she's doing is good for the land and its people, when really her goal is to enslave the whole world."

"How could anyone who is a slave think that it's good?" asked Colleen.

"Because the Spell makes you forget yourself," said Nemon. "You start to think that there's no other life to live. First, you drift off to sleep, then those goblins come and take you to the pits, and there you stay, slaving away digging treasure for her or making shoes for the goblins. And after a while, you just give in to it and start to forget that there was ever anything else."

"That sounds awful," said Colleen.

"Aye," said Nemon. "Aye."

As the hours passed, and the sleepiness seemed to gather about them like a dense fog, they helped each other ward it off. They told stories, sang songs, and now and then even gave one another a little shake.

Through it all, Dvalenn snored loudly, and Oracle simply sat, occasionally interjecting a bizarre word.

Soon the sun was sinking below the horizon, and they were all blinking heavily with sleep when Zelo cried out, "There it is! See the lights?"

Frederick peered ahead and, sure enough, a large tree lay just ahead, and among the branches were several glimmers of light.

"Pixies!" cried Rose happily. "See how they shine!"

Indeed, as they rode up to the tree, Colleen could see several little winged pixies flitting here and there among the tree's branches, their bodies and gossamer wings shining in the failing light of evening.

"Hey there, ho there!" called Humble. "Pixie friends and goblin foes, we have come to visit your tree!"

The pixies, seeing the gnomes and leprechauns among the big people and their horse, danced and flitted about all the more, and called down from the tree branches in high singing voices, "Ho, gnomes and leprechauns! What a strange sight you are, riding with the big people to the south! What brings you to our tree in this sleepy wood?"

"We need a place to spend the night," said Mrs. Wigglepox. "Would you allow us to stay with you for the evening?"

Two pixies then swooped down out of the tree and flitted about them, just out of reach.

"How do we know you are not spies of the Goblin King?" said one of them.

"Because we are his enemies," she said. "He has taken my husband and this human girl's mother captive, and we are on a journey to rescue them. But first we are going to see the Lady Danu for advice and help."

"Three little leprechauns, one *big* leprechaun, three gnomes, two human children, and a dwarf who has fallen asleep, are going to rescue them from the goblin dungeons? Surely you jest!" said one of the pixies, its high voice somehow a mixture of mirth and sadness.

"We have no other choice," said Colleen. "We can't just sit back and do nothing."

The pixies stopped their flitting about and hung in the air before them, looking hard and long at all their faces.

"Some say there is no Goblin King," said one of the pixies.

"That'd be me!" called a voice from above them.

They all looked up to see a rather dim-looking fairy sitting on a branch. Her shine was nearly gone, and they could see no wings on her back.

"And there's no such thing as the Witch either," she continued. "All that sort of talk is nonsense."

"Hello," said Colleen. "What do you mean, no Witch?"

"Just that," said the pixie. "There's no such thing. Have you ever seen one?"

"Oh, shut up, Intelli," yelled one of the other pixies. "Don't you mind her. She's gone all drab, she has, poor thing."

"My name is Apetti. This is my sister Irassi," said the pixie, indicating the fairy flying next to her.

"And that one up there," she said, pointing to the wingless fairy on the tree branch, "is our sister Intelli."

"I've not gone all drab," yelled Intelli. "You're the nutter, what with you flitting here and there and talking to imaginary *shadows* and all that. There's no such thing as shadows either!"

"Is too!" shouted Apetti. "Mam said so!"

"Mam said so!" mocked Intelli. *"Mam said so!"*

"Shut up, both of you!" shouted the third pixie. "I want to hear what these people have to say."

Apetti stuck her tongue out at Intelli and then looked glum, and Intelli turned her back on them all and mumbled, "Who knows, they might not exist either. They might just be a dream or a bit of bad acorn or..." and off she went, mumbling about not believing in things.

"My apologies," said Irassi. "My sisters are constantly fighting and arguing and bickering about something. I do wish they would make amends."

"It's your fault," mumbled Apetti. "You're the one who always wants to go find the Waking Tree or chase away shadows or go on some other fool adventure. Why can't we just stay here and enjoy the sun and the tree. It's so much easier!"

"If you weren't so bothered with your silly *pleasures* all the time," retorted Irassi, "then maybe we'd get somewhere."

Apetti and Irassi began to argue about this and that, and then Irassi threatened to leave, and Apetti pulled her hair. They began to fight, buzzing about like angry bees until Intelli shouted, "Will you two stop that bickering! I'm trying to think of important things!"

"You must forgive my less intelligent sisters," said Intelli to no one in particular. "Irassi always wants to do something grand. Apetti just wants to have fun staying here at the tree, and the two of them just can't cooperate any more. If they would only listen to me..."

Then as quickly as they had started, Apetti and Irassi stopped fighting, and Apetti said, "Oh come on, this is no fun. We're being rude. Let's play a game with our new friends here. Forget about that old Goblin King and all that and let's play!"

Intelli rolled her eyes, and Irassi said, "Games! Games! That's all you ever want, Apetti. I say we go with them. I want to go and help them out. Now you two shape up, we're going!"

All three of them began to quarrel again, and Mrs. Wigglepox sighed heavily.

"This is what happens to fairies under the Spell," she said sadly. "They've lost all their powers because they're not unified like they used to be."

"They've lost their powers?" asked Frederick.

"Well," said Mrs. Wigglepox. "Fairies, and pixies in particular, work as a team. Together, they have the gift of not just wind walking, but *world* walking, and of world *seeing*."

"What's world walking and world seeing?" asked Colleen.

"It's both seeing into and traveling between the worlds. I have a mind to think that that's how that mirror in the wood was made – fairies helped make it – a whole lot of them, I would guess. You see, when they act and think and live as *one*, then their powers all come together and they can *see* and *shift*, as it were, between the worlds."

"Do you mean that maybe the reason we have stories of fairies in our world is that, well, we really *did* have fairies there?" asked Frederick.

"No doubt," said Mrs. Wigglepox. "See, of all the little people, it was the fairies that were given this great gift of world seeing and walking. And if three of them were one, it was as though they were one soul, and together they could even see and travel into the Blessed Realm, and the stories that they told... why you would be amazed! It's said that it was the fairies that first met the Great Wizard, Anastazi the Great. Perhaps it was they who helped him find or make the Timeless Hall, but...”

Mrs. Wigglepox was going to say more, but Intelli cut her off.

“Blessed Realm? There is no such thing! I've never been there and I'm a pixie!”

“I want to go there!” shouted Irassi, “But these two won't let me. Apetti just wants to lie around and play games, and Intelli doesn't even want to try because she doesn't believe in anything and is always lost in thought. But I say we go!” Once again, they went off into a heated debate.

“The Spell, the Spell,” said Oracle in a moment of clarity, then slipped back to his ramblings and said, “It dakesmonwull.”

“Nutter!” cried Intelli.

“This is getting us nowhere,” said Mrs. Wigglepox. “We've got to get going and find somewhere else to spend the night.”

Sadly, Colleen flicked the reins, and they rolled away. But it was only a short time before they came to a good-sized cave in a cliff face that could be seen a short distance from the road. Its dark mouth opened wide, as if in some great yawn in response to the sleep that hung heavy about them.

“How about that?” asked Frederick. “Looks like as good a place as any.”

Colleen turned Badger off the road and through the trees toward the gaping mouth and stopped in front of it.

Stalactites of wet green moss hung from its upper rim, creating the illusion of great jagged teeth.

“This place is scary,” said Rose after a moment. “I don't like it.”

“Well, it's the best we can do for the night,” said Mrs. Wigglepox. “Best get inside. But do be careful, Colleen.”

They slowly went in, passing the dangling moss and entering into the dim light of the cavern.

"Maybe I was wrong," said Frederick. "I have a bad feeling about this place."

Even as he said it, there was a grinding sound, and the light of the cave began to fade. Lily and Rose shrieked in fear, and they all turned about and watched in terror as the mouth of the cave began to close, clenching its moss teeth together. In the next moment, they found themselves in absolute darkness.

The hair on the back of Frederick's neck prickled, and his blood ran cold as a cackling laughter came echoing from deep within the blackness before them. A sickening feeling rose in the pit of his stomach. They were trapped.

Chapter 32 – Chasing the Goblin

Adol McGunnegal sat in his room on the farm, staring out the window. He desperately missed his children, and felt terrible at having sent them all to Wales, now four days ago. But what could he do? He had to provide for them somehow, and he felt as though this opportunity was Providence lending him aid.

Yet he still could not shake a strange feeling that something was not quite right. There was an uneasiness about the farm. Even the wild birds and animals were more skittish than normal. Was it just his imagination, or just the stress of having lost his wife those months ago, his father-in-law just days before, and now having sent his children away, getting the better of him? And to make matters worse, Badger had wandered off, or been stolen, and he had not found any trace of him, nor had any neighbors seen him.

For the past few nights, he had not slept well, and his meetings with Rufus had also been uneasy. He asked too many questions, and Adol began to believe that his children had been onto something – something important. Was there something here on the farm that was valuable beyond imagination? He and Rufus had signed a contract, giving Rufus and Mabel legal ownership of the farm if he failed to pay back the taxes within three years. There had also been a good deal of legal language that he did not understand, but that Rufus assured him were just minor points, and not to be concerned.

He sat for a long time, pondering these things, searching his heart and mind for some answers to the tension that he felt. He was about to get up and lock the house when something outside the window caught his eye. The sun was just dipping low in the west, casting long shadows across the farm, and he was sure that he had spotted someone, or something, dash away in the direction of Grandpa McLochlan's hut.

Adol stood and lifted the lid of the trunk on which he had been sitting. He rooted around in it for a few seconds and then produced a large club. It was an old thing, passed down through his family, from when, he didn't know. Probably used for tenderizing meat, he thought, but it was the closest thing to a weapon that he had.

Quickly, he slipped down the stairs and out the kitchen door, dashing silently, almost too silently for such a big man, across the field and toward the McLochlan hut.

When he arrived, he found the cellar doors open. In the shadows that filled the basement, he could barely make out another shadow – something cloaked in black crouching by one wall. It was holding something in its gray, bony hand – something round and made of glass. Adol surged into the basement with a tremendous bellow, his club swinging over his head.

The creature sprung to its feet and spun around, hissing. The black hood covering its head hid most of its features, but Adol could make out two yellow eyes and a distorted gray-green face. It stood, poised, only for a moment, and then turned and *leaped.* For a moment, Adol thought that it would collide headlong with the back wall of the cellar, but instead, it dove *through* something and *vanished.*

Adol dashed forward, his club held ready, expecting to see the black figure hiding in a hole or something. But instead, there before him was a framed doorway of sorts, with a brown forest beyond, and the black creature rising from having tumbled into the leaves. The thing hissed at him again and the scene before him began to swirl.

"No!" he bellowed, and dove headlong at the swirling mist.

But he was too late, and he crashed hard into his own reflection. He stared at himself for a fraction of a second, threw down his club, grabbed and lifted the huge frame as easily as another man might lift a hat from a rack. He expected the black creature to be behind it, but only a stone wall was there, with a triple spiral carved on it. He put the mirror down, looked about the room again, and picked up his club.

Where had this mirror come from? Had Grandpa McLochlan hidden it down here all these years? Had Ellie known about it? A moment ago, it had been – a doorway? He ran his hands along the edge of the mirror, feeling the intricately shaped brass branches and leaves that made up its frame, searching for some secret to open it again. But the mirror held only his own image and that of the basement. And what of the crystal that the creature had been holding? What had that been? He stared at his reflection for a long time, waiting to see if the window would open again. But the night grew black outside, and soon all was dark. Slowly, he turned and left the basement, looked back once, then walked back to the house, pondering what all this could mean. Strange things were happening around the farm, and he intended to find out why. There were plans to be made.

* * *

The goblin lay sprawled in the leaves for several minutes, staring at the mirror and its own reflection. It had dropped the crystal ball when it dove through. Realizing this, it began to frantically search through the leaves. At last, it found the perfect sphere and stuffed it into a pocket in its black robe. It sat for a long, long time, breathing heavily and staring, waiting.

At last, it rose, went to the mirror, and took the crystal into its gray hand. The mirror changed. Darkness filled the scene beyond the portal.

Cautiously, it looked around to be sure no one had seen, and then it slipped back through the mirror. It then went to the door and peered out. There was the man, walking in the moonlight back toward his house. It waited until the man was far away, and then slipped into the night.

With glee, it cackled as it ran. "I have it! I have it!" Then it reached the wall, climbed over, and sped toward the center of the bog.

Chapter 33 – The Hag and the Hermit

Colleen pushed down the feeling of hysteria that was rising up within her, but she could not help but feel as though they had just been eaten alive. The mouth of the cave had closed down like some great maw and shrouded them in absolute darkness. And what had been that laugh? Who lived here in this dank place of fear?

"Look!" hissed Frederick. "What's that?"

There before them, a bobbing orange light appeared. It appeared to be floating in the air and was coming toward them. It stopped some distance away, and they could see a thin figure with long, stringy, white hair dimly outlined by the light. A moment later, an old woman's voice called to them from the darkness.

"Follow me," it said, and the figure turned and walked back the way it had come.

Hesitantly, they followed, inching forward through the darkness until they rounded a bend. There, the dim light of a small fire sent shadows dancing across the walls of a chamber. Hunched beside the flames was what appeared to be a woman with wild, unkempt hair, bare feet, and wearing a ragged brown dress that hung in tatters down to her thin, boney knees.

She turned her head in their direction, and gave them a nearly toothless grin.

"Ah, a fine, fine catch," she whispered, then cackled madly.

Her tongue darted out of her mouth, licking her lips, and shot back in again, almost snake-like. Then she clenched her gnarled hands into fists, shook them victoriously over the fire, and laughed again. "A fine catch, indeed!"

She rose and took a step toward them. Her hollow, sunken eyes were wide with a look of covetous delight.

"I have just the perfect place for you, my young lovelies," she said.

Then her expression changed to almost a look of pity and she said, "Ah, poor things. You must be tired after a long day's journey. Come in and rest by the fire. Here, let me help you. Do you have any good gingerbread cookie recipes?"

Something about this old woman deeply disturbed Colleen. First, she was as big as they were, and she looked to be human. No one they had met had mentioned anything about another human living here in this land. Then there was all that talk about *catching* them.

But she seemed harmless enough, and the fire did look welcoming after their long journey.

"Please, ma'am," said Colleen, "who are you?"

"Just a little closer, dearie," she crooned. "That's right, come up to the fire and warm yourselves. Just a little closer... *HA!*"

"Look out!" cried Mrs. Wigglepox, as something came swooping down from the darkness above them. Colleen was snatched into the air and carried upward. She screamed as she felt herself gripped by unseen hands and thrust roughly into a cage that hung suspended from the ceiling. The door of the cage slammed shut of its own accord, and she grabbed its iron bars and shook them. The cage swung back and forth and she could see that it was suspended by a chain from the ceiling.

Frederick cried out, "Hey, hey!" and then flew past her and into an adjacent cage. She could barely make out his face in the dim light.

"What's going on!" he shouted.

Badger whinnied and stamped, then began to neigh wildly. They both looked down and could see the old woman waving a thin stick in her hand, as though she were conducting an orchestra, and saying something that they could not quite make out. The horse quieted, hung his head, and appeared to fall asleep.

The woman walked past him and up to the cart, then in a louder voice said, "And what have we here? A family of leprechauns! Maybe I'll keep you for myself as pets!"

"You just keep away from us!" shouted Mrs. Wigglepox, and pushed Lily and Rose behind her.

The old woman reached out a hand to grab them and they ran to the far side of the cart.

"What fun!" she crowed, and climbed into the cart after them.

"You leave them alone!" shouted Colleen.

The hag looked up at her and grinned.

"Patience, love. Momma's going to make us a nice pie." She laughed madly and grabbed all three of the leprechauns.

"And look here!" she cackled in delight. "Three gnomes!"

Then she proceeded to scoop up Humble, Neman, and Zelo.

Lily and Rose screamed, and Mrs. Wigglepox beat on the bony fingers that gripped them. The old woman climbed down from the cart and began to hum a tune. She walked over to one wall and produced what looked to be a birdcage and, into this, she placed the Wigglepoxes and the gnomes.

"Frederick, we've got to do something!" said Colleen. "She's going to eat them!"

Frederick shook his cage, kicked at the door, and even tried throwing his body against the bars. But he only succeeded in making it swing wildly, banging into Colleen's.

The old woman was humming a tune and boiling water in a pot now, and began cutting up roots and putting them into the water.

"Oracle!" shouted Colleen. "Do something!"

A moment later, Oracle's head peeked over the back of the wagon. He looked as though he had just awakened from a nap. He yawned and stretched, then stood up and banged his cane on the wood of the seat.

From the direction they had come into the cave, the sound of stone grinding on stone could be heard, and a voice yelling, "Mal? Are you home, Mal?"

The hag stopped what she was doing and called out, "Who's there? Come so soon?" Then, in a regretful voice, she said, "And I've not even had time to cook the pie."

She sighed heavily and walked past the wagon, seeming not to see Oracle, and continued out to the front of the cave.

Colleen strained to hear what was being said, for a conversation between the hag and someone else seemed to be going on. Soon the voices grew closer and they could clearly hear someone saying, "No, no, it's no trouble at all, Mal. I shan't stay for long."

"I'm in the middle of making dinner, Cian. Come back tomorrow and we can talk," said the hag.

But apparently, the visitor was insistent and bustled right on into the cave, the hag trailing behind, wringing her hands. To Colleen's and Frederick's great surprise, the visitor turned out to be a little man nearly as tall as Oracle, and quite obviously a leprechaun. As soon as he came into the circle of firelight, he stopped, looked about, looked up into the shadows of the ceiling, and frowned.

"Now, Mal, how many times have I told you not to trap people for the goblins. And what is this – a family of leprechauns in a cage, and three gnomes? And a boy and girl, no less! For shame!"

The hag looked down at her hands and dug her shoe in the dirt. "But, it's just a few of them, and the goblins only take them to see *her*. It's no harm done. And they trade with me for such catches, you know. What else can a poor old hag do for a living in these dark times?"

"*Trade* with you, Mal? You mean they give you their putrid ooze in exchange for prisoners. These are *people*, Mal. You can't trade in people. I've told you this before. I'm afraid this is the last time. I'm really going to have to send you away," said the leprechaun.

The hag stopped suddenly and cocked her head as if listening. "Hmm," she said. "Seems as though I might have an extra catch today!" she said. With that, she leaped to one side and waved a hand. Out of the darkness from above, a shadow swooped down upon the leprechaun. But just as it did, a stick came flying out of the wagon and struck the shadow.

Colleen and Frederick were not quite sure what they had seen, but it seemed to them that Oracle had thrown his cane, and that when it struck the shadow, the darkness of it seemed to crack into pieces and shatter. Something that looked like gray ash floated down on top of the leprechaun, which he brushed from his shoulders.

"You really should keep your place a bit tidier, Mal," he said.

The hag's face grew hard and full of anger. She waved her hands again and muttered an incantation. There was a sound like a gong that made everyone in the room, except the hag, hold their ears. Then the hag screamed and ran for the cave entrance. Her last words before she disappeared were, "I'll have a catch yet!"

The leprechaun looked about the room once again, went over to the cage that held the Wigglepox family and gnomes, and broke it open.

"Thank you, kind sir," said Mrs. Wigglepox as he placed them on the ground. "Can you get our friends down as well?"

"Let's see what can be done," he said. He walked over to the far wall and found two ropes tied to fixtures on the wall. These ropes went up to the ceiling where they were strung through pulleys and then were tied to the chains that held the cages.

"I'm a bit short," he said, as he tried to reach the knot that tied the ropes.

After several times jumping, he managed to hang onto the end of the rope, pull himself up further, and began to untie the knots.

"I'm not sure if it's a good idea to untie…" began Frederick as he watched.

But before he could finish what he was saying, the knot gave way and both cages began to fall to the ground. Both Frederick and Colleen braced themselves for the inevitable crash.

But the crash never came. Just before hitting the ground the cages both stopped abruptly – the ropes had knots in them that had jammed in the pulleys.

"Well, friends," said the little man. "You had best get out of those cages and come over to the fire."

"The doors are locked," said Frederick.

"I dare say you could open them," he said.

Colleen suddenly felt very foolish. Of course, she could open them. She found the key that Doc had given her and slipped it into the lock on the door.

"Why didn't I think of that a few minutes ago?" Colleen said.

The leprechaun shrugged and walked over to the fire. "Please, come and sit for a time and we will talk."

Hesitantly, Colleen took a few steps forward.

"If I may ask, who are you?" she said.

"Ah, there will be time for introductions soon enough," said the leprechaun. "Come, now, sit with me by the fire and we shall talk."

Colleen glanced at Mrs. Wigglepox, who nodded her head. They all walked over to the fire and sat down across from the little man.

"I'm Colleen McGunnegal, and this is Frederick, Humble, Neman, Zelo, Edna, Lily, and Rose. May we ask your name, sir?" asked Colleen.

The little man smiled. "I am only a poor recluse living as best I can in these troubled times."

"Who was that old woman? Was that the Witch?" asked Frederick after a moment.

"No, no," he said. "Her name is Mal. I have been trying to help her for years. She came here long, long ago, though, and has been capturing little people and giving them to the goblins in exchange for ooze. Still, I hold out hope for her. She and the goblins built this place as a trap of sorts for passersby. But her luck has not been so good recently. She and I have an odd relationship."

"I'd have almost thought you were friends with her by the way you talked," said Frederick.

"Friends? For my part, yes, I try to be a friend to her. But she doesn't care much for me, although she is afraid of me."

"Afraid of you?" said Frederick. "But you... you're too *tall* to be one of the little people, like Oracle over there, and too short to be a dwarf... what *are* you? Why would she be afraid?"

The little man laughed a clear, hearty laugh that echoed in the chamber.

"But I *am* one of the little people," he said. "Mrs. Wigglepox could tell you that."

They all turned to her and she looked down, a bit embarrassed.

"I don't understand," said Colleen. "Then why are you so... so *big*?"

"I am not *big*," explained the little man. "It's just that these others are rather *small*."

"It's true," said Mrs. Wigglepox. "We are small. But, good sir, please, won't you tell us who you are?"

He looked hard at Mrs. Wigglepox for a moment, nodded his head, and said, "My name is Cian."

"I heard the old woman call you that, but surely, you are not *the* Cian?" she said.

"What's wrong, Mrs. Wigglepox?" asked Frederick, and he stood, looking suspiciously at him.

But the little man continued to stare at Mrs. Wigglepox, an odd twinkle in his deep brown eyes.

"But you couldn't be... *him,*" she gasped.

He laughed again and said, "But I am. You know it in your heart."

"What's going on?" asked Colleen. "Mrs. Wigglepox, what *is* the matter?"

But Mrs. Wigglepox only stared and said nothing.

"Right then," said Frederick. "Let's have it plain. So, your name is Cian. A funny name, but I've heard worse. See here now, how about telling us who you really are and what your business is?"

The little man smiled up at Frederick and said, "Please, Frederick, sit and be at ease. Give Mrs. Wigglepox and me a moment."

Frederick slowly sat down and Cian and Mrs. Wigglepox stared at each other, as if they were searching each other's faces for some deep secret.

At last, Mrs. Wigglepox spoke. "I believe you. But it's *really* hard to believe! How did you escape *her*?"

"Ah, Mrs. Wigglepox, that is a tale. But I think our guests here deserve some explanation," he said.

He looked at Colleen, at Frederick, and at all the little people, who all were mesmerized by this little man.

"I am Cian," he said, "last of the Sons of the Elders of the Little People."

They all stared at him.

"You mean that you are a son of one of the Seven that woke up on the First Morning inside the Waking Tree?" asked Rose.

Cian smiled broadly at her and said, "Yes, daughter! And you are of my tribe!"

"That makes you my great, great, great... Grandfather!" said Rose, and she ran forward, jumped up into his lap, and hugged the button on his brown coat.

His smile broadened even more and his face turned a bit red.

"Indeed I am," he replied, gently picking her up and hugging her, then placing her back on the ground.

"But, Grandfather, you are rather big, as big as Oracle," she said to him sheepishly.

They glanced back at the wagon, but Oracle seemed to have disappeared.

"And who is this Oracle?" asked Cian.

"Why, he's a leprechaun, as big as you, although he looks much older," said Colleen. "But he seems to have vanished. He is a bit disturbed, you know."

"I should like to meet this big leprechaun," said Cian curiously. "But perhaps he does not wish to meet me, or perhaps later. I heard rumor of your coming and thought you might pass this way. I hoped that you would not meet Mal, the old hag of these parts. She can be troublesome."

"Troublesome!" said Mrs. Wigglepox. "She was going to make a pie out of us!"

"It was providential for you that I came along, then," said Cian. "But come, perhaps we can make use of her fire and make something better than a leprechaun pie."

He smiled and winked at Lily and Rose, then began to dig through a pouch that hung at his side, adding spices to Mal's stew that she had begun to cook.

They all settled down, watching him for several minutes, and then Frederick spoke up, wanting to break the silence.

"You know, it's the fault of those crazy pixies just back a-ways," said Frederick. "We couldn't convince them to let us stay with them for the night, so we moved on. What a bunch that is! But at least Intelli seemed to try to think about things and not just buzz about. She seemed to be the most reasonable of the three."

"Ah, Intelli!" said Cian as he stirred the pot. "Yes, she is often lost in thought. But for her that has become simply sitting on a dead branch and listening to a constant babble of thoughts, while there is a whole universe of mysteries just waiting for her to experience. She was made to wander between the worlds! But she just sits there, becoming more and more skeptical that anything at all is true or real."

He sighed and then continued. "But all of that is a side effect of the Spell. The pixies live deeply wounded under its influence. They have become rather scatterbrained. It shows the evil craft of the Witch, for the pixies were once one of her greatest foes. Now she has divided, and so conquered them. They are no longer a threat to her."

"Sounds too deep for me," said Frederick.

"Deep calls to deep," said Cian.

"People keep telling me that!" said Frederick. "What's that supposed to mean?"

"I think you will know soon enough," Cian replied, looking thoughtfully at Frederick. "As for these little folk, and Mal, it will take a lifetime of work to heal them of the wounds they have taken, unless the Spell can be broken. But that is one reason I come here on occasion – to help them along their way and to keep them from falling to the final end of the Spell, and to teach them to find what is truly deep."

"What is the *final end* of the Spell?" asked Colleen.

She wondered what could be the end of a life lived under this terrible black magic.

"It is different for different people," he said. "Some, as you know, fall into the sleep and may never waken. They will just go on and on into endless and deepening nightmares. But for the pixies, it is different. If they cannot find a way to be reunited to each other and live in unity, and so fight the Spell, they will eventually *fade*. Their wings will wither and disappear, even as Intelli's have already begun to. Their brightness will become a dull gray. They will abandon each other in the end, and wander aimlessly about looking for something to bring them happiness, but never finding it, for their *real* life can only be found with each other."

"That's so sad!" said Colleen. "Can you help them?"

"Yes," said Cian. "But they must want the help first. On occasion, I stop by and remind them of this, and give them a word or two of encouragement. If they are ever to be healed of the Spell's influence, then they must wholly turn away from their troubled way of life and return to their natural state."

Colleen thought about this for a moment and then asked, "What does it mean for a pixie to be in its natural state?"

Cian smiled a sad smile, then said, "The fairy folk are naturally creatures of light. But the source of their illumination is not within themselves. The Spell has tricked them into trading who and what they really are for a cheap copy.

"You see, Intelli must turn away from her one-dimensional reasoning. She has begun to think that she can be illumined simply by thinking about things. She has forgotten that she must seek contemplation of the other worlds and the light that fills them.

"Irassi believes that self-determination is the path to finding light. She wants everything her own way. She is fond of saying, 'If you can't trust yourself, who can you trust?' But she must turn from her self-will, and away from her personal ambitions, toward selfless love of her sisters and all others, and learn that real light is gained through humility and service.

"Then there is Apetti. Poor thing, she seeks fulfillment in distractions and pleasures. If she would only gaze into the Blessed Realm at the Uncreated Light that ever dwells there and everywhere, then all her passions would be transformed and she would never seek the cheats that the Spell offers her again. She would truly live."

He sighed, and then said, "If they would do these things, then they will be given wings that would carry them as one across the boundaries of the worlds, and free them to live as they were intended, and they would truly be filled with a light that would never fade."

Cian looked thoughtful for a moment, and then said, "Then there's poor old Mal. She wasn't always a hag, you know. Once she was like a princess, so sweet and beautiful. But she gave herself over to the Witch in exchange for power. Do you think that what she got was a fair trade?"

"Sounds like she got the short end of the stick," said Frederick.

"Indeed," said Cian. "Everyone who deals with the Witch is cheated in the end. I suppose they actually cheat themselves."

"What about our people?" asked Mrs. Wigglepox. "I know the Spell keeps us from wishing, but what can we do about it?"

"Ah, much! But first, you must be aware of how you are wishing. You know there are four levels of wishing," said Cian. "The first is the *wish of words*. That is just *saying* 'I wish for this' or 'I wish for that', but nothing deeper in you is moved or engaged. Little magic is stirred by such wishes.

"The second is the *wish of the mind*. That's when you wholly concentrate on your wish and your mind doesn't go beyond the words of your wish. That's better, but still doesn't stir the deep magic.

"Then there is real wishing, when your mind descends into your *heart*. That's where the real magic lives, and where the leprechaun finds her true self – her *wishing self*. That is where the real work of wishing can be done."

Everyone was quiet for a moment, and then Rose spoke up. "Please, sir, you said that there were four kinds of wishing. What is the fourth?"

"Ah!" said Cian, a satisfied smile on his face. "Now *that* is where the deepest magic of all is found. It is the *silent wish*. No words can express it. It goes beyond words, beyond the mind, beyond the imagination, perhaps even beyond the heart. It is the wishing that touches the *beyond*, and takes the leprechaun into magical realms that are free of all spells and witches and words and images and every sensible thing, to the very *uncreated source* of all wishes. Some call it the *wish of contemplation*. It is the place where the fairies go when they too find their true selves. It is the place that all creation is intended to go and find its fulfillment."

Silence filled the room. No one spoke. Frederick stared at the flickering fire before him. The embers glowed red, the flame filling their charcoal bodies with mysterious light. What kind of beings were fairies and leprechauns that could be like these coals – filled with fiery light, and yet not be turned to ash? And what about him? He felt empty somehow, as though he were just a black burned twig, outside of the fire, apart from these strange beings that surrounded him. They could literally slip into other worlds. Still, hadn't he done the same? He had come through the mirror. Was there a doorway that he might step through, even into this Blessed Realm of which they all spoke?

A sudden feeling of longing stirred deep inside him, a yearning to run madly down every trail and path of all the worlds – to go and explore and experience and see everything. To find himself amid the vast ocean of creation. To find his place in it all. For a moment, he felt as though he would burst with excitement and expectation. Had he begun that journey already? He tried to think this through, and his brain began to hurt. He shook his head, and the feeling quietly slipped away, like water through his fingers. He suddenly felt a great loss, as though for a fleeting moment, he had been on the verge of experiencing something remarkable, but rather than embracing it, he had tried to analyze it, and so lost it completely.

He looked over at Colleen. She was sitting cross-legged, staring into the flames. The Wigglepoxes and gnomes seemed deeply thoughtful.

Cian seemed to sense his feelings and smiled at him.

"Well, come, I think it is time for a tale," said the leprechaun. "Perhaps Oracle will join us to hear it. Come close and I will tell you the tale of the Waking Tree and of the Seven Elders, and of the coming of the Witch."

Mrs. Wigglepox, Lily, Rose, and the three gnomes all quickly gathered around Cian. Frederick and Colleen looked at each other and then drew in closer as well.

Cian looked serious for a few moments, as if remembering, and then began to chant in a clear voice that filled the chamber.

"In days of old the Wondrous Three
Shown down their single Light.
And pierced the void of nothingness,
Filling its dark night.

With a word the Triune spoke
And worlds did come to be
And on one grand isle,
They made the Waking Tree.

Grand it was, so tall and fair,
Its branches pierced the Sky.
And in its depths the Three in One
Made seven brothers and their wives to lie.

Each they gifted with strong gifts
To share among their kin.
That should some evil come their way
Together they might win.

To one was given understanding,
And love for all that's good.
To the second, fortitude,
To live just as he should.

To the third 'twas temperance
To guide him 'long the way.

And to the fourth 'twas justice
To make the night like day.

To the fifth was faith,
Great obstacles to move.
And to the sixth, charity,
To help and heal and soothe.

And to the last 'twas given hope,
That sadness might not stay,
But be dispelled by his clear voice
And find a brighter day.

To each was also given power
With which to live and be,
And plant the seeds of the future
Beyond the Waking Tree.

To wish, to see,
To walk, to grow,
To dig, to find,
To believe, to know.

To meditate and contemplate
To spread the forest fair,
That from the Waking Tree
Might come a world so rare.

And for long years all was well,
And peace and grace did reign.
Until the Door was opened,
And Anastazi came.

Tall he was, his robes of blue,
His hair of silver-gold.
His wisdom found no match
In those days of old.

And others came soon after
Through the Silver Door.
And Little People ventured forth

Other lands to explore.

Lugh of Cian, Elder's son,
Did find a world so fair,
And found that Men revered him,
And feared his power there.

A darkness crept into his heart,
A lust for power grew.
And Lugh did grant men wishes
In exchange for what they knew.

Much evil in the world of Men
His wicked hands did sow.
His evil wishes dragons brought,
And sorrow men did know.

And when at last he did return
To the land of Little Folk,
He lusted more for power
O'er Leprechaun and Oak.

And 'tis said that he himself
Did cause the Witch to be,
And when she came he saw his chance
To seize the Waking Tree.

What dark councils they did have!
What plots and evils planned!
For soon the Goblins came
And joined their evil band.

Then after years of dark toil,
Their dreadful trap they sprang.
And from the sea a dark tide swept,
And an evil song they sang.

All would have died, both Folk and Tree,
Except that on that day,
Anastazi the Great they met,
Along their burning way.

His eyes of lavender did flash,
As he stood upon a hill,
And looked down on Goblin hosts,
Their voices cruel and shrill.

Like a shining star
Amid a sea of black,
Anastazi's voice rang out,
And halted their attack.

But the Witch strode forth, robed in gloom,
And in that fateful hour,
She wove her spells of darkness,
To fight the Elf's bright power.

But brave he was, and none could match
The Elven Lord's great strength.
And around him Little Folk
Gathered and fought back.

The battle raged throughout the day,
A clash of dark and light,
Until the Elven Lord and Witch
Came face to face to fight.

Her weapon was enchanted fire,
Her tongue was filled with lies.
With promises of power she sought
To draw him to her side.

But he cursed such vain gifts
And drew near to strike the blow
That would put an end
To Goblin, Witch and foe.

Her fire roared, his lightning flashed,
He seized her in that place.
And drew the blackened hood
Off of her hidden face.

But when he looked into her eyes,
Anastazi shrunk away,
And did not slay the Witch,
But left her there that day.

And so she fled the way she came,
Sailing south into the sea.
And Anastazi left as well,
Fading into memory.

But great harm there was done,
And greater treachery,
For Lugh's betrayal cast a curse
Upon all the Tuathi.

And all who had involved themselves
In his wretched blame,
Began to shrink in size and heart,
And small, indeed, became."

His chanting voice faded and all was silent for some time until Colleen spoke.

"Cian, what happened to Anastazi the Great? Why didn't he kill the Witch?" she asked.

"No one knows," he said. "But it is said that he left that field of battle greatly distressed, as if his heart had been broken."

"Has anyone seen him or the Witch since then?" asked Frederick.

"The Witch – yes, we have seen her, though rarely," he said. "She relies on her goblins to do her bidding. But Anastazi – there have only been rumors about him. No one that I know of has seen him since that day thousands of years ago."

They were quiet for a moment and then a thought struck Frederick, and he asked, "Sir, why is she called the *Court* Witch?"

"Ah," said Cian, "it is because she pretends to be the court witch of the Goblin King."

"Pretends?" asked Frederick.

"Aye, pretends. She is the real power behind the goblin throne in the land of the Little People. It is said that no one has ever seen the goblin king himself for hundreds of years, except in his royal chamber, and that is deep in the pits of his dark fortress somewhere in the sea. She uses him, I think, to control the goblins."

He paused and then his eyes brightened.

"But see here, we have other friends visiting us this night!" he said, pointing to the cave entrance.

They all turned to look, and indeed, just at the ends of the fire light, a number of gnomes had gathered and several fairies.

"Come, come, friends!" said Cian, and they all scurried in, seven in all, eying the big people cautiously as they came.

"They know that when I come, Mal runs off to find the goblins and will be gone for quite some time. We will be safe for a while," Cian said. "Deep down inside there is a piece of her that isn't a hag, you know. That is true of anyone who serves the Witch. There is always hope."

"The mice of the wood told us you were coming," said one gnome. "We saw Mal go running through the woods all in a fluster."

"Well, here we all are, and there are tales to be told!" Cian said.

Introductions were made, and Cian explained that these few little people lived nearby under the roots of an old tree. They had eluded both Mal and the goblins, always setting a watch for them, and they would come and listen to Cian when he came by.

There was a great deal of chatter among them all for several minutes as Cian tried to explain why the big people had come and what they were doing, and that they were not with the Witch, and that they needed help and guidance.

Through all of this, Oracle remained hidden in the wagon.

Cian raised a hand and called for quiet, and when they were still, he said, "Dear friends, you have all been introduced to our big people friends here, but in the wagon, there is a sleeping dwarf. He has fallen under the Spell and cannot wake himself. And there is a shy little person too, I think."

Some of the little people ran to the wagon and climbed up the wheels to peer in at Dvalenn, while others went and stroked the legs of Badger, who was awake now, and didn't seem to mind at all. Oracle had buried himself beneath the hay, and no one seemed to notice him.

It took some moments for Cian to call them all back to order again, but when he had, he continued.

"This is Colleen, a *girl* from the Land of Men who comes with gifts to our aid. And this is Frederick, a *boy* from the same land, of noble blood, who will do great deeds and be tested sorely before the end. And I believe that some of you may know Mrs. Wigglepox and her children and these fine gnomes who are traveling with them," he said.

They all bowed, and the little people bowed in return.

Cian went on to tell of their journey, but Frederick was not listening. He was thinking about what Cian had just said. *I will do great deeds and be tested sorely before the end. Just what is that supposed to mean?* he thought to himself. *And just what is "the end"?* He was determined, before this night was through, to ask Cian those questions.

* * *

Colleen also was thinking similar thoughts. Just what *gifts* did she have to give these little people? She was just a thirteen-year-old girl, after all.

But Cian seemed to know their thoughts, and he called to them and said, "Listen to me, my friends. Tonight, you must stay in this cave. Stay within the ring of light that the fire casts. Your presence in the forest is known now, and the Witch's people will be looking for you."

"But won't they come here first?" asked Colleen.

"Yes, they will come," Cian replied. "Mal has alerted them."

"Then we should leave and find another place to spend the night!" said Frederick.

"No," said Cian. "You must stay here tonight. But you will come to no harm, and the goblins that come will not find you as long as you stay within the fire's light."

"But won't they see us if we are in the light?" asked Frederick. "Wouldn't it be better to go deeper into the darkness of the cave and hide there?"

"Ah, Frederick, running into the dark will not hide you from goblin eyes. But they hate the light and fear the fire. As long as you remain in the light, the goblins will not come near you."

"But they will see us, won't they?" asked Colleen. "Surely, even if they don't like the light, they will just wait outside the cave until we starve to death."

"No," he said. "Do not be afraid. You will see. Already they are coming."

Chapter 34 – Bite of the Goblin

There was a harsh sound outside, coming faintly into the cave.

"Goblins!" whispered Mrs. Wigglepox, her voice fearful.

There was a rush of whispers and nervous looks among the little people, but Cian seemed unconcerned, and slowly rose from his place by the fire and said, "Remember, no matter what you see or hear, stay in the ring of light. Do you understand? Stay in the light!"

Then he casually strode past them all and toward the cave entrance.

"Cian!" whispered Mrs. Wigglepox, but he did not seem to hear her, and disappeared around the corner.

"Oughtn't we to go after him or something?" said Frederick to no one in particular.

"No," said Mrs. Wigglepox. "He said to stay here. I suspect he knows what he's doing."

"But won't he be captured by the goblins?" asked Frederick.

Then, a rather large leprechaun, if seven inches tall could be considered large, went up to Frederick and said, "Good sir, would you come with me to the edge of the light and listen?"

Frederick looked down at him, then looked at Colleen, nodded, and followed the little man to the very edge of the fire light.

Colleen cautiously followed them, staying close behind Frederick, and then the whole group tiptoed forward.

"Now listen!" whispered the big leprechaun.

Frederick strained his ears, but could only hear muffled voices outside, some of them high and harsh, and others gruffer.

There were loud exclamations and shouting, and the haggardly voice of Mal yelling above the din.

"There it is!" she squealed.

"Catch it, quick, before it goes back in the cave!" yelled another voice.

There was a good deal of running about in the sticks and leaves, with four or five harsh voices all yelling things like *"there it goes!"* or *"where did it go?"* and *"there it is, you ninny!"* and similar things, until all the voices were confused.

This went on for several minutes, until the clear voice of Cian rang out, seemingly from some distance away and said, "Hear me, brother goblins!"

There was a sound of a *"Huh?"* and a *"Duh!"* and something like a *"Hoo!"* and then a *"There it is, up on the top of the cave!"* followed by a great deal of scrambling around again.

But Cian's voice continued, "Brother goblins! I have a word for you!"

The running about stopped, and one of the goblin voices said, *"What does it mean?"*

By the sound of it, Frederick imagined to be a rather slow-minded goblin.

"It means it wants to talk, you idiot! But never mind that, let's get it and take it to the Witch!" said another harsh voice.

"And then make pies with what's left in the cave!" said Mal.

"To the Witch!" cried another.

"Ah, the Witch!" said Cian loudly. "Do you know what the Witch has done with your king?"

"What does it mean, 'done with the king'?" said the slow-sounding goblin.

"I will tell you what she has done with him!" exclaimed Cian. "She has used him, and is even now using him. When did you last see your king outside of his royal throne room?"

There was some muttering among the goblins that Frederick could not make out, but Cian continued on.

"Yes, do you know why he does not leave the throne room?" asked Cian.

"It's because he's the king!" shouted one of the goblins. *"Now*

come down here, and we'll take you to see him!"

"No," said Cian. "He does not leave his royal throne room because he cannot! He has been bewitched by the Witch herself, and she desires to rule over you. In fact, she *does* rule over you."

"What does it mean, she rules over us?" asked the dull-sounding goblin.

"Shut up, Nous. Don't listen to it. The Witch warned us not to listen to these little brutes. They've got poison tongues," said another.

"What ya mean, it's got a poison tongue, Haram?" asked Nous.

"Never you mind, just climb up there and bring it down," said Haram.

"You climb up and bring it down," said Nous. *"If it's got a poison tongue, I'm not going up there. It might bite me. And besides, what did it mean about the Witch, anyway?"*

"I'm in charge here," said Haram, *"and I says you're going to climb up there and grab it and bring it down. Now here's a sack - go and get it!"*

There was a *whack*, and Frederick imagined the hand of Haram slapping Nous hard.

"You'll be sorry for that!" yelled Nous, and returned the *whack*.

There was a great deal of yelling and tussling as Haram and Nous began to roll about and fight and the other goblins cheered on one or the other.

"Farewell, friends!" came the voice of Cian through the din. "Remember my words! You are all slaves to the Witch, as is your king! I counsel you to go and see this for yourselves! When did you last speak to your king, and when did he last answer you? I tell you, he cannot answer for himself, but only as the Witch moves him. Go to him and see!"

"There it goes!" yelled another goblin. *"It's getting away!"*

The fighting stopped, and Haram yelled, *"After it!"*

"You go after it," said another goblin. *"Just what if it's right? I*

haven't seen the king for years. Have any of you?"

"We haven't been to the fortress for years, you idiot!" yelled Haram.

"Well, I say it's time we go back," said another.

"Right," said Nous. *"I've had enough of this running around chasing these little beasts, what with their poison tongues and all. I'm going back to the Island on the next ship."*

Without another word, he turned and trudged away through the forest.

There was some murmuring among the other goblins, and then Haram screamed, *"Get back here, Nous, or you'll be mighty sorry!"*

There was a pause, then a *twang* that sounded like a bowstring. Faintly, Frederick thought he heard a yell.

"Anyone else want to desert the troop?" asked Haram.

There was silence, and then Haram said, *"That's what I thought. Now follow me and we'll pick up the trail of that little beastie."*

"What about Nous?" said a goblin.

"You want to join him?" said Haram.

Then they could hear the sound of footsteps trailing away through the leaves, and a moment later, Cian walked into the circle of light from the cave entrance.

"The goblins and Mal will follow my trail far from here and then lose it," he said. "They will not return tonight, I think. But they have wounded one of their own, and he lies dying in the wood."

"Can we help him?" asked Colleen.

"You have a good heart, Colleen," said Cian. "Yes, we can help him if we bring him here to the fire."

"Come on, then," she said to Frederick. "Let's bring him in."

"You want to bring a goblin in here?" said Frederick.

"We can't just let him die out there," she said.

"You know," said Mrs. Wigglepox, "that goblin out there would leave you to die, or worse, if he found you wounded in the forest."

"Well, I'm not a goblin," she replied, "and it wouldn't be right to just leave him."

Frederick looked doubtful.

"Are you coming or not?" asked Colleen.

"All right, then," he replied, and the two of them headed for the cave entrance.

Cian and all of the little people followed after them.

They found the body of the goblin fallen in the leaves, an arrow protruding from its back.

Dark blood stained the forest floor, but it was still alive, its breath coming in labored gasps.

It wore an entirely black robe and on its feet were hard black boots. Its head was covered by a black hood, and at its side hung a wicked-looking blade. Dirty yellow claw-like fingernails made its gray, gnarled hands look rather like birds' feet.

Frederick reached to pull the arrow out, but Colleen stopped him.

"He might bleed to death if we pull it out," she said. "Let's get him by the fire. I remember Badger was accidentally shot by our neighbor with an arrow. He missed a target he was aiming for and the arrow went wild and hit poor Badger right in the shoulder. Dad took a hot knife and sealed the wound with it after he pulled out the arrow."

"Let me handle it, Colleen," said Frederick. First, he drew the goblin's blade and threw it into the woods, then with a grunt and with Colleen's help, managed to get the goblin over his shoulder.

The goblin gurgled a groan, but lay limp as Frederick slowly carried him into the cave and laid him down by the fire where Cian had cleared a spot.

"You know," said Frederick, "I thought these goblins were bigger, but this one is no taller than I am. But oh, man, it stinks!"

"Do not underestimate them," said Cian. "Although they may be your size, or even smaller, they are strong and of evil temper. And they sometimes possess dark powers that make them even more dangerous."

"Well, bad or not, we still need to help him," said Colleen, and she pulled the knife at her side from its sheath and began to heat the blade in the fire.

Soon the tip was quite hot, and she said, "Frederick, pull out the arrow."

Frederick looked worried, but gripped the shaft of the arrow, and with a tremendous yank, pulled the arrow from the goblin's back.

The creature groaned, and then lay still. A sticky wet stain quickly formed on its black robe.

"Quick, Frederick, you've got to tear away that robe it's wearing. I didn't think of that."

Frederick grimaced, but bent down and tried to tear the robe away from the little hole that the arrow had made. Soon his hands were covered in the creature's dark blood.

"I can't do this," he said with disgust.

Then Cian, who had been standing watching, stepped forward and said, "Please friends, allow me."

Frederick and Colleen stepped back and Cian bent down over the goblin. He carefully rolled it over and pulled the dark hood from its face.

Colleen gasped and stepped back, and Frederick's eyes went wide.

It was a hideous creature, with gray-green mottled skin, an overly large bulbous nose, and large, hairy, pointed ears. Its black tongue lolled out of a wide mouth full of crooked, sharp, and yellowing teeth. Its grayish-purple hair was thin and unwashed and hung in limp, wet strands across its wrinkled forehead. Its breath stank, making them want to gag and its eyes were shut tightly in a grimace of pain.

But Cian looked at the creature with sad eyes and carefully stroked the dirty hair from its face, caressing the beast with pity, even care.

"He is near death," he said.

"Oughtn't we to seal the wound?" asked Colleen.

"He will not live through such an ordeal," said Cian.

Colleen and Frederick looked at one another for a moment, and then Colleen said, "Frederick, we've got to try. Here, help me roll him over."

They bent over him and were about the roll him over on his stomach when a voice came from the darkness and said, "Leave the hobgoble."

They turned to see a little figure hobbling forward from the direction of the wagon. Several of the little people gave a gasp.

"Now see here, Oracle," began Colleen, "maybe it is a goblin, and an ugly one at that, but still, it doesn't seem right to just let it *die* without at least trying to help. I mean, I know it's your enemy and all that, but my dad always says that you're supposed to help any anyone who's in need, even your enemies."

Oracle walked from the darkness. His hood covered his face and, in one hand, he held a small, round pot by its handle and, as he approached, the children could see that something shiny was inside it.

Frederick's eyes went wide as he peered inside, this time at the sight of two pure gold nuggets that sat in the bottom of the pot. They shone like the gold in Doc's cavern, and even more so, for as Oracle reached in the pot and pulled out one of the nuggets, it reflected the light of the fire so that it seemed to be on fire itself.

The little people in the cave gave an audible "*ooohhhh!*" as Oracle placed the pot next to the goblin, knelt down next to him, and stroked his face.

Cian stared, a look of shock and astonishment and wonder on his face. He was about to speak, but Oracle held up a hand and silenced him.

Then Oracle slowly pulled back his hood and their eyes met. A look of recognition washed over Cian's face. He opened his mouth to speak, but Oracle said, "Shhh! Wisssshhhh!"

Cian stood and took a step back, then hesitantly, he stepped forward and knelt down beside Oracle.

Shutting his eyes, Oracle held the gold in his left palm and placed his right hand on the goblin's head and muttered something. Cian placed his hand on the gold nugget, his face filled with surprise and joy.

Colleen watched as a rainbow descended from the ceiling – or rather through the ceiling from somewhere *beyond* the cave, and enveloped the kneeling forms of Oracle, Cian, and the unconscious goblin.

The gold in Oracle's hand blazed with light for a moment, shining through both of the leprechaun's hands, and then seemed to move, blending itself with the rainbow and enveloping the goblin. Then, both rainbow and gold faded away until only the light of the fire remained.

Oracle bowed his head slightly, then he touched the goblin's bony hand, and it opened its eyes and blinked twice.

"I had a funny dream," it said in a voice that was gruff and thick.

Seeing Oracle and Cian, it jumped in surprise. Then its eyes darted to Frederick and Colleen and the other little people, and it backed away on all fours until it hit its head on the cave wall with an audible "*humph!*"

"Do not be afraid, Nous," said Cian. "You are safe with us."

"You're the one with the poison tongue, ain't you?" said Nous, his voice fearful, shrill, hissing, and slurring all at the same time.

Cian laughed, then said, "I see you are fully recovered, friend. No, I do not have a poison tongue. I only speak the truth. And see, we have removed the arrow that Haram shot you with."

Cian bent down and picked up the black arrow and held it up for Nous to see.

Nous paused, and then reached behind his back to feel for his wound.

"Well, he must have missed or something," said Nous. "And I... I must have tripped over a root and been knocked cold. Yeah, that's it."

He seemed to be speaking to himself now, not looking at the others.

"No, Nous," said Colleen. "That other goblin shot you and you almost died. See your blood on the arrow? I think Oracle and Cian made you well. I think they made a wish for you."

Nous narrowed his eyes and looked at the leprechauns.

"Leprechauns, make a wish for a goblin? Ha! That would be the day!" he spat.

But he reached around his back again and felt his torn robe. It was wet, and he looked in wonder at the blood on his hand.

"But..." he began, and he screwed up his face as if some deep thought was struggling to get to the surface.

"But, leprechauns..." he began again, but then screwed up his face even further.

Then he began what seemed to be an argument with himself. He got up and began to pace back and forth, seemingly having forgotten the presence of the others.

"Now let's get it straight," he said. "The Witch says they're evil, that they want all the goblin gold and would sneak into our own world and rob everyone blind. That's right."

Nous nodded to himself and then began again. "That's why she's put the sleep on 'em – to keep 'em out. Best they work in the mines and dig gems and gold for us rather than sneakin' about and getting it all for themselves and wishin' harm on us. Bad enough we're stuck in this world."

His face seemed to grow angry then, and he said, "They did it! They're the ones who locked the door! Curse them! And she promises to pay them back for it!"

Then Nous caught sight of Oracle and Cian, eyed them suspiciously, looked confused, and continued his monologue.

"But then... then... why would *it*," and he pointed at the leprechauns, "... why would *it* make a wish to... to make me better?"

He paced on, back and forth, mumbling now to himself and looking at the blood that still stained his hand. Colleen and Frederick and all the little people watched with growing interest.

"I think it's having an argument with itself," whispered Frederick to Colleen.

"Yes," she whispered back. "He seems quite confused."

Just then, the goblin voice grew louder and they heard it say, "Ah, but *it* doesn't know, does it? *It* doesn't know how many of those little things I've snatched up and taken to the *ship*, does it? Ha! Hundreds, I'd reckon. Lost count years ago. 'Course now they're getting a bit scarce since we've loaded must of 'em up. And what about that *big* one last year? Now *that* was a catch."

The goblin laughed in glee, and then grew serious again and said, "Too bad about old Pwca. That big one was a witch in her own right, she was. Made him vanish right into thin air, poor thing."

Then the goblin slowly turned and stared at Colleen. Its yellow eyes turned into slits, and it showed its equally yellow teeth in a snarl.

"Waits one second. That one!" It pointed its bony hand at Colleen and began to breathe heavily. "That one looks a good bit like that other big one we put on the ship that made Pwca disappear!"

Suddenly, it leaped forward, springing with a speed and agility that surprised them all.

Somehow, though, both Frederick and Colleen saw it coming. Colleen jumped to the side just as Frederick jumped in front of the goblin. At the same time, Oracle stuck his cane out, tripping the goblin and sending it sprawling into Frederick.

The two of them tumbled to the ground and rolled over and over, both yelling and kicking and punching. The goblin managed to end up on top and began to batter poor Frederick mercilessly.

"Hoblestop! Frederstop!" cried Oracle, and danced about, waving his cane in the air.

Frederick spun his body to one side and wrapped one leg over the goblin's neck, grabbed one of its flailing arms, and straightened his legs, pushing with all his might.

The goblin was slammed to the ground and began to thrash about violently, but Frederick held onto its arm for dear life, holding the arm between his legs while trying to keep the twisting body away at the same time.

Soon, all the little people were running to and fro, trying to avoid the fight.

"Enough!" shouted Cian.

"Hoblestop!" yelled Oracle.

"Stop!" shouted Colleen.

"I'm trying!" shouted Frederick. "Ouch!"

Then they began to tumble about again, but somehow Frederick got behind the goblin and put his arm around its throat in a chokehold and wrapped his legs around its body. Putting his other arm behind its head, he squeezed the sides of its neck. It thrashed madly for several long seconds and then went limp.

Frederick jumped away from it and stood up. His left eye was red and swollen, and he had many scrapes on his arms and face.

"Frederick, you killed it!" cried Colleen.

Frederick looked down at the goblin and said, "No, just knocked it out. See, it's still breathing."

They all looked and indeed, the goblin's chest rose and fell. A line of drool was running from its mouth.

"Where did you learn to do that?" asked Colleen.

"I get picked on a lot in school," he replied, smiling shyly. "A friend of mine taught me a trick or two."

"Are you all right, Frederick?" asked Cian. "Did the goblin bite you?"

"What? I'm all right. And I don't think it..." he began, but then noticed his left arm.

Indeed, there was a bite on his arm – two puncture wounds where the goblin had broken the skin with its yellow fangs.

"Frederick, I must tell you something," said Cian. "The bite of a goblin is never a good thing. Strange things happen to one bitten by their kind."

Colleen looked worried and said, "What's wrong? What's going to happen?"

"It depends on the person. Those who are strong may ward off the Phage. Others who do not resist..." Cian paused.

"Say it," said Frederick.

"... they become goblins," he said, and looked down.

Frederick looked in horror at the wound on his arm and then at the hideous goblin lying on the ground.

Oracle hobbled over and looked at Frederick's wounded arm.

"You should have let it die, Oracle," said Frederick. "Why did you let it live if you knew it could do such a thing? Why should any of them be allowed to live?"

Oracle only bowed his head, looking sad.

Frederick looked desperately around the room and his eyes fell on the fire and the hot knife still sitting beside it. He hesitated only a moment and dashed over and grabbed the blade.

"What are you doing?" cried Colleen.

There was a mad look in Frederick's eyes as he walked back to the goblin with the knife in his hand, its tip red-hot.

"Frederick, don't...," whispered Colleen.

He lifted the knife, gazing at its glowing tip, and then looked at the goblin.

"Don't...," pleaded Colleen.

All the little people were silent, watching.

The goblin opened its eyes and saw Frederick standing over it with the knife.

Frederick stood for a long moment, staring down at the creature, his own breath labored. The creature stank and it sickened him. How many others had it killed or taken away? How much damage had it done in this world of suffering? How many others had it infected with this foul Goblin Phage? It deserved to die!

He looked again at the knife in his hand, then at the goblin that cringed at his feet. He swallowed hard and his breathing became ragged. The bite marks on his arm throbbed, and thoughts of hatred toward this vile creature spun in his mind.

"Kill it!" whispered something in his ear. *"Pay it back for all that it has done!"*

Tears rolled down his face as the pain in his arm grew intense. Then, suddenly, he saw Lily and Rose staring up at him, their faces filled with fear and pleading.

"Don't do it," whispered Lily.

The red-hot knife, the cringing goblin, his bleeding arm, and the faces of the little people swirled in a haze before him. Doubt, fear, pain, and uncertainty clamored in his mind.

"Please…," she whispered again, her voice pleading.

He stared at her for a moment and something in his heart gave way. With a cry, he turned and ran into the darkness.

Sobbing, he stared at the knife in his trembling hand, then at his wounded arm. *"Maybe if I…,"* he thought, and in a moment of decision, brought down its hot tip on one of the oozing wounds. He cried out in pain, pulled the knife back, and then did the same to the second bite mark. Then he dropped the knife, sank down against the cave wall, and wept.

The goblin looked after him, amazed.

"The boy… the boy did not… did not kill," it croaked, rubbing its throat. "Why?"

"Because he is not a murderer, Nous," said Cian. "Nor are any of us. We are not like the Witch. You are free to go if you wish. Or you may stay and eat with us if you would prefer."

"It did not kill…," mumbled Nous, looking at the darkness where they could still hear Frederick quietly sniffing.

"And that one made a wish..." grunted Nous, looking at Oracle. "And that one helped it," he whispered, looking at Cian.

"And that one," he grunted, turning to look at Colleen, "is sister to the Pwca-killer, but it did not kill either."

The look of deep confusion flooded the goblin's features again as it tried to grasp these things.

"It's called 'mercy'," said Cian gently to Nous, and he walked over to him and placed his hand on the goblin's arm.

Nous flinched from the touch, as if it were hot.

"Do not be afraid, Nous," said Cian. "No one here will harm you."

Nous looked around the room and shook his head in amazement.

Slowly, he got to his feet, looked once toward Frederick, and slowly backed away toward the cavern entrance.

Then he moved faster, then turned and fled from the cave.

Cian gave a deep sigh and said, "Frederick, please, may I see your arm?"

Frederick slowly came back into the circle of light. His dirty face was streaked with tears, and he held his arm close to his body.

"Can you... can you heal this too?" he asked Cian, a look of hope in his eyes. "Oracle... Oracle... can you...?"

Cian looked closely at his arm, and then looked at Oracle, who stood next to him, gazing at the punctures. The bite marks on Frederick's arm were oozing blood and something gray. Tiny black spidery veins ran in all directions from the bite marks.

"Hobgoble bite infectonates. Problemicky," said Oracle.

"It may be that we could help," said Cian after a moment. "But there is dark magic at work in the goblins, Frederick. Leprechaun magic is strong, to be sure – a gift to our people. But the Goblin Phage comes from a strong magic as well – from the Great Worm that rules their world."

"The Great Worm?" asked Colleen.

"Never mind that," said Frederick. "Could you at least try?"

Cian looked at Oracle, who walked to where his pot sat, picked it up, and sadly shook his head.

"We have no more gold, Frederick," said Cian. "I am sorry."

"Hobgoble bite dreadible, atrociable," babbled Oracle.

"But there's one more piece of gold in that pot!" said Frederick.

"You cannot ask Oracle to do that, Frederick," said Cian.

"But why not?" he cried.

"It would be his last wish," said Cian.

"Well, Lily did the same thing, and nothing has happened to her," he pleaded.

"Has it not?" he said.

Colleen was not sure if it was a question or a statement.

They all turned and looked at Lily, who had been standing quietly watching, tiny tears rolling down her face.

Then little Rose strode forward, and in her hand was her own little pot. She placed it on the ground, and with her two tiny hands, she drew out one lump of gold that filled the whole thing.

"I will give my last nugget for Frederick," she said. "I'm not afraid."

Mrs. Wigglepox rushed to her side and said, "No, Rose. If anyone is to grant their last wish for Frederick, it will be me. He saved Lily back in the Crystal Cavern. I owe him that much."

She too drew out her little pot, and in it, they saw a single nugget.

"But can't you do something without it?" he asked, his eyes pleading.

"Under this Spell of the Witch, our strength fails us. The goblins have taken our treasure," said Mrs. Wigglepox.

Frederick looked from one leprechaun to another, and then he said,

"What will happen to a leprechaun who makes their last wish?"

There was a moment of silence, and then Cian spoke. "We become mortal."

Frederick opened his mouth to speak, and then shut it again. He looked at the Wigglepox family, who now had their arms around each other and were looking up at him.

Oracle drew out his last piece of gold, held it out to Frederick and said, "Touch and wish."

Frederick knelt down on the ground beside them, his shoulders sagging, and his head drooping. He looked at the bite marks on his arm, and the black tendrils creeping outward from it. The flesh around the bite was now gray.

Then he took an unsteady breath and said, "No."

"Frederick? Come on, you need to wish it away," said Lily.

"No. I can't let any of you sacrifice yourself for me. Besides, it might not be that bad. I'll be all right, you'll see," he said. But his voice was thick with emotion as he said it.

"Brave Fredersmouth," said Oracle, coming up to him. "Deep, deep is the snaple bite of the hoblegoble."

"What does that mean?" asked Colleen.

"It means that you must be careful, Frederick," said Cian. "This Goblin Phage is not only a physical thing. It is something that affects you more deeply than that. You must be careful that you do not become a goblin in a boy's body, or a boy in a goblin's body."

"Be careful? How do I... I mean... is there something I should or shouldn't do?" asked Frederick desperately.

"From now on, Frederick, the choice of how goblin-like you become is in your hands."

"I don't understand, Cian," he said. "What, exactly, am I supposed to do?"

"Become truly human, my boy," he said. "It seems to me that somehow you humans can be full of light if you want. It is light that drives back the Phage. That is why the goblins hate it and move about in the darkness and avoid the sun as much as possible."

Frederick looked confused, and felt even more so.

Cian looked at him seriously and said, "Don't be afraid. You will understand in time. I also think that the Lady Danu will be able to help you, if you are willing when you see her. Just remember that light and only light will drive back the Phage. The Phage breeds in the darkness."

He paused, looked carefully at Frederick, and then leaned in closer toward him. He furrowed his brow, and spoke in a serious, low voice. "One thing more, Frederick- you may begin to ... remember things."

"Remember things?" he said in a quavering voice.

"Yes, boy, remember things – things that you did not remember before. Places, voices, sights that you have never seen before. Dark places filled with dark shadows," he said.

The glow of the fire made Cian's face strange and frightening as he continued on.

"You may dream of unholy places - of pits and darkness and dangers. It is part of what the Phage does. It opens the mind of those contaminated with it to the influence of the Great Worm and its minions. I have never heard of a human contracting the Phage before, so I do not know how it will affect you. Strange that this should happen now, but there is a reason, Frederick, though we do not yet see it. But come now, you must rest. Do you have blankets? Come, lie by the fire."

Frederick did not understand all that Cian had said, and he fingered the wounds on his arm. They burned and itched and throbbed all at once, and he feared what might come of them.

But he lay down by the fire and curled into a ball and eventually drifted off to sleep, and each one in the cave did the same. It had been a terrible day.

Once in the night, Frederick dreamed that he was walking deep underground into a dark chamber. Before him was a black throne with a huge hunched goblin on it, and behind the throne stood another figure cloaked in a black robe and leaning on a staff.

He awoke covered in sweat, and Colleen was leaning over him with a concerned look on her face.

"I'm all right," he mumbled, and rolled over, falling into a fitful sleep.

* * *

Colleen lay awake for a long time, thinking about all that had happened to them. *Where had Oracle gotten that pot of gold?* she wondered. Who was he anyway? And who was this Cian fellow? She thought that Cian had recognized Oracle when he first saw him. Oracle was obviously a nutty old leprechaun. Or was he?

She was scared for herself and even more for Frederick. And she didn't know just what to think or do. She hoped that they would reach this Lady Danu the next day and not have to spend another night in this wood so full of nightmares. Would they make it in time, or would Frederick become a goblin as the leprechauns feared?

At last, Colleen began to doze off to the sound of Oracle snoring and Frederick muttering something about worms. They had been catapulted into a terrifying and wondrous land, but tomorrow they would discover just what this strange new world had done to them.

She shivered once and fell into a troubled sleep.

Continued in "Taming the Goblin"...

Author's Note

I hope you've enjoyed *Into a Strange Land*, the first book of The McGunnegal Chronicles series. My goal has been, and always will, be to provide great clean adventure stories for all ages that also whisper of deep things.

Please consider giving the book a review on Amazon. I would really appreciate it.

If you are enjoying this series, please *like* The McGunnegal Chronicles Facebook page at: www.facebook.com/McGunnegalChronicles.

Look for the audio version of these books on Audible.com.

Thanks again, and enjoy reading!
Ben Anderson

Book 2 – Taming the Goblin

Be sure to check out the next book in the series, *Taming the Goblin*, where the strangeness of the McGunnegals continues to unfold as Colleen begins to glimpse the latent power of the ancient bloodline that runs true in her veins.

Frederick also has something within him - the poison of the Goblin Phage that threatens to transform him into one of the hideous creatures of the night. He must leave Colleen in this strange land in order to save himself, and to seek the help of a long-dead king back in the world of Men.

Colleen goes on without him, but has again encountered the goblin, Nous, whose life she once saved. She must convince her companions that he is worth befriending, trust him to lead them to the Witch's dungeons, and there help her to free its captives, all the while hoping that he does not betray them all.

Look for the third book in the series, *The Witch and the Waking Tree,* where more grand adventures await, and an unexpected ending brings *The Strange Land Trilogy* to a thrilling conclusion.

Book 4, *Hidden Worlds*, begins a whole new series of adventures with the McGunnegals.

44638013R00179

Made in the USA
Middletown, DE
10 May 2019